7/8

HANGMAN

Also by Daniel Cole

Ragdoll

HANGMAN

DANIEL COLE

An Imprint of HarperCollins*Publishers*

HANGMAN. Copyright © 2018 by Daniel Cole. All rights reserved. Printed in the United States of America. No part of this book may be used or reproduced in any manner whatsoever without written permission except in the case of brief quotations embodied in critical articles and reviews. For information, address HarperCollins Publishers, 195 Broadway, New York, NY 10007.

HarperCollins books may be purchased for educational, business, or sales promotional use. For information, please email the Special Markets Department at SPsales@harpercollins.com.

Originally published in the United Kingdom in 2018 by Trapeze.

FIRST U.S. EDITION

Library of Congress Cataloging-in-Publication Data has been applied for.

ISBN 978-0-06-265398-7

18 19 20 21 22 LSC 10 9 8 7 6 5 4 3 2 1

"What *if* there is a God?
"What *if* there is a heaven?
"What *if* there is a hell?
"And what *if* . . . just what *if* . . . we're
   all already there?"

PROLOGUE

Wednesday, 6 January 2016

9:52 A.M.

"There is no God. Fact."

Detective Chief Inspector Emily Baxter watched her reflection in the interview room's mirrored window, listening for any reaction to this unpopular truth from her eavesdropping audience.

Nothing.

She looked terrible: fifty rather than thirty-five. Thick black stitches held her top lip together, pulling taut every time she spoke, reminding her of things she would rather forget, old and new. The grazed skin on her forehead was refusing to heal, tape splinted her fractured fingers together, and a dozen other injuries were concealed out of sight beneath her damp clothing.

With a deliberately bored expression, she turned to face the two men sitting across the table from her. Neither spoke. She yawned and started playing with her long brown hair, running her few functional fingers through a dusty section, matted together by three days' worth of dry shampoo. She couldn't have cared less that her last answer had clearly offended Special Agent Sinclair, the imposing, bald American now scribbling onto a piece of elaborately headed notepaper.

Atkins, the Metropolitan Police liaison, was an unimpressive sight beside the smartly dressed foreigner. Baxter had spent the majority of the previous fifty minutes attempting to work out what color his off-beige shirt had started out life as. His tie hung loosely around his neck, as if a philanthropic hangman had tied it, the dangling end failing to conceal a recent ketchup stain.

Atkins eventually took the silence as his cue to step in:

"That must've led to some pretty *interesting* conversations with Special Agent Rouche," he stated.

He had sweat running down the side of his closely shaven head, courtesy of the lighting above them and the heater in the corner, which was billowing out hot air and had transformed the four sets of snowy footprints into a dirty puddle on the linoleum floor.

"Meaning?" asked Baxter.

"Meaning that according to his file—"

"Screw his file!" Sinclair interrupted. "I used to work alongside Rouche and know for a *fact* that he was a devout Christian."

The American flicked through the neatly indexed folder to his left and produced a document decorated in Baxter's own handwriting. "As are you, according to the application for your current role."

He held Baxter's gaze, relishing that the confrontational woman had contradicted herself, as if the balance of the world was restored now that he had proven she did indeed share his beliefs and had merely been attempting to provoke him. Baxter, however, looked as bored as ever.

"I've come to the realization that, in general, people are idiots," she started, "and a great many have the misguided notion that mindless gullibility and a strong moral compass are in some way linked. Basically, I wanted the pay rise."

Sinclair shook his head in disgust, as if he could not believe his ears.

"So you lied? Doesn't exactly support your point about that strong moral compass, now does it?" He smiled thinly, making more notes.

Baxter shrugged: "But does say a *hell* of a lot about mindless gullibility."

Sinclair's smile dropped.

"Is there some reason you're trying to convert me?" she asked, unable to resist jabbing at her interviewer's temper so that he jumped to his feet and leaned over her.

"A man is dead, Chief Inspector!" he bellowed.

Baxter didn't flinch.

"A lot of people are dead . . . after what happened," she mumbled, before turning venomous, "and for some reason *you* people seem intent on wasting everybody's time worrying about the only person out there who deserves to be!"

"We're asking," interjected Atkins, trying to defuse the situation, "because some evidence was found close to the body . . . of a religious nature."

"Which could have been dropped by anyone," said Baxter.

The two men shared a look, which she recognized as meaning that there was more they were not sharing with her.

"Do you have any information on Special Agent Rouche's current whereabouts?" Sinclair asked her.

Baxter huffed: "To the best of my knowledge, Agent Rouche is dead."

"Is that *really* how you want to play this?"

"To the best of my knowledge, Agent Rouche is dead," repeated Baxter.

"So you saw his bo—"

Dr. Preston-Hall, the Metropolitan Police's consultant psychiatrist and the fourth person sitting at the small metal table, cleared her throat loudly. Sinclair broke off, understanding the unspoken warning. He sat back in his chair and made a gesture toward the mirrored window. Atkins scribbled into his tatty notebook and slid it across to Dr. Preston-Hall.

The doctor was a well-presented woman in her early sixties, whose expensive perfume had been reduced to acting as a floral air freshener that failed to mask the overwhelming smell of damp shoes. She had an effortlessly authoritative air and had made it quite clear that she would end the interview at any point should she deem the line of questioning detrimental to her patient's recovery. Slowly she picked up the coffee-stained book and read through the message with the air of a schoolteacher intercepting a secret note.

She had been silent for almost an entire hour and clearly felt no need to break it now, offering Atkins only a simple shake of the head in answer to what he had written.

"What does it say?" asked Baxter.

The doctor ignored her.

"What does it say?" she asked again. She turned to Sinclair. "Ask your question."

Sinclair looked torn.

"Ask your question," Baxter demanded.

"Emily!" the doctor snapped. "Do not say a word, Mr. Sinclair."

"You might as well just say it," challenged Baxter, her voice filling the small space. "The station? You want to ask me about the station?"

"This interview is over," announced Dr. Preston-Hall, standing up.

"Ask me!" Baxter shouted over her.

Sensing his last chance for answers slipping away from him, Sinclair elected to persevere and worry about the consequences later:

"According to your statement, you believe that Special Agent Rouche was among the dead."

Dr. Preston-Hall raised her hands in exasperation.

"That wasn't a question," said Baxter.

"Did you see his body?"

For the first time, Sinclair saw Baxter falter, but rather than enjoying her discomfort, he felt guilty. Her eyes glazed over as his question forced her back underground, trapping her momentarily in the past.

Her voice cracked when she finally whispered her answer:

"I wouldn't have known if I had, would I?"

There was another strained silence, in which everyone reflected on just how disturbing that simple sentence was.

"How did he seem to you?" Atkins blurted the half-formed question when the quiet became unbearable.

"Who?"

"Rouche."

"In what way?" asked Baxter.

"Emotional state."

"When?"

"The last time you saw him."

She considered her answer for a moment and then smiled genuinely:

"Relieved."

"Relieved?"

Baxter nodded.

"You sound fond of him," continued Atkins.

"Not particularly. He was intelligent, a competent coworker . . . despite his *obvious* flaws," she added.

Her huge brown eyes, emphasized by dark makeup, were watching Sinclair for a reaction. He bit his lip and glanced again at the mirror as if cursing someone behind the glass for such a testing assignment.

Atkins took it upon himself to finish off the interview. He now had dark sweat patches underneath his arms and had failed to notice that both women had subtly scraped their chairs back a few inches to retreat from the smell.

"You had a team search Agent Rouche's house," he said.

"I did."

"You didn't trust him, then?"

"I didn't."

"And you feel no residual loyalty towards him now?"

"None whatsoever."

"Do you remember what the last thing he said to you was?"

Baxter looked restless: "Are we done here?"

"Almost. Answer the question, please." He sat, pen poised over his notebook.

"I'd like to go now," Baxter told the doctor.

"Of course," Dr. Preston-Hall answered sharply.

"Is there some reason that you can't respond to this simple question first?" Sinclair's words cut across the room like an accusation.

"All right." Baxter looked furious. "I'll respond." She considered her reply and then leaned across the table to meet the American's eye.

"There . . . is . . . no . . . God," she smirked.

Atkins tossed his pen across the table as Sinclair got up, sending the metal chair clattering to the floor as he stormed out of the room.

"Nice job," Atkins sighed wearily. "Thank you for your *co-operation*, Detective Chief Inspector. Now we're done."

Five weeks earlier . . .

CHAPTER 1

Wednesday, 2 December 2015

6:56 A.M.

The frozen river creaked and snapped as if shifting in its sleep beneath the sparkling metropolis. Various vessels, ice-trapped and forgotten, drowned gradually in the snow as the mainland was temporarily reunited with the island city.

As sunrise crept over the cluttered horizon, and the bridge basked in the orange light, it cast a stark shadow across the ice below: between the imposing archway, a framework of wires crisscrossed in the powder, a web of threads that had caught something overnight.

Tangled up and bent out of shape where it hung, like a fly that had torn itself apart in its desperation to break free, William Fawkes's broken body eclipsed the sun.

CHAPTER 2

Night pressed against the windows of New Scotland Yard, the lights of the city smudged behind a layer of condensation.

With the exception of two brief toilet breaks and a visit to the stationery drawer, Baxter had not left her cupboard-sized office in Homicide and Serious Crime Command since arriving that morning. She stared at the tower of paperwork on the edge of her desk, balancing precariously over the wastepaper bin, and had to fight all of her natural instincts not to give it a gentle prod in the right direction.

At thirty-four, she had become one of the youngest female chief inspectors ever appointed within the Metropolitan Police, though this rapid ascent up the ladder had been neither expected nor particularly welcomed. Both the supervisory vacancy and her subsequent overpromotion into it could be attributed solely to the Ragdoll case and her apprehension of the infamous serial killer the previous summer.

The last chief inspector, Terrence Simmons, had been forced to retire due to ill health, which everybody suspected had been exacerbated by the commissioner's threat to fire him should he refuse to leave voluntarily, the customary reflex gesture for a disillusioned public, like sacrificing an innocent to appease the ever-wrathful gods.

Baxter shared the sentiment held by the rest of her colleagues: disgusted to see her predecessor being used as a scapegoat but, ultimately, relieved that it wasn't her. She had not even considered putting in an application for the newly vacated position until the commissioner had told her that the job was hers should she want it.

She looked around her chipboard cell, with its dirty carpet and dented filing cabinet (who knew what important documents were entombed within that bottom drawer she had never been able to open?), and wondered what the hell she had been thinking.

A cheer rose up out in the main office, but the sound didn't even register with Baxter, who had returned to a letter of complaint about a detective named Saunders. He had been accused of using a profanity to describe the complainant's son. Baxter's only doubt regarding the claim was the relative tameness of the word used. She started to type an official reply, lost the will to live halfway through, screwed up the complaint, and threw it in the general direction of the bin.

There was a timid knock at the door before a mousy officer scuttled in. She collected up Baxter's near- (and not-so-near-) misses and dropped them into the bin before flaunting her world-class Jenga skills by placing another document on top of the unsteady tower of paperwork.

"I'm very sorry to disturb you," said the woman, "but Detective Shaw is about to make his speech. I thought you might want to be there."

Baxter swore loudly and rested her head on the desk:

"Present!" she groaned, reminding herself too late.

The nervy young lady waited awkwardly for further instructions. After a couple of moments, and unsure whether Baxter was even still awake, she quietly left the room.

Dragging herself to her feet, Baxter walked out into the main office, where a crowd had gathered around Detective Sergeant Finlay Shaw's desk. A twenty-year-old banner, which Finlay had actually purchased himself for a long-forgotten colleague, had been Blu-tacked to the wall:

SORRY YOU'RE LEAVING!

An array of stale supermarket doughnuts sat on the desk beside him, various "reduced" stickers documenting the contents' three-day journey from unappetizing to inedible.

Polite laughter accompanied the rasping Scottish detective's exaggerated threat to give Saunders one final punch in the face before he retired. They were all laughing about it now, but the last incident had resulted in one reconstructed nose, two disciplinary hearings, and hours' worth of form-filling for Baxter.

She hated these things: so awkward, so false, such an anti-climactic send-off after decades of service with so many close calls and so many horrific memories for him to take home as souvenirs. She stood at the back, smiling along in support of her friend, watching Finlay fondly. He was the last proper ally she had in this place, the one remaining friendly face, and now he was leaving. She hadn't even bought him a card.

Her office phone started to ring.

She ignored it, watching Finlay fail miserably to pretend that the bottle of whisky they had clubbed together to buy him was his favorite.

His favorite was Jameson—same as Wolf.

Her mind wandered. She remembered buying Finlay a drink the last time they had met up socially. Almost a year had passed since then. He had told her that he never regretted his own lack of ambition. He had warned her that the DCI role wasn't right for her, that she would be bored, frustrated. She hadn't listened, because what Finlay couldn't understand was that she wasn't looking so much for a promotion as she was a distraction, a change, an escape.

The phone in her office started to ring again and she glared back at her desk. Finlay was reading through the variations of "Sorry to see you go" that had been scrawled across a *Minions* card, of which somebody had mistakenly believed him to be a fan.

She checked her watch. She really needed to finish at a decent time for once.

*

Setting the card aside with a chuckle, Finlay began his heartfelt goodbye. He planned to keep it as short as possible, having never much enjoyed public speaking.

". . . Seriously, though, thank you. I've been knocking about this place since it was Brand-Spanking-New Scotland Yard . . ." He left a pause, hoping that at least one person might laugh. His delivery had been terrible, and he had just blown his best joke. But he continued regardless, knowing that it was only downhill from here.

"This place and the people in it have become more than just a job and colleagues—you've become a second family to me."

A woman standing in the front row fanned her tearful eyes. Finlay attempted to smile at her in a way that conveyed both that the feeling was mutual and that he had some idea of who she was. He looked up into his audience, searching for the one person for whom his parting message was actually intended.

"I've had the pleasure of watching a few of you grow up around me, transforming from cocky little trainees into"—he felt his own eyes prickling now—"strong, independent, beautiful, and brave young women . . . and men," he added, concerned that he may have just outed himself. "I want to say what a pleasure it has been to work alongside you and how *truly* proud I am of you. Thank you."

He cleared his throat and smiled at his applauding colleagues, finally spotting Baxter. She stood beside the desk in her office with the door closed, gesticulating wildly as she spoke to someone on the phone. He smiled again, sadly this time, while the crowd dispersed, leaving him alone to collect his things and vacate the premises one final time.

Memories slowed his progress as he took down the photographs that had inhabited his workspace for years, one image in particular, creased and discolored with age, hijacking his thoughts: an office Christmas party. A crepe-paper crown covered Finlay's balding head, much to the amusement of his friend Benjamin Chambers, arm around Baxter, in what must be the only photograph in existence of her actually smiling. And there on the end, failing miserably to win the bet that he could lift Finlay off the ground, was Will . . . Wolf. Carefully tucking the picture into his jacket pocket, he finished packing the remainder of his things.

On his way out of the office, Finlay hesitated. He didn't feel as though the forgotten letter he had discovered right at the back of his desk drawer belonged to him. He considered leaving it behind, considered tearing it up, but in the end he dropped it to the bottom of his box of crap and made his way over to the lifts.

He supposed it was just one more secret he would have to keep.

At 7:49 P.M., Baxter was still sat at her desk. She had sent out text messages every twenty minutes apologizing for running late and promising to get out as soon as she possibly could. Her commander had not only caused her to completely miss Finlay's retirement speech but was now sabotaging her first social arrangement in months. She had demanded that Baxter remain where she was until her arrival.

There was no love lost between the two women. Vanita, the media-savvy face of the Metropolitan Police, had quite openly opposed Baxter's promotion. Having worked with her on the Ragdoll murders, Vanita had advised the commissioner that Baxter was argumentative, opinionated, and had a total lack of respect for authority, not to mention that she still considered her responsible for the death of one of the victims. Baxter regarded Vanita as a PR-bowing snake who had not thought twice about throwing Simmons under the bus at the very first sign of trouble.

To make matters worse, Baxter had just opened an automated email from their records department, reminding her, for the umpteenth time, that Wolf still had several outstanding files to return. She scanned the extensive list, recognizing a couple of the cases . . .

Bennett, Sarah: the woman who had drowned her husband in their swimming pool. Baxter was reasonably confident that she'd lost that one down the back of a radiator in the meeting room.

Dubois, Léo: the straightforward stabbing that had gradually escalated into one of the most complicated multi-agency cases in years, involving drug smuggling, black-market weaponry, and human trafficking.

She and Wolf had had a great time on that one.

She spotted Vanita entering the office with two other people in tow, which did not bode well for her hopes of getting out by 8 P.M. She didn't bother to get up as Vanita sauntered in, greeting her with such practiced pleasantness that she could almost have believed it.

"DCI Emily Baxter, Special Agent Elliot Curtis with the FBI," Vanita announced, flicking back her dark hair.

"It's an honor, ma'am," said the tall black woman, holding out her hand to Baxter. She was wearing a masculine-looking suit, had tied back her hair so tight that it looked shaved, and was wearing minimal makeup. Although she looked to be in her early thirties, Baxter suspected that she was younger.

She shook Curtis's hand without getting out of her seat while Vanita introduced her other guest, who seemed more interested in the destroyed filing cabinet than he was the introductions.

"And this is Special Agent—"

"How *special* can they be, I wonder," Baxter interrupted, playing up, "when we've got two just in my pitiful excuse of an office?"

Vanita ignored her:

"As I was saying, this is Special Agent Damien Rouche with the CIA."

"Rooze?" asked Baxter.

"Rouch?" tried Vanita, now doubting her own pronunciation.

"I believe it's Rouche, like 'whoosh,'" added Curtis helpfully, turning to Rouche for advice.

Baxter looked puzzled as the distracted man smiled politely, gave her a fleeting fist bump, and helped himself to a seat without saying a word. She placed him in his very late thirties. He was clean-shaven with pasty skin and salt-and-pepper hair styled into a slightly overgrown quiff at the front. He looked at the snaking tower of paperwork between them, then down at the bin waiting expectantly beneath, and grinned. He wore a white shirt with the top two buttons undone and a navy suit that looked tired but well fitted.

Baxter turned to Vanita and waited.

"Agents Curtis and Rouche just got in this evening from America," said Vanita.

"That would make sense," replied Baxter more patiently than she had intended. "I'm in a bit of a rush tonight, so . . ."

"If I may, Commander?" Curtis asked Vanita politely, before turning to Baxter. "Chief Inspector, you heard, of course, about the body that was discovered nearly a week ago. Well—"

Baxter looked blank and shrugged, stopping Curtis before she had even started.

"New York? Brooklyn Bridge?" asked Curtis, astounded. "Strung up? Worldwide news?"

Baxter had to stifle a yawn.

Rouche rummaged around in his coat pocket. Curtis waited for him to produce something useful but instead he removed a family-sized packet of Jelly Babies and ripped it open. On noticing her angry expression, he offered her one.

Ignoring him, Curtis opened her bag and produced a file. She found a series of enlarged photographs and put them down on the desk in front of Baxter.

Suddenly it dawned on her why these people had come all this way to see her. The first photo was taken from street level looking up. Silhouetted against the glow radiating off the city was a body, hanging between cables a hundred feet above. The extremities had been contorted into an unnatural pose.

"We've not made this public yet, but the victim's name was William Fawkes."

For a moment Baxter stopped breathing. She had already been feeling faint from lack of food, but now she felt as though she might actually pass out. Her hand trembled as she touched the distorted shape framed by the iconic bridge. She could feel their eyes on her, watching her, perhaps resurrecting the doubts they'd

had about her vague version of events surrounding the dramatic
conclusion to the Ragdoll murders.

With a curious expression, Curtis continued:

"Not *that* one," she said slowly, reaching over to slide the top
photograph off the pile to reveal a close-up of the naked, overweight, and unfamiliar victim.

Baxter held her hand to her mouth, still too shaken to respond.

"He worked for P. J. Henderson's, the investment bank. Wife,
two kids . . . But someone's clearly sending us a message."

Baxter had regained enough composure to flick through the
remaining photographs, which depicted the cadaver from various angles. One complete body, no stitches. A man in his fifties,
stripped naked. His left arm hung loose, the word "Bait" carved
deeply into his chest. She flicked through the other photographs
and then handed them back to Curtis.

"Bait?" she asked, looking between the two agents.

"Perhaps now you can see why we thought you should be
aware," said Curtis.

"Not really," replied Baxter, who was rapidly returning to her
normal self.

Curtis looked stunned and turned to Vanita:

"I had expected your department, over any other, to want to—"

"Do you know how many Ragdoll copycat crimes there have
been in the UK in the past year?" Baxter interrupted. "Seven that
I know about, and I actively try to *avoid* knowing about them."

"And that doesn't concern you at all?" asked Curtis.

Baxter didn't see why she should spare this particular horror any
more time than the five that had landed on her desk that morning.

She shrugged: "Freaks be freakin'."

Rouche almost choked on an orange Jelly Baby.

"Look, Lethaniel Masse was a highly intelligent, resourceful,
and prolific serial killer. These others are no more than sickos
defacing the dead before their local plod picks them up."

Baxter shut down her computer and packed her bag in preparation to leave:

"Six weeks ago, I handed a packet of Smarties to a three-foot version of the Ragdoll trick-or-treating on my doorstep. Some beret-wearing ponce decided to stitch a bunch of dead animal bits together. That mess is now the newest addition to the Tate Modern and being enjoyed by record numbers of equally poncy and equally beret-wearing, beret-wearing ponces."

Rouche laughed.

"Some sick bastard is even making a TV show about it. The Ragdoll is out there now, everywhere, and we're all just going to have to learn to live with it," she finished.

She turned to Rouche, who was staring into his bag of Jelly Babies.

"Does he not talk?" she asked Curtis.

"He prefers to listen," Curtis said bitterly, sounding as though she had grown tired of her eccentric colleague after just one week of working together.

Baxter looked back at Rouche.

"Have they changed these?" he finally mumbled through a Technicolored mouthful when he realized that all three women were waiting for him to input to the meeting.

Baxter was surprised to find that the CIA agent spoke with an impeccable English accent.

"Changed what?" she asked, listening carefully in case he was putting it on to wind her up.

"Jelly Babies," he said, picking his teeth. "They don't taste like they used to."

Curtis was rubbing her forehead in embarrassment and frustration. Baxter raised her hands and looked to Vanita impatiently.

"I've got somewhere to be," she said bluntly.

"We have reason to believe that this isn't just another meaningless copycat, Chief Inspector," insisted Curtis, gesturing to the photographs in an attempt to steer the meeting back on track.

"You're right," said Baxter. "It's not *even* that. Nothing's been stitched together."

"There's been a second murder," snapped Curtis loudly, before reverting to her professional tone. "Two days ago. The location was . . . *favorable* in the sense that we were able to quell the media leakage, at least temporarily. But realistically we don't expect to be able to keep an incident of this"—she looked to Rouche for assistance; none came—"*nature* from the world for more than another day or so."

". . . the *world*?" asked Baxter skeptically.

"We have a small request of you," said Curtis.

"And a big one," added Rouche, even better spoken now that he had finished his mouthful.

Baxter frowned at Rouche, Curtis did the same, and then Vanita glared at Baxter before she had time to protest. Rouche glared at Vanita just to keep things even as Curtis turned back to address Baxter:

"We'd like to interview Lethaniel Masse."

"So that's why both the FBI and CIA are involved," said Baxter. "Stateside murder, Blighty suspect. Well, knock yourself out." She shrugged.

"With you present, of course."

"Absolutely not. There's no reason you could *possibly* need me there. You can read questions off a card by yourselves. I believe in you."

Rouche smiled at the sarcastic aside.

"Of course we will be delighted to assist you in any way that we can, won't we, Chief Inspector?" said Vanita, eyes wide with anger. "Our friendships with the FBI and CIA are both important relationships that we—"

"Christ!" blurted Baxter. "Fine. I'll come and hold your hands. So what's the small request?"

Rouche and Curtis glanced at one another, and even Vanita shuffled uncomfortably before anyone dared speak.

"*That* . . . was the small request," said Curtis softly.

Baxter looked about to blow.

"We would like you to look over the crime scene with us," Curtis continued.

"Photographs?" asked Baxter in a strained whisper.

Rouche stuck out his bottom lip and shook his head.

"I have already agreed to the temporary secondment to New York with the commissioner and will be stepping into your shoes while you're away," Vanita informed her.

"They're big shoes to fill," replied Baxter snippily.

"I'll cope . . . *somehow*," said Vanita, her professional facade slipping for a rare moment.

"This is ridiculous! What the *hell* do you people think I could possibly contribute to a completely unrelated case on the other side of the world?"

"Nothing at all," Rouche answered honestly, disarming Baxter. "It is a *complete* waste of all our time . . . Times? Time?"

Curtis took over the conversation:

"I think what my colleague is *trying* to say is that the American public won't see this case as we do. They'll see Ragdoll murders here, Ragdoll-esque murders there, and they'll want to see the person who captured the Ragdoll Killer hunting these new monsters."

"Monster*s*?" asked Baxter.

It was Rouche's turn to roll his eyes at his colleague. She had clearly said more than she had meant to at this early stage; however, the resulting silence told Baxter that the woman had raised her guard once more.

"So this is all just a PR exercise, then?" asked Baxter.

"And yet," said Rouche with a smile, "isn't everything we do, *Chief Inspector*?"

CHAPTER 3

Tuesday, 8 December 2015

8:53 P.M.

"Hello? Sorry I'm so late," called Baxter from the hallway as she kicked off her boots and entered the living room. A variety of delicious smells drifted in on the cold breeze coming from the kitchen doorway, and the inoffensive sound of whichever singer-songwriter Starbucks had been promoting that week crooned out of the iPod speaker in the corner.

Four places had been set at the table, the flickering tea lights lending the room an orangey glow that emphasized Alex Edmunds's flyaway ginger hair. Her gangly ex-colleague loitered awkwardly, empty beer bottle in hand.

Although tall herself, Baxter had to stand on tiptoes to embrace him.

"Where's Tia?" she asked her friend.

"On the phone to the babysitter . . . again," he replied.

"Em? That you?" called a well-spoken voice from the kitchen.

Baxter remained quiet. She was far too exhausted to get dragged into helping with dinner.

"I've got wine in here!" the voice added playfully.

That tempted her into the showroom-perfect kitchen, where several top-of-the-range pans were bubbling away under the muted light. A man wearing a smart shirt beneath a long apron presided over them, giving them an occasional stir or burst of heat. She walked over and planted a quick kiss on his lips.

"I missed you," said Thomas.

"You mentioned something about wine?" she reminded him.

He laughed and poured her a glass from an open bottle.

"Thanks. I need this," said Baxter.

"Don't thank me. Courtesy of Alex and Tia."

They both raised their glasses to Edmunds, standing in the doorway, and then Baxter jumped up onto the work surface to watch Thomas cook.

They had met at rush hour, eight months earlier, during one of London's recurrent, but unfailingly crippling, Tube strikes. Thomas had intervened when an enraged Baxter had unreasonably attempted to arrest one of the workers picketing for better pay and safer working conditions. He had pointed out that by restraining the hi-vis-clad gentleman and following through on her threat to force him, against his will, to walk the six miles back to Wimbledon with her, she would technically be guilty of kidnap. At which point she had arrested Thomas instead.

Thomas was a gentle and honest man. He was handsome in a manner as generic as his taste in music and was over ten years her senior. He was secure. He knew who he was and what he wanted: a tidy, reassuringly quiet, comfortable life. He was also a lawyer. It made her smile to think of just how much Wolf would have hated him. She often wondered whether that was what had attracted her to him in the first place.

The smart town house serving as the venue for the dinner party belonged to Thomas. He had asked Baxter several times over the previous couple of months to move in with him. Although she had slowly started to keep some of her possessions there, and they had even redecorated the master bedroom together, she had point-blank refused to give up her flat over Wimbledon High Street and had kept her cat, Echo, there as a constant excuse to return home.

The four friends sat down to enjoy dinner together, exchanging stories that had grown less accurate but more amusing with age and expressing intense interest in the answers to the most mundane questions regarding work, the correct way to cook salmon, and parenthood. With Tia's hand in his, Edmunds had spoken animatedly about his promotion at Fraud and reiterated several times how much more time he could now spend with his growing family. When asked about work, Baxter neglected to mention the visit from her overseas colleagues and the unenviable task that awaited her in the morning.

By 10:17 P.M. Tia had fallen asleep on the sofa, and Thomas had left Baxter and Edmunds to talk while he cleared up in the kitchen. Edmunds had swapped to wine and topped up their glasses as they chatted over the dying flickers of the tea lights.

"So how are things at Fraud?" she asked quietly, glancing back over to the sofa to ensure that Tia was definitely asleep.

"I told you . . . great," said Edmunds.

Baxter waited patiently.

"What? Things are good," he said, crossing his arms defensively.

Baxter remained silent.

"They're OK. What do you want me to say?"

When she still refused to accept his answer, he finally smiled. She knew him far too well.

"I am *so* bored. It's not that . . . I don't regret leaving Homicide."

"It sounds like you do," suggested Baxter. She attempted to talk him into coming back every time they saw one another.

"I get to have a life now. I *actually* get to see my daughter."

"It's a waste, that's all," said Baxter, and she meant it. Officially, she had been the one to bring in the notorious Ragdoll Killer. Unofficially, it had been Edmunds who had broken the case. He alone had been able to see through the cloud of lies and deception that had blinded her and the rest of their team.

"I'll tell you what—you give me a nine-to-five detective job and I'll sign the paperwork tonight." Edmunds smiled, knowing that the conversation was over.

Baxter backed down and sipped her wine, while Thomas crashed about in the kitchen.

"I've got to visit Masse tomorrow," she blurted, as if it were an everyday occurrence to go calling on serial killers.

"What?" Edmunds spluttered up a mouthful of his half-price Sauvignon Blanc. "Why?"

He had been the only person she had trusted with the truth of what had happened the day she captured Lethaniel Masse. Neither of them could be sure how much Masse remembered. He had been subjected to a vicious beating and close to death, but she had always feared how much he had been aware of, how easily he could ruin her should his psychotic brain so decide.

Baxter told him about her conversation with Vanita and the two "special" agents, explaining how she had been seconded to accompany them to attend the crime scene in New York.

Edmunds listened silently, his expression becoming increasingly uneasy as she continued.

"I thought this was over," he said when she had finished.

"It is. This is just another copycat like the others."

He didn't look so sure.

"What?" asked Baxter.

"You said the victim had the word 'Bait' carved into his chest."

"Yeah?"

"Bait for who? I wonder."

"You think that was meant for me?" asked Baxter with a snort, reading Edmunds's tone.

"The guy has Wolf's name and now, lo and behold, you're being dragged into it."

Baxter smiled affectionately at her friend.

"It's just another copycat. You don't need to worry about me."

"I always do."

"Coffee?" asked Thomas, surprising them both. He was standing in the doorway drying his hands on a tea towel.

"Black, please," said Edmunds.

Baxter declined, and Thomas disappeared back into the kitchen.

"Have you got something for me?" she whispered.

Edmunds looked uncomfortable. Glancing toward the open kitchen doorway, he reluctantly produced a white envelope from the pocket of his jacket, draped over the chair behind him.

He kept it on his side of the table as he tried, for the umpteenth time, to convince her not to take it from him.

"You don't need this."

Baxter reached for it and he pulled it away from her.

She huffed.

"Thomas is a good man," he said quietly. "You can trust him."

"*You're* the only person I trust."

"You're never going to have anything real with him if you carry on like this."

They both glanced at the doorway as they heard the rattle of ceramic against ceramic from the kitchen. Baxter got to her feet, snatched the envelope out of his hand, and sat back down just as Thomas entered the room with the coffees.

Tia was unrelentingly apologetic when Edmunds gently shook her awake just after 11 P.M. On the doorstep, while Thomas wished Tia good night, Edmunds embraced Baxter.

"Do yourself a favor—don't open it," he whispered in her ear.

She gave him a squeeze but didn't respond.

Once they had gone, Baxter finished off her wine and pulled on her coat.

"You're not leaving?" asked Thomas. "We've hardly seen each other."

"Echo'll be hungry," she said, sliding her boots back on.

"I can't run you. I've had too much to drink."

"I'll get a taxi."

"Stay."

She leaned as far toward him as she could, keeping her damp boots planted firmly on the doormat. Thomas gave her a kiss and a disappointed smile.

"Good night."

*

A little before midnight, Baxter opened the door to her flat. Not feeling the remotest bit tired, she slumped onto the sofa with a bottle of red. She switched on the television, flicked aimlessly through the planner when there was nothing on, and scrolled through the selection of Christmas movies she had been stockpiling.

She finally decided on *Home Alone 2* as she didn't really care if she fell asleep during it or not. The first movie was, secretly, one of her all-time favorites, but she found the second an uninspiring imitation, falling into the age-old trap of believing that by relocating the same story to New York City, they would create a bigger and better sequel.

She poured the remainder of the bottle into her glass as she half watched Macaulay Culkin perform his light-hearted acts of attempted murder. Remembering the envelope stuffed in her coat pocket, she removed the folded paper, Edmunds's plea for her not to open it replaying in her head.

For eight months he had been jeopardizing his career by abusing his power at Fraud. Every week or so he had provided Baxter with a detailed report of Thomas's finances, subjecting his assorted accounts to the standard checks for suspicious and fraudulent activity.

She knew that she was asking too much of him. She knew that he considered Thomas a friend and that he was betraying his trust. But she also knew why Edmunds did and would continue to do this for her: he wanted her to be happy. She had been so debilitatingly crippled by trust issues ever since she had allowed Wolf to walk out of her life that Edmunds knew she would abandon a settled future with Thomas if he did not constantly assess her new boyfriend's trustworthiness.

She put the unopened envelope down on the coffee table beside her feet and tried to concentrate as one of the Wet Bandits had his head set ablaze by a blowtorch. She could smell the scorched flesh. She remembered how quickly the tissue could char and die, the screams of pain as the nerve endings burned away . . .

The man on the television removed his sore head from the toilet before carrying on as if nothing had happened.

It was all a lie; you really couldn't trust anyone.

She finished off her glass in three large gulps and tore open the envelope.

CHAPTER 4

Wednesday, 9 December 2015

8:19 A.M.

London had frozen overnight.

The weak winter sun felt distant and remote, a noncommittal cold light that had failed to thaw the frosty morning. Baxter's fingers grew numb as she waited for her lift out on Wimbledon High Street. She checked the time: twenty minutes late, time that could have been spent in the company of a hot coffee inside her cozy apartment.

She jigged about on the spot to keep warm as the cold air bit her face. She had even been reduced to wearing the ridiculous woolly bobble hat and matching gloves that Thomas had bought for her at Camden Lock Market.

The dreary pavement had been upgraded to a sparkling silver on which people tottered about, suspicious that the ground had its own agenda to break their legs if given half the chance. She watched two men shout to one another across the busy street, the mist from their breath rising above their heads like speech bubbles.

When a double-decker bus stopped at the traffic lights, she caught her reflection in its steamed-up windows. In embarrassment, she pulled the bright orange hat off her head and shoved it into her pocket. Above her own disgruntled image, a familiar advertisement was wrapped around the outside of the vehicle:

Andrea Hall, The Ventriloquist Act: Messages from a Killer

Apparently not content with the fame and fortune acquired through the misery of others while acting as the official news personality of the Ragdoll murders, Wolf's ex-wife was *actually* arrogant enough to have released an autobiographical account of her experiences.

As the bus pulled away, the enormous photograph of Andrea that dominated the rear panels smiled down at Baxter. She looked younger and more attractive than ever and had cut her striking red hair into a trendsetting short style that Baxter would never have dared risk. Before her smug visage could travel too far out of range, Baxter opened her bag, took out her lunch box, and removed the key ingredient to her tomato sandwich, which exploded satisfyingly across the giant stupid woman's giant stupid face.

"Chief Inspector?"

Baxter winced.

She had failed to notice the enormous black minivan pulling up at the bus stop behind her. She dropped her lunch box back into her bag and turned around to find the special agent watching her with a concerned expression.

"Whatcha up to?" asked Curtis cautiously.

"Oh, I was just . . ." Baxter trailed off, hoping that the immaculate and professional young woman would consider that ample explanation for her unusual behaviour.

"Throwing food at buses?" Curtis offered.

". . . Yes."

As Baxter approached the vehicle, Curtis slid the side door open, revealing the spacious interior that the tinted windows obscured.

"*Americans,*" she whispered in disdain under her breath.

"How are we this morning?" asked Curtis politely.

"Well, I don't know about *we,* but *I'm* bloody cold."

"Yes, I apologize for the delay in getting to you. We hadn't expected the traffic to be quite so bad."

"It's London," said Baxter matter-of-factly.

"Jump in."

"Sure there's room?" Baxter asked sarcastically as she crawled ungracefully into the vehicle. The cream leather squeaked as she settled into one of the seats. She wondered whether she should make it clear that the noise had originated from the leather and not from her, but reasoned that it must happen to every passenger as they sat down.

She smiled across at Curtis.

"Excuse you," said the American, who pulled the door closed before shouting through to the driver that they were ready to go.

"No Rouche today?" asked Baxter.

"We're picking him up en route."

Shivering as the van's heater began to thaw her out, Baxter wondered briefly why the agents had not thought to book themselves into the same hotel.

"You're going to have to get used to that, I'm afraid. New York's under two feet of snow." Curtis rooted through her satchel and produced a smart black beanie hat similar to the one she was wearing. "Here."

She passed it to Baxter, who looked momentarily hopeful, until she realized that it had the letters "F," "B," and "I" printed in bold yellow across the front—a sniper-friendly target if ever she saw one.

She tossed it back to Curtis.

"Ta, but I've got my own," she said, taking the orange eyesore out of her pocket and pulling it down over her head.

Curtis shrugged and watched the city roll past for a moment.

"Have you seen him since?" she eventually asked. "Masse?"

"Only in court," replied Baxter, trying to work out where they were heading.

"I'm a little nervous." Curtis smiled.

Baxter was momentarily mesmerized by the young agent's perfect movie-star smile. She then noticed her flawless dark complexion and was unable to tell whether she was even wearing makeup to achieve the effect. Feeling a little self-conscious, she fiddled with her hair and stared out the window.

"I mean, Masse is an *actual* living legend," Curtis continued. "I heard that they're already studying him in the academy. I'm sure one day his name will be mentioned in the same breath as Bundy and John Wayne Gacy. It's . . . it's an honor really, isn't it? For want of a better word."

Baxter turned her huge, angry eyes on the other woman.

"I *suggest* you find a better word," she snapped. "That sick sack of shit murdered and mutilated one of my friends. You think this is fun? You think you're gonna get an autograph?"

"I didn't mean any offen—"

"You're wasting your time. You're wasting *my* time. You're even wasting *this* bloke's time," said Baxter, gesturing to the man in the driver's seat. "Masse can't even speak. Last I heard, his jaw was still hanging off."

Curtis cleared her throat and sat up straight. "I would like to apologize for my—"

"You can apologize by being quiet," said Baxter, ending the conversation.

The two women sat in silence for the remainder of the journey. Baxter watched Curtis's reflection in the window. She didn't look angry or indignant, only frustrated with herself for the careless comment. Baxter could see her lips moving silently as she rehearsed her apology or vetted the topic of their next unavoidable interaction.

Starting to feel a little guilty about the outburst, Baxter remembered her own unchecked excitement, just a year and a half earlier, on first laying eyes on the Ragdoll, realizing that she had stumbled into the middle of something enormous, fantasizing about the knock-on effects it could have on her career. She was about to say something when the vehicle turned a corner and parked up outside a large semidetached house in a leafy residential suburb. She had no idea where they were.

She stared out in confusion at the mock-Tudor property, which somehow managed to look simultaneously homey and neglected. Impressive weeds erupted through deep cracks in the steep driveway. The muted colors of disconnected Christmas lights clung desperately to the peeling paint of the tired windowpanes, while smoke drifted lazily out from the bird's-nest-covered chimney.

"Funny-looking hotel," she commented.

"Rouche's family still live over here," explained Curtis. "I think they come out to see him occasionally, and he gets back when he can. He told me he just lives out of hotels in the US. Then again, that's the nature of the job, I suppose. Never being able to settle in one place for long."

Rouche emerged from the house eating a piece of toast. He seemed to blend into the frosty morning: his white shirt and blue suit mimicked the scattered clouds drifting across the sky above, the silver streaks in his hair glistening like the icy concrete.

Curtis climbed out to greet him as he skidded down the drive-way, colliding toast-first into her.

"Christ, Rouche!" she complained.

"Couldn't you have got anything bigger?" Baxter heard him ask sarcastically before they both climbed in.

He took the window seat opposite Baxter and offered her a bite of his breakfast, grinning as he looked at the woolly orange mess atop her head.

The driver pulled out and they were on their way again. Curtis busied herself with some paperwork, while Baxter and Rouche watched the buildings flicker past, blurring into a single indecipherable shape with the whir of the engine.

"God, I *hate* this city," blurted Rouche as they crossed the river, his eyes glued to the impressive vista. "The traffic, the noise, the litter, the crowds swelling through its narrow arteries like a heart attack waiting to happen, graffiti decorating anything unfortunate enough to find itself within arm's reach."

Curtis smiled apologetically at Baxter as Rouche continued:

"It kind of reminds me of school: *that* party at the rich kid's house, you know? The parents are away and in their absence all of the artistic and architectural brilliance is trampled, defaced, and ignored to accommodate the trivial lives of those who never fail to underappreciate it."

They sat in strained silence as the van crawled toward a junction.

"Well, I *love* where you live," said Curtis enthusiastically. "There's so much history everywhere."

"*Actually*, I'm with Rouche on this one," said Baxter. "Like you said, there's history everywhere. *You* see Trafalgar Square; *I* see the alleyway opposite where we fished a prostitute's body out of the bins. *You* see the Houses of Parliament; *I* see the boat chase down the river that made me miss . . . something that I shouldn't have missed. It is what it is, but it's home."

For the first time since setting off, Rouche turned his attention away from the window to take a long, studying look at Baxter.

"So when did you leave London, Rouche?" asked Curtis, who evidently did not find the peaceful silence as comfortable as the others did.

"In 2005," he replied.

"It must be hard being so far away from your family all the time."

Rouche appeared in no mood to talk about it but reluctantly answered:

"It is. But as long as I hear their voices every day, we're never really that far apart."

Baxter shifted uncomfortably in her seat, a little embarrassed by the heartfelt sentiment, made worse when Curtis made an unnecessary and insincere "Awwww!"

They were dropped off in the visitors' car park at Belmarsh Prison and made their way to the main entrance. The two agents surrendered their weapons as they were fingerprinted, then ushered through the airlock doors, X-ray machine, metal detector, and manual searches before being told to wait for the prison governor.

Rouche looked tense as he took in his surroundings, while Curtis excused herself to visit the "restroom." After a few moments, Baxter could no longer ignore the fact that Rouche was singing "Hollaback Girl" by Gwen Stefani under his breath:

"You OK?" she asked.

"Sorry."

Baxter watched him suspiciously for a moment.

"I sing when I'm nervous," he explained.

"Nervous?"

"I don't like confined spaces."

"Well, who does?" said Baxter. "That's like not enjoying being poked in the eye: it's obvious. It's pointless even voicing out loud because no one wants to be trapped somewhere."

"Thank you for your concern." He smiled. "While we're on the subject of looking nervous, are *you* all right?"

She was surprised that he had picked up on her apprehension.

"After all, Masse did have a *pretty* good punt at . . ."

"Killing me?" Baxter helped him. "Yeah, I remember. It's nothing to do with Masse. I'm just hoping Governor Davies isn't still working here. He doesn't like me much."

"*You?*" asked Rouche, in what he hoped had (but had not) come across as dismayed aghast.

"Yeah, *me,*" said Baxter, a little offended.

It was a lie, of course. Baxter's trepidation was indeed rooted in coming face-to-face with Masse again, not because of what he was but because of what he might know and what he might tell.

Only four people knew the truth concerning what had occurred inside that Old Bailey courtroom. She had expected Masse to contradict her hastily formulated version of events; however, no opposition was ever made to her statement. And as time wore on, she began to let herself hope that he had lost consciousness, too injured during his altercation with Wolf to be aware of her shameful secret. Every day she had wondered whether the past would catch up with her, and now she felt as though she was flaunting her good fortune by sitting down with the one person who could ruin her in an instant.

At that moment Governor Davies came around the corner. His face dropped when he recognized Baxter.

"I'll get Curtis," she whispered to Rouche.

She paused at the door to the toilets on hearing Curtis's voice coming from inside. This struck Baxter as bizarre, as they had given up their mobile phones back at security. She gently leaned against the heavy door until she could make out the young American agent talking to herself in the mirror:

". . . No more *stupid* comments. *Think* before you speak. You *can't* make a mistake like that in front of Masse. 'Confidence in oneself demands confidence from others.'"

Baxter knocked loudly and swung the door open, making Curtis jump.

"Governor's ready for us," she announced.

"I'll just be a moment."

Baxter nodded and went to rejoin Rouche.

The governor escorted the group in the direction of the high-security unit.

"As I'm sure you're well aware, Lethaniel Masse sustained some lasting injuries prior to his apprehension by Detective Baxter here," he said, making an effort to be pleasant.

"Detective chief inspector now," she corrected him, ruining it.

"He has undergone numerous reconstructive surgeries on his jaw but will never have full use of it again."

"Will he be able to answer our questions?" Curtis asked.

"Not coherently, no. Which is why I've arranged for an interpreter to sit in on your interview."

"Who specializes in . . . mumbling?" asked Baxter, unable to help herself.

"Sign language," said the governor. "Masse learned it within weeks of arriving here."

The group was led outside through another security door, where the recreation areas stood eerily empty as a coded message was announced over the Tannoy system.

"How is Masse as a detainee?" asked Curtis, the interest evident in her voice.

"Exemplary," answered the governor. "If only they were all so well behaved. Rosenthal!" he called to a young man at the far end of the five-a-side football pitch, who almost slipped on the ice as he jogged over to them. "What's going on?"

"Another fight in House Block 3, sir," panted the young man. One of his shoelaces was undone and trailed along the floor behind him.

The governor sighed. "I'm afraid you'll have to excuse me," he said to the group. "We had an influx of new inmates this week and there are always teething problems while they size each other up and adjust the pecking order. Rosenthal here will take you to see Masse."

"Masse, sir?" The young man looked less than enthused by the order. "Of course."

The governor hurried away as Rosenthal led them toward the prison within a prison, surrounded by its own walls and fences. When they reached the first security gate, he patted his pockets frantically and started retracing his steps.

Rouche tapped him on the shoulder and handed him an ID card.

"You dropped this back there," he said kindly.

"Thank you. The boss would *literally* kill me if I lost that . . . again."

"Not if one of the escaped mass murderers you're in charge of got to you first," Baxter pointed out, making the young man go bright red with embarrassment.

"Sorry," he said, before buzzing them through, only to confront them with another series of security checks and searches.

He explained how the high-security unit was divided into "spurs" of twelve individual cells and how warders were allowed to work only a three-year stretch before being transferred back into the main prison.

Inside, beige walls and doors surrounded the terra-cotta-colored floors and the framework of rust-red railings, gates, and staircases. Above their heads, large nets stretched between the walkways, sagging in the center where rubbish and other, more aerodynamic objects had accumulated.

The building was surprisingly quiet, as the prisoners were still confined to their cells. Another guard showed them to a room on the ground floor, where a dowdy, middle-aged woman was waiting for them. She was introduced as their sign-language expert, and then the guard took them through the painfully obvious rules before finally unlocking the door.

"Remember, if you need anything, I'll be right outside," he emphasized twice, then pushed open the door to reveal the imposing figure sat with his back to them.

Baxter could sense the guards' uneasiness around their most notorious inmate. A long chain linked Masse's handcuffs to the top of the metal table, running down the length of his dark blue boiler suit to attach the shackles that bound his feet to the concrete floor.

Although he did not look around, keeping the deep scars that were cut into his scalp facing them as they filtered into the room, he tilted his head back and sniffed the air inquiringly, breathing them in.

The two women looked at one another, instantly unnerved, while Rouche sat down, selflessly choosing the seat nearest to their suspect.

Despite the chains binding him to the room he could not leave, it was Baxter who felt trapped as the heavy door closed behind them and she slowly took her seat opposite the man who, despite his incarceration, still posed such a threat to her.

As Masse watched her glancing around the room, looking anywhere to avoid meeting his eye, a lopsided grin formed on his ruined face.

CHAPTER 5

Wednesday, 9 December 2015

11:22 A.M.

"Well, that was a complete waste of time," sighed Baxter as they stepped back out into the spur's main atrium.

Masse had not even attempted to answer a single question during Curtis's half-hour monologue. It had been like visiting a caged animal at the zoo, Masse present in name only—a subdued and defeated shadow of the sadistic monster that still kept her up at night, feeding off the fumes of a reputation that he could no longer live up to.

Wolf had utterly broken him, body and soul.

She could not know for certain whether his attention had kept returning to her because he knew what she had done or simply because she had been the one famously credited with his arrest. Either way, she was glad that it was over.

Rosenthal had been waiting for them in "the Bubble," the secure staff area at the far end of the spur, and was already making his way over.

"We'll need to conduct a thorough search of Masse's cell," Curtis advised him.

The inexperienced guard looked uncertain.

"I . . . *er* . . . Does the governor know?"

"You're not serious?" Baxter asked Curtis in exasperation.

"I've got to agree with Baxter," said Rouche, "but in a politer way, of course. Masse isn't involved. This isn't the best use of our resources."

"On what we've seen so far, I'm inclined to agree," started Curtis diplomatically, "but we have a strict protocol to follow, and I cannot leave the premises until such time as we rule out, without a shadow of a doubt, any possibility of Masse's involvement."

She turned back to Rosenthal:

"Masse's cell . . . please."

Dominic Burrell, or "the Bouncer," as he was better known to inmates and staff alike, had been imprisoned for beating a complete stranger to death simply because the man had made the mistake of looking at him "funny." He had spent the majority of his incarceration in House Block 1 but had recently been transferred to the high-security unit following two similarly unprovoked attacks on warders. He was generally avoided where possible, given his reputation and obsession with bodybuilding, despite his unimpressive stature of five feet six inches.

He watched from his cell as the group on the ground floor were escorted up to Masse's empty room, which stood directly opposite his own. As they began their cramped search of the six-by-ten-foot room, he lost interest and continued tearing the fabric of his mattress into long strips, assisted by the razor-sharp wedge of plastic fashioned out of melted food packaging.

When he heard the guards unlocking the first cell door in order to line the inmates up for lunch, he flipped the mattress back over and wrapped the long piece of material around his waist to conceal it beneath his clothing. He was ushered out onto the walkway and noted that Masse was only two people ahead of him in the queue. Once the prison guard had moved on, he shoved past the man between them, who was evidently aware of his reputation and backed away without argument.

Standing on his tiptoes, he whispered into Masse's ear: "Lethaniel Masse?"

Masse nodded, disguising their conversation by keeping his
eyes forward.

"I'm here to deliver a message."

"Wha' mes-sage?" Masse slurred painfully.

Leaning around to check on the warder's location, he placed a
firm hand on Masse's shoulder and gently pulled him closer until
his lips were grazing the fine hairs of his ear:

"You . . ."

As Masse turned his head, the Bouncer locked his enormous
arm around his throat and dragged him backward into the empty
cell beside them. As per prison rules, the men in front and behind
reassumed their places in line, neither interfering nor alerting the
guards to the fight.

Through the open door, Masse made eye contact with one
of the men in line, who just stood there watching him suffocate
impassively. He tried to call out, but the few incoherent mumbles
that he managed through his mangled jaw failed to attract the
attention of anybody who could help him.

Masse wondered for a moment whether the burly man intended
to rape him when he ripped his top open, but then he felt the
sting of the blade tearing into his chest and realized that he was
going to die.

He had felt it only once before—the unfamiliar sensation of
fear, tainted with a twisted fascination as he finally appreciated
what each of his countless victims had experienced in their final
moments, the helplessness they had felt at his hands.

Curtis, Baxter, and Rouche had been advised to finish up their
fruitless search of Masse's cell and leave before the lunchtime prisoner movements. While the doors on the first floor were opened
up, Rosenthal had escorted them down to ground level and across
the atrium. They had almost reached the red iron gate when the
first whistle blows pierced the calm above them.

It was difficult to make out what was happening as three warders
struggled to reach whatever the jeering prisoners were blocking.

More whistles joined the panicked calls for assistance as the shouts grew more excitable, echoing deafeningly around the empty metal building as the prisoners occupying the cells on the ground floor joined the cacophony.

"Let's get you out of here," said Rosenthal as bravely as he could muster. He spun back around and inserted his ID card into the reader on the wall; a red light blinked in response. He tried again. "Shit!"

"Problem?" asked Baxter, keeping one eye on the events developing above.

"We're in lockdown," he explained. He was clearly beginning to panic.

"All right. So what do we have to do in a lockdown situation?" Rouche asked the young man calmly.

"I-I don't . . ." he stuttered.

The whistle calls above were growing more desperate, while the shouting somehow grew even louder.

"The Bubble, perhaps?" Baxter suggested.

Rosenthal looked at her wide-eyed and nodded.

The noise above rose to a crescendo as someone was lifted over the walkway railings and dropped into the empty void at the core of the atrium. The half-naked body ripped the netting from the wall on one side and landed facedown just a few meters away from the group.

Curtis screamed, attracting the attention of the men above.

"We need to go. Right now!" said Baxter, but she froze when the dead body made a sudden and unnatural movement toward them.

It took her a moment to realize that the length of knotted material trailing down the destroyed netting had been wrapped around the bloody victim's neck. Just then the makeshift rope pulled taut, dragging the corpse up into the air as a second, more muscular body, dropped alongside it.

"He's still alive!" gasped Rosenthal in horror as the counterweight thrashed about desperately while the frayed noose took its time to choke him.

"Go! Go! Go!" ordered Baxter, shoving Curtis and Rosenthal after Rouche, who had almost reached the door to the Bubble.

"Open the door!" he yelled.

The whistles went silent one by one as the riot escalated. There was a chilling cry from somewhere above and then a burning mattress dropped into the middle of the atrium, the chaos fueling the inmates' excitement like fresh blood to shark-infested waters.

The first of the prisoners had clambered down the broken netting as the group reached Rouche at the Bubble's secure door.

"Open up!" shouted Rouche, hammering frantically on the metal.

"Where's your card?" Baxter asked Rosenthal.

"It won't work. They need to open it from inside," he panted.

More inmates had made the perilous descent onto their level, while the first man benevolently unlocked cells at random with a blood-smeared security pass.

Rouche rushed around to the front, where he could see a warder inside through the protective glass.

"We're police officers!" he yelled through the impenetrable window. "Open the door!"

The terrified man shook his head and mouthed the words "I can't. I'm so sorry," gesturing to the approaching ensemble of the country's most dangerous men.

"Open the door!" shouted Rouche.

Baxter joined him at the window.

"What now?" she asked as calmly as she could.

There was nowhere for them to go.

An enormous inmate climbed down from above. He was wearing a prison officer's uniform that looked absurdly small for him. The trousers were cropped halfway up his shin, and his stomach was on show beneath the hem of the shirt. The ensemble would have looked almost comical had it not been for the fresh scratch marks torn across his face.

Curtis was pounding on the door, pleading desperately.

"He isn't going to open it," said Rosenthal, slumping down onto the floor. "He can't risk them getting through."

The rioters were rushing toward them, eyeing Rouche and Rosenthal with burning hatred and the women with hunger. Rouche grabbed Baxter by the arm and shoved her into the corner behind him.

"Hey!" she shouted, trying to fight him off.

"Stay behind us!" he shouted to the women.

Rosenthal seemed confused by the word "us" until Rouche dragged him back up onto his feet.

"Go for their eyes," Rouche shouted to the petrified young man seconds before the pack engulfed them.

Baxter kicked out wildly. There were hands and sneering faces everywhere. A strong fist grabbed a clump of her hair and dragged her a couple of feet, but she was released when a fight broke out between two of her attackers.

She scrambled back against the wall, looking for Curtis, but the powerful arm returned for her. From nowhere Rosenthal appeared, leaping onto the man's back, sinking his fingers deep into one of the tattooed inmate's eyes.

Suddenly, the lights went out.

Only the eerie illumination of the crackling fire in the center of the atrium remained, two silhouettes hanging above the dying flames like the aftermath of a witch hunt.

There was a loud bang. The space filled with smoke. Then another.

Men in full riot gear and protective masks entered through the iron gate on the far side of the hall as the inmates covered their faces and ran for cover, dispersing in all directions like hyenas chased off a kill.

Baxter spotted Curtis lying unconscious a few meters away and crawled over to her.

She wrapped the FBI agent's ripped shirt back around her. A large bump protruded from her head, but she appeared otherwise unharmed.

Baxter felt her nose and mouth burning and could taste the CS gas as it diffused into her section of the room. Through her failing vision, she watched the spectral shapes fan out into the haze surrounding the fire, welcoming the searing pain in her airways because it meant that she was still alive.

After forty minutes of eyebaths in the medical center, Baxter was finally permitted to join Rouche and Governor Davies. Having recovered more quickly than the other two, Rouche had kept her updated with the latest news while she ungraciously received her treatment.

They had learned that one of the dead prisoners had been a man named Dominic Burrell. More troublingly, however, the other had been Masse. From the CCTV footage, they had confirmed that it was Burrell who had murdered Masse prior to taking his own life.

Curtis was awake but still shaken by the ordeal, and Rosenthal had a broken collarbone but was in high spirits.

Now that Baxter could see, she suspected that Rouche was more injured than he was letting on. He was limping and appeared to be taking intentionally shallow breaths. She noticed him holding his chest painfully when he thought nobody was watching.

The governor had ensured that once all the inmates were returned to their cells, the scene had been left untouched. He then explained, as politely as possible, that there was nowhere else for the prisoners to go and, as such, the high-security unit was operating as usual, only with two dead bodies hanging from the rafters. So the sooner they did whatever they needed to do, the better.

"I'm ready when you are," said Baxter, who looked a tad crazed now that her eyes were bloodshot and inflamed. "Should we wait for Curtis?"

"She said to go on without her."

She was a little surprised that the FBI agent would volunteer to miss out on her own crime scene but decided not to push the matter:

"Then let's."

*

Baxter and Rouche stared up at the two bodies dangling six feet apart above their heads. She noticed that he was holding his chest again. They had managed to persuade the lead detective to give them five minutes alone with the scene before he and his team took over.

Entirely protected from the elements by the numerous security doors and quite sensible lack of opening windows, the bodies hung surreally still, suspended from opposite ends of the same piece of knotted material, which had been looped around the railings on the first floor.

Baxter was too disturbed by the macabre scene to feel the weight lift off her shoulders: whatever Masse had or had not known was irrelevant now.

She was safe.

"So when we both told Curtis that your case and my case were in no way related, it actually turns out that they really, really are," said Baxter flippantly. " 'Bait,' " she read aloud. The scruffily scrawled letters on Masse's chest now looked black with congealed blood. "Just like the other one."

She moved position to look up at Dominic Burrell's muscular body, also stripped to the waist, also sporting a mutilated message across his chest.

" 'Puppet,' " she read. "That's new, right?"

Rouche shrugged noncommittally.

"*Right?*" Baxter asked again.

"I think we'd better talk to Curtis."

Baxter and Rouche returned to the medical center to find that Curtis was feeling much better. In fact, she was in the middle of conducting an interview with a handsome man in his late thirties, dressed in civilian clothes, and whose mid-length, dark brown hair flopped down loosely in a style that looked a little young for him.

Not wanting to interrupt, Rouche went to make them another coffee. Not hesitating to interrupt, Baxter didn't:

"You good?" she asked Curtis, who looked a touch annoyed at having to pause midsentence.

"Yes. Thank you," she replied, dismissing Baxter as politely as possible.

Making an inquiring gesture toward the attractive man, Baxter felt as though she were caught between two supermodels—the three-meter gap between them and the doorway hadn't done him justice.

"This is . . ." Curtis started reluctantly.

"Alexei Green." The man smiled. He got to his feet and shook her hand firmly. "And you, of course, are the famous Emily Baxter. It's an honor."

"Mutually," Baxter replied nonsensically, his stupid cheekbones putting her off.

Going red, she quickly excused herself and hurried off after Rouche.

Five minutes later, Curtis was still engrossed in the interview. In fact, unless Baxter was mistaken, the straitlaced agent appeared to be flirting.

"Do you know what?" said Rouche. "Screw it. We need to bring you up to speed, especially now. Let's talk outside."

They stepped out into the crisp but sunny afternoon. Baxter pulled her bobble hat back over her head.

"Where to start?" he started somewhat unsurely. "The banker William Fawkes, who was strung up on the Brooklyn Bridge—"

"Mind if we just call him 'the Banker' from now on?" asked Baxter.

"Sure . . . We believe he had one arm hanging loose because his killer didn't finish. This is backed up by eyewitness reports describing someone or something falling from the bridge into the East River."

"Is it possible they survived the fall?" Baxter asked, pulling her hat down to cover even more of her frozen face.

"No," replied Rouche decisively. "One, it's roughly a hundred-and-fifty-foot drop. Two, New York was knocking minus nine degrees that night: the river was frozen solid. Three, and most significantly, the body washed up the next morning. And you'll never guess what he had scarred across his chest . . ."

"'Puppet,'" they chimed together.

"So we've got two dead victims with the same word carved into them, two dead killers with a *different* word carved into *them*, taking place on opposite sides of the Atlantic?" summarized Baxter.

"No," said Rouche, tucking his cold hands under his armpits. "You're forgetting about the one Curtis mentioned yesterday that we've kept under wraps so far, the one we brought you in to help us investigate."

"Making this victim and killer number three."

"All murder-suicides, just like today," Rouche added.

Baxter looked surprised:

"Any theories yet?"

"Only that things are likely to get a *hell* of a lot worse before they get any better. After all, we're chasing ghosts, aren't we?"

Rouche poured the rest of his tasteless coffee onto the ground. It sizzled and steamed like acid. He closed his eyes and tilted his head up into the sun before pondering out loud:

"How do you catch a killer who's already dead?"

CHAPTER 6

Wednesday, 9 December 2015
7:34 P.M.

Baxter managed to open the front door to Thomas's house just using her chin and stumbled into the hallway holding a cat carrier in one hand and a Waitrose bag in the other.

"Just me!" she called out to no response.

As the downstairs lights were on, she knew that Thomas was home. The television chatted quietly to itself as she walked muddy footprints through to the kitchen. She placed the shopping bag and the cat down on the table, then poured herself a large glass of red wine.

She slumped into one of the chairs, kicked off her boots, and massaged her aching feet as she stared out at the dark garden. The house was blissfully quiet, bar the comforting hum of the heating firing back up and the muffled rain of the upstairs shower through the floorboards.

She removed the family-sized bags of Monster Munch and Cadbury's Buttons from her shopping bag but was distracted by her own ghostly reflection in the black windows. She realized that this was the first time she had seen herself since the ordeal earlier that day and totted up the numerous scratches that covered her face and neck, the long, weeping graze across her forehead only counting as one. She shuddered as she remembered the hands clawing at her, dragging her across the floor, the helplessness she had felt on kicking one malevolent face away just for it to be replaced by another.

She had showered twice before leaving her apartment and still felt dirty. She rubbed her face wearily and ran her hands through her damp hair before topping up her glass.

Ten minutes later, Thomas entered the kitchen in his dressing gown.

"Hey. I didn't think you were coming over ton—" He stopped short when he saw the cuts decorating her face. He rushed across the room and sat down beside her. "Jesus! Are you all right?"

He took one of her crisp-dusted hands in his and squeezed it gently. Baxter forced an appreciative smile and wriggled it out of his grasp, picking up her wineglass as an excuse for not wanting to be touched.

"What happened?" he asked.

Thomas was an unfailingly mild-mannered man, except when it came to his borderline overprotectiveness of Baxter. The last time she had returned home with a split lip, he had used all of his influence as a lawyer to make her assailant's time in custody as miserable as possible, and to ensure he was sentenced to the maximum term at the end of it.

She actually considered confiding in him for a moment.

"It's nothing." She smiled weakly. "Got involved in a fight at the office. Should've just left them to it."

She watched Thomas relax a little, satisfied in the knowledge that no one had deliberately tried to hurt her.

Desperate to know more but picking up on Baxter's reluctance to elaborate, he helped himself to a crisp.

"Starter, main, or dessert?" he asked, gesturing to the bag.

She tapped the open bottle of wine: "Starter."

She pointed to the enormous bag of Monster Munch: "Main."

She picked up the bag of Buttons: "Dessert."

Thomas smiled fondly at her and leaped to his feet.

"Let me make you something."

"No, I'm fine. I'm not really hungry."

"Just an omelet. It'll take five minutes," he said, already setting to work on the emergency dinner. He glanced at the cat carrier on the kitchen table. "What's in the box?"

"Cat," replied Baxter automatically, hoping that she was right: Echo had been uncharacteristically quiet since arriving at the house.

It suddenly occurred to her that it might have been polite to ask him whether he was prepared to look after her pet while she was away before turning up with it. It then occurred to her that she had never actually told him, out loud, that she *was* going away.

She really couldn't be bothered to get into an argument.

"And as much of a pleasure as it always is to see Echo," started Thomas, his tone changing already, "how come he decided to pop across town on such a chilly evening?"

Baxter figured that she might as well get it over with.

"I've been seconded indefinitely to work with the FBI and CIA on a high-profile murder case. I'm flying out to New York in the morning and have no idea when I'll be home."

She let that sink in for a few moments.

Thomas had gone very quiet.

"Anything else?" he asked.

"Yeah. I forgot Echo's food, so you'll have to get some. Oh, and don't forget to give him his pills." She rummaged around in her bag, then shook the box in her left hand: "Mouth." And then the box in her right: "Butt."

She could see Thomas grinding his teeth as he banged the pan around on the metal hob. Oil splashed and hissed as it escaped the nonstick confines of Jamie Oliver's invention.

Baxter got up: "I need to make a call."

"I'm making you dinner!" snapped Thomas as he pelted the pan with grated cheese.

"I don't want your *bloody* angry omelet," she snapped right back at him before heading upstairs to talk to Edmunds in private.

*

Edmunds had just been peed on.

Tia had taken over nappy duties while he went to change his shirt. He was carrying the soiled garment to the washing machine when his phone went off.

"Baxter?" he answered while washing his hands.

"Hey," she greeted him casually. "Got a minute?"

"Sure."

"So . . . interesting day."

Edmunds listened attentively as she gave a detailed account of her time at the prison. She also passed on the limited information that Rouche had shared with her outside in the grounds.

"A cult?" he suggested sensibly once she had finished.

"Certainly seems the most likely explanation, but apparently the Americans have whole teams assigned to cult activities and religious sects. They've said the murders don't fit with any of the groups they're monitoring."

"I don't like this whole 'Bait' thing. It was one thing killing someone with Wolf's name, but now they've managed to get to Masse. It feels like that message is for you, and if it is, you're involved now. You're giving them exactly what they want."

"I agree it's one possibility, but what else can I do?"

"Alex!" Tia called from the bedroom.

"Just a minute!" Edmunds shouted back.

The neighbor next door thumped against the wall.

"She's peed on me too now!" yelled Tia.

"OK!" Edmunds called back in frustration.

The neighbor started thumping again, knocking a family photograph clean off the shelf.

"Sorry about that," he said to Baxter.

"Would it be OK to call you when I've got more?" she asked.

"Of course. Be really careful over there."

"Don't worry—I'll be on twenty-four-hour Puppet watch," she assured him.

"Actually," said Edmunds, his tone deadly serious, "I think we need to be more concerned about whoever it is who's holding the strings."

*

The moment Baxter reached the bottom of the staircase, she knew that an argument with Thomas would be unavoidable. The television had been paused. Andrea was frozen mid-report, and the headline at the bottom of the screen read:

Ragdoll Killer dead following visit from Chief Inspector

She *really* hated that woman.

"You went to see Lethaniel Masse today?" Thomas asked quietly from somewhere inside the room.

Baxter huffed and entered the living room. Thomas was sat in his chair with the remainder of the bottle of wine.

"Uh-huh." Baxter nodded as though it were of no importance.

"You didn't tell me."

"Don't see why I would." She shrugged.

"No. Why would you? Why would you?!" shouted Thomas, getting up. "Just like why would you tell me that there was a riot there today?"

"I wasn't involved in that," she lied.

"Bullshit!"

Baxter was a little taken aback. Thomas hardly ever swore.

"You turn up here battered and bleeding . . ."

"It's a few scratches."

". . . risking your life among out-of-control prisoners because you were paying a visit to the most dangerous man in the entire country!"

"I don't have time for this," said Baxter, fetching her coat.

"Well, of course you don't," yelled Thomas in frustration as he followed her into the kitchen. "You've got a flight to New York in the morning, which you *also* neglected to tell me about." He paused. "Emily, I don't understand why you feel you can't share these things with me," he said softly.

"Can we talk about this when I get back?" she asked, matching his calm tone.

Thomas looked at her for a long moment and then nodded in defeat as she slipped her boots back on.

"Look after Echo for me," she said.

She got up and walked out to the hallway. Thomas smiled as she pulled on the matching hat and gloves that he had bought for her as a joke. It was baffling to him that this woman, attempting to blow the hair out of her eyes as a pompom wobbled on top of her head, could have gained such a formidable reputation among the few colleagues whom she had permitted him to meet.

She reached for the door.

"What on earth is this case you've been asked to help with?" he blurted.

They both knew that it was more than just a passing question: it was a plea for her to open up to him before she left; it was an opportunity for her to prove that things would be different from now on; it was him asking whether they could ever have a future together.

She gave him a peck on the cheek.

The door clicked shut behind her.

Rouche was woken by the sound of "Air Hostess" by Busted buzzing out of his mobile phone. He answered it as quickly as he could to hush the irritating ringtone.

"Rouche," he said in a hoarse whisper.

"Rouche, it's Curtis."

"Is everything all right?" he asked urgently.

"Yes. Fine. I didn't wake the family, did I?"

"No." He yawned as he made his way downstairs to the kitchen. "Don't worry—they'd sleep through anything. What's up?"

"I couldn't remember whether we were picking you up at six thirty or seven tomorrow."

"Seven," Rouche answered pleasantly, checking the time.

It was 2:52 A.M.

"Oh, right," she mumbled. "I thought it might have been six thirty."

Rouche suspected that this had not been the real purpose of

her unsociably timed call. When she remained silent, he sat down on the cold floor and made himself comfortable.

"Scary day," he said. "It was good to get home and talk it through with someone."

He allowed the silence to run its course, giving his colleague the opportunity to seize the prompt should she want to.

"I . . . um . . . I don't really have anyone," she finally admitted. She spoke so softly that he could barely hear her.

"You're a long way from home," he reasoned.

"That doesn't really . . . I still wouldn't have anybody."

He waited for her to continue.

"The job just takes precedence over everything else. I wouldn't have the time it takes to cultivate a relationship. I've lost touch with almost all my friends."

"What do your family say about it?" he asked, hoping he wasn't putting his foot in it.

Curtis sighed heavily. He winced.

"They'd say I've got the right work ethic. I'm just in the wrong job."

Rouche adjusted position to huddle up against the cold, knocking over a broken cupboard door, which in turn toppled a pile of tiles across the dusty room.

"Shit."

"What was that?" asked Curtis.

"Sorry. We're redoing the kitchen and it's a bit of a mess," he told her. "So tell me about your family."

They talked about nothing in particular until Curtis's murmured responses faded into silence. He listened to her shallow breaths and tiny snores for a while, finding the sound a surreally peaceful way to finish such a traumatic day.

Eventually, he hung up.

Too tired to make the arduous journey back upstairs, he rested his head against the cupboard, closed his eyes, and drifted off to sleep amid the splintered units and exposed concrete at the heart of his home.

CHAPTER 7

Thursday, 10 December 2015

2:16 P.M.

14:16 12-10-2015 -5°C/23°F

Baxter watched the numbers on the dashboard display blink in warning from her warm seat in the back of the FBI vehicle. She glanced down at her own watch, realizing that she had forgotten to reset it on the plane as it still read "7:16 P.M." She must have missed the announcement. All three of them had slept through the seven-and-a-half-hour flight following their night of broken sleep.

It had been a painfully slow journey into Manhattan from the airport. The city's traffic had been reduced to trundling through its streets at walking pace as vehicles slid and spun over a week's worth of compacted ice and filthy slush.

Baxter had visited New York twice in her youth. She had ticked off all the usual tourist traps, marveled at the movie-set skyline surrounded by water, and experienced that feeling of being at the very center of the world as people from every corner of the earth jostled for position on a two-mile-wide island. Now, she just felt tired and wanted to go home.

Rouche sat quietly beside her. He had suggested that their driver take them in via the Brooklyn Bridge. As they approached the second enormous stone tower, he pointed to where the Banker's body had been strung up:

"His wrists and ankles had been bound, suspending him between these two cables either side of the road, watching the people passing beneath. It was like a premonition hung over the gateway to the city for the entire world to see, an example of the horrors to befall those who dare step beyond that point."

The car flickered into shadow as they passed through the archway.

"Could we just stick to the facts that we know for certain, please?" asked Curtis from the passenger seat. "You're creeping me out."

"Anyway, as you know, he didn't get to finish. The killer was just attaching the left arm on to the outer cable when he lost his footing, plummeted through the ice, and drowned," Rouche explained. "Which must have been annoying for him."

The irreverence with which Rouche had trivialized the killer's death-inducing fall caught her by surprise and, despite her foul mood, Baxter smirked.

Rouche couldn't help but smile back: "What?"

"It's nothing," she told him, turning to stare out the window as they descended into the frozen city. "You just reminded me of someone, that's all."

The condition of the roads had gradually deteriorated the farther they traveled from Midtown. By the time they entered Washington Heights, huge snow banks bordered the roads, functioning like bumpers at a bowling alley as they nudged vehicles back on course.

Baxter had never been north of Central Park. The same wide roads crisscrossed at regular intervals, but the ordered buildings stood modestly beside one another, allowing the low winter sun to spill over the streets rather than having to jab between eclipsing skyscrapers. She was reminded of a model village that her parents had taken her to as a child: a toy version of New York City.

Within moments of their driver parking up/sliding gently up to a parking meter, that nostalgic comparison had been shattered.

A large white tent had been erected over the entrance to the 33rd Precinct, where a snowy-haired officer was performing the dual role of security and traffic management. As they climbed out, he was inanely directing the drivers of undirectable cars away from the cordon that extended out into one of the city's uncommonly curved sections of road.

"As I mentioned when we first met, due to the location we've been able to keep this one under wraps," Curtis explained to Baxter as they entered through the building's new tented porch.

Just below the top of the tent, the blue New York Police Department sign adorned the front wall above a set of double doors. A few meters to the right of the entrance, the rear half of a Dodge four-by-four protruded from the building. Six inches of concrete pillar jutted up out of the ground behind it like a broken tooth. Even without approaching the vehicle, Baxter could see the dried, dark blood that had been flicked generously across the cream upholstery.

Two police officers came out through the double doors, walked past the scene of destruction embedded in their workplace as though it were no more than an unwelcome choice of decoration that they had not been consulted about, and exited through the slit in the canvas.

"Let me take you through what we know," said Curtis, pulling down the bright yellow tape encircling the vehicle.

"Mind if I make a call?" asked Rouche.

She looked a little surprised.

"I know all this," Rouche pointed out.

Curtis gave him a dismissive wave and he stepped outside, leaving the two women alone.

"Hey, before we get too into this, I wanted to ask: Are you doing all right?"

"All right?" asked Baxter guardedly.

"Yeah. After yesterday."

"I'm fine." Baxter shrugged, as if she couldn't even remember to which incident Curtis was referring. "So . . . the truck in the wall . . ." she prompted, steering the conversation away from personal questions.

"Our victim was Robert Kennedy, thirty-two, married. Been in the force nine years, detective for four."

"And the killer?"

"Eduardo Medina. Mexican immigrant. Worked in the kitchens of the Park-Stamford Hotel in the Upper East Side. And before you ask, no. We've found no link between him and Kennedy, the other killers, or the other victims."

Baxter went to ask something.

"Or the Ragdoll murders . . . *yet*." Curtis sighed.

Rouche put his phone back into his jacket pocket as he returned from outside. He joined Baxter as Curtis stepped into the middle of the covered road.

"We've got security-camera footage—"

"From the school opposite," spat Rouche, interrupting her. "Sorry. Carry on."

"So we've got security-camera footage of Medina parking up on West 168th and dragging Kennedy's unconscious body out from the backseat. The camera angle wasn't favorable, but we can confidently ascertain that during this five-minute period, he carried an already-branded Kennedy around to the hood of the vehicle under a sheet and splayed him out across it. One rope to one limb, just like the body on the bridge."

Baxter glanced back at the wrecked vehicle. A length of thick rope trailed out over the rubble, ending level with the back tire.

"Medina strips naked, the word 'Puppet' carved into his chest, and pulls the sheet off Kennedy. He floors it up Jumel Place, and this is where we've got to be grateful for the weather, because he takes the corner too fast"—Curtis walked the path of the car's trajectory—"and loses control, and instead of careering straight through the main entrance, he plows into this wall, killing them both on impact."

"Nobody else was hurt," Rouche added.

They followed Curtis inside, squeezing past the truck and stepping over a section of the broken wall into an office.

The front end of the vehicle had crumpled back as far as the smashed windscreen. Debris and dust had been thrown ten meters across the room in every direction, but beyond that, the rest of the office appeared relatively unaffected by the tidy area of destruction in the corner.

Baxter stared down at the masking-taped outline of a body.

"Are you *kidding* me?" she whispered in disbelief. "Well, that's one way to contaminate a crime scene. We're not in a *Naked Gun* movie."

The legs and torso had been stuck flat to the floor; however, the arms and head climbed up onto the truck's flattened front grille.

"Give them a break," said Rouche. "They did this under exceptional circumstances."

"We probably shouldn't put too much stock into the positioning of the body," said Curtis. "As I'm sure you can appreciate, Kennedy was one of them, so they got him off this thing as quickly as possible and commenced CPR. One of the rookies did *this* while they were working on him."

"And we're sure neither Medina nor any of his family had a vendetta against the police?" asked Baxter, skeptically.

"Not that we've found," replied Curtis. "I know. It doesn't make any sense when he has so obviously gone all out to rile up the entire NYPD. Everybody knows when you kill a cop, the entire police force is gonna come down on you like a ton of bricks. Whether this is some sort of cult, online group chasing fame, or Ragdoll appreciation society, targeting a cop was probably the stupidest move they could have made, and whatever they're trying to achieve, they've just gone and made it ten times harder for themselves."

Baxter was reminded of something Edmunds had said to her the previous night:

"Somebody's holding the strings," she said, "coordinating these murders, using these Puppets for their own gain. We know the victims aren't chosen at random because the other two are both Ragdoll-related. We're now three murders in. We have absolutely no idea who they are, where they are, or even what they want. The *last* thing these people are is stupid."

"So why declare war on the police?" asked Rouche, fascinated.

"Why indeed?"

Several loud voices filled the tent.

"Special Agent Curtis?" someone called.

Baxter and Rouche followed Curtis back through the hole in the wall. A news crew was setting up their equipment, eyeing the scene greedily every time they looked up. Curtis went off to speak to a group of black-suited people.

"Looks like you're up," Rouche whispered to Baxter. He removed an emergency tie from his pocket and looped it around his neck. "How does it feel to be the official face of a propaganda campaign?"

"Shut up. They can film me doing my job but can piss right off if they—"

"Rouche?" an overweight man called as he abandoned Curtis's group. He wore a huge padded winter jacket, which did not complement his already top-heavy silhouette. "Damien Rouche?" he said, smiling broadly and holding out a sausage-fingered hand.

Rouche hastily finished the untidy knot he was tying and spun around, looking unusually presentable:

"George McFarlen." He smiled, glancing down accusingly at the FBI badge dangling around the man's neck. "You bloody turncoat!"

"Says the British CIA agent!" He laughed. "So it was you who got caught up in all that unpleasantness at the prison, was it?"

"Afraid so. But someone up there must have been looking out for me."

"Amen to that." McFarlen nodded.

Baxter rolled her eyes.

"Hey, are you still shooting?" the man asked Rouche.

"Not really, no."

"No! Well, that's a *damn* shame." McFarlen appeared genuinely disappointed as he turned to address Baxter. "This guy here still holds the agency record at fifty yards to this day!"

Baxter nodded and followed it up with a noncommittal noise.

Picking up on her feigned interest, McFarlen turned his attention back to Rouche:

"Family still out in England?" The domineering man did not
even wait for an answer. "How old's that daughter of yours now?
Same as my Clara: sixteen?"

Rouche opened his mouth.

"What an age." McFarlen shook his head. "It's all just boys
and bitching. I'd suggest you lay low here and head back when
she's twenty!"

An inappropriately booming laugh filled the crime scene as
the man somehow unearthed the hidden hilarity of his comment.
Rouche smiled politely, then received a well-meaning but eye-
watering slap to the back before McFarlen ambled away.

Baxter winced as Rouche held his painful chest.

"I'm pretty sure that qualifies as assault," she joked.

Curtis came to fetch her. She introduced Baxter to Special Agent
in Charge Rose-Marie Lennox. The haggard woman appeared to
be the FBI equivalent of Vanita: a bureaucrat masquerading as
an operational agent, complete with token sidearm just in case
anyone ever attempted to steal the photocopier from her office.

"We are all *so* grateful for your assistance," Lennox told her
sycophantically.

"OK," said the reporter, taking position in front of the camera.
"We're on in three, two, one . . ."

"Wait. What?" asked Baxter. She made to walk off, but Lennox lightly took hold of her arm as the reporter described a
press-appropriate version of events.

Finally, the reporter introduced Lennox, who began reciting
her well-rehearsed responses.

". . . a sick and cruel attack on one of our own. I believe I speak
for all of my colleagues when I say that we will not rest until . . . I
can confirm that we are looking into links between this murder,
the incident on the Brooklyn Bridge a week ago, and the death of
Lethaniel Masse yesterday . . . We will be working alongside the
Metropolitan Police in England, who have graciously provided

us with the expertise of Chief Inspector Emily Baxter, who of course captured . . ."

Baxter lost interest and looked back at Rouche and Curtis as they assessed the wreckage. She watched Curtis call Rouche over to look at something on the driver's door, completely missing the reporter's question:

"What?"

"Chief Inspector," the woman repeated through the most insincere smile Baxter had ever had the misfortune to witness. "What can you tell us about the scene behind us? What are you working on right now?" She gestured toward the devastation with a sad face even more unconvincing than the smile-scowl.

The cameraman turned to Baxter.

"Well," she sighed, making no effort at all to disguise her disdain, "I *was* investigating the death of a police officer, but *now*, for reasons unknown to me, I'm stood here like an idiot talking to you."

There was an uncomfortable pause.

Lennox looked insanely angry, and the abrupt response appeared to trip up the reporter, who had not had time to form her follow-up question.

"Why don't we let you get back to work, Chief Inspector? Thank you." Lennox smiled reassuringly, placing a gentle hand on Baxter's arm as she shrugged and walked away. "As you can see," the special agent in charge told the reporter, "we've *all* taken this loss to heart and just want to get on with finding whoever is responsible."

Lennox saw the news team off and then called Curtis outside. They crossed the road and perched against the fence to Highbridge Park, the border where the compacted ice on the sidewalk became unspoiled powdery snow. Lennox lit up a cigarette.

"I heard about what happened at the prison," she said. "Are you all right? Your father would have my head if anything happened to you."

"Thank you for your concern, but I'm fine," lied Curtis. She was irritated that despite all she had done to prove herself in her own right, she was still receiving preferential treatment because of her family connections.

Lennox had apparently picked up on her tone because she decided to move on:

"That Baxter's an irritable bitch, isn't she?"

"She just doesn't suffer fools gladly," replied Curtis, before realizing that she had just inadvertently insulted her superior. "Not that you're a fool, of course. I just meant . . ."

Lennox waved off the comment with a waft of smoke.

"She's strong and she's smart," said Curtis.

"Yes . . . That's what I'm afraid of."

Curtis wasn't sure what she meant by that.

Although she had never touched a cigarette in her life, the warming glow of the burning tobacco dancing through the freezing air suddenly looked more tempting than it ever had before.

Lennox turned to face the baseball field at the top of the snowy hill.

"She's a tourist here," she told Curtis. "No more. We'll shove her in front of the cameras a few more times, take a few photos to appease the public, and then we'll stick her on a plane home."

"I really think she might be able to help us."

"I know you do, but there's always a lot more going on than there seems. Just as Officer Kennedy's murder is a direct insult to the NYPD, a taunt intended to make the public question the omnipresent authority that governs them, Baxter's presence here poses a similar threat to us."

"I'm sorry—I don't follow," said Curtis.

"We've got the NYPD, FBI, and CIA working on this and getting nowhere. We need Baxter here to show that we're doing all we can, but at the same time, we need to get her out before the Metropolitan Police can claim any of the credit for its resolution. When we're under attack, a show of strength is required. We need to prove to the world that *we* can deal with our own problems. Make sense?"

"Yes, ma'am."

"Good."

A group of schoolchildren began traipsing deep footprints through the park. Another set started a snowball fight a little too close for comfort.

"Carry on as normal," instructed Lennox. "Let Baxter tag along wherever you go, but should you come across any significant leads, I want you to keep her out of the loop."

"That might be difficult."

"Orders sometimes are." Lennox shrugged. "But it'll only be for a few more days. We'll send her packing after the weekend."

One of the police officers had brought Baxter and Rouche cups of coffee while they waited for Curtis to return. Along with the chipped mugs, he'd handed them a brief but nonetheless unsolicited pep talk:

"You are gonna get the bastards behind this."

Baxter and Rouche simply nodded until the angry man appeared satisfied and wandered off. Even though the tent was shielding them from the wind, it was still below freezing and they were beginning to feel it.

"If we have time, want to grab some dinner with me and Curtis tonight?" asked Rouche.

"I . . . um . . . I don't know. I've got some calls to make."

"I know this great, quirky little pizzeria in the West Village. I always go when I'm in New York. It's tradition."

"I . . ."

"Come on. All three of us are going to be exhausted and starving by this evening. You've got to eat something." Rouche smiled.

"Fine."

"Great. I'll book us a table."

He took out his phone and scrolled through his contacts.

"Oh, I forgot to ask," said Baxter. "What did you and Curtis find on the driver's door?"

"Huh?"

Rouche had the phone to his ear.

"When I was screwing up that interview, it looked like you had found something."

"Oh, *that*? It was nothing," he told her.

Someone at the pizzeria picked up and he strolled away.

CHAPTER 8

Thursday, 10 December 2015

11:13 P.M.

Curtis was trapped.

She scanned the shabby hotel room, weapon raised, watching for any sign of movement. She wanted to scream for Rouche, but doubted that he would hear her anyway and didn't want to alert the intruder to her precise whereabouts. She could feel her pulse thumping in her ears in time to her racing heart as she stared at the door, meters away and yet so far out of reach.

She knew that she would have to go for it at some point.

She had already changed into her nightwear: a retro My Little Pony vest top, bright green shorts, and thick woolly socks. Very slowly, she crawled across the bed and reached for her suit jacket draped over the back of a chair.

She took a bracing breath and leaped from the bed, throwing the flip-flop she had been brandishing behind her. Struggling with the lock, she fell out into the corridor as the door swung shut behind her.

Composing herself, she got back to her feet and knocked gently on the door to the adjacent room. Rouche materialized, looking a little disheveled himself: white shirt untucked and barefooted. The combination of jet lag and too much wine at dinner had taken its toll on all of them.

He regarded his visitor for a moment and rubbed his tired eyes, trying to focus.

"Are you wearing a My Little Pony T-shirt?"

"Yes," panted Curtis.

He nodded: "*OK.* Did you want to come in?"

"No. Thank you. I actually came over to ask whether you're any good with spiders."

"Spiders?" Rouche shrugged. "Yeah, sure."

"I don't want any of that scooping-it-up-on-a-piece-of-paper crap, setting it free outside so the horrible thing can climb back up again. I need it dead . . . gone," she instructed him.

"I understand," said Rouche, grabbing a shoe and his room key.

"This thing is *way* too big to be messing around with," Curtis continued, appreciating his compliance.

Rouche suddenly looked a little unsettled: "How big are we talking?"

Baxter had managed to put her tartan pajama shirt on inside out, an oversight that she had not made with the matching bottoms, which she was merely sporting back to front.

She drank another large glass of bitter-tasting tap water, while some irritating guests down the corridor knocked and slammed doors. Collapsing onto the bed, she felt as though the ceiling were twisting slightly, making her nauseous. The sounds of the city drifted in through the window as she groped blindly for her phone, selected Edmunds's name, and called the number.

"What?" shouted Edmunds, sitting bolt upright in bed.

Leila started crying in her cot in the corner of the room.

"What time is it?" groaned Tia, having only just got her back to sleep.

As the disorientation dissipated, Edmunds realized his phone was ringing downstairs. He managed to negotiate the maisonette's staircase, saw Baxter's name on the display, and answered:

"Baxter? Everything all right?"

"Yeah, good . . . It's good," she slurred.

"Is that Emily?" Tia called from upstairs as Leila wailed.

"Yeah," Edmunds stage-whispered, conscious of their miserable neighbor.

"I think your baby's crying," Baxter informed him helpfully.

"Yeah, we know, thanks. The phone woke her up," he said. "Woke all of us up."

"At twenty past six?" she asked before going very quiet. "*Ah, you know what I've gone and done, don't you?*"

"Counted the wrong way?" suggested Edmunds.

"I've counted it the wrong way."

"Yes."

"On the clock, I mean."

"Yes! I know. Baxter, are you drunk?"

"No. Definitely not. I've just had a bit too much to drink."

Tia tiptoed downstairs with Leila in her arms, who had finally settled down.

"Come to bed," she mouthed to Edmunds.

"One minute," he whispered back.

"I'm really sorry," said Baxter guiltily. "I just wanted to catch you up on the crime scene I was at today."

"Which one?" asked Edmunds.

Tia looked quite angry now.

"Detective bound to the front of a truck while still alive and driven through the wall of a police station."

Edmunds was torn.

"I'll give you a call in the morning," said Baxter. "Your morning . . . No! My morning . . . Wait . . ."

"No, it's OK." Edmunds smiled apologetically at Tia. "Tell me now."

"Where did you last see it?" asked Rouche, aware that by wielding his shoe as a weapon, he had left his bare feet worryingly exposed.

"It jumped under the wardrobe, I think," said Curtis from the elevated safety of the bed.

"Jumped?"

"Well, sort of pounced."

"Pounced?"

He was losing confidence.

"No, more like . . . What's the spider equivalent of galloping?"

"Still galloping, I suppose!" he said, voice rising as he edged gradually toward the wardrobe, checking the floor around him for sneak attacks.

"Perhaps we should ask Baxter to do it?" suggested Curtis.

"I'm doing it!" Rouche snapped. "We don't need Baxter. I'm just making sure I don't miss."

Curtis shrugged. "I didn't get a chance to properly thank you today," she said, clearly a little embarrassed.

"Thank me?"

"For last night."

"Any time at all," he said sincerely, glancing back to smile at her, but Curtis's eyes were wide with fear.

Rouche slowly followed her gaze to the floor. An enormous spider, the size of a saucer, was sitting on the carpet in front of him.

He froze.

"Get Baxter," he whispered.

"What?"

Suddenly, it ran straight for him. Rouche shrieked, discarded the shoe, and sprinted for the door.

"Get Baxter!" he yelled as they both bundled back out into the corridor.

So not to keep Tia and Leila awake, Edmunds had braved the freezing rain and run barefoot across his muddy slice of garden to the shed. He switched on the feeble light and dried off his laptop.

The Wi-Fi signal was strong enough for him to open up the

news story and a map of Manhattan. Baxter proceeded to give him a slurred, albeit detailed, account of what had happened.

"I don't understand it," sighed Edmunds.

Baxter was disappointed. She had grown accustomed to expecting the impossible from her best friend.

"I'm sticking with the cult theory. I can't see another explanation," he said.

There was a knock at the door on Baxter's end.

"Sorry. Hold on."

Edmunds listened to the distant voices while he cleared some more space around him:

"Hey. Oh, you're on the phone."

"Yep."

"We've got a slight situation in Curtis's room. Nothing urgent, though . . . Do you know what? I'm sure we can sort it out."

"It's fine. Can I just finish my call first?"

"Sure. Thanks."

"I'll only be a few minutes."

A door closed. There was some loud rustling and then Baxter's voice returned louder than ever:

"Sorry about that . . . So the only link we've got still is that two of the victims are Ragdoll-related."

"And that's barely a link at all," said Edmunds. "One of them was just some bloke who happened to share Wolf's name; the other victim was the actual Ragdoll Killer. There's no consistency there at all."

"In which case, it's got to be better to focus on the killers. We know there must be a link somewhere."

"The Puppets," said Edmunds. "I agree. We have absolutely no hope of predicting who they might target next without knowing what they're trying to achieve, which we'll never understand unless we know what links them."

"Why drum up all this press attention, have the world's ear, and then not say anything?"

"My guess: they're not satisfied with just the ear; they want the world's undivided attention. This is going to escalate."

"Correct me if I'm wrong, but you don't sound particularly disappointed about that," remarked Baxter, picking up on Edmunds's excited tone.

"Send me everything you've got on the killers in the morning and I'll start looking into it. And, Baxter . . . please be careful. Remember: *bait*."

"I will."

"Have you spoken to Thomas?"

"No."

"Why not?"

"We had an argument before I left."

"About what?"

"Stuff."

Edmunds sighed: "Don't mess it up by being stubborn."

"Thanks for the advice. You'd make a great marriage counselor."

He wasn't sure Tia would agree with her on that.

"Good night."

"Night."

Edmunds hung up. It was 4:26 A.M., but he was wide-awake and freezing cold. He looked around at the neglected space and then began tidying away his tools, suspecting that he might need to use the shed again before the resolution of this case.

Baxter was fast asleep on Curtis's bed.

Curtis and Rouche had taken a side each and were sat alert and poised to strike with the makeshift armory they had assembled. Although Rouche had refused to let her use the room's weighty Bible as a projectile, they were armed with two pairs of shoes, one flip-flop, a can of hair spray, and both of their government-issued firearms (only to throw at the atrocity, unless things really got out of hand).

Baxter had been no use whatsoever. She had stomped in impatiently, only to dive for the "safe zone" once the situation had been explained. She had kicked off her boots and fallen asleep within minutes.

"Another?" asked Rouche, adding his empty miniature bottle to the assorted pile on the bed.

"Why not?" replied Curtis, finishing her own.

Rouche crawled across to a chair, opened up the minibar, and selected them each a drink.

"Cheers," he said.

They toasted and took a sip.

"Do you ever get tired of this?" asked Curtis after a moment.

"*This?*" asked Rouche, shoe in hand.

"Not *this* in particular, just this: shitty hotel rooms, creased shirts . . . being alone."

"You're sharing a bed with two other people," he pointed out.

She smiled sadly.

"No," he said. "But if I ever *did* get tired of it, I don't think I could keep doing it for long."

"It must be so hard being away from your wife and daughter."

"And yet I still do it. If you don't have those ties and are already struggling—"

"I'm not struggling!" Curtis snapped.

"I'm sorry: poor choice of words."

"I just . . . Is this what life's going to be forever?"

"It will if you don't change it," Rouche told her.

Curtis threw a shoe past his head, which dented the flimsy partition wall and disturbed Baxter in her sleep.

"Shadow . . . sorry." She shrugged.

"It's none of my business, so feel free to toss another shoe at me if I'm speaking out of turn, but ruining your life just to prove that you made the right decision isn't really proving anything at all."

Curtis nodded thoughtfully.

"Baxter's PJ pants are on the wrong way around," she said after a few moments.

"Yes, they are," said Rouche, without even needing to look.

Baxter was now snoring gently. Curtis looked at her a moment before saying, softly:

"My senior agent has told me not to share anything of importance with her."

"Why?"

Curtis shrugged: "She's only going to be around for a couple
more days anyway."

"Shame. I quite like her."

"Yeah. Me too."

"Get some rest," he told her. "I'll keep watch."

"You sure?"

Rouche nodded. Within five minutes Curtis was asleep beside
him, and within ten he had nodded off as well.

Curtis's alarm went off at 6 A.M. After spending the entire night
on her bed, all three of them looked a little confused when they
first opened their eyes.

"Morning," croaked Rouche.

"Morning," said Curtis, mid-stretch.

Baxter had no idea what was going on.

"I'm going to take a shower," Rouche announced.

He got up and made his way over to the door. He stopped
abruptly, stared at the floor, and groaned.

"What?" asked Curtis.

She cautiously walked over to join him beside the flattened
corpse stomped into the carpet.

"Baxter must've stood on it when she came in," he chuckled,
exhausted.

He tore off a strip of toilet paper, scooped up the evidence, and
then flushed away their first successful capture as a team.

Things were looking up.

CHAPTER 9

Friday, 11 December 2015

9:07 A.M.

Lennox subtly tapped her finger over one of the three cue cards she had placed in front of Baxter as they had taken their seats:

I can't speculate on that.
I can confirm that is correct.
There is nothing to suggest that.

Baxter leaned a little closer to the small microphone, which sat expectantly on the black cloth that had been draped over the line of spare desks to make them look more official:

"I'm afraid I can't speculate on that."

She picked up on Lennox's almost inaudible tut as she sat back in her chair and another reporter asked the man sitting beside her a question. Lennox scribbled a quick note and slid it over to her, at no point looking anything less than enthralled by the question asked and the deputy assistant director's answer.

Baxter took a moment to decipher the scrawl:

Never say, "I'm afraid . . ."

Usually this would have been enough to send her storming out in a temper, regardless of the roomful of journalists and cameras recording her every move; however, out of respect, she bit her tongue and remained seated.

The purpose of the press conference was to confirm the identity of the deceased detective and, in answer to rampant Internet speculation and conspiracy theories, to officially confirm that the murders of "the Banker," Lethaniel Masse, and Detective Robert Kennedy were all linked.

Baxter wasn't concentrating. She was still reeling over the scribbled note and had made a point of screwing it up in front of Lennox, who was slowly approaching the end of her own meandering answer:

". . . and our colleagues overseas, such as Detective Chief Inspector Baxter here."

The moment she finished, a young man in a cheap suit was rewarded for his attentiveness by raising his hand before anybody else.

Lennox gestured to him.

"So, Chief Inspector, what do *you* believe is the motive behind these murders?" he asked.

The room awaited her response.

Lennox needlessly tapped one of the cue cards.

"I can't speculate on that," read Baxter.

"A source at the prison revealed that the two dead bodies had words cut into them: 'Puppet' and 'Bait,'" continued the man, unwilling to walk away with only a noncommittal five-word answer. "Photographs from the Brooklyn Bridge would suggest that there may have been similar markings on the deceased. Can you confirm whether this is consistent on all of the bodies discovered thus far?"

Lennox hesitated for a moment and then rested her finger over a different card. Although surprised, Baxter obeyed the silent command:

"I can confirm that is correct," she said robotically.

The room erupted into a hum of mumbled conversations and hissed whispers. Baxter noticed Curtis and Rouche standing against the back wall and was reassured by their presence. Curtis gave her a professional nod, while Rouche cheerily gave her two thumbs-up, making her smile.

"And, Chief Inspector! Chief Inspector!" the man called over the restrained commotion, pushing his luck by asking a third question. "Considering that the three victims thus far have been a police officer, a man named William Fawkes, and the Ragdoll Killer himself, the word 'Bait' carved into each of them, I can only presume that you and your colleagues have considered the possibility that these messages are, in fact, intended for you?"

A deathly hush followed as the room of impatient journalists waited for her response to what was, in all fairness, a rather good question.

Lennox pushed the "can't speculate" card in front of her. Of course she would, thought Baxter bitterly. Lennox was hardly going to admit that she had dragged her halfway across the world only to put her in harm's way.

"That is just one of several possibilities that we are currently looking into," she said. By "we" she had meant Edmunds, of course.

Lennox looked a little annoyed that Baxter had gone off-card but appeared content with the professional and concise answer.

"Chief Inspector Baxter!" someone in the front row called.

When Baxter automatically looked in the woman's direction, she took it as an invitation to stand up and ask her disarmingly direct question:

"Are there going to be more murders?"

Baxter remembered her conversation with Edmunds the previous night. Lennox rapped her fingers on the "can't speculate" card once again.

"I . . ." Baxter hesitated.

Lennox turned to Baxter and tapped the card more urgently. At the back of the room, Curtis looked worried and was shaking her head. Even without the short script, Rouche mouthed the words "I can't speculate on that."

"Chief Inspector? Are there going to be more murders?" the woman asked again as the audience remained quiet.

Baxter thought of the official press release that had accompanied her arrest of Masse: the story she had had to tell to save herself, the diluted explanation of Wolf's involvement.

It was all just dead bodies and endless lies . . .

"I believe that this is going to escalate . . . Yes."

As the room jumped to its feet, firing questions to the flash of cameras, Baxter sensed heads either side turn in her direction. Apparently she had been mistaken in thinking that the public would want the truth for once.

It was a depressing realization that they thrived on these empty promises and insincere reassurances. When it came down to it, perhaps the PR snakes were right: people would rather get stabbed in the back than ever see it coming.

"So this is what we've got so far." Special Agent Kyle Hoppus directed them over to one of ten chaotic whiteboards lining the walls. "These are our killers."

MARCUS TOWNSEND	EDUARDO MEDINA	DOMINIC "THE BOUNCER" BURRELL
Brooklyn Bridge	33rd Precinct	Belmarsh Prison
39yrs/White US	46yrs/Latino	28yrs/White British
Ex-financial trader	Chef Park-Stamford Hotel	Arrested 2011 for murder
Bankrupted when markets crashed '08	Immigration problems: half of family still in Mexico	Incarcerated past 4 years
Periods of living rough	Vendetta against authorities?	How related to Ragdoll murders unless contacted while inside?
Financial links to victim?		Visitation records show sees psychiatrist once per week and family on birthdays
Investigated for insider trading '07		Obvious vendetta against police
Vendetta against police?		

The FBI's New York Field Office was located on the twenty-third floor of a disappointingly mundane building off Broadway. With the exception of the standard New York exposed brick-work, Baxter could have been back in New Scotland Yard: the whitewashed high ceilings, the same fuzzy blue material decorating the partitions between desks, and an almost identical, not hard-wearing enough, hard-wearing carpet.

Hoppus gave them a minute to read through what little information had not been scribbled out or written over. Baxter thought him suspiciously amiable considering his position of seniority.

"As you can probably tell, having exhausted every possible link between the killers, between the victims, between the killers and the victims, and between all of them and the Ragdoll murders, we're currently focusing on the fact that each of our killers had good reason to resent the police," Hoppus explained.

"We've got a team still working through their financials, another going through their computers and phone records with a fine-tooth comb . . . obviously. But truth be told, we're struggling here. No overwhelming religious or political views, with the possible exception of Medina, who's a Catholic and strong Democrat supporter like the majority of Mexican immigrants. No prior history of violence apart from Burrell. Basically, as far as we can fathom, these people did not know and have never been in contact with one another," he finished.

"Yet committed three undoubtedly coordinated murders within days of each other," pondered Rouche out loud. "*Creepy.*"

Hoppus did not respond but did give Curtis a quizzical look as to why she had brought this strange man up to see him.

"Would I be able to get a copy of their files?" Baxter asked him. She decided not to mention that she planned to send them across the planet to a Fraud officer with no involvement in the case whatsoever.

"Of course," said Hoppus a little shortly. He clearly considered it an insult that she thought she might find something that his entire team had overlooked.

Rouche moved closer to the board to study the three small photographs that had been affixed above the names. Burrell's was the mugshot from his arrest. Townsend was wearing a T-shirt embellished with a familiar logo.

"Townsend was in the Streets to Success program?" asked Rouche.

"He was," replied Hoppus, who had been speaking to Curtis and Baxter.

"Still?" asked Rouche.

Hoppus looked confused: "He's dead."

"I mean . . . at time of death. He hadn't dropped out or anything?"

"No. Still enrolled." Hoppus was unable to keep a tone of annoyance out of his voice.

"Hmmm." Rouche turned his attention back to the board.

He had learned from a previous case that Streets to Success was a scheme intended to get the city's escalating number of homeless back into employment and to a level of self-sufficiency. They provided mentorship, accommodation, education, counseling where required, and job opportunities to people the world had given up on. An admirable endeavor; however, it was difficult to imagine the gaunt and ghostly-looking man in the photograph ever finding his way back into society.

Rouche had seen enough addicts to know when a person was more addicted to a drug than to life.

He moved on to the photograph of Eduardo Medina. The top of someone's head remained in the bottom corner where the picture had been roughly trimmed. From Medina's positioning, Rouche could tell that he must have had his arms around this missing person; he looked happy.

"What's going to happen to his family now?" blurted Rouche, interrupting Hoppus yet again.

"Whose?"

"Medina's."

"Well, considering that the asshole murdered a cop in cold blood, I'd be surprised if they did anything short of deport his son, who was over here with him, and block the rest of his family and relatives from *ever* entering the country again."

"So he's *really* screwed them over, then?" concluded Rouche.

"I'd say that's an understatement," said Hoppus, turning back to Curtis.

"But he was doing his very best for them up until the murder?"

Hoppus visibly flinched in annoyance and turned back to face Rouche.

"I suppose. He pulled long shifts at the hotel, sent money back to his family. He was in the process of getting his daughter over here."

"Doesn't sound like a baddy to me," said Rouche.

The usually personable Hoppus reddened with anger.

"Christ," Curtis whispered to herself, embarrassed.

"A 'baddy'?" spat Hoppus, now turning all of his attention on the CIA agent, whose own attention was still occupied with the photograph. "This man strung a *police officer* to the front of his truck and drove it through a wall!"

"You misunderstand me," replied Rouche pleasantly. "I didn't say he hadn't done a very bad thing. I'm just not convinced that he was a bad man."

The office had gone eerily quiet as Hoppus's colleagues picked up on their boss's uncharacteristic outburst.

"I agree with Rouche." Baxter shrugged, ignoring Curtis's look of betrayal. "Medina's your best bet at working out what's going on. Burrell was a piece of shit anyway. Townsend was screwed up and in contact with God-knows-who on the streets. Medina was a hardworking man trying to do right by his family. An abrupt change in his life will be much more obvious than in the others."

"That's what *I* said," mumbled Rouche.

"Point taken," said Hoppus begrudgingly, still not looking particularly happy with any of them.

"Agent Hoppus was just explaining the other branch of the investigation to us," Curtis told Rouche, trying to get them all back on the same page.

He tore himself away from the wall to join them.

"I was just saying that the tech team was plowing through recent Internet search traffic for words such as 'Puppet,' 'Masse,' 'Ragdoll,' and 'Bait' prior to this morning's press conference when the search engines became saturated. They've also turned up forums and sites where people are already trying to find out how to get involved."

"Sick bastards," uttered Baxter.

"Couldn't agree more," said Hoppus. "We're logging the IP addresses of anyone who visits and are continuing to monitor them in case they attract someone who's actually involved."

"As awful as it sounds," started Curtis, "we're basically waiting for another body, aren't we?"

"I probably wouldn't suggest we announce that to the public . . . but yeah, we're completely in the dark here," agreed Hoppus as one of his junior agents came over to join them.

"Apologies for the interruption, sir. Special Agent in Charge Lennox is downstairs with some reporters. She's asked to borrow Chief Inspector Baxter."

"Leave me alone!" sighed Baxter in frustration.

The junior agent looked momentarily afraid that he was to relay that message back down to Lennox.

"On the bright side, you can only improve on the last one," Rouche told her cheerily.

Curtis nodded encouragingly.

"What was it? 'We're basically waiting for another body'?" asked Baxter. She turned to the young man: "OK, lead on."

"She was joking . . . *right*?" Hoppus asked nervously as they watched her leave the office.

Baxter could feel her phone vibrating against her ribs as she recited the same generic answers to the same generic questions that she had been asked earlier in the day. Although not a fan of Wolf's ex-wife, she had no doubt that the blandly unimaginative journalists whom she had encountered thus far on her trip could learn a trick or two from Andrea Hall's school of shameless scaremongering.

Despite her irritation at being dragged away for yet another PR exercise, she realized that she was looking forward to rejoining Rouche and Curtis upstairs. The Ragdoll case had only lasted a little over a fortnight and yet, for more reasons than she would care to admit, it had left her feeling empty: unresolved. This unexpected continuation to the case had already reinvigorated her as a detective. She felt useful and part of a team. More, though, it made her realize just how much she regretted taking the DCI role.

The same young man who had come to collect Baxter attempted to interrupt the live interview:

"Special Agent in Charge," he whispered nervously.

Lennox carried on with her spiel.

"Agent Lennox," he tried again.

Baxter could see that the young man looked torn about what to do as his supervisor continued her perfectly delivered response.

"Lennox!" Baxter barked as the cameras continued to roll. "I think this bloke needs to talk to you."

"And you, Chief Inspector," he added, looking grateful.

"Duty calls." Lennox smiled to the cameras.

They moved well away from the reporters, who were watching them carefully.

"What couldn't *possibly* wait until I'd finished?" she whispered angrily at the young man.

"I didn't think it would look good if you knew what was going on after the rest of the world did," he explained.

"And what *is* going on?"

"There's been another murder . . . a second cop."

CHAPTER 10

Friday, 11 December 2015

5:34 P.M.

Detective Constable Aaron Blake had become separated from his partner in the chaos. Between them, they had managed to shut down half of London with their ad hoc traffic diversion, as six lanes were directed off the Mall in the hope that the vehicles might miraculously fit down the far narrower Marlborough Road. The situation wasn't being helped by the blanket of freezing fog that had descended over the city. Blake had, at least, been able to see Buckingham Palace lit up against the dark sky when they had arrived on scene. Now, he couldn't see more than five feet in front of him.

The opaque air was tinted an otherworldly blue by the lights of the emergency vehicles. The fog had drenched his dark hair and soaked through four layers of clothing. It muffled the sound of the stationary motorists as he groped blindly back toward the crime scene, guided by the spotlight blazing off the rear of the fire engine.

"Blake!" Saunders called to his colleague as he materialized out of the mist like a cheesy magician. He too was soaked through, his highlighted blond hair now an unnatural orange where it stuck to his sneering face.

Baxter's very first decision after becoming chief had been to pair together the two detectives that nobody wanted to work with. Neither had been enamored with the news. Saunders was known for being the mouthiest, crudest, and most chauvinistic man still clinging, somehow, to a job at Homicide and Serious Crime Command, whereas Blake had gained his reputation by being a gutless, backstabbing, conniving shit.

"Didn't come across the forensics guys on your travels, then?" asked Saunders in his Cockney tones.

"You gotta be jokin'," replied Blake. "I lost the bloody road back there for a few minutes."

"Shittin' Christ, this is an absolute cack-up."

Blake was distracted when a gold shape floated by, several feet above Saunders's head, accompanied by the clacking of hooves on concrete.

"What now?" huffed Saunders, taking out his ringing phone. "Chief?"

Baxter had phoned Vanita on her way back up to the field office. She was surprised to hear her commander sounding so calm and decisive, now en route to assume control of an *actual* crime scene instead of hiding behind her desk. Vanita had passed on the few sketchy details that she had, and informed Baxter of the personnel already on scene, which had done nothing to ease her concerns.

"Saunders, can you give me a sitrep?" Baxter asked him from across the Atlantic.

She found herself a vacant desk and helped herself to a pen and paper.

"Absolute shit-fest," was his concise answer. "'Av you seen what the weather's like in London? Ridiculous. We can't see our hands in front of our faces. I got men on horses sneaking up on me, rearing up from out of the mist; it's like bloody Sleepy Hollow here."

"Have you secured the crime scene?" Baxter asked.

A piercing siren buzzed out of her phone.

"Sorry, hold on . . ." Saunders's voice became distant: "Oh, fantastic! Another police car! And just what do you think you're gonna achieve that the other two dozen units couldn't? . . . Yeah, right back at you!"

"Saunders!"

"Yeah, sorry."

"Have you secured the crime scene?"

"Well, the fire boys were first ones 'ere and they did their bit. But yeah, we've strung up some tape nobody can see."

"What resources have you got there with you?"

"All the bastards. The lot: two fire engines, at least three ambulances. I lost count of police cars somewhere in double figures. I spoke to some bloke from MI5, the royal horsey-men; even some bloke from the RSPCA was running about for a while. Forensics are apparently somewhere, but we ain't found 'em yet."

"Just keep the scene secure. Vanita will be there shortly," Baxter told him. "Have you got Blake with you?"

She disliked the two men equally but, as a general rule, tended to get more sense out of Blake.

"Yeah, give us a sec . . . Blake! Chief wants to speak to you . . . Yes, *you*. What you doing your hair for? She can't see you . . . I can't even see you!"

There was a crackle on the other end of the line.

"Chief?" said Blake, feeling the moisture on the cold screen pressing into his cheek as he stared up at the clear night sky. He was overcome with a surreal feeling, as if he had climbed far above the mess below and poked his head up through the top of a cloud.

"I need you to walk over to the crime scene and tell me *exactly* what you see."

Illusion ruined, Blake followed the instructions and ducked beneath the tape that they had set up around the vehicle's charred skeleton. He switched on his flashlight, the diffused beam emphasizing the dark smoke still escaping the wreck, entangling itself in strands of white fog as it rose up to pollute the bitter night.

"OK. I'm on the Mall, palace end. Got one completely burned-out police car pretty much in the dead center of the road." Broken glass and plastic trim crunched and snapped beneath his feet as he moved in closer. "We've got two bodies in the driver and passenger seats. Witness saw smoke coming from inside the car as it pulled away from Trafalgar Square. Seconds later, it was an inferno."

At this point Blake normally would have made some tasteless joke or inappropriate comment, but the combination of the eerie atmosphere, the significance of this fourth murder by an unknown entity, and the grotesque scene before him had encouraged a rare moment of professionalism. He just wanted to do his job well.

"How close did it get to the palace?" asked Baxter.

"Not that close. I'd say we're about two-thirds of the way down, but it's a long old road. I think we've got to assume that was their intention, though, if the fire hadn't spread so quickly."

"Tell me about the bodies."

He had known this was coming. All the doors were wide open from when the firefighters had searched for anybody else inside. Blake covered his nose and kneeled down beside the blackened remains.

"They're, um . . . they're in a bad way." He gagged but didn't bring anything up. "Jesus. The smell is . . ." He could feel himself gagging again.

"I know," said Baxter sympathetically. "What do you see?"

Soot-stained water was still dripping off the exposed chassis and freezing into tar-like puddles around his feet. He shone his Maglite around the interior of the car.

"I can definitely smell petrol, lots of petrol. Could just be the tank, but going off what the witnesses said, my guess is the interior was soaked in it. Got a male in the driver's seat. Christ, I can't even tell what color his skin was."

He ran the light all the way up the charred body, the beam hovering nervously over the chest area before illuminating the now skeletal face.

"A little under six foot, thin, naked from the waist up. The whole body's completely burned away apart from an area on his chest, which looks almost untouched."

"Puppet?" asked Baxter, already knowing the answer.

"Must've used a flame-retardant varnish or something over the scars," said Blake, turning his flashlight to what little was left of the other body. "Same story for the female in the passenger seat: naked from the waist up, the word 'Bait' still just about legible. Looks fresh. She's wearing one of our utility belts and black boots, so we're confident it's Constable Kerry Coleman. It's her patrol car, and she was flagged up as not responding to radio calls just over an hour ago."

There was a crunching sound behind Blake. He looked back to find Saunders lifting the tape for the forensics team.

"Forensics have just arrived," he told Baxter. He got up and moved away from the car. "Want me to let you know what they find?"

"No. Vanita will be there any moment now. Report to her. I'll be back tomorrow."

"All right."

"And, Blake . . ."

"Yeah?"

"Good work."

He chose to focus on the compliment rather than the surprised tone in her voice as she gave it:

"Thanks."

Baxter tore her page of scribbles from the notebook and went to join the rest of the team in Lennox's office. She passed on Blake's assessment of the scene, and they discussed the clear pattern that was beginning to emerge. The UK now mirrored the US murders, only on a delayed timescale: both sides of the Atlantic had one Ragdoll-related victim apiece, and were now level pegging on dead police officers as well.

"I need to get back there," Baxter told Lennox. "I can't be here when I've got people murdering colleagues on my doorstep."

"I completely understand," said Lennox kindly, only too happy to have a valid excuse to send Baxter packing earlier than anticipated.

"It's the same case," Rouche pointed out, "whether you investigate it here or there."

"I can't stay."

"I'll have someone book the flight," said Lennox before anyone else could try to dissuade Baxter from leaving.

"Tonight?"

"I'll do my best."

"Thank you."

"No, Chief Inspector," said Lennox, holding her hand out to her, "thank *you*."

Baxter had been booked on a flight back to the UK the following morning. She had spoken to Vanita on several occasions throughout the afternoon and to Edmunds twice. She had even left Thomas a voicemail to tell him that she was coming home, which made her feel like an incredibly open and attentive girlfriend.

Despite the difficulties in identifying incinerated remains, it had not taken the team back in London long to attach a name to Constable Coleman's killer: Patrick Peter Fergus, whose undamaged mobile phone had been retrieved from a discarded rucksack.

The real-time GPS tracking system, by which the dispatchers allocate resources to incidents, had shown Coleman's vehicle making an unscheduled stop on Spring Gardens. Armed with a time and location, the oft-debated "Big Brother" nature of the capital had then played to their advantage. Nine separate surveillance cameras had captured elements of the anticlimactic murder.

A white-haired gentleman, carrying a bag and dressed in jeans and a polo shirt, had been walking down Whitehall. While he was waiting at a crossing, Constable Coleman's patrol car had pulled up at the lights. Instead of crossing the road, he had walked over and knocked on her window, pointing toward the quiet side street, smiling pleasantly as he did so.

Building works either side of the road had reduced the pedestrian traffic, meaning that no one witnessed the man calmly stoop down to pick up a brick. And then, as Constable Coleman stepped out of her car, he had struck her once across the forehead before carrying her around to the passenger seat. From the assorted cameras, they were able to discern the events taking place within the vehicle: the knife, the fireproof coating, the bottle of petrol—all stashed inside the bag that he had been carrying innocently through the crowds.

Baxter shivered as she ended a call to one of the night-shift detectives. Vanita had scheduled a press conference first thing to announce the identity of their murdered colleague, but apart from that, there had been no further developments. The tech team had scoured the recovered phone, finding nothing of significance. The blatant randomness of the murder, as depicted in the footage, negated the need to look for links to Constable Coleman. She had simply been in the wrong place at the wrong time, presenting a man intent on killing a police officer with an opportunity to do so.

Baxter was standing outside the Reade Street Pub in Tribeca. The cozy, old-fashioned bar was known to be the haunt of FBI agents and, as such, was one of the best-behaved spots in the city. Curtis's colleagues had persuaded her to join them for a drink at the end of their shift. She, in turn, had guilted Baxter and Rouche into tagging along too.

Baxter supposed that she had better head back in, but had found it strangely relaxing watching the night engulf the late afternoon, the city's windows illuminating one by one like fairy lights. A frozen sigh escaped her lungs before a wall of warmth, music, and raucous laughter greeted her as she stepped back inside.

Rouche and Curtis were stood in a large group by the bar. The loudest member was telling a story involving his by-the-book colleague, while Curtis smiled along uncomfortably.

"... So she comes storming out of this shit-hole apartment block, covered *literally* head to toe in white powder. In one arm she's dragging the dealer out by the neck; in the other she's carrying this little Scottie dog." Everyone laughed appropriately as the man took a swig of his bottle. "We've got TV cameras, all the neighbors out with their phones. There's even a helicopter hovering overhead. So what does she do?"

He looked to Rouche, as if actually expecting him to guess

which of the infinite possibilities available to her through free will Curtis had chosen to go with.

He shrugged.

"She walks straight up to our, now, assistant director, drops the poor animal into his arms, covering him in powder, and says: 'I'm keeping the dog!'"

Curtis's colleagues all laughed riotously.

"Ah! Ah-a!" force-laughed Rouche, looking bemused.

"See, the sick bastard had tried to feed the entire two kilos to the dog when he heard the sirens coming. The boss had to sit in a vet's all night waiting for it to crap out some evidence!" He looked Rouche dead in the eye: "Guess what she named him?"

A pause. He was doing it again. Rouche was quite tempted to explain that he had no possible way of knowing, not being psychic, which, if he had been, would have meant he could have avoided this awkward conversation altogether.

"Coke . . . Cocaine . . . Ummm . . . Co-Canine?" he tried.

An uncomfortable silence met his answer.

"Dusty," said the man, as though Rouche had just slapped him across the face. "She called him Dusty."

Spotting Baxter approaching, Rouche excused himself and hurried away to intercept her.

"I'm buying you a drink," he told her, directing her to the other end of the bar.

She wasn't about to argue: "Red wine."

"Small? Large?"

"Large."

Rouche ordered for them.

"You know, watching the footage of that officer's murder really got to me," he said as they waited for the barman to return. "I was almost more repulsed by how nonviolent it was . . . Not that I wanted her to suffer," he added quickly. "Just that . . ."

"It was too easy," Baxter finished for him. She had felt exactly the same way. "Just pick a person off the street, anyone, hit them on the head hard enough with whatever's lying around, and they're gone."

"Right." Rouche nodded, handing the barman his credit card. "She didn't stand a chance, did she? It was just too random . . . opportunistic."

They each took a sip of their drink.

"Curtis and I will take you to the airport in the morning," he told her.

"That's not necessary."

"We insist."

"Well, if you insist."

"Cheers," said Rouche, raising his glass.

"Cheers," replied Baxter, her tension dulling from feeling the first acidic bite on her tongue.

It took Baxter a few attempts to successfully insert her key card. Once inside her room, she kicked off her shoes, tossed her bag onto the bed, switched on the bedside light, and then wobbled across to open the tiny window.

She was desperate to get out of her work clothes, and pulled off her smart trousers en route to the bathroom. Halfway through unbuttoning her shirt, her phone went off. She climbed onto the bed to retrieve it from her bag, stopping short when she saw that the text message was from Thomas.

"What the hell are *you* still doing up?" she wondered out loud before realizing how late it was and that she should have been asleep hours earlier.

Can't wait to see you. I think Echo has fleas x

"You've got fleas," she mumbled in irritation.

It did not even occur to her that he might appreciate a reply, but it did remind her that she still needed to forward Edmunds the files on the killers that Hoppus had given her. She typed out a barely coherent email to Edmunds, making eleven spelling mistakes in just sixteen words, attached the documents, and pressed "send."

She tossed the phone away from her and her eyes fell on the ugly scar that adorned the inside of her right thigh, a lasting reminder of the Ragdoll case, of Masse . . . of Wolf. The sight of it always caught her off guard.

She shuddered as she absentmindedly ran her fingers over the raised skin. Goose bumps spread across her body as she remembered the cold. Not like the mild chill blowing in from the winter outside but truly cold, frozen to her core. It was something that she had never experienced before. She pictured the blood pouring out of her, her temperature plummeting as the warm liquid evacuated her body.

She got back up to close the window and then pulled on her pajama bottoms as quickly as she could, hoping to forget that this part of her, which she so despised, was there all over again.

CHAPTER 11

Saturday, 12 December 2015

7:02 A.M.

Baxter had hit the "snooze" button five times before managing to drag herself out of bed. She skipped her shower in favor of brushing her teeth, stuffing her things into her case, and quickly putting on some makeup. She stepped out into the corridor just two minutes late, looking reasonably presentable, to find that she was the first to be ready.

Less than a minute later, a feeble groan emanated from Rouche's room. The lock clicked loudly and he stumbled out looking decidedly worse for wear. She suspected that he had slept in his crumpled suit. He had obviously attempted to have some influence over his unruly hair, which had ignored his input, and despite wearing sunglasses, was still forced to shield his eyes from the corridor's lighting.

"Morning," he croaked, sniffing the armpit of his jacket.

Judging from the face he pulled, he would not be getting a hug goodbye.

"How is it that you look so . . . ?" Rouche paused, not wanting to say anything that might be deemed inappropriate.

"So . . . ?" whispered Baxter, conscious that people in the neighboring rooms might still be asleep.

She wondered whether he had dozed off behind the sunglasses.

". . . well," he finally settled on. Those sexual-harassment seminars his entire department had been forced to attend hadn't been a complete waste of time after all.

"Practice," answered Baxter. "Far too much practice. Sunglasses are a nice touch . . . *subtle*."

"I thought so." Rouche nodded, quickly realizing that nodding would be off the cards for the rest of the day.

"Why have you even got sunglasses? It's minus five out there."

"Reflections," said Rouche defensively. "When you're driving, to protect against glare."

"Glare?" Baxter sounded skeptical.

At that moment the door to Curtis's room opened and the immaculate agent stepped out with her phone pressed to her ear. Ever the professional, she had nursed a bottle of beer all evening and left the pub at 9 P.M. After making her excuses to her colleagues, she had found Baxter and Rouche tucked away at a little table by the window. Unfortunately, by then they were on their third drink, had just ordered food, and were in no hurry to leave.

She nodded to Baxter and then took a long, angry, judgmental look at the state of her disheveled colleague. She shook her head and walked away toward the lift.

Rouche looked back at Baxter innocently.

"Did the glasses help?" she asked with a smirk as she rolled her case past him.

It was decided that it was probably best that Curtis drove. Baxter sat in the back, while Rouche opened the passenger-side window and directed as many of the heater vents in his direction as possible. Within moments of leaving the hotel, their black FBI vehicle had been swallowed up by a sea of taxicabs, decelerating toward a complete standstill like a run of yellow paint drying.

The police radio chattered away in the background, a cheerful tone preempting each reply between the dispatcher and the officers on the road. The city that never sleeps had had an especially restless night from what Baxter could gather, although she was having to read between the lines, not being familiar with the NYPD incident codes. Curtis had been good enough to translate the more interesting calls for her.

It was already lunchtime back in London, and the team had put the morning to good use. Baxter had been sent updated details on their latest killer, Patrick Peter Fergus, and read it out to Curtis and Rouche:

"Sixty-one years old. Working for the vaguely named Consumer Care Solutions Limited as a cleaner for the past two and a half years. Previous run-ins with the police: just a pub brawl thirty-odd years ago. Only family is a mother with dementia out in Woking . . . Jesus!"

"What is it?"

"He had a part-time evening job as a Santa Claus. That's where he was heading when he instead decided on the spur of the moment to murder an innocent policewoman."

Rouche seemed to sober up in an instant and turned back to look at Baxter:

"You're serious?" he asked.

"Please don't let Andrea get hold of that," she groaned, speaking to no one in particular. "'The Santa killings.' You can see it coming a mile off."

She looked out the window as they lurched a few feet at a time past City Hall Park. The dark gray sky above was yet to follow through on its threat to snow. A green signpost told her that they were gradually sneaking up on the Brooklyn Bridge.

She received a text message from Thomas and tutted: "What now?"

What time are you back?
Bought stuff for a late-night dinner! x

She was considering her reply when she was distracted by a transmission on the hushed radio. It had not been the message that had caught her attention—she had completely missed the entire thing—it was the tone of the dispatcher's voice.

In the thirty minutes that Baxter had been half listening, she had heard the professional woman task units to a serious domestic-abuse call, a dead heroin addict, and a man threatening to kill himself. At no point had her calm-and-collected demeanor faltered . . . until now.

"So what's the plan when you—" started Rouche, who had not picked up on what the two women had heard.

"Shhhh!" snapped Curtis, turning the radio up as they rounded the corner and started to ascend the ramp to the bridge.

"10-5," said a slightly distorted male voice.

"He's asking her to repeat it," Curtis interpreted for Baxter's sake.

The same cheerful tone sounded, jarring with the dispatcher's thinly veiled concern.

"42 Charlie. 10-10F . . ."

"Possible firearm," whispered Curtis.

". . . main concourse, Grand Central Terminal. Reports of possible shots fired . . . 10-6."

"She's asking him to stand by," said Curtis as they edged farther toward the first stone tower, where they had already had to cut a man down from the entrance to the city.

The woman's voice returned, fast and alert:

"42 Charlie. 34 Boy. 34 David. 10-39Q . . ."

"What's that?" asked Baxter.

"Other. I don't think she knows what's going on, but she's already calling backup."

". . . main concourse, Grand Central Terminal. Reports of one perp, armed, carrying a hostage . . . believed to be deceased."

"What the hell?" said Rouche.

"10-5," responded one of the officers, expressing the same sentiment but in digit form.

"A dead hostage isn't a hostage," said Rouche. "It's a dead person."

The woman wasn't making any sense. It was clear that she wanted to give the officers further details but was unable to over the open channel, which anyone with a thirty-dollar scanner could listen in to.

"10-6 . . . Grand Central Terminal. 10-39Q . . . 10-10F . . . 10-13Z . . . 10-11C . . ."

"Alarms going off now," said Curtis. "Backing up a civilian-clothed officer."

"One armed perp. Shots fired!" the dispatcher passed on unnecessarily. Her transmitter had picked up the sharp clicks from the headphones as she listened in on the call. "Confirm: 10-10S. Perp is attached to a dead body."

Rouche turned to Curtis: "Attached? This is one of ours, isn't it?"

Curtis hit the sirens.

"Sorry, Baxter, looks like you're stuck with us a little longer," said Rouche, before turning back to Curtis. "We'll have to go over the bridge and— What are you doing?!"

Curtis was turning them around to face three lanes of oncoming traffic. She weaved between the vehicles, scraping through gaps that looked impossibly small. She mounted the pedestrianized area outside City Hall Park, the traders and tourists gesturing and jumping out of the way. The tires squealed as they drifted left and then swung right, in a haze of burned rubber, onto Broadway.

Even Baxter double-checked that her seat belt was done up. She closed the text message from Thomas and put her phone away, watching the bluish city speed past the tinted windows; she'd tell him later that she wouldn't be coming home after all.

Curtis was forced to leave the car two hundred meters from the station due to the endless crowds spilling out through the main entrance and into the road. They sprinted between the gridlocked traffic on 42nd and toward the sound of an automated evacuation announcement. They passed three police cars, abandoned at varying distances from their destination, and then hurried inside through the Vanderbilt Avenue entrance.

Rouche led the way, cutting a path through the fearful faces. As he did so, the disquieting realization that nobody was saying a word to one another dawned on him. He spotted an NYPD officer guarding the entrance to the main concourse and fought through the silent evacuation to reach him.

He took out his ID: "Rouche, CIA."

The young man held a finger to his lips and gestured through the archway before whispering almost inaudibly: "He's right there."

Rouche nodded and matched his volume: "Who's in charge?"

"Plant." He pointed them down the corridor. "East Balcony."

The group made its way around to the opposite end of the hall to find a flustered officer on the radio to the control room. His graying mustache twitched in time to his quietly delivered diatribe.

"Keep me updated," he said, curtly bringing the transmission to a close before looking up at the newcomers.

"Plant?" asked Rouche. The man nodded. "Special Agent Rouche, CIA." He gestured to his colleagues: "Curtis, FBI. Baxter . . . don't have time to explain. What've we got?"

Baxter stole a brief glance into the grand main hall, the cerulean ceiling an artificial sky to the vast expanse of deserted marble below. She scanned what she could see of the upper level, where the stairs up to the West Balcony merged before their final ascent toward three enormous arched windows.

Her eyes were drawn to the iconic brass clock atop the information booth in the center. Suddenly, there was a flash of skin, distorted through the kiosk's glass windows, gone as quickly as it had appeared. She stepped back behind the wall, heart now racing, her eyes wide and alert, because what she had seen had frightened her.

"Four shots fired," Officer Plant informed them, "none at us, all up at the ceiling. He's"—Plant stared into space for a moment—"he's got someone, a man, who's . . . He's got someone sewn onto him."

A pause.

"Can you elaborate?" asked Rouche, showing no reaction whatsoever, acting as though he were taking any other description of a suspect.

"He has a deceased white male stitched onto his back."

" 'Bait' carved into his chest?"

Plant nodded.

Rouche unconsciously glanced at Baxter.

"Has he said anything to you?" he asked the officer.

"He was distressed—crying and muttering—when I arrived, but we had to pull back when he started firing rounds into the air."

"And do we know how he got here in this . . . condition?"

"Witnesses saw him climbing out of a van in front of the main entrance. I've passed details on to dispatch."

Rouche nodded: "Good. Where are your men?"

"One west, one upper level, two on the platforms keeping people on trains."

"OK," said Rouche decisively after a moment's deliberation. He removed his crumpled jacket and unclipped his firearm. "Here's what we're going to do: you tell your men not to fire on this suspect under any circumstance."

"But what if he—" started Plant.

"*Any* circumstance. Understood?" Rouche reiterated. "He is *far* too important."

"Rouche, what the *hell* do you think you're doing?" asked Curtis. She looked appalled as he took out his handcuffs and locked his wrists together.

"Do it now," Rouche instructed Plant, ignoring her.

"I'm not letting you go in there," she told him.

"Look," whispered Rouche, "believe me, I like this plan even less than you, but we can't catch dead people. This could be our only chance at working out what's going on. Somebody needs to go out there. Somebody needs to speak to him."

Curtis looked to Baxter for support.

"He might just shoot you before you even open your mouth," said Baxter.

"Good point," said Rouche. He considered his options for a

moment. He awkwardly pulled out his mobile phone and called Curtis's number. After setting it to hands-free, he dropped it into his shirt pocket. "Keep the line open."

"Go ahead," said Plant, replying to a voice in his ear. "10-4." He turned to Rouche. "ESU are three minutes out: full tactical team."

"Which means he'll be dead in four," Rouche told them. "I'm going out there."

"No!" whispered Curtis, reaching for him but grasping only air as he stepped out into the cavernous hall.

Rouche raised his restrained hands above his head and very slowly started to approach the clock in the center. With the exception of the evacuation announcement triggering every thirty seconds, the lonely echo of his footsteps was the only discernible sound.

It was just them.

Not wanting to startle the man from whom he so desperately needed answers, he started to whistle the first tune that came into his head.

Curtis was holding her phone up for them all to listen to, the slow clicking of Rouche's heels against the marble delayed through the tinny speaker. She half expected to hear the roar of a gunshot after every step.

"Is he whistling that Shakira song?" asked Plant, now seriously questioning the sanity of the man whose orders he was following.

Curtis and Baxter chose not to answer him.

Rouche was halfway to the clock. The expanse of shiny marble that surrounded him was growing in all directions, as if he were floating out to sea. He realized that the distance to safety had not seemed quite so far, judged while standing in it. He spotted one of the other officers watching in awe from the wings, which did nothing to calm his nerves as he approached whatever horror awaited him.

Almost level with the information kiosk, Rouche ceased whistling and faltered in his step . . . because a dead man stood facing him. Twenty paces away. He had been stripped completely naked, the word "Bait" still bleeding from his chest, his head slumped forward as if trying to decipher the carelessly carved tattoo. Obscured from Rouche's sight, the man to the rear began to cry, animating the mutilated body before him, shoulders shaking in time to the sobs.

It was, without doubt, the most terrifying thing that Rouche had ever seen.

"Yeah . . . No, thank you," mumbled Rouche, suffering an abrupt change of heart. He casually turned on the spot to commence the return journey when a distraught voice finally addressed him:

"Who are you?"

Rouche winced. He sighed heavily and slowly turned back to face the dead man.

"Damien," answered Rouche. He took a few tentative steps closer.

"You're police?"

"Of sorts, yes. I am unarmed and handcuffed."

Rouche continued to approach a step at a time, confused as to why the man had not turned around to verify his claims. But he was staring skyward, transfixed by the night sky a hundred and twenty-five feet above. Rouche followed his gaze up to the incredible ceiling sparkling with stars, constellations realized as fully formed entities painted in gold: Orion, Taurus, Pisces . . . Gemini.

The twins were depicted sitting beside one another, almost twisted together. Four legs extended confusingly, unclaimed by either brother: a single entity, inseparable.

Distracted, Rouche realized that he was now only a few paces from the celestial imitation. He felt bile rising in the back of his throat as he heard the "dead" man whimper between wheezy breaths.

"Jesus Christ . . . Hostage is still alive," he whispered as loudly as he dared, praying that his colleagues would hear him. "Repeat: hostage is still alive!"

*

Curtis's hand was trembling as she turned to Plant:

"We need EMTs. And make sure ESU know the situation before they come storming in here."

Plant moved away to do as he was told.

"We're too far away," said Baxter, feeling as shaken as Curtis looked. "If anything goes wrong . . . We need to get closer."

Curtis nodded: "Follow me."

Rouche had drawn level with the double-man. A thin layer of dark blood looked to bond the faux twins as much as the huge black stitches threading their tented skin together. He forced a neutral expression onto his face before finally regarding the person responsible for the atrocity.

His naked skin was waxy and pale, tears merging with sweat despite the chill. He was a little overweight, eighteen years old at most, with scruffy, childish hair like the Gemini twins above. The word etched into his chest looked healed, a part of him now. His sleep-starved eyes slowly descended from the heavens to rest upon Rouche, a pleasant smile on his face despite the loaded weapon in his hand.

"Mind if I sit?" asked Rouche, attempting to appear as non-threatening as possible.

When he did not respond, Rouche slowly got down onto the cold floor and crossed his legs.

"Why ask a question and then not wait for the answer?"

Rouche instinctively glanced at the gun in the man's twitching right hand.

"I can't talk to you. I . . . I shouldn't," he continued, becoming agitated. He held a hand to his ear and looked around the empty concourse as if he'd heard something.

"I feel rude." Rouche smiled apologetically. "You were polite enough to ask me my name, yet I still have no idea of yours."

He waited patiently. The man looked torn and held a hand up to his forehead as though he were in pain.

"Glenn," he said, bursting into tears.

Rouche continued to wait.

"Arnolds."

"Glenn Arnolds," Rouche repeated for the benefit of his colleagues. He had no idea how clearly they were picking up the conversation. "Gemini," he said conversationally, staring up at the ceiling. He was aware that he was taking a huge risk broaching the subject but sensed that they were just about out of time.

"Yeah," said Glenn, smiling through the tears as he treated himself to another look up at the stars. "It's always nighttime to me."

"What does it mean to you, Gemini?"

"Everything."

"In what way?" asked Rouche with interest. "That . . . you aspire to be?"

"That I am. That he made me."

The "dead" man facing the empty hall made an anguished groan. Rouche willed him not to regain consciousness, unable to imagine anyone ever recovering from the trauma of waking up stitched onto another person.

"He?" asked Rouche. "Who is *he*?"

Glenn started shaking his head violently and hyperventilating. He gritted his teeth and pressed his hand against his forehead:

"Can't you hear that?" he yelled at Rouche, who remained quiet, unsure as to what the correct answer would be in the man's eyes. Eventually, the discomfort appeared to ease. "No . . . I can't be talking to you about this. *Especially* not about him. I'm *so* stupid! This is why he told me to just walk in and do it!"

"It's OK. It's OK. Forget I asked," said Rouche soothingly, so tantalizingly close to the name of the person pulling the strings and, at the same time, one wrong word away from a bullet in the head. Members of the Emergency Service Unit flickered past the entrances as they surrounded the hall. "He wanted you to just walk in and do what?"

Glenn did not even hear the question as he sobbed, unconsciously raising and lowering the gun as he chastised himself for being so weak.

Rouche was losing him.

"Is this your brother?" Rouche raised his voice desperately, gesturing to his victim, who was becoming increasingly vocal.

"No. Not yet," Glenn answered. "But he will be."

"When?"

"When the police officers free us."

"Free you?" asked Rouche. "You mean *kill* you?"

Glenn nodded. A red dot appeared on his bare chest. Rouche's eyes tracked it until it settled on his forehead.

"Nobody wants to kill you, Glenn," he lied.

"But they will. He said they would. They'll have to . . . after we kill one of you."

Again Rouche's gaze was drawn to the gun.

"I don't believe you want to hurt anybody," Rouche told the distraught man. "Know why? Because you could've done it already, but you didn't. You started firing into the air to scare people away from you . . . to save them. Didn't you?"

Glenn nodded and broke down.

"It's all right. I'll make sure nothing happens to you. Put the gun down."

A moment's deliberation and then Glenn leaned forward to drop to his knees, but as he did so, he cried out in pain, tearing one of the deep stitches out of his skin. The man to the rear screamed in horror as the pain dragged him back to consciousness. He began to thrash about, straining the remaining links between them, the red dot dancing over their bodies as they struggled.

Rouche saw the look of betrayal on Glenn's face as he watched the laser cross his chest.

He knew what was coming.

"Don't shoot! Don't shoot!" Rouche yelled, getting back to his feet. He took a step closer to the forced-twins, the red dot appearing on the skin of his own raised arm, blocking the officer's shot.

Glenn glanced up at what he was about to become one final time and then raised the gun toward Rouche.

"Don't shoot him!" Rouche shouted again: the information was worth so much more than his life.

As Glenn was pulled off-balance by the thrashing man, a sharp crack transformed the red dot into a bloody hole through his throat. Having missed its mark, Rouche heard the click of the rifle reloading too late as the dying man took aim.

He closed his eyes, held his breath, and let the hint of a smile form across his face.

The gunshot was deafening.

CHAPTER 12

Saturday, 12 December 2015
11:23 A.M.

The watery vending-machine coffee in Curtis's hands had gone cold over twenty minutes earlier. She was staring up blankly at the muted television as it failed to distract its audience from the pains and miseries that had led each of them to the emergency room at NYU Langone Medical Center. Baxter was sat beside her, still trying to compose the brief text message that she had been working on for the previous half hour. She gave up and put her phone away.

"I don't think I can do this anymore," mumbled Curtis. "If he dies . . ."

Baxter sensed that she was supposed to respond with something, but wasn't sure what. She had never been much of a shoulder to cry on. So she attempted a sympathetic smile, which seemed to do the trick when Curtis looked across at her.

"I should never have let Rouche go out there," Curtis continued.

"Wasn't our decision to make," said Baxter. "It was his. He made a call, for better or worse."

"Worse . . . definitely worse."

Baxter shrugged: "That's the job. We find ourselves in these screwed-up situations and all we can do is make a call."

"Yeah, well, I made a call too," said Curtis. "You sound like you're talking from experience. Was there a decision that you regretted?"

Baxter had not been ready for the intrusive question. Had she been, she would have forced herself not to conjure the smell of wood polish, the feeling of blood-sodden material clinging to her skin, the vibration through the floor as the Armed Response Unit approached . . . Wolf's bright blue eyes . . .

"Baxter?" Curtis asked, snapping her out of the memory.

She was unsure how long she had been lost in it this time, imagining herself choosing differently, torturing herself as she did so often by watching these theoretical scenarios play out to far favorable resolutions . . . to happy endings.

She laughed at herself for being so naive. There are no happy endings:

"I've made decisions that I don't, and probably never will, know were right," Baxter told her. "You just have to live with them."

"For better or worse," said Curtis.

Baxter nodded: "For better or worse."

A woman at reception was pointing a doctor in their direction. They got up and followed him through to a private room.

"We couldn't save him," was the flustered man's sledgehammer of an opening line.

Curtis walked out, leaving Baxter to finish up. When she came back out into the waiting room, Curtis was nowhere to be found. She took out her phone and held it up to her ear:

"Rouche? It's Baxter. He didn't make it. We need to talk."

It was almost impossible to get lost in Manhattan; however, as Curtis walked aimlessly down First Avenue, she was struggling to decide on the best route back to the field office. Her encyclopedic knowledge of the streets, alleyways, and landmarks spanning a huge area around Midtown did not extend this close to the borders of the island.

The unsettled sky was still resisting the urge to snow, but the bitter wind was making everyone's life quite miserable enough in its absence. She braced herself against it and walked on, positive that she was going to be sick at any moment. She could feel the guilt eating away at her insides, a tangible and toxic weight that she just wanted cut out and dropped to the bottom of the river that reappeared in her peripheral vision at every intersection.

She had killed an innocent man.

Her stomach twisted as she admitted it to herself for the first time. She ran into the darkened entrance of an underground car park to vomit.

As if it had not already been the worst day of her life, she and Rouche had had an enormous argument only minutes after pulling the trigger, even though he had been the one to force her hand. *He* had chosen to confront Glenn Arnolds unarmed and unprotected. *He* had inexplicably remained out there rather than retreating to safety when the situation deteriorated. It was *his* fault that she had been left with an impossible ultimatum: she could watch her colleague die or risk killing an innocent person.

She had made a call.

It had been the first time that Curtis had ever discharged her weapon in the field. Ever the overachiever, she had fired a single shot, a single bullet that had claimed the lives of two people as it passed through the base of Glenn Arnolds's skull, killing him instantly, only to embed itself in the back of his victim's.

If she had just aimed a few millimeters higher . . .

When she had so desperately needed friendship and reassurance, Rouche had told her that she had made the wrong decision, that she had killed their investigation, that she should have just let him die. For some reason, his reaction had upset her more than anything else.

With tears prickling her eyes, she took out her phone and called the number that anybody else would have labeled "Home." The words "Curtis residence" flashed up on the screen.

"Please be Mom," she whispered.

"Senator Tobias Curtis," a deep voice answered brusquely.

Curtis remained silent. She considered hanging up.

"Elliot? Is that you?" asked the senator. "Elliot?"

"Yes, sir. I was actually hoping to speak to Mom."

"So you don't want to speak to me, then?" he asked.

"No . . . I do. I just . . ."

"Well, which is it? You either do or you don't."

Tears were escaping Curtis's eyes now. She just needed someone to talk to.

"Well?"

"I'd like to talk to Mom, please," she said.

"Well, you can't. I don't want your mother involved. Do you think I don't know what's happened? Lennox called me the moment she found out. As you *should* have done."

Curtis felt a fleeting moment of relief: he already knew. She turned the corner onto a street that she actually recognized and swapped to the other ear to give her frozen hand a respite from the cold.

"I killed someone, Daddy . . . Sorry. Sir."

"The victim's dead?" the senator asked quietly.

"Yes." She burst into tears.

"Jesus Christ, Elliot!" he bellowed. "How could you be so careless? Do you have *any* idea what this is going to do to me when the press get hold of it?"

"I-I . . ." stammered Curtis. Even she was shocked by his utter disregard for her well-being.

"I can see the headlines now: 'Idiot Daughter of United States Senator Guns Down Innocent.' I'm finished. You know that, don't you? You've finished me."

Curtis was so upset by his words she could barely walk. She slumped onto an icy step and wept into the phone.

"Pull yourself together, for God's sake," he barked before sighing and swapping to as gentle tone as he could muster: "I'm sorry. Elliot?"

"Yes?"

"I apologize. This has all come as quite a shock and perhaps I overreacted."

"It's OK. Sorry if I disappointed you."

"Let's not worry about that. Let's worry about what to do next. Lennox will take you through exactly what to say to minimize the damage to the FBI, to me, and to whatever is left of your career."

"What about the man I killed?"

"Well, the damage is done there," said the senator dismissively, as if leaving him off the Christmas-card list. "You do and say whatever Lennox tells you, and if your team makes any advances or arrests in connection to this 'Puppet' nonsense, *you* need to be the one making them and looking like the hero. Do you understand me?"

"Yes, sir."

"Good."

"I love you."

The line disconnected. He must not have heard her.

It was someone's birthday. It was *always* someone's birthday. The day on which someone became a temporary department-wide celebrity, pressured by social etiquette into spending the best part of a day's wages on Krispy Kremes.

Edmunds sat back down at his desk, obligatory doughnut in hand, exploding whatever had been concealed inside all over his keyboard as he bit into it. He could feel his shirt pulling uncomfortably as he reached for the bin. He had put on almost a stone since transferring back to Fraud. Although his gangly frame could never look overweight, he could feel the extra pounds there in everything he did.

He stared at the screen of foreign bank accounts in front of him until his eyes glazed over. He had not done a jot of work for almost an hour while watching the early night settle over the city outside. He was distracted. He knew that Baxter had sent him the files on the first three killers that morning, which he'd not even had a chance to look at, due to a teething one-year-old, a sleep-deprived wife, and the ever-inconvenient demands of full-time employment. He found himself wishing away the hours until he could settle back down in his shed and focus on the investigation.

After a quick scan of the office to locate his boss, he opened up the BBC News website, which was updating with reports from Grand Central Terminal. He stole a look at his mobile phone again, surprised not to have heard anything from Baxter. As he read through the horrific eyewitness accounts, he had to remind himself how the press latched on to these stories, exaggerating and inventing as they went. Having said that, even if there was only an element of truth to any of it, it was still undoubtedly one of the most disturbing things he had ever heard.

Unable to resist any longer, he opened up his email, downloaded the attachments to Baxter's garbled message, and set to work.

Rouche had remained behind at Grand Central while Curtis and Baxter accompanied the casualty attached to Glenn Arnolds's corpse in the back of the ambulance. Following his near-death experience, all Rouche had wanted was to hear his wife's voice. He knew that he had behaved abysmally toward Curtis in his haste to leave the crime scene and make his phone call. He owed her more than an apology.

He had made his way to the medical center on foot and met Baxter outside the main entrance. Within minutes they had crossed FDR Drive and found a bench looking out over the East River.

"If this is about how I acted towards Curtis, I know," started Rouche. "I'm an arse. I'll get dinner tonight to apologize."

"It's not."

"So it's about me going out there unarmed to speak to him?"

"Do you want to die, Rouche?" Baxter asked bluntly.

"Excuse me?" He laughed. He looked bewildered.

"I'm being serious."

"What? No! Look, someone had to go out there and—"

"I'm not talking about that."

"You mean me telling them not to shoot him? We needed him alive. I *so* nearly got a name out of—"

"I'm not talking about that either," Baxter interrupted.

The conversation paused as a homeless man, wheeling a cart, passed behind them.

"I wasn't with Curtis when she stepped out to save you. I was along the side wall behind the Puppet-man . . . facing you."

Rouche waited for her to elaborate.

"I saw you smile."

"Smile?"

"When that first shot didn't take him down and he raised the gun at you. You closed your eyes . . . and you smiled."

"Trapped wind?" tried Rouche.

"I know what I saw." She looked at him, waiting for an explanation.

"I don't know what to tell you. I don't remember smiling. I don't really see what I would have had to be smiling about. But no. I assure you that I *don't* want to die . . . Promise."

"OK," said Baxter. "But from personal experience, when someone starts being reckless with their own life, it tends to be everyone around them who ends up getting hurt."

After a moment's silence, a pigeon abandoned its branch on the monochrome tree behind them. They both watched it soar toward Roosevelt Island and the Queensboro Bridge beyond.

"I screwed up today," said Rouche, still staring out at the river. "I should've known that man was alive sooner. A few more seconds could have made all the difference."

"How could you *ever* have known that?" asked Baxter.

"He was bleeding."

"Bleeding?"

"Bright red and streaming out of him." Rouche shook his head, frustrated with himself. He turned to face her. "The dead don't bleed."

"I'll be sure to remember that," she assured her intense colleague.

"Come on," said Rouche. "We've got work to do."

"What work? Arnolds didn't tell us anything."

"Sure he did. He told us that he didn't choose to do it, that he had been instructed to, manipulated. It raises questions about our other killers, doesn't it? Perhaps none of them are devoted members of some imagined secret cult—perhaps they're all just being manipulated into doing these things by a single person."

"*He*," said Baxter, remembering what she'd heard while eavesdropping in on the tinny speakerphone conversation.

"He." Rouche nodded. "We've been going about this all wrong. I think there *is* a link between our killers: they all had a vulnerability, something to blackmail, someone to threaten. If we can work out what those things were, we'll be able to work out who might be in a position to exploit them."

"So where do we start?"

"The team searching Arnolds's apartment found an appointment card. He was seeing a psychiatrist."

"He did seem to have a few . . . *issues*," said Baxter tactfully.

"And who better to tell us what those issues were than his shrink?"

CHAPTER 13

Saturday, 12 December 2015

2:15 P.M.

Curtis had not been at the field office when Baxter and Rouche stopped by. Neither had she returned any of their calls. Unsure whether she had just taken an extended lunch to clear her head or, quite understandably, stood down for the remainder of the day, they decided to press on without her.

The address of the practice, scrawled across the back of Rouche's hand, had led them to a grand building on East 20th Street overlooking Gramercy Park. They climbed the steps between the imposing columns of the ornate portico.

Baxter felt a little underdressed as they crossed an impressive reception area and were instructed to take a seat. Overwhelmed by the number of buttons on the coffee machine, she poured herself a glass of water and sat down opposite Rouche, classical music softening the silence.

"We'll catch up with Curtis at the hotel," Rouche told her, more for his own benefit, seeing as Baxter had not spoken a word in over five minutes. "She probably needs a bit more time."

"She might need more than that," said Baxter, looking pointedly around at where they were.

"Hmmm."

"What? It might help."

"They'll suggest it, no doubt."

"Do you have a problem with that?" asked Baxter, a little defensively.

After the dust had settled on the Ragdoll case, and she was able to stop long enough to actually process what had happened, she had been to talk to someone. She had always considered it a provision for weaker people than her, for people unable to cope with the trials of everyday life, but she had been wrong. It had been far easier to express her feelings to a complete stranger than to anybody who knew her, who might judge her, who expected more from her. Over several sessions, she had gradually come to terms with the death of one of her closest friends: Benjamin Chambers, a man who had been more of a father figure to her than a colleague.

"I have no problem with other people doing it," answered Rouche, "but it's certainly not anything I'd ever consider."

"Yeah, you're just too strong a person to have any issues, aren't you?" snapped Baxter, aware that she was revealing something deeply personal with the outburst. "You are *perfect*."

"I am *far* from perfect," said Rouche calmly.

"You think? Ordering your colleagues to let you die. Screaming at the friend who killed an innocent man to save you. Smiling as some nutjob points a gun at you."

"Not this again."

"I'm just saying, if anybody needs to talk through some of their shit . . . it's you."

"You done?" asked Rouche.

Baxter kept quiet, suspecting that she had perhaps crossed a line. They sat in silence for a moment until the scowling receptionist lost interest.

"I pray," said Rouche, back to his amiable self. "That's where I went while you were at the hospital. That's where *I* talk through my 'shit' *every single day* because I fear I might have more than anybody."

Something in Rouche's tone told Baxter that he meant it.

"You misunderstand my misgivings," he continued. "I pass no judgment on the person looking for help; we *all* are. It's the person paid to listen that I don't trust. Because the idea of someone out there knowing everything about me that I try *so* hard to hide away terrifies me—as it should everyone else. *No one* should have *that* much power over you."

Baxter had never thought about it like that before, projecting a certain professional detachment onto the authoritative doctor. Had she been fooling herself into believing that someone in such a profession was bound by a set of laws and decorum more stringent than those that Baxter flaunted so regularly within her own? Had she tried to ignore that the woman had a mouth located just a few inches below her greedy ears just like everybody else?

She had just begun dissecting each and every conversation that she had had with the counselor when they were invited in to see Dr. Arun. His luxurious office was a more relaxed take on the reception area, with a tree standing watch beside the window. He offered them seats at his tidy desk. A thick file sat atop, labeled with Glenn Arnolds's name.

"May I see some identification before we start?" asked the doctor firmly but politely. He raised his eyebrows on reading Baxter's Metropolitan Police–issued card but did not question it.

"So I believe you require some information on one of my patients. I presume there is no need to tell you that most of what is documented here is protected by doctor-patient confidentiality."

"He's dead," blurted Baxter.

"Oh!" said Dr. Arun. "I'm very sorry to hear that. But it does not change the fact that—"

"He murdered someone," Baxter continued. It was not technically true but was far simpler than the actual story.

"I see."

"In quite possibly the darkest and most disturbing way that either of us has ever seen."

"*Right,*" said the doctor, his mind immediately jumping to the horrific reports coming out of Grand Central Terminal. "OK. What do you need?"

Glenn Arnolds had been diagnosed with acute schizoaffective disorder at the age of ten, attributed to the untimely death of his twin brother the previous year: a blood clot in the brain. Glenn had gone through life expecting to suffer the same fate at any given moment, not helped any by his propensity for severe headaches. He had lived his life literally waiting to die while mourning the death of his twin. This had led to him becoming increasingly reclusive and depressed, and had prompted a tendency to regard life as cheap and fleeting, just as his brother's had been.

He had transferred to the Gramercy Practice three years earlier, had a flawless attendance record, and had been making significant progress in both one-on-one and group sessions. With the exception of mild depressive episodes, his psychotic symptoms had been kept at bay by prescription meds. In summary, he had never shown the slightest indication of violence toward anybody.

"How was he paying for the pleasure of your company?" Rouche asked the doctor.

Baxter wondered whether he had phrased the question intentionally to make the psychiatrist sound like a prostitute.

"Doesn't look like you guys come cheap," he added.

"Health insurance," answered Dr. Arun with just a hint of injustice in his voice. "*Very good* health insurance. I believe that when his twin died, his parents signed him up for the best they could afford. Since the mental illness was diagnosed afterwards . . ." The doctor finished his sentence with a shrug.

"And in your 'professional opinion' . . ."

Baxter glared at him.

". . . how did Glenn seem to you over the past couple of weeks?" asked Rouche.

"I'm sorry?"

"Did he present any indication that he might have relapsed? Or could he have stopped taking his meds?"

"Well, I wouldn't know," said Dr. Arun in confusion. "I have never met him."

"What?" asked Baxter.

"We had our first session scheduled for next week. I'm sorry. I thought you knew. I've taken over Dr. Bantham's client list. He left the practice last Friday."

Baxter and Rouche looked at one another.

"Last Friday?" she asked. "Was this a planned resignation?"

"Oh yes. I was interviewed for the role a good two months ago."

Baxter sighed, having thought they were onto something.

"We're still going to need to talk to him," Rouche told the doctor. "Think you could find us some contact details?"

There had been no answer on either phone number supplied by the scary receptionist. She had printed off a home address for Dr. Bantham in Westchester County, approximately a fifty-minute drive from Manhattan. With the FBI still attempting to identify Glenn Arnolds's victim, Glenn Arnolds's body somewhere between the hospital morgue and the forensic lab, and Curtis ignoring them, they elected to risk a wasted journey up to Rye to pay the doctor a visit.

Baxter didn't have high expectations as she read the directions out to Rouche:

"With the golf course on the left, we should cross over Beaver Swamp Brook any second, then it's the next right turn off Locust Avenue."

"Lovely."

They pulled into an idyllic cul-de-sac. It had clearly been snowing heavily north of the city. Inches of powder balanced on the beautifully pruned hedges lining the sweeping driveways, which had been brushed clear to reveal the wet gravel beneath. Perfect snowmen stood proudly in generous gardens, surrounded by sets of small footprints. Wood siding of various hues adorned each home, giving the wintry scene a Scandinavian edge. It was hard to picture the pandemonium of Times Square less than an hour's drive away.

"I have a suspicion that the town planner wanted to keep this place secret," said Rouche as he looked for house numbers. He was unable to resist enviously imagining his family coming home to one of these perfect properties. "What's this one, Dog Shit Drive?"

Baxter laughed, as did Rouche at the unfamiliar sound.

They turned into a driveway at the end of the road just as the twilight activated the automatic sensors leading up to the triple garage. It was not looking hopeful. None of the lights were on inside the house, and unlike the neighboring properties, an unspoiled layer of snow covered the driveway, garden, and path up to the front door.

They parked up and stepped out into the silent garden. Wind chimes played softly on the breeze from the porch of another house, and they could hear a car speeding along a road somewhere far off in the distance. Baxter was shocked by the cold; it felt several degrees cooler than it had back in the city. They crunched loudly toward the front door in the fading light, the tall trees that surrounded them draining of color and definition with every passing second.

Rouche rang the doorbell.

Nothing.

Baxter trampled the flower bed to peer through a large window, the dark bulbs of fairy lights nailed into the frame reminding her of Rouche's neglected family home. She squinted, letting her eyes adjust to the darkness. She thought she could make out the hint of a warm glow coming from another room.

"Might be a light on," she called to Rouche as he knocked at the door.

She stomped over more flower beds, turned the corner, and peered through the side windows, where she thought she had seen the light. But the house was completely dark inside. She sighed and made her way back to Rouche.

"Probably on holiday. It *is* nearly Christmas," she said.

"Probably."

"Wanna try the neighbors?"

"Nah, not tonight. It's too cold. I'll leave a card, and we can make some phone calls in the morning," said Rouche, already heading back toward the warm car.

"*Plus* you promised us dinner tonight," Baxter reminded him.

"Well, yeah, *if* we find Curtis. I wasn't rude to you."

"You were a bit rude."

Rouche smiled. "Yeah, maybe a bit rude."

They climbed back into the car and turned up the heater. Rouche reversed down the long driveway, guided by the twinkling lights of the house opposite. With one final glance back at his dream home, the car wheelspun down the curb, and they drove away back to Manhattan.

A few minutes passed, in which the night swallowed up the last of the dying light. And then, somewhere inside the lifeless house, the warm glow returned, burning against the darkness.

Thomas woke up at the kitchen table with Echo's rear end pressed into his face. He sat up as the clock on the cooker changed to 2:19 A.M. The remnants of the dinner he had cooked for himself and Baxter sat in the center of the table beside his phone: no new text messages, no missed calls.

He had kept abreast of the latest developments from New York throughout the day, assuming that Baxter would be involved in some capacity. He had fought the overwhelming urge to contact her, just to ensure that she was all right, to let her know that he was there should she need to talk.

He had felt her slipping away from him over the past couple of months, not that he could say he ever truly *had* her in the first place. It seemed that the harder he tried to hold on to her, the further he ended up pushing her away. Even Edmunds had warned him off pressuring her. He had never considered himself a needy person, in fact quite the opposite. He was self-assured and independent. But the ridiculously unreasonable demands that Baxter's job made of her had left him in a state of perpetual anxiety.

Was it "clingy" to want to know whether his girlfriend was still alive?

She would go nights without sleep, entire days fueled by coffee alone. She could be roaming any part of the city, at any hour, in the company of the very worst that London had to offer. She had grown so accustomed to the horrors she witnessed that she had become desensitized to it. And *that* was what worried him most: she was not afraid of anything.

Fear was a good thing. It kept one alert, careful. It kept one safe.

He got up, took the plate he had set aside for Baxter, just in case, and scooped the contents into Echo's food bowl, who looked down at him as if he had just soiled a perfectly good pile of biscuits.

"Night, Echo," he said.

He switched off the lights and went up to bed.

The dark bags under Edmunds's eyes looked ghastly as they were thrown into shadow by the light radiating off his laptop. He switched on the kettle and had to remove his thick jumper because the small fan heater had excelled itself. Had the lamp he was working by not been resting on top of a lawnmower, he might have convinced himself he was somewhere more glamorous than his own decrepit shed.

He had spent hours wading through the killers' financials. Blake had also been good enough to keep him in the loop regarding the Met's investigation into the sixty-one-year-old cop-killing arsonist, Patrick Peter Fergus. This was on the proviso that Edmunds put in a good word with Baxter, which, of course, he had no intention of doing.

Due to his incarceration, Dominic Burrell's accounts had taken a matter of minutes to work through; however, the same could not be said for their first killer, the bridge-diving Marcus Townsend. Despite being written as an endless list of transactions and balances, his financial history had been a riveting read. Edmunds could track it right back to his first tentative foray into illicit trading, watching his confidence growing proportionally to his various bank balances.

It had been a disaster waiting to happen. As the trades became more and more blatant, Edmunds could sense the addiction behind the numbers until the sudden cessation in mid-2007, the very worst thing that Townsend could have done. Edmunds could picture the scene: the police arriving at his offices, looking through the records, spooking him into incriminating himself through a drastic drop in personal profits, and Townsend admitting his guilt in trying to save himself. From there, it had been a tragic story for Townsend: fine after fine hacking away at his fortune before the value of whatever assets he still possessed crashed along with the worldwide markets.

He had been ruined.

Before moving on to Eduardo Medina's accounts, Edmunds opened up the website for the Streets to Success initiative, in which Townsend had still been enrolled when he strung a body up over the Brooklyn Bridge. It was inspirational stuff, seeing the photographs of homeless people, who looked too far detached from society to ever return, dressed in shirts and ties on their first day of work. Perhaps that was why Edmunds lingered on the site for longer than he normally would have.

He came across a hyperlink, contained within one of the true stories, that caught his attention. He clicked on it and was redirected to another part of the site. He only read down to the third item on the list before excitedly throwing the dregs of his coffee across his lap. He checked his watch, counted out the hours on his fingers, and phoned Baxter.

Baxter was fast asleep. They had eventually caught up with Curtis back at the hotel, where Rouche had made a heartfelt apology, and she had reluctantly agreed to join them for some food. All a little drained after the eventful day, they had called it a night in order to get an early start in the morning.

Baxter reached for the buzzing phone: "Edmunds?" she groaned.

"Were you asleep?" he asked, a little judgmentally.

"Yes! Funnily enough. It's all right for you—it's . . . Wait, no, it's not. What are you still doing up?"

"Going through the files you sent me," he said, as though it were obvious.

Baxter yawned.

"Are you OK?" he asked.

He had finally learned how to speak to Baxter. If she wanted to talk about what had happened that morning at Grand Central, she would. If not, he would receive a one-word response and move on until such time as she did.

"Yeah."

"I need you to get hold of some more stuff for me," said Edmunds.

"I know. I'll get you the files on the Mall and Grand Central tomorrow."

"I've already got the London file."

She didn't even want to know how he had managed that, so decided not to ask.

"I need complete medical records for all of them," said Edmunds.

"Medical? OK. Looking for anything in particular?"

"I don't know. It's just a hunch."

Baxter trusted Edmunds's intuition even more than her own.

"I'll send them to you tomorrow. I mean, later."

"Thanks. I'll let you get back to sleep. Good night."

"Edmunds?"

"Yeah?"

"Don't forget why you left the team in the first place."

Edmunds understood the underlying sentiment. This was Baxter's way of saying that she was worried about him. He had to smile.

"I won't."

CHAPTER 14

Sunday, 13 December 2015

7:42 A.M.

"Possession!"

Baxter stood half dressed in her hotel room, immediately regretting switching on the television. Although no surprise to find the murders a topic of debate on one of the country's biggest breakfast shows, the conversation appeared to have veered into uncharted territory.

"Possession?" one of the perfect-looking news presenters prompted the unfailingly controversial televangelist.

"That's correct—possession," Pastor Jerry Pilsner Jr. confirmed in a thick Southern drawl. "The work of a single ancient entity, leaping from one broken soul to another, driven by an insatiable lust for torment and pain, which it inflicts indiscriminately upon the weak and unvirtuous . . . There is only *one* way to protect ourselves . . . The *only* salvation is God!"

"So," started the show's female presenter carefully, "are we talking about . . . *spirits* here?"

"Angels."

The woman looked lost and turned to her male counterpart to let him know it was his turn to ask the next question.

"Fallen angels," the pastor elaborated.

"And . . ." faltered the male presenter, "are you saying that these fallen angels—"

"Just one," the pastor interrupted. "It only takes one."

"So this fallen angel, whoever they are—"

"Oh, I know *precisely* who he is," their interviewee interjected again, stumping the presenters completely. "I've always known who it was. I can even give you his name, if you'd like . . . One of his names . . ."

Both presenters leaned forward in anticipation, clearly aware that they were forging sensationalist-TV gold.

". . . *Azazel*," whispered the pastor as the show cut to a perfectly timed commercial break.

Baxter realized that the hairs on the back of her neck were standing on end as a cheerful advert for the latest invention in fruit-flavored sweets flashed and shouted at her from the screen.

The pastor had made a passionate case and, to be fair, had come up with a way of linking the bizarre murders together, which was more than the Met, NYPD, FBI, and CIA combined had managed. But then she felt a shiver when the news program returned with footage of the pastor's white wooden church, isolated at the end of a dirt track that cut a scar across a vast barren field.

The congregation had swarmed from as far as three towns over, emerging from the tree line like eidola, dressed in their Sunday best, desperate to stake their own claim to salvation. The crowd surrounding the fragile building swelled to five people deep, drinking in every word as the preacher addressed those who wanted to be saved.

Baxter found something about the scene deeply sinister: these people in nowheresville America huddling together like sheep, surrendering themselves entirely to their opportunistic shepherd, who had no reservations about unabashedly exploiting other people's real-world misery to promote his delusional bullshit: having the nerve to call the victims, two of whom were honest police officers, "weak and unvirtuous."

God, she hated religion.

Unable to tear herself from the screen, she watched as the pastor bestowed his parting thoughts to his adoring audience before him, and the countless others seeking salvation from the comfort of their sofas at home.

"You know, I look around at you fine people here today, at my own self in the mirror, and do you know what I see?"

The congregation waited with bated breath.

"Sinners . . . I see sinners. Ain't *not one* of us perfect here. But as people of the Lord, we dedicate our lives to making ourselves better!"

The audience broke into applause, murmurs of agreement, and the sporadic call of "Amen."

"But then," continued the pastor, "I look further afield. I look at this world we're living in, and do you know how that makes me feel? It frightens me. I see *so* much hate, *so* much cruelty, *so* much malice.

"Can we *even* look to the Church for help? When just the other week, *yet* another member of the clergy—a man supposedly at one with God—was alleged of molesting a seven-year-old boy! This is *not* a good place! I *love* my God, but He is *not* here!"

A professional at the very top of his game, the pastor broke eye contact with his transfixed audience to address the camera directly.

"I'm speaking to all the nonbelievers out there . . . I want you to ask yourselves:

"What *if* there is a God?

"What *if* there is a heaven?

"What *if* there is a hell?

"And what *if* . . . just what *if* . . . we're *all* already there?"

Baxter hung up the phone and sighed heavily. Through the partially obscured glass, she was able to make out Lennox getting up from behind her desk to give Curtis a reassuring, but no doubt uncomfortable, hug. Apparently the special agent in charge would not be throwing her to the wolves as predicted. Baxter tried to imagine Vanita doing the same for her and shook her head at the absurd thought.

She had just had a thirty-five-minute conversation with her superior back in London. They had barely had a chance to check in the previous day after the events at Grand Central Terminal. Following a protocol-dictated display of concern for Baxter's emotional state, Vanita had asked her to take her through the details to ensure that it matched the report that the Americans had sent over. They discussed the imminent probability of a similarly disturbing murder occurring in London, the frightening lack of progress all around, and agreed that Baxter should remain out in New York as the Metropolitan Police's representative while Vanita held the fort at home.

She typed out a quick text to Thomas while waiting for Lennox and Curtis to finish. She had completely forgotten to tell him she was not coming home and realized that she probably had not helped the situation developing between them any with her lack of contact.

Hey. How is Echo? Talk later? ☺

Lennox emerged from her office, Curtis trailing close behind:

"Can I have everyone working on the murders today in the meeting room, please?"

Over a third of the office got to their feet and crowded into the space, some having to stand outside, listening in, reminiscent of the scenes outside Pastor Jerry Pilsner Jr.'s church. Baxter squeezed through and joined Rouche, Curtis, and Lennox at the front. Across the large whiteboard, Rouche had written out details of their five killers:

US	UK
1. MARCUS TOWNSEND *(Brooklyn Bridge)* *MO: strangulation* *Victim: Ragdoll-related*	**3. DOMINIC BURRELL** *(Belmarsh Prison)* *MO: stabbing* *Victim: Ragdoll-related*
2. EDUARDO MEDINA *(33rd Precinct)* *MO: high-speed impact* *Victim: police officer*	**4. PATRICK PETER FERGUS** *(The Mall)* *MO: blunt-force trauma* *Victim: police officer*
5. GLENN ARNOLDS *(Grand Central)* *MO: Unpleasant* *Victim: - ?*	

"Everyone here?" asked Lennox pointlessly, seeing as several people were stood behind a wall. "Good. For those of you who have not yet met: Detective Chief Inspector Baxter with the Metropolitan Police and Special Agent Roooch with the CIA."

"Rouche," Rouche corrected her.

"Ruch?" she tried.

"It's not pronounced Roach?" asked a muscular man sitting in the front row.

"No," said Rouche in bewilderment that a) the man believed him stupid enough not to know his own name and b) several other members of the audience made their own attempts at his surname in a drone of incorrect pronunciation:

"Rooze?"

"Roze?"

"Rooshy?"

"Rouche," Rouche corrected again politely.

"My neighbor *definitely* pronounces it Roach," insisted the man in the front row.

"Is that perhaps because their name *is* Roach?" reasoned Rouche.

"It's Rouche," Curtis told the room. "Like 'whoosh.'"

"OK! OK!" Lennox shouted over the din. "If we could *please* get back on track. Quiet! Over to you, Agent . . . Rouche."

He got to his feet.

"So . . . these are our killers," he started, pointing to the board, "presented in an easy-to-read, bite-sized format just to ensure that we're all up to speed. Can anyone tell me anything that we can ascertain from it?" he asked, as if addressing a class of schoolchildren.

Mrs. Roach's neighbor cleared his throat:

"Pieces of shit have murdered two of our own, and for that, they're going down . . . *Yeah!*" The burly man cheered his own comment and then proceeded to applaud himself as several of his colleagues followed suit. "Come on!" he shouted excitedly.

"OK." Rouche nodded patiently. "Anything a little more tangible? Yes?"

"The murders in New York and London definitely mirror each other."

"Absolutely," said Rouche, "which means that we can look forward to an 'unpleasant hyphen question mark' murder in London at any moment, raising the question why? For what reason would someone want to declare war on both of these cities and these cities alone?"

"The stock markets?" someone shouted out.

"Concentration of wealth?"

"Media focus?"

"And we need to explore all of those avenues," Rouche told them. "OK. What else does the list tell us?"

"The MO," a voice called from behind the wall. The officer pushed her way through to the front. "Every MO has been different, which suggests a degree of independence. Clearly these people are provided with a target, perhaps a time frame, but it would appear that the rest is up to them."

"Excellent!" said Rouche. "Which brings me to my next point—

we need to focus on these people as individuals. Glenn Arnolds didn't want to hurt anybody . . . not really. He was being used. We want to split you into five teams. Each team takes one of our killers. Your job will be to identify anything about them that could have been exploited. Off the top of my head: Townsend—money, Medina—immigration status, Burrell—prison perks like drugs or placement, Fergus—ill mother, Arnolds—his dead brother and general mental health."

His audience was attentively scribbling notes.

"Also, Baxter here has requested a copy of each of their medical records forwarded to her at your earliest convenience," he added.

Rouche noticed the inquiring look that Lennox shot Curtis.

"I'll free up anyone else I can," Lennox told him.

Rouche nodded in gratitude.

"Anything you turn up," said Rouche, addressing the room once more, "please do contact myself, Curtis, or Baxter immediately. Between us, we'll have an overview of the entire case and should be able to spot any similarities or patterns. Thank you kindly."

Rouche's conclusive farewell also served to dismiss the room.

Lennox went over to speak to him, Baxter, and Curtis privately:

"I've got a string of press conferences and meetings," she told them. "I may require you throughout the day, Chief Inspector."

Baxter had figured as much.

"Your plans?" Lennox asked none of them in particular.

"Forensic Services first. They've got both the bodies from yesterday and hopefully an ID on . . . our victim," said Rouche, choosing his wording carefully with Curtis present. "We've got the Arnolds team trying to get hold of his psychiatrist and interviewing his friends and neighbors, so will probably be chasing up one of those later on."

"Very well." Lennox stopped Curtis on the way out while Baxter and Rouche went on. "What does she want the medical records for?"

"I'm not sure."

"Find out. Remember our talk. After what's happened, it's more

important than ever that *we* break this case. If she's keeping anything from you, I'll have no reservations about sticking her on the
next plane home."

"I understand."

Lennox nodded and then stepped aside to let Curtis catch up
with her colleagues.

"So Glenn Arnolds *was* still taking his meds?" asked Curtis in
confusion.

"No, but he was taking meds," answered the petite woman cryptically, peering over the top of her reading glasses to address her.

Curtis recalled meeting the forensic pathologist on several occasions in the past. After all, Stormy Day was not a name easily
forgotten. If recollection served, the feeling of being utterly confused while in the woman's company was completely normal.
Stormy passed Curtis and Rouche a file containing a copy of a
printout: results from the blood test performed as part of the
autopsy. It meant absolutely nothing to either of them.

They were sat in the reception area of the OCME Hirsch Center
for Forensic Services. Situated on East 26th Street, it occupied one
of the numerous ancillary buildings to the main medical center,
meaning that the two cadavers had traveled only three blocks south
from the NYU Langone emergency room. They were meeting in
this unconventional spot because, unbeknown to Curtis, Rouche
had phoned ahead to request that they have no further involvement with the bodies.

She would have been offended had she known, but he had seen
the relief on her face when asked to take a seat in the light, airy
reception area instead of being led into the darkened labs at the
heart of the building, where she would have been confronted with
the wax-skinned corpse of the man she had shot.

Baxter was yet to join them. She had not even managed to escape the field office before Lennox had "borrowed" her for some
press conference or other.

Stormy gestured to the incomprehensible page in Curtis's hand:

"I don't know exactly what he was taking, but he really, *really* shouldn't have been taking them. There was virtually no sign of the antipsychotic medications he'd been prescribed, but there were trace amounts of ETH-LAD and benzodiazepines."

Curtis looked blank.

"One of the side effects of benzodiazepine is suicidal tendencies."

"Oh."

"And ETH-LAD is like LSD's little brother. Possibly two of the worst things that someone with Arnolds's history could be taking: hallucinations, a diminished grip on reality. And this was *on top* of the withdrawal symptoms from the antipsychotics. The guy would have been a state, though I bet that ceiling at Grand Central would have come to life!" Realizing that her hippie roots were probably best saved for a less conservative audience, she cleared her throat and continued: "I've sent a sample of his blood down to Quantico for extensive testing and asked to see any other medication they find at his home."

"I'll chase that up for you," said Curtis, making a note.

"That's all I've really got for you on Arnolds besides the obvious. To be honest, it's a bit of a bizarre situation. Normally his body would have remained at the crime scene, but because of the nature of the incident, he's covered in another man's blood and tissue, went for a journey in an ambulance, and had to be cut free in the emergency room. Basically, half of New York City has probably poked his corpse by now. The level of contamination and postmortem interference is problematic, to say the least."

"What about our victim?" asked Rouche.

"Noah French. Reported missing two days ago. He worked in one of the ticket kiosks at Grand Central."

Rouche looked impressed.

"Didn't even need to run any tests to work it out," Stormy continued. "He had a tattoo on his forearm: 'K.E.F. 3-6-2012.' Had to be a son or daughter. We checked the initials against birth records in the New York area for that date and got one result back."

"Genius." Rouche smiled.

"I thought so. He'd been drugged: some form of opiate. Details are all in the file." Stormy was distracted by something at the front desk. "Is *she* with you?"

They turned around to see Baxter gearing up for an argument with the man behind reception, who clearly had no idea what she was talking about. Stormy got up to intervene before the situation escalated.

Rouche turned to Curtis:

"We've got a proper lead," he said. "We *need* to speak to this psychiatrist."

"Yeah. *We* will," said Curtis.

She flicked back to the blood results, opened up the metal rings, and removed the printout.

Rouche looked confused.

"Er, what are you doing?" he asked.

"Following orders."

"By removing evidence?"

"By keeping our first real break in the case between the FBI and CIA."

"I don't really . . . I don't feel very comfortable with that," said Rouche.

"And you think I do? But that's why they're called *orders* and not *treats*."

Stormy was heading back over with Baxter in tow. Curtis still had the printout in her hand:

"Hide this."

She tossed it at Rouche, who threw it back at her:

"I don't want it! I'm gonna tell her."

"Don't!"

Rouche's coat was draped over the back of the sofa. Curtis stuffed the wrinkled sheet of paper into one of the pockets just as Baxter sat down beside them. She ignored Rouche's disapproving look as Stormy continued.

*

Baxter had accompanied Lennox to the press conference, which had been scheduled in order to formally release details of the incident at Grand Central Terminal. She had been both surprised and impressed by Lennox's refusal to bow to the pressure of naming the agent responsible for an innocent man's death. She had emphasized that the only person to blame had been a mentally unstable man, who had engineered a man's death by forcing the hand of an agent, who had acted both heroically and as dictated by protocol.

Lennox had been savvy enough to make her agent appear the victim, and the journalists' questions had quickly softened in their accusatory tone. Baxter had done her bit by churning out the same rehearsed answers as usual when asked how the investigation was progressing.

When she eventually got out, she checked her phone to find several updates. As requested, the teams had sent over the killers' medical records as soon as they had received them. So far, she had the notes on Eduardo Medina, Dominic Burrell, and Marcus Townsend. She forwarded them straight to Edmunds before heading off to Forensic Services.

Edmunds glanced down at the screen of his phone, which buzzed as he received three consecutive emails. On seeing Baxter's name, he got up and went into the toilets, locking himself in a cubicle before downloading the attachments. He flicked through the first report and found what he was looking for in seconds. He opened up the second and found the same word a few pages in. He clicked on the third report and started to read. Suddenly, his eyes lit up. He burst out of the cubicle, exited the toilets, and rushed toward the lifts.

Baxter, Rouche, and Curtis had just finished up with the forensic pathologist. As they stepped back out onto First Avenue, Baxter's phone went off. She would have ignored the call had it been anybody else:

"Edmunds?" she answered, moving away from her colleagues.

"They were *all* having counseling of some sort!" he greeted her excitedly.

"Who?"

"The killers. That's what links them! I was on that Streets to Success website and it said that they offer counseling to help people get back on their feet. It got me thinking. My notes on Patrick Peter Fergus say he suffered a breakdown due to the financial burden of his ill mother. Makes sense he'd go see someone. And guess what?"

"Go on."

"Marcus Townsend *did* take Streets to Success up on their kind offer of complimentary life-coaching sessions. Eduardo Medina spiraled into depression after his daughter's immigration application fell through—he was at an AA group the night before the murder—and Dominic Burrell had compulsory weekly meetings as part of his rehabilitation plan."

Baxter was smiling. Edmunds was yet to let her down:

"Glenn Arnolds, unsurprisingly, had serious mental health issues since childhood," she said excitedly. "We've been looking for his psychiatrist anyway."

"Better look harder: that's five out of five!" Edmunds almost shouted. "OK. You can say it."

"Say what?"

"That you'd be lost without me."

Baxter hung up.

Curtis had spent the brief phone call devising a way to leave Baxter behind with Lennox while she and Rouche disappeared up to Westchester County to interview the elusive Dr. Bantham. She fell silent when Baxter approached them wearing a rare grin on her face:

"We *need* to find the psychiatrist," she told them decisively.

Rouche looked to Curtis and smirked.

CHAPTER 15

Sunday, 13 December 2015

12:22 P.M.

". . . So if *Azaz* is Hebrew for 'strength' and *El* means 'God,' there's an argument that, in *that* particular order, 'Azazel' means 'strength over God' . . . And here it says that animals deemed 'dark,' such as bats, snakes, and feral canines, are 'particularly susceptible vessels to sustain unclean spirits between hosts.'"

"Could we *please* talk about something else?" complained Curtis from the driver's seat as she indicated to turn off the interstate. "You're really starting to creep me out."

Rouche had caught one of the channel-hopping Pastor Jerry Pilsner Jr.'s numerous television appearances that morning and had spent the entire journey googling their supernatural suspect.

Baxter had tried her damnedest to sleep through most of it.

They started down a rural road, the branches of the bare trees like knotted fingers grasping out at lonely vehicles.

"OK, but get this . . ." said Rouche excitedly, scrolling down the screen of his phone.

Curtis huffed.

Awake again, Baxter wiped a bit of drool from the corner of her mouth.

"'Hunted by the archangel Raphael, Azazel the fallen is unburdened of his blackened wings and bound in the darkness of the deepest pit on God's creation. For buried beneath the sharpest of rocks in the harshest, most remote desert of the earth, Azazel remained—in a grave lined with the shredded feathers of his own decimated mantle, never again to see the light till he burn within the fires of Judgment Day.'"

"Thanks for that," yawned Baxter.

"I hate you, Rouche," Curtis told him, shivering off the unpleasant story.

"Last little bit," Rouche promised, clearing his throat. "'In that endless darkness, Azazel fell into madness, and unable to break free of his chains, he tore his spirit free of his shackled body to wander the earth forever as a thousand different souls.'"

Rouche put his phone down in his lap:

"I've creeped myself out now."

The first delicate snowflakes were landing gently against the windscreen as they pulled into the Banthams' icy driveway. The forecasters had predicted heavy snowfall later in the day, warning of possible blizzard conditions overnight and into the morning.

As Curtis followed Rouche's tire tracks from the previous day up to the garages, Baxter gazed out at the house, which looked just as uninhabited as it had the previous afternoon, except that a set of deep footprints had been trodden into the otherwise untouched lawn.

"Someone's been here," she said hopefully from the backseat.

Curtis parked up, and they stepped out into the cold. Rouche noticed a neighbor watching them curiously from the property opposite and hoped that she would leave them in peace. She started to approach, almost slipping over twice as she negotiated the driveway.

"You two go ahead," he told them.

Curtis and Baxter approached the front door while he went to intercept the nosy woman before she could delay them further by breaking a hip.

"Can I help you?" he whispered to himself, anticipating the typical greeting of an interfering neighbor.

"Can I help you?"

"Just looking for Dr. James Bantham," he said, dismissing her with a smile.

Curtis rang the doorbell while the woman looked on suspiciously. She showed no sign of leaving.

"Cold out," said Rouche, subtly suggesting to the woman that she might be more comfortable retreating to the warmth of her own goddamn business.

Baxter knocked loudly when there was no answer.

"They've got good security," said the neighbor, making no attempt to disguise the implication.

"No kidding," replied Rouche, taking out his identification. "They've got three police officers on their doorstep."

The woman thawed instantly, despite her blue hands looking as though they might drop off at any second.

"Have you tried their cell phones?" she suggested as she retrieved her own.

"Yes."

"Have you got Terri's number, though?" she asked, holding the phone up to her ear. "Lovely woman. And the kids. We all look out for each other arou—"

"Shut up!" Baxter yelled from beside the front door. The woman looked outraged. After a moment, Baxter turned to Curtis: "Can you hear that?"

She crouched down and opened the letterbox, but the sound had stopped.

"Call it again!" she shouted back at the nosy neighbor.

A few seconds later, the quiet hum of a phone vibrating against a hard surface returned.

"Phone's in the house," she called back to Rouche.

"Oh," said the neighbor. "Well, that's weird. She always has her phone with her in case the boys need her. She must be home. Perhaps she's in the bath."

Rouche registered the genuine concern on the woman's face:

"Baxter! Listen again," he shouted.

He took out his own phone and redialed the number he had attempted to contact the doctor on the previous day, his heart fluttering a little in the pause as he waited for the call to connect.

Baxter pressed her ear into the narrow gap in the door as she strained to listen.

"*Oh, the weather outside is frightful . . .*"

Startled, she fell back onto the wet floor as the Christmas tune blared from directly behind the door.

"*But the fire is so delightful . . .*"

Rouche turned to the bewildered woman: "You, go!"

He was already reaching for his weapon as he sprinted toward the house.

Baxter watched from the damp ground as Curtis kicked at the lock.

"*And since we've no place to go . . .*"

Curtis kicked again. This time, the door swung open, sending the phone and its festive ringtone skidding beneath an impressive Christmas tree.

"FBI! Anyone home?" she shouted over the last line of the chorus.

Rouche and Baxter followed her inside. As he rushed upstairs, Baxter headed through the hallway and into the kitchen.

"Dr. Bantham?" she could hear him calling somewhere above.

The house was warm. In the center of the impressive country kitchen, four half-eaten lunches sat cold and forgotten. A thick skin covered the surface of the bright orange soup.

"Anyone home?" shouted Curtis from another room as Rouche continued to trample about upstairs.

Baxter looked down at what was left of the golden-crusted rolls beside three of the four bowls and then down at the floor, where occasional flakes and crumbs marked a path back the way she had come. She followed the sporadic trail halfway down the hallway to what looked like a narrow cupboard door.

"Hello?" she called before cautiously pulling it open to discover a set of steep wooden stairs descending into the dark. "Hello?"

She took one step down to search the wall for a light switch. The wood creaked beneath her modest weight.

"Curtis!" she called.

She took out her mobile phone and switched on the built-in flashlight. The staircase was thrown into stark white light. She took two more tentative steps. Every inch she descended, she claimed a little more of the basement back from the darkness. As she placed her foot to step again, she trod on something unstable and felt her ankle twist beneath her.

She fell, landing in a heap against a cold stone wall.

"Baxter?" she heard Curtis call.

"Down here!" she groaned.

She lay still on the musty floor, breathing dust and damp, as she mentally assessed the damage one limb at a time. She was bruised, had removed the scabs on her forehead, and could feel her ankle throbbing in her boot, but appeared to have got away with only minor injuries. Her phone sat two steps above the floor, casting a spotlight on the bread roll that had tripped her.

"Shit," she winced as she sat herself up.

Curtis appeared in the doorway: "Baxter?"

"Hi." She waved up.

There were heavy footfalls overhead as Rouche rushed to join them.

"Are you all right?" Curtis asked. "You should've turned the light on."

Baxter was about to retort with something cutting when Curtis reached up and pulled a cord by the door, which made a satisfying click.

"I might've found something useful," started Curtis, but Baxter wasn't listening.

She was watching the darkness with wide eyes, not even daring to breathe. The lone dusty bulb that hung from the ceiling slowly started to glow, casting an orange haze.

"Baxter?"

Baxter's pulse doubled in pace as the shape closest to the light took human form and then another beside it. Both were lying face-down on the ground, bloody burlap bags covering their faces. She was already getting up to leave as the bulb reached full intensity, the fight-or-flight instinct taking hold. As she climbed onto her knees, she saw two more bodies beyond the others, identical in positioning, the same bloodstained bags over their heads, but only half the size of the two adults.

"What is it?" asked Curtis urgently.

Baxter scrambled up the staircase, debilitated as much by panic as by her twisted ankle. She fell out into the hallway and kicked the door shut behind her as she tried to calm her breathing. She kept one boot pressed firmly against the base of the wood, as if afraid that something might climb out after her.

Curtis was poised with her phone at the ready, anticipating the need for backup. Rouche kneeled beside Baxter and waited patiently for her to explain. She turned to face him, panting warm breath across his face:

"I think . . . I found . . . the Banthams."

Rouche was sitting on the porch outside, watching the snow fall over the assortment of vehicles that now filled the long drive-way. Catching one of the insubstantial flakes, he rubbed it into nonexistence between his fingers.

A memory returned to him: his daughter playing in the garden when she was younger, four or five, wrapped up against the cold as she tried to catch snowflakes on her tongue. She had stared up in fascination at the white clouds literally disintegrating above her. Without the slightest hint of fear in her voice, she had asked him whether the sky was falling.

It had stayed with him for some reason, that surreal idea of witnessing the world die, of being helpless to do anything more than watch it happen and catch snowflakes. He realized, as the clouds continued to bleed, that the memory meant something else entirely to him now, having witnessed these incomprehensible acts of violence and cruelty play out beneath a snowglobe sky.

More was coming, of that he was sure, and there was nothing any of them could do but watch.

*

Surrounded by their peers, and lit with bulbs from this millennium, the basement had taken on the appearance of any other crime scene, albeit one populated with professionals in tears and frequent requests to "step out for a moment." The forensic field team claimed the lower level to preserve the scene, while their colleagues worked in the kitchen, where the family had been gathered before their deaths. Two photographers were going from room to room documenting everything, and the Canine Unit had already been through the property.

Baxter and Curtis were upstairs. They had not said a word to each other in almost an hour as they searched for anything that might assist their investigation.

There were no obvious signs of a struggle. Curiously, the murdered doctor had been branded with "Puppet" rather than "Bait," while no markings featured on any of the other bodies. The family had been restrained and then executed in turn with a single bullet to the back of the head. The estimated time frame: eighteen to twenty-four hours since death.

There was always a heightened atmosphere at crime scenes involving children. Baxter felt it as much as anyone despite not having any of her own, not ever planning to, and avoiding them wherever possible. People worked in a state of anger-fueled professionalism, prepared to go without sleep, without food, without seeing their own families in dedication to the task at hand, which was probably why Baxter snapped when she spotted Rouche sat outside, doing nothing.

She stormed downstairs, ignoring the throbbing in her ankle, marched out through the open front door, and shoved him backward off his seat.

"Ow!" he moaned, rolling onto his front.

"What the *hell,* Rouche?!" she yelled. "Everyone else is in there trying to help while you're sat out here on your arse!"

The ESU Canine Unit walking the perimeter stopped in the distance, the officer shouting at the German shepherd when it started barking aggressively in their direction.

"I don't do dead kids," Rouche said simply as he got up, watching the dog lose interest and continue walking.

"Who does? Do you think *any* of us want to be in there? But it's our job!"

Rouche didn't say anything. He started brushing off the snow.

"You know I worked the Cremation Killer case, right?" continued Baxter. "Me and Wolf . . ." She hesitated. She actively avoided bringing up her infamous ex-partner's name. "Me and Wolf had to deal with *twenty-seven* dead girls in as many days."

"Look, I had a bad experience . . . on a job, and since then I just don't do dead kids . . . ever," Rouche explained. "It's kind of a thing. I'm taking care of stuff out here. OK?"

"No, not *bloody* OK, actually," said Baxter.

She grabbed a handful of snow and ice off the ground on her way back inside. Rouche winced as he shook out his top. Moments later, a solid snowball connected viciously with the side of his head.

It was dark by the time they closed up the crime scene for the night. The predicted heavy snowfall had arrived as promised, sparkling against the black sky in the floodlit front garden. Baxter and Curtis walked outside to find Rouche huddled up in the same spot as before.

"I'll give you two a moment," said Curtis, excusing herself.

Baxter pulled her woolly hat over her head and sat down beside him to look out over the tranquil garden. From the corner of her eye, she could see the nasty cut on his forehead.

"Sorry about the head," she said into a cloud of mist formed by her warm breath. She watched the neighbors' Christmas lights flashing alongside those of the police vehicles.

"No need to apologize." Rouche smiled. "You didn't know it was going to hurt."

Baxter looked guilty: "I put a rock in it."

Rouche cracked a smile and then they both laughed.

"What did I miss out here?" she asked.

"Well, it's snowing."

"Thanks. I got that."

"I don't get it. They're killing their own now? How does that fit the pattern?" Rouche sighed. "I've told the teams that the priority is to identify and locate the other counselors, and I've requested Bantham's complete client list from the Gramercy Practice. I've also ordered full blood workups for all of the Puppets."

Rouche realized that they still had not told Baxter about the illicit drugs found in Glenn Arnolds's system. He planned to confront Curtis about it later that evening.

"Just in case," he added when Baxter looked intrigued. "But the main thing I've been up to is gathering evidence." He pointed to where a miniature tent had been erected in the pristine white garden. "Our killer's footprints."

"We can't know that for certain."

"*Actually,* we can."

Rouche took out his phone and flicked through to a photograph he had taken earlier that afternoon. He handed it to Baxter: a light speckling of snow decorated the sky, the idyllic house, which was now destined to haunt her, sitting dark and still below. Their FBI vehicle was parked in front of the garages, neat tire tracks carved into the ice behind it. Now scrubbed clean by the snow, a deep set of footprints had taken the shortest route possible by cutting across the garden.

"It could have been a neighbor or a paperboy," said Baxter.

"It wasn't. Look again."

She focused on the screen and zoomed in on the picture.

"There are no footprints leading *to* the house!"

"Exactly," said Rouche, "and it didn't snow here last night. I checked. I went round before the cavalry turned up. I eliminated yours, mine, Curtis's, and the nosy neighbor's; *this* was the only other set."

"Which means . . . the killer must have been here yesterday! They were in there while we were stood on the doorstep!" gasped Baxter. "Shit! We could've had them!"

She handed the phone back to him.

They sat in silence for a moment.

"Think whoever killed these people is the one holding the strings? Your *Azazel*?" she asked.

"I don't know."

"Christ, Rouche. What the hell's going on?"

He smiled sadly, extended his hand beyond the shelter of the porch and into the building blizzard.

". . . The sky is falling."

CHAPTER 16

Sunday, 13 December 2015

6:13 P.M.

The snowstorm had hit earlier than predicted, drowning New York State under inches of fresh powder from above as the freezing wind raged unchecked below. Before the car's heater had even warmed up, they had been diverted off the New England Thruway and, judging by the wreckage half a mile ahead, away from the blizzard's first victims of the night. Curtis had followed the flashing orange instructions bestowed by a hastily erected information sign and joined the procession of slow-moving vehicles before eventually picking up Route 1.

Baxter could feel herself dozing off in the back of the car. Outside the window, the world was nothing but static on a screen. Inside, the heater was billowing leather-scented hot air from the sleepily lit dashboard. The sound of the tires cutting a path through the snow was as relaxing as listening to a gentle stream, while the police scanner chatted away idly, the assorted voices discussing car accidents, barroom brawls, and burglaries.

The day had taken its toll on her; it had on everybody involved. At the scene, she had allowed professional bravado to take over, the same world-weary attitude that had seen her through some of the toughest jobs of her career. But now, sat in the back of the dark car, all she could see was that basement, the bodies slumped forward: bound and blind, surrendered, an entire family massacred.

Although she knew it was completely unreasonable, she felt bitter toward Thomas, toward Tia, toward the handful of friends with whom she still occasionally kept in contact. What depths of surreal horror had their days plunged to? Did they get rained on heading into work? Perhaps the wrong kind of milk in their Starbucks coffee? Had a colleague made a snide remark?

None of them understood what it was like to be a homicide detective. Not one of them could even comprehend the things that she was expected to see, to remember.

None of them was strong enough.

It was not uncommon to feel resentment toward people with simpler, more mundane lives. Without doubt it was the reason that so many of her colleagues were in relationships with other people on the force. There were excuses, of course—the shifts, working in such close proximity, the preordained common interests—but Baxter suspected that it went deeper than that. As unpleasant as it was to admit, in the end everyone and everything outside of the job just started to feel a little . . . trivial.

"OK with you, Baxter?" Rouche turned around to look at her.

She hadn't even realized anyone had spoken: "Huh?"

"Weather's getting worse," Rouche repeated. "We were saying we might stop off somewhere and get a bite to eat."

Baxter shrugged.

"Whatevs," he vocalized for Curtis's sake.

Baxter glanced back out the window. An ice-glossed sign declared that they were now entering Mamaroneck, wherever that was, while snow fell more heavily than she had ever seen. Barely able to make out the buildings lining the main street, Rouche and Curtis squinted through the storm as they searched for somewhere to stop.

"Could you chuck me my jacket, please?" asked Rouche, apparently optimistic that they were going to find somewhere.

Baxter grabbed the coat from the seat next to her. As Rouche thanked her and pulled it through the gap between the two front seats, she saw something drop out of one of the pockets and land by her feet. She reached around in the footwell until she found the scrunched-up sheet of paper. She was about to hand it back to him when she noticed Glenn Arnolds's name printed at the top of it.

With her dark eyes watching the back of Rouche's head, she carefully unfolded it.

"What's that on the left?" asked Curtis, pointing to where several vehicles had pulled off the main road.

"'Diner and Pizza'!" said Rouche excitedly. "That all right with everyone?"

"Sounds good," answered Baxter distractedly as she attempted to read the crumpled sheet by the intermittent light of passing buildings, shards of orange fleetingly highlighting sections of the page.

She was able to ascertain that it was a forensic blood report. Although the list of medications and chemicals meant nothing, the pathologist had clearly circled certain items that must be significant in some way.

Why would Rouche have kept this from her? She was considering whether to call him out on it there and then when he turned around to smile at her:

"I don't know about you, but I'm ready for a beer."

She smiled back, screwing the paper into a ball on her lap as Curtis followed the vehicle in front into the overflowing car park. After some convincing by Rouche, she reluctantly abandoned the car on a verge. Baxter donned her woolly hat and gloves. Rouche left his ID badge in the windscreen, which he considered more than ample explanation for mowing over whatever flower bed or lawn lay concealed beneath the snow.

They stepped out onto the churned-up surface of the car park, bracing themselves against the cold as they approached the diner. A queue of at least two dozen people snaked out from the main doors, sheltering beside the glass windows that teased them with warmth, conversation, and hot food, only hardening their resolve to eventually get inside. While Rouche and Curtis went to claim their spot at the back of the queue, Baxter excused herself to make a phone call.

She walked out of earshot, to the main street, where a tiny church posed like a picture from a Christmas card, only ruined by the Dunkin' Donuts opposite. She called Edmunds's number. After a few rings it went to voicemail.

"Need to talk. Call me," was her abrupt message.

Rather than join her colleagues, who had not moved an inch since she'd left them, she took a seat on a wall and waited, hoping that he might call back at any moment.

She *really* needed to speak to him.

A family at the front of the line were invited inside, allowing Curtis and Rouche to take two satisfying paces closer to the entrance. They watched Baxter's silhouette across the street, the glow from the screen of her phone lighting up her face.

"I really thought we were getting somewhere," said Curtis sadly. "And now this: another dead end."

Rouche could tell that she was thinking about Glenn Arnolds, about the innocent man she had been forced to kill. In truth, he was amazed that she was still operational considering how devastated she had been just twenty-four hours earlier. Their late-night conversation following the prison riot had given him an insight into her powerful political family. Ever since, Lennox's favoritism, protectiveness, and willingness to make exceptions for Curtis had seemed downright blatant.

It struck him as odd that Curtis could not see that her determination to succeed in her chosen career, her track record for high-profile cases, and her swift promotion up the ranks that she flaunted to spite her family was actually *because* of them and who she was. Anyone else would have been taken off the case and subjected to weeks of evaluations and assessments, but because Curtis wanted to redeem herself, here she was.

"We *are* getting somewhere," said Rouche with a reassuring smile. "We weren't supposed to find the Banthams, not yet. All the other bodies have been paraded in front of us, but these . . . no theater, no audience. These were hidden away. And that means we're on the right track. A dead Puppet; maybe Bantham *was* being coerced into murder . . . *maybe* he resisted."

Curtis nodded before they shuffled a few feet farther along in the queue:

"I just wish we could have saved them," she said.

As Rouche had said at the time, Arnolds had been their first and possibly only living suspect. He alone could have given them the information that they so desperately needed, and Curtis had lost them that advantage. He could tell from the look on her face that she was wondering whether they might have been able to reach the Bantham family in time had she chosen differently.

"We need to work as a team," said Rouche.

Curtis followed his gaze back to Baxter, who looked to have thrown her phone over a locked fence in a temper and was struggling to retrieve it.

They both smiled.

"I've got orders," she told him.

"Stupid orders."

Curtis shrugged.

"It's not practical to cut Baxter out of the investigation. Look what happened today," said Rouche.

"Why *don't* we look at today?" Curtis snapped back. "She knew to focus on the psychiatrist—how? It didn't come from us. Perhaps *she's* keeping things to herself as well. Did you ever think about that?"

Rouche sighed and regarded her for a moment:

"And what happens the day Lennox tells you to cut me out?"

Curtis looked a little uneasy. She hesitated: "I cut you out."

She held his gaze and nodded as if unsure of herself yet refusing to apologize or back down.

"Simple as that?" asked Rouche.

"Simple as that."

"I'm going to make this easy for you," Rouche told her. "*I'll* tell her about the meds. No one's ordered me not to, and I'd ignore them if they had."

"If you do, I *will* report it back to Lennox. I *will* document that you disregarded my express wishes. And she *will* have you removed from the case."

Curtis couldn't even meet his eye now. She turned around to find that another group had been allowed in and moved forward. They were almost at the entrance. After a few moments, she looked back at him.

"And now I feel bad," she told him. "The chili cheese fries are on me."

Rouche still looked a little hurt.

Curtis sighed: "And a milkshake."

The good news was that Baxter had been reunited with her phone, courtesy of every swear word in her arsenal and a big stick. The bad news was that Edmunds still had not called back. She now couldn't stop shivering, and the snow caking her boots had soaked through to her socks. She phoned his number again and waited for it to go to voicemail:

"It's me. Bad day. Looks like you were right about the psychiatrist, but . . . it's complicated. I'll tell you about it later. There's something else too: the CIA agent, Damien Rouche, I need you to look into him for me. And before you start, no. I'm not just being paranoid, and I know not everybody in the world's out to get me, but I found something, and I need you to trust me on this. Just . . . just see what you can find out, OK? OK. Bye."

"Chili cheese fries . . ." started Rouche, standing just a couple of meters away.

Baxter shrieked and slipped, landing heavily on the ground.

Rouche went to help her up.

"I'm fine," she snapped as she got back to her feet, holding her painful rear end.

"I just wanted to let you know that our table's ready and the chili cheese fries are on Curtis."

"I'll just be a minute."

She composed herself as she watched him cross the street back toward the diner. How much had he heard? She supposed it didn't matter.

He was hiding things from her.

And one way or another, she was going to find out why.

CHAPTER 17

Monday, 14 December 2015

8:39 A.M.

Just checked—he's actually an evil super-villain who eats kittens. Good call! ;) I'll try phone at lunch x

Edmunds hit the "send" button, knowing that he would no doubt pay for it when Baxter woke up.

"On your phone again?" a nasal voice asked from the desk opposite as he slid his mobile back into his pocket.

Edmunds ignored the question and logged back in to his computer, which had locked him out while he had been otherwise engaged. He despised the sniveling, arse-kissing creature that he was forced to work alongside: Mark Smith. Incredibly, his name was probably the most interesting thing about him. Edmunds did not even have to look to know that the brush-haired thirty-year-old was wearing a suit two sizes too big for him with a yellowing, pit-stained shirt beneath. The man made the entire office smell like bed.

Mark cleared his throat: "I said, I see you're on your phone, yet again," he pushed when Edmunds failed to respond.

Channeling Baxter, Edmunds leaned around his computer and stuck his middle finger up at the petty little man:

"Can you see this?" he asked before returning to his screen.

Edmunds's uncharacteristic hostility was completely justified. It was hard to imagine now, but there had been a time when he had allowed himself to feel intimidated by his colleagues, spurred on by this unimposing ringleader. It had built and built, until he had dreaded going into work each morning.

That had been a while ago, before he had transferred up to Homicide and Serious Crime Command for a brief spell to work on the Ragdoll murders, before he had met his persistently irritable, occasionally obnoxious, frequently volatile, and effortlessly inspiring mentor in Baxter.

Nobody ever talked down to her. She simply would not allow them to. She point-blank refused to take any shit off anybody, superior or not, whether they were in the right or not.

He smiled just thinking about his best friend's pigheadedness. She could be an absolute nightmare at times.

He vividly remembered the day that he finally decided to apply for the transfer. He had always wanted to be a homicide detective. He had studied criminal psychology at university, but his natural aptitude for numbers and spotting patterns combined with his confidence issues had deposited him in a dependably secure position on the Fraud team. He had met Tia. They had moved in together, finding an ex-council maisonette that seemed resolutely impervious to any attempt to spruce or modernize. And then she had fallen pregnant.

His entire life appeared to be etched in stone . . . and *that* had been the problem.

After one particularly bad day at the office, courtesy of Mark and his fellow mono-browed lackeys, Edmunds had excused himself from the meeting and finally submitted his application to follow his dream. His colleagues had laughed in his face when they found out. He and Tia had argued when he'd arrived home, and she had relegated him to the sofa for the first time in their relationship. But he had been determined, motivated into action by his hatred of his colleagues, the tedium of his job, and the undoubted waste of his abilities.

His decision to return to Fraud had been one of the hardest of his life, walking back in on that first day to take a seat at the same desk he had vacated less than half a year earlier. The entire department presumed that he had failed to make the grade, that he lacked what it took to make it in Homicide, unsurprised that he was more suited to spreadsheets than dead bodies. However, the truth was that he had thrived during his short time there. He had played an integral part in the resolution of the Ragdoll murders. Because of that, he had returned to Fraud with a chip on his shoulder. These people had no idea what he had accomplished while working on the biggest case in living memory.

Nobody did.

The pinnacle of his investigative achievements had been obscured under a cloud of secrecy from the public, raining down a torrent of half-truths contrived to protect the integrity of the Metropolitan Police and, as a by-product, Detective Fawkes. He was one of the few people who knew the Met's shameful secret and the truth of what happened within that blood-soaked courtroom, but he had no choice except to remain silent for Baxter's sake.

Bitterly, he had kept the official press statement relating to Wolf's disappearance, reading it from time to time to remind himself that the grass wasn't always greener . . . In fact, he was finally coming to realize that it did not matter where you stood.

It was all burned:

> . . . as such, Detective William Fawkes is wanted for questioning in relation to a number of issues arising during the Ragdoll investigation and the alleged assault of Lethaniel Masse at the time of his capture, which has led to lasting medical problems.
>
> Anyone with information regarding his current whereabouts should contact the police immediately.

That had been it.

They wanted to ask him some questions.

It made Edmunds sick even to think about it. Wolf had tumbled quickly down the priority list, managing to evade their half-arsed attempts to locate him accordingly.

Edmunds had been tempted to conduct his own investigation, but his hands were tied: should he pursue Wolf, he risked exposing Baxter's involvement in his escape. He could do nothing but obediently swallow the injustice of Wolf going free as he listened to the diluted version of events render his contribution to the case no more than water-cooler gossip.

That was why he held his colleagues, his job, his life in such contempt: everyone still thought he was nothing.

"You know we're not allowed phones on in here," Mark mumbled as he booted up his computer.

Edmunds had almost forgotten he was there:

"God, I hate you, Mark."

He felt his phone buzz in his pocket and made a show of taking it out and replying to the text from Tia.

"So . . ." started Mark.

"Don't talk to me."

". . . where did *we* go yesterday?" he asked, struggling to contain his excitement. "I couldn't find you anywhere for a while in the afternoon. I needed to ask you something. I asked Gatiss if maybe he knew where you'd gone, but he didn't know either."

Edmunds could hear the smile in Mark's voice. The smug little snake had slithered straight into the boss's office the moment he stepped outside to speak to Baxter about things that actually mattered.

"I did mention to him that you were probably taking an important phone call," continued Mark, "seeing as you'd felt the need to have your mobile on you and check it every few minutes throughout the day."

Edmunds clenched his fists. He had never been a violent person, and was not built for it anyway, but somehow Mark always knew which buttons to push. He allowed himself a few moments to fantasize about shoving the man's ugly head through his computer screen and then turned back to his own to find that it had

locked him out again. It wasn't even 9 A.M., which meant his day
had not yet officially begun.

He sighed heavily.

Baxter dozed off for a split second. She sat up to discover that
she hadn't missed anything; the gibberish-spurting woman was
still spurting gibberish.

She, Rouche, and Curtis had claimed three adjacent rooms at
the NYPD's 9th Precinct in order to get through the seventeen
Streets to Success participants more quickly. Each of whom had
accepted the charity's well-intentioned but, in hindsight, possibly
counterproductive offer of free "Life Coaching."

It struck her that in this particular drug-addled woman's case,
it hadn't really worked.

Of their five identified killers, only Glenn Arnolds had been a
patient of Dr. Bantham and the prestigious Gramercy Practice.
The budget option, a Phillip East, had provided services to both
Eduardo Medina and, in the rather vague capacity as "life coach,"
Marcus Townsend through the charity. They had already ascertained that Dominic Burrell had links to Dr. Alexei Green, whom
Curtis had interviewed, and even flirted with, back at the prison,
but they had found no record of Patrick Peter Fergus ever being
in therapy.

Both the UK and the US teams' repeated attempts to contact
East and Green had proved fruitless, further confirmation of the
counselors' involvement, even if they could not see the whole picture yet. With no idea whether the two men were masterminding
the murders or going to turn up in a similar state to Dr. Bantham,
Curtis had suggested they begin working through the client lists.
So far, though, it had been a complete waste of time.

Baxter dismissed her interviewee and got up to make herself a
coffee. Rouche was deep in conversation in the neighboring room.
She watched him suspiciously for a moment as he joked and
laughed with someone sitting out of view but then realized that

she still had not informed Edmunds of what they had discovered at the Bantham family home.

There had been one further development. Overnight, the Canine Unit had followed a scent from the house to a turnout a few hundred meters beyond the brook. One of the neighbors had noticed a blue or green van parked there on the morning of the murder, although the rural nature of the roads in the area made the chances of picking anything up on the traffic cameras slim to none.

She needed to bring Edmunds up to speed.

She walked past the assorted people waiting to be interviewed and stepped out onto East 5th Street. Taking a seat on one of the benches opposite the precinct, she settled into the former occupant's bum imprint. She regarded the buildings adjacent to the police station: typically New York. Renovation work was being carried out on one of them; tunnels hung from empty windows, past the customary snow-covered fire escapes and down to the dumpsters below. It looked like a giant game of snakes and ladders.

Depressed by the thought, she took out her phone and called Edmunds.

One step forward. Two steps back.

Edmunds waited for his supervisor to leave the office before loading up Thomas's financial activity for the previous week. After a quick glance to make sure the printer was free, he clicked the "print" button and got up from his desk. It spat the warm pages out and he collected them up, noting that it was longer than usual, presumably because of Christmas fast approaching.

He felt his phone go off in his pocket and looked down at the screen as subtly as he could. He felt Mark's eyes burning into his back as he stuffed the printout into his jacket pocket and rushed outside to take the call.

The moment Edmunds was out of sight, Mark leaned over to his station and knocked the mouse to prevent the screen from locking him out. He got up and walked around to take a seat at Edmunds's terminal.

"What are you up to?" he whispered to himself as he flicked through the open pages: BBC News, a map of Manhattan, work email.

Mark's eyes lit up when he saw a tab for Edmunds's personal email account; however, to his disappointment, when he clicked on it, it was on the "sign out" page. It didn't matter, though. He had what he needed: the personal financial records of a Mr. Thomas Alcock on-screen and no paperwork to support the invasion of privacy anywhere on his desk. An illegal search on a civilian was a very serious offense.

Mark could hardly contain his excitement as he printed off his own copy of Thomas's records to present to Gatiss as evidence.

At long last he had him.

CHAPTER 18

Monday, 14 December 2015

10:43 A.M.

Baxter shivered.

Her spur-of-the-moment decision to call Edmunds had left her insufficiently attired for a lengthy conversation out in the cold. He listened in silence as she told him about the Bantham family, about the suspicious vehicle spotted close to the scene, and about the bloodwork printout that had been stuffed into Rouche's pocket.

"Something's off," she continued. "I'm not just being paranoid. He's always on his phone, allegedly to his wife, and I mean *all* the time. You turn around at a crime scene and he'll just be gone, talking to this mystery person instead of doing his job."

"What are you meant to be doing right now? Probably not speaking to me," Edmunds pointed out, playing devil's advocate.

"It's different."

"Maybe he *is* talking to his wife."

"Oh, come on. No one talks to their wife *that* much. Plus, he doesn't like her enough to live on the same continent, so doesn't really strike me as the needy type," said Baxter through chattering teeth. She had brought her legs up to make herself as ball-like as possible. "He's quite . . . secretive, in a weird way, and now I know he's keeping important pieces of evidence from me. Would you *please* just look into it for me?"

Edmunds hesitated, positive that no good could come from poking around in her colleague's business:

"Fine, but I—"

"Hold on," Baxter interrupted as Rouche and Curtis came rushing out of the precinct's main entrance. She got to her feet.

"They've found Phillip East!" Curtis called across the street to her.

"Gotta go," Baxter told Edmunds.

She hung up and rushed toward the car. As she caught up with them, Rouche thrust her coat and bag into her arms.

"Ta, but you forgot my hat," said Baxter, so as not to appear too grateful to the man she had just asked her friend to investigate.

They climbed into the car. Curtis reversed out onto the street and wheelspun as she pulled away. As Baxter put on her coat, her woolly hat and gloves landed in her lap.

Edmunds returned to the office, his mood buoyed slightly by the sight of Mark's empty desk. He logged back in to his computer and was about to continue work on the mind-numbing task that he had been dipping in and out of all day when he realized he was being watched. Mark was looking out from Gatiss's office but diverted his gaze when Edmunds met his eye.

A little disconcerted, he closed down all of his extracurricular tabs and then tucked Thomas's financial records away at the bottom of his bag, just in case.

Disappointingly, Phillip East's attorney had beaten them to the field office and was already inside the interview room, no doubt advising his client not to answer any of their questions.

Lennox had been awaiting Curtis's arrival. She handed one of her team a mobile phone and then greeted them by getting straight to the point:

"He's lawyered up. Find out what you can while we have him, but I sincerely doubt we'll be able to keep him more than another half hour based on the encyclopedia of threats his attorney just reeled off at me."

"Who's the lawyer?" Curtis asked as they all walked across the office.

"Ritcher," replied Lennox.

"Oh crap."

Curtis had had dealings with him before: a notoriously competent and obstructive defense lawyer usually hired to assist the rich and powerful out of the trouble that their money and arrogance tended to attract. Worse, he reminded her of her father. She genuinely doubted that they were going to get anything out of East now.

"Good luck," said Lennox as they arrived at the interview room. She blocked Baxter's path with an outstretched arm. "Not you."

"Come again?" asked Baxter.

Rouche also went to argue when Lennox continued: "Not with Ritcher in there. You'll earn us a lawsuit per syllable."

"But—"

"You can watch. End of discussion."

Rouche hesitated, but Baxter waved him off and stomped into the small annex next door. He entered the interview room and took a seat next to Curtis. On the other side of the table, Ritcher looked every bit as self-important and venomous as his reputation suggested. He was in his late fifties with a long, angular face and a full head of thick, white, wavy hair. In comparison, his client looked starved of both sleep and food, his unimposing frame struggling to fill the threadbare suit he sported. His sunken eyes darted around the room.

"Good morning, Mr. East," said Curtis pleasantly. "Mr. Ritcher, always a pleasure. Can I offer either of you a drink?"

East shook his head.

"No," replied Ritcher. "And for your information, you've now got four questions left."

"Have we?" asked Rouche.

"Yes."

"Really?"

Ritcher turned to Curtis: "It's probably advisable to tell your colleague not to antagonize me."

"Is it?" asked Rouche.

Curtis kicked him beneath the table.

In the other room, Baxter shook her head despairingly:

"Should've let me in there," she mumbled.

"I've got a question," said Ritcher. "What gives the FBI the right to drag my client in here like some sort of petty criminal without so much as an explanation, let alone any hint of unlawful activity?"

"We tried phoning," said Rouche flippantly, "but *your client* and his family had elected to abandon their lives and go into hiding." He turned to the doctor. "Hadn't you, Phillip?"

"We just need to ask Mr. East a few questions relating to our investigation. That's all," said Curtis, in a futile attempt to pacify the ill-tempered lawyer.

"Yes, your *investigation*," sneered Ritcher. "Your supervisor was good enough to provide me with an insight into the inner workings of the FBI's finest before relieving us of our personal possessions, of course, lest we feel the need to share your unrivaled ingenuity with the outside world: a psychiatrist turns up dead who provided a service to one of these Puppet freaks and you, quite brilliantly, now suspect all of these people's caregivers of wrongdoing . . . Inspiring stuff."

"Your client provided counseling to *two* of our killers," said Curtis.

Ritcher sighed: "Correction: he counseled *one* of them in a somewhat official capacity. To the other, he gave up his *own* free time in aid of a charitable organization for the homeless. An admirable endeavor, I'm sure you'll agree."

East's wide eyes flicked to Rouche and then back down to the table.

"Have you represented Phillip before?" Rouche asked the obstructive lawyer.

"I don't see how that's relevant."

"I do."

"Very well," said Ritcher in exasperation. "This is, in fact, my first time representing . . . Mr. . . . . East," he said pointedly.

"Who's paying for your services . . . and how?"

"Now, I *know* that's not relevant."

"Because I suspect you don't come cheap," continued Rouche. "Chief shit-unsticker to the rich and shitty."

Ritcher smiled and leaned back in his chair as Rouche went on: "Forgive me for finding it just a *little* suspicious that a part-time counselor, rest-of-time office administrator, wearing a thrift-store suit, decides to enlist the services of CSU . . ."

Everyone looked puzzled.

". . . chief shit-unsticker," Rouche clarified, "just to answer a few questions, which he couldn't do before because he and his family had gone into hiding."

"Was there a question concealed somewhere within your name-calling and meandering pontifications?" asked Ritcher.

"Asking questions isn't getting us anywhere," said Rouche. "You don't answer them. No: I'm *telling*." He gestured to the file in front of Curtis while East watched him nervously. Curtis looked uneasy but slid it over to him. Rouche started flicking through. "Call me a skeptic, Phillip, but when I heard you were missing, I presumed you were running out of guilt. Having met you, I can now see, quite clearly, that you were running out of fear."

Rouche stopped on one of the pages. After a moment, he had to look away. He removed the photograph from the file and tossed it into the center of the table.

"Good Lord!" gasped Ritcher.

"Rouche!" shouted Curtis.

East, however, appeared transfixed by the black-and-white image of the entire Bantham family bound, bagged, and slumped over in a neat line, just as Baxter had found them.

"That's James Bantham, a psychiatrist . . . one of you," Rouche explained. He noticed East unconsciously pull the fabric of his baggy shirt away from his chest. "That's his wife lying beside him and their two boys behind her."

East looked torn. He was unable to take his eyes off the photograph. The sound of his quickening breath filled the small room.

"Bantham never told us anything," said Rouche with exaggerated regret. "He probably thought he was protecting them."

Ritcher reached out and turned the haunting photograph facedown on the table.

"Goodbye, Agent Rouche," he said, getting up.

Irritatingly, the only person in history to actually pronounce Rouche's name correctly at first go was the one person he would rather forget it.

"W-we've still got questions!" stuttered Curtis.

"I'm sure you do," replied Ritcher.

"Phillip," said Rouche as the lawyer tried to hurry his client out of the room. "Phillip!"

East looked back at him.

"If we could find you, they *will* find you." Rouche knew that he was speaking the truth despite being none the wiser as to who "they" were.

"Ignore him," Ritcher instructed, ushering him out to collect up their confiscated possessions.

"Shit!" said Curtis as she watched the two men walking away through the busy main office. "We didn't get anything."

"We can't let him go," said Rouche. He removed his handcuffs from his pocket.

"But Lennox said—"

"Screw Lennox."

"She'll have you taken off the case before you even get him back to the interview room."

"At least there'll still be a case."

He shoved past her and rushed after the two men waiting for the lift.

"Phillip!" he called across the office.

The doors slid open and they stepped inside.

"Phillip!" Rouche shouted again, running for the closing doors. "Wait!"

He knocked someone out of the way as he sprinted the final few meters, sticking his hand into the narrowing gap. The sheets of metal juddered and parted once more to reveal Ritcher and East. Sharing the small box with them, almost unrecognizable wrapped up in her coat and hat, was Baxter.

"What floor?" she asked innocently.

Rouche tucked the handcuffs back into his pocket, producing one of his business cards instead, which he handed to the counselor.

"In case you do think of anything . . ." he said, letting the doors slide shut between them.

Curtis caught up with him as the audience he'd attracted started to lose interest.

"You let him go?" she asked in confusion.

"No, I didn't."

The last half hour of the day was dragging, and Edmunds was eager to get home to immerse himself in the murder case once more. The latest update from Baxter had occupied his thoughts all afternoon, and as appalling as it was to admit, it had excited him. He adored the challenge of an unsolvable puzzle, and this case had not disappointed. He had been sure that the counseling link would tie it all together, but if anything, it had only complicated matters further.

"Could we borrow you a moment?" asked Mark, directly behind him, making Edmunds jump.

He had been staring blankly at his screen, oblivious to everything else.

"In Gatiss's office," Mark added, unable to hide his smile.

Edmunds had expected some sort of comeuppance for the previous afternoon, so he got up and followed Mark across the room. He only hoped that the slap on the wrist would not take too long.

The moment he crossed the threshold, he saw Thomas sitting opposite Gatiss at his desk. Evidently, this was not about the phone call. As Mark closed the door behind them, Edmunds took a seat, glancing nervously at his friend beside him.

Mark pulled up a chair at the end of the desk.

"I'm sorry to have to call you in here like this, Mr. Alcock," said Gatiss.

Edmunds's boss was a stocky man, completely bald with angry little eyes.

"That's quite all right," replied Thomas pleasantly.

"A situation has been brought to my attention, concerning you, I'm afraid. Therefore I thought it best to ask you in and get to the bottom of it right here and now."

Edmunds really didn't like where this was going. He had always been so careful to cover his tracks.

"First things first," said Gatiss. "Do you two know one another?"

"Yes, we do," answered Thomas, smiling at Edmunds. "Alex is a close friend and used to work with my . . . girlfriend."

Both Thomas and Edmunds pulled a face. The term was not particularly fitting when used to describe Baxter. Mark was watching attentively, his greedy eyes drinking in every detail of the avalanche about to wipe Edmunds from his life.

"And, Edmunds. A little awkward, I appreciate, with your 'friend' sat right beside you. Do you believe Mr. Alcock guilty of any unlawful activity?"

"Of course not."

Mark made a little squeak, he was so excited.

"Interesting. Well, Mr. Alcock, it may come as a shock to you to learn that your friend has been illegally utilizing our fraud-detection software to look into your private bank accounts and credit cards," said Gatiss, turning his furious eyes on Edmunds.

Mark proudly produced the printout and placed it on the desk in front of them.

"Well . . . not really," said Thomas in confusion, "because I asked him to."

"You what?!" blurted Mark.

"I'm sorry?" asked Gatiss.

"God, I feel terrible if I've landed him in trouble over this," said Thomas. "I have a bit of a rocky history with gambling. I begged Alex to keep an eye on my financial records and asked him to challenge me if he suspected that I was . . . *indulging* again. Unfortunately, I know myself: I would never admit it of my own accord. He's a very good friend."

"Four months without a single bet," said Edmunds proudly, unable to help grinning as he patted Thomas on the back.

"It's still illegal!" Mark snapped over him.

"Mark! Just get out!" ordered Gatiss, finally losing his patience.

Edmunds subtly itched the side of his head with his middle finger, a gesture only Mark could see as he got to his feet and left the room.

"So you had full knowledge of these searches that Edmunds was carrying out?" Gatiss asked Thomas.

"Full knowledge."

"I see." He turned back to Edmunds. "But Mark has a point. No matter how well intentioned, abuse of our resources is a criminal offense."

"Yes, sir," agreed Edmunds.

Gatiss sighed heavily as he considered his options:

"I'm issuing you with an official warning. Do *not* make me regret my leniency on this matter."

"I won't, sir."

Edmunds escorted Thomas out of the building. The moment they were clear of the doors, they burst into laughter.

"Gambling problem," snorted Edmunds. "Quick thinking."

"Well, I couldn't very well tell the truth, could I? That my girlfriend has such crippling trust issues that she'll leave me if I'm not subjected to weekly audits." It was said lightly, but it was clear that Thomas was hurt that after eight months together, Baxter still did not completely trust him.

As he and Thomas had grown closer, Edmunds had found himself in an impossible situation. He could betray his new friend by continuing the illegal searches, but by doing so, preserve Thomas's relationship with Baxter. Or he could refuse to carry out Baxter's request, in which case she would end the relationship instantly rather than risk getting hurt again. In the end, he had decided to come clean to Thomas, who had handled the news admirably. He had only sympathized with Baxter's debilitating paranoia. Having nothing to hide, he had given Edmunds his blessing to continue supplying her with regular reports, reasoning that he would rather that than be without her.

Thomas was the right man for Baxter. Edmunds was confident of that. In time, she would see it too.

"Follow that car!"

Baxter had never been quite so excited to say anything as she had been to utter those words after climbing into the back of a yellow cab in New York City.

Ritcher and East had gone their separate ways outside Federal Plaza. She had hoped that East would make his way by subway; however, the deteriorating weather had persuaded him to splash out for a taxi. Terrified that she was going to lose their best lead, she had almost got herself run over flagging down her own ride.

It had been like a cup game trying to keep eyes on the correct yellow cab as they stuttered through the Financial District. The traffic thinned once they'd left the island and got onto the freeway. Confident that there was no longer any chance of losing East, Baxter took out her phone. She knew that Rouche and Curtis would be waiting to hear from her, ready to follow behind.

She glanced out the window in search of a road sign and then typed out a quick text:

278 towards Red Hook

Once she'd pressed "send," she recognized the familiar Louisiana inflection coming through the radio: "It's about breaking you down piece by piece until there's nothing left," explained Pastor Jerry Pilsner Jr.

"And . . . from my very limited knowledge of exorcisms and

the such . . . mainly from horror movies," the host joked, "this happens in stages, doesn't it?"

"Three stages. That's right."

"But . . . that's all this is, isn't it? The stuff of scary movies? You aren't seriously claiming that this is what is happening to these 'Puppet' people, are you?"

"I am *entirely* serious. Three stages, the first being 'Diabolical Infestation.' This is where the entity chooses its victim, experiments with their susceptibility . . . makes its presence known.

"The second stage is 'Oppression,' in which the entity has a firm hold over the subject's life, escalating its psychological victimization, making its target doubt their own sanity."

"And the third?" the host asked.

"'Possession'—the point at which the victim's will is finally broken. The point at which they invite the entity in."

"Invite?"

"Not in the traditional sense," clarified the pastor. "But there is always a choice. Should you *choose* to surrender . . . you are *choosing* to grant it permission."

Baxter leaned forward to speak to the driver: "Could you turn that off, please?"

CHAPTER 19

Monday, 14 December 2015
12:34 P.M.

Baxter's taxi idled outside one of the eastern entrances to Prospect Park as Phillip East paid for his own ride a hundred meters down the street. He remained in the same spot for over a minute, scanning the passing cars and the park opposite anxiously. Apparently satisfied that he had not been followed, he walked a little way back up the road toward her before turning into a grand art deco apartment block.

She climbed out of the cab and paid the driver far too much. She couldn't help but suspect that he had deliberately fumbled about looking for change, knowing full well that having followed this man across New York, she would elect to lose the $8.50 over losing her quarry. Dodging the traffic, she headed in through the main entrance after East.

For a sickening moment, she thought she had lost him, but then heard a door unlock somewhere along the ground-floor corridor. Following the sound, she saw East pass through a doorway at the end of the hallway. She strode down the corridor, thrown into gloom by a broken bulb overhead, and made a note of the apartment number.

Baxter headed back outside and crossed over the road to claim a bench at the entrance to the park, from where she would be able to watch the building without attracting attention. She braced herself against the cold and took out her phone to update Rouche.

Curtis and Rouche had been twelve minutes away fifteen minutes earlier. Baxter was stamping her feet in the slush, in part to keep warm but mainly because she was growing more impatient by the second.

"Merry Christmas!" smiled an enthusiastic older gentleman as he passed her, who correctly interpreted Baxter's scowl as an invitation to get the hell away from her.

She had just called Rouche again to find out what was holding them up when an unfamiliar vehicle parked illegally outside the apartment block.

Baxter got to her feet.

"Five minutes tops!" Rouche promised apologetically down the phone. "Baxter?"

She changed position to see better. A hooded man climbed out. He slid the side door open and removed a large rucksack.

"Baxter?"

"We might have a problem," she told him, already crossing back over the road as the man entered the grand lobby. "A green van's just pulled up. Driver acting suspiciously."

She heard Rouche pass the message on to Curtis. Seconds later, the wail of sirens buzzed out through her phone. Jogging along the sludgy path that led up to the glass doors, she reached to pull one of them open when she saw the man crouched over his bag inside, just a few meters away. She almost slipped as she abruptly halted, pressing her back against the brick wall to stay out of sight.

"Two minutes, Baxter. We're almost there," Rouche shouted over the siren. "Wait for us."

Baxter glanced around the wall. Through the glass door, she could see that the man was assembling something. She was still unable to make out a face. After a moment, he removed a gun, elongated by the silencer attachment screwed onto the barrel. He concealed it inside his jacket, closed the bag, and stood back up.

"We don't have two minutes," whispered Baxter. "East's family might be in there."

She hung up before Rouche could protest. She had to do something, especially with the Banthams fresh in her mind.

She moved through the main entrance and saw the figure retracing East's steps down the poorly lit corridor to stop outside his apartment door. She needed to buy more time so removed her keys from her bag, clinking them piercingly in the silent lobby. Feeling the figure turn in her direction, she sauntered unhurriedly along the corridor toward him as though she were just an oblivious resident.

She walked as slowly as she dared, while the man watched, making no effort to conceal the fact that he was waiting for her to pass.

Once she was just a few steps away from him, she looked up and smiled sweetly:

"Merry Christmas!"

The man did not respond. The hood of his winter jacket came up around the front of his face, fastened together over his nose and jaw. She was only able to ascertain that he was Caucasian, was of average height and weight, and had dark brown eyes. He had one hand inside his jacket, no doubt wrapped around the handle of the gun.

There was still no sign of Rouche and Curtis, so she dropped the keys to the floor, as per her impromptu plan.

"Bugger," she said, kneeling down to retrieve them.

She selected the longest and sharpest, Thomas's house key, to wedge between her knuckles to form a makeshift weapon. She saw the man roll his eyes in exasperation and seized her opportunity.

Rising up suddenly, she jabbed her spiked fist under the man's hood, sinking the key into his cheek. They both fell back into the apartment door as the man cried out in pain.

He shoved her against the wall opposite and pulled the weapon from his jacket as she threw herself into him, using the heel of her hand to break his concealed nose, knowing that his watering eyes would hinder his vision.

Wolf had taught her well.

The man lashed out blindly, striking her with the heavy gun. A lock clicked and then a concerned face peered out through a crack in the doorway. Distracted away from Baxter, the man kicked the door wide open, knocking East onto his back.

There were screams from somewhere inside as three muted gunshots fired in quick succession.

"No!" shouted Baxter.

She pulled herself back up and scrambled inside after him.

"Green van!" yelled Rouche as Curtis pulled around the traffic and accelerated down the wrong side of the road.

He already had his weapon drawn and had removed his seat belt, desperate to get to Baxter. Curtis cut the sirens and slammed her foot on the brake, feeling the ABS judder beneath her foot. The car squealed to a halt less than a meter behind the van's faded back doors.

Rouche leaped out and had taken only a few steps toward the entrance when there was a loud smash from one of the ground-floor windows. As he turned to look, a man climbed out, landing badly and rolling across the snow. Rouche locked eyes with him for a split second before he scrambled to his feet and took off in the opposite direction.

"Find Baxter!" Rouche shouted to Curtis as he started after their suspect.

With her own weapon raised, Curtis ran in through the entrance and along the ground-floor corridor in the direction of the broken window. Several people were loitering outside their own apartments, looking toward an open door surrounded by damaged plaster.

"Baxter?" she shouted.

Gun first, she moved into the doorway and was confronted with a dead body. East was on his back, staring blankly up at the ceiling. Dark red blood had soaked into the beige carpet beneath him.

"Baxter?" she called again, a distinct tremor in her voice.

She heard crying in another room and cautiously proceeded, pausing to kick open the bathroom door and confirm that the small kitchen was empty. She moved into the living room to find it half destroyed. Furniture lay in pieces. A large glass table had been reduced to sparkles in the carpet. A woman was shielding her three young children in her arms, clearly unsure whether Curtis was there to save them or kill them.

On the other side of the room, Baxter lay crumpled over, as if she had been thrown through the broken bookcase. Her left arm was bent awkwardly behind her.

"Baxter!" Curtis gasped.

She rushed over to her colleague and checked for a pulse, exhaling in relief when she felt the angry pounding in her fingertips, and then smiling when she heard Baxter groan a swear word.

"My . . . my husband?" East's wife asked between distressed breaths.

She shook her head.

As the woman broke down, Curtis radioed in to request an ambulance.

Rouche was deep within the warren of icy alleyways that serviced the huge apartment complex and surrounding properties. He had gotten himself completely lost while chasing phantom footsteps that led only to another dead end, the thin sliver of sky overhead a featureless ceiling to the claustrophobic passageways.

He paused when he reached a crossroads, concrete corridors stretching out in all directions.

He closed his eyes to concentrate.

The slap of running feet passed directly behind him.

He spun around.

On seeing no one there, he turned the corner, following the only possible route that the fleeing man could have taken, his shoulders scraping through the narrow gap. As he rounded the next wall, he raised his arms in front of him defensively and slipped onto his back.

An enormous husky was on its hind legs, teeth bared and growling as it chewed frenziedly at the chicken-wire fence standing between them.

Slowly, Rouche lowered his arms. Satisfied that the animal couldn't get through, he got back up onto his feet. But as the dog continued to tear at the unyielding wires between them, a chill coursed up his spine.

Rouche was drawn closer, his face barely six inches from the beast's as he stared into its dark eyes . . .

Suddenly, the dog whimpered as if injured, dropped back onto all fours, and disappeared down another passageway.

Rouche listened to the padded feet fade into the silence and then shook his head, feeling a little foolish for allowing the TV pastor and his fanatical theories to get to him. He picked his weapon up off the floor and headed back into the dark maze.

Just over five minutes later, he arrived at the apartment. He paused over East's body in the hallway. Three bullet holes had been scattered across his chest, the thick carpet squelching underfoot as he crouched down over him. Just visible where the bullets had ripped through his shirt, the familiar crude marking: "Puppet."

He rubbed his tired eyes. "Shit."

Tia had been crashed out on the sofa since 7 P.M. At 9:20 P.M., Edmunds headed back downstairs, having eventually managed to get Leila off to sleep. Since coming home from work, he had cooked dinner, cleaned out Bernard's litter tray, done a pile of laundry and two days' worth of washing-up. He scooped Tia up in his arms and carried her to bed, feeling like a model husband.

For once, he felt like he had earned the right to continue working into the small hours with what little energy he had left. He went through into the kitchen to make himself a strong coffee. He had to wake up. He still needed to drive across the city.

After his official warning that afternoon, he could not risk using any of the fraud software to carry out his investigation of Rouche. He had utilized the limited resources left available to him to gather some very basic information. Even armed with what little he had found, there were glaring irregularities that warranted further exploration.

He wondered whether Baxter might be onto something after all.

Through backdated structural spider diagrams that he had found buried in the Human Resources area of the intranet, Edmunds had discovered that a former colleague from Homicide and Serious Crime Command had worked alongside Rouche during his time in Narcotics. Edmunds had been fortunate enough to catch him on duty.

The man had described Rouche as "sharp as a tack," "a little eccentric," but overall "pretty chilled," which more or less correlated with Baxter's description of him; however, when asked about Rouche's religious beliefs, the man had burst out laughing.

"I'm more religious than he is, mate," he told Edmunds, which was saying something when it came from the death-metal-loving detective whose infamous faded forearm tattoo read:

God is dead

The man then recited a thirdhand story told to him by a friend in Protection Command, where Rouche had transferred in 2004: "Fired. At least, that's what everyone presumed. There was no send-off, no replacement arranged. He was literally there one day, gone the next. Never to be seen again. Boss went apeshit, unsurprisingly."

Edmunds thanked the detective for his help and made a loose arrangement to meet for drinks that neither of them had any intention of following through on.

He had been able to obtain Rouche's home address before leaving the office and calculated that it would be less than a half-hour drive at that time of night. He tiptoed into the hallway, donned his coat and scarf, removed the car keys from the hook, and crept out.

*

"You see this small, shadowy area here? That's a chip in your elbow joint," explained the doctor cheerfully.

"Fantastic," sighed Baxter. "Can I go now?"

She had been confined to the hospital room for almost three hours while the doctors and nurses prodded and poked at her, and her patience was beginning to wane. The altercation with the hooded man had left her aching and bruised all over. Her face was decorated in dozens of tiny cuts courtesy of the glass table, which, in turn, had exploded across the apartment floor courtesy of her face. And now she had three strapped-up broken fingers and a chipped elbow to add to her growing list of ailments.

The doctor excused himself and requested that a nurse equip her with a sling.

"You were very brave today," said Curtis once they were alone.

"Stupid, more like," said Baxter, wincing in pain.

"Bit of both, perhaps." Curtis smiled. "Rouche said there were burlap bags and duct tape in the rucksack they recovered from the crime scene. Enough for all five of them. You saved them."

Feeling awkward, Baxter ignored the praise: "Where's Rouche?"

"Where else?" Curtis replied, which she took to mean that he was on the phone as usual.

Picking up on Baxter's despondent expression, Curtis felt obliged to give her a pep talk: "This isn't another dead end. You know that, right? They've dragged Ritcher back in. The family are under police protection and being interviewed as we speak. We've now got full access to East's financial and phone records, and the DNA evidence from your keys and clothes are being fast-tracked through Forensics. We're making progress."

A flustered nurse returned with a bright purple sling in her hands.

"This is for you," she announced, handing it to Baxter.

Both Curtis and Baxter regarded the eyesore with reservation.

"Have you got a black one?" they chorused together.

"I'm afraid not," she replied sharply. "Now, this is optional . . ."

"Optional?"

"Yes."

"Then *this* is for you," said Baxter, handing it straight back to the woman. She turned to Curtis and smiled: "Let's go."

Edmunds double-checked the address he had been given for the Rouche family home under the weak interior light of his dilapidated Volvo. He was parked up outside the dark house. Even from the car, he could see the patches of paint peeling away from the windows and weeds escaping through the cracks in the steep driveway. An air of neglect surrounded the old house, which had the potential to be so much more.

He could imagine the tumbledown property feeding the imaginations of the local children: the haunted house on the hill. Despite never having met Rouche, Edmunds felt angry with him. He, Tia, and Leila had to survive on a rough estate, the privilege for which left them floundering barely above the breadline. But even with their limited means, they made a real effort to take pride in where they lived, despite a total lack of support from their unapologetically content neighbors.

By making an effort, Edmunds had inadvertently turned his modest home into a target for some of the more resentful residents, aggrieved by the audacity of his lower-middle-class existence. Just that morning, he had found his tasteful white and ice-blue Christmas lights severed in half, and he could not afford to replace them. But here was Rouche with a beautiful family home on a picturesque street in a prosperous residential suburb of the city and he had just left it to rot.

Edmunds climbed out of his car and pushed the driver's door closed as quietly as he could. Checking once more that no one was around, he climbed the driveway up toward the dark house. Unfortunately, there was no vehicle. A number plate could have been a useful source of information, but there were two bins around the side that would serve just as well.

By flashlight, he began rooting through the recycling for anything relating to the secretive CIA agent. Suddenly, the narrow
passageway was thrown into light. Edmunds crouched down behind the bins as an elderly gentleman emerged from the house
next door and poked his head over the fence. He pulled his long
legs closer into his body.

"Bloody foxes," he heard the man complain.

There was the sound of footsteps, a door closing, locking, and
then the light went out. Edmunds felt he could risk breathing
again. After his official warning that afternoon, all he needed was
to get caught trespassing on a CIA agent's property. Accordingly,
he cursed himself for being so reckless, but his body betrayed his
true feelings: the buzz of adrenaline demanding that his heart
pump harder, the mist from his staccato breaths becoming more
regular, like a steam train gathering speed.

He wanted to ensure that the old neighbor had lost interest
before he attempted to leave so continued down the side passage
and into the back garden, where long grass slashed wet stains
across his trouser legs. A pristine Wendy house stood out of place
beside broken fence panels and a vacated rabbit hutch.

There was still a light on inside the house. He peered in through
the patio doors, when a phone started to ring in the hallway.
After five rings he heard a woman's voice answer: "Hello, my
love! We're both missing you so, so much!"

Edmunds cursed under his breath as he hid from view and
crawled back toward the passageway. He passed the bins and
hurried back down the driveway without being seen. Climbing
into his car, he pulled away without turning his lights on, knowing that it would hinder any attempt to identify his vehicle. Once
safely back on the main road, he switched on his headlights and
sped away, his heart still racing.

He'd found nothing and yet he had a grin on his face the entire
way home.

CHAPTER 20

Monday, 14 December 2015

7:54 P.M.

Curtis and Rouche were hit by a wall of hot air as they entered their hotel. A familiar, irritable voice cut over the roar of the industrial heater above them. They followed the sound into a shabby bar area. Some sporting event or other looked minutes away from starting on a chunky television, and the overly bright lights revealed every flaw in the 1980s decor, the dark wallpaper stained with nicotine and thirty years of spilled drinks.

"I said I can manage!" Baxter told the barman while slopping her large glass of red wine onto the floor.

She slumped down into a booth by the window, jarring her injured arm as she did so, and swore loudly.

"And *that's* why you wear a sling," muttered Rouche, before whispering: "Think she'd notice if we just turned round and left?"

He realized he was talking to himself because Curtis hadn't made it beyond the fuzzy television. Despite her uninspiring sur-roundings, she stood straight-backed with her hand over her heart as the American national anthem was performed by a stadium-sized choir of beer-swigging hot-dog aficionados.

"Americans," Baxter tutted, shaking her head as Rouche took a seat, placing a small discolored book on the sticky table between them. "You should get up there with her, seeing as you hate home so much."

Rouche glanced back at Curtis, who looked to have tears of pride glistening in her eyes:

"Nah, my karaoke track's 'Since U Been Gone,' thanks."

As he turned back to face Baxter, "The Star-Spangled Banner" reached its thunderous conclusion to an applause worthy of a Bon Jovi encore.

"Should you . . ." Rouche hesitated. He gestured to the drink in front of her. "Should you be drinking that if you're on painkillers?"

Baxter glared at him: "I think I deserve it, don't you?"

He elected to drop the subject. Curtis joined them at the table, eyeing Baxter's enormous wine with similar concern. Presumably the barman had filled it to the brim in the hope that it would prevent the ill-tempered woman returning for a second glass.

"Should you really be drinking that if . . ." Curtis trailed off when she noticed Rouche shaking his head in warning. She abruptly changed the subject, picking the book up off the table to read the front cover: "*Father Vincent Bastian: An Account of the Exorcism of Mary Esposito* . . . You're not *still* on this, are you?"

Rouche snatched the book from her and flicked through to a dog-eared page:

"OK. Listen to this—a written statement from somebody who was *actually* possessed . . . 'The night stalked me, even during the day. And although the sun burned, it was burning in a black sky—the colors muted as if lit by candlelight, and I was a shadow, forced to share myself with him.'"

He looked up at their blank faces. Baxter took a long sip of her wine.

"Like our Gemini-man said while he stared up at the stars in Grand Central: 'It's always nighttime to me,'" Rouche explained. "Come on, tell me that's not relevant."

"It's not relevant!" Baxter and Curtis replied in unison.

"And then back at the apartment block today, I followed the sound of running footsteps to . . ." He had been about to bring up his encounter with the feral dog but trailed off on seeing their expressions.

"You're reading too much into this, Rouche," Baxter told him, wiser for the wine. "You're making links that aren't there. Not everything is gods and ghosts. Sometimes it's just people being dicks."

"Hear, hear." Curtis nodded, keen to change the subject yet again. "Lennox assumes you'll be leaving us now that you've been wounded in the line of duty."

"Yeah, I bet she does," scoffed Baxter, ending that conversation. "So, any progress?"

"The van's meant to have been scrapped," Rouche told her. "Full of DNA. It'll take days to separate out who's who. The wife and kids don't seem to know anything. East arrives home a couple of days ago—"

"You mean the day we started looking into Bantham?" asked Baxter.

"Exactly," said Rouche. "He starts frantically throwing things into bags, yelling at them all that they needed to leave."

"He made up some story about an ex-patient of his being fixated on him, but the wife said he had been acting strangely for weeks," Curtis added.

"She didn't think to ask him why he had the word 'Puppet' carved across his chest, then?" Baxter asked flippantly.

"She said they hadn't been . . . intimate since all this started." Curtis shrugged.

Baxter sighed heavily and finished off her wine:

"I might head up. I need a shower after having all those people prodding at me."

"Need any help getting undressed?" asked Curtis.

"No. Thank you." Baxter frowned as though she had just been propositioned. "I'll manage."

There was a knock at Curtis's door.

"I could use some help getting undressed," said Baxter, who was unable to see the grin on her colleague's face because she was half in, half out of her shirt, which she'd managed to get stuck somewhere above her head.

"Let me grab my key," laugh-coughed Curtis, hurrying back into her room as voices filled the corridor.

"What are you looking at?" she heard Baxter snap at someone.

Curtis escorted her back to her room, where a British news station was quietly summarizing the specifics of Parliament's latest unpopular decision. After some maneuvering, Curtis was finally able to free her. Embarrassed, Baxter covered herself with a towel.

"Thanks."

"You're welcome."

"Bitch!"

Curtis looked stunned: "I'm sorry?"

"Not you," Baxter clarified, her eyes on the television as she fumbled around for the remote control to turn up the volume.

Being the middle of the night back in England, the same prerecorded pieces were playing on a loop. It was the turn of Andrea Hall's final report of the evening, which caught Baxter's attention when her own tired face appeared on the large screens behind the stylish newsreader. The reporter's trendsetting red hair had developed a striking blond streak, which would no doubt be replicated by women all over the country before lunchtime.

"I'm sorry," said Andrea, getting choked up. "Of course, as many of you will know, Detective Chief Inspector Baxter and I are very close personal friends . . ."

"Bitch!" Baxter repeated, seething, while Curtis remained sensibly silent.

". . . I, along with the rest of the team here, wish her a very speedy recovery following this 'altercation' with a suspect." Andrea took a deep breath and moved on with the stoic professionalism one would expect of someone who didn't actually give a toss.

"OK. Let's speak to Commander Geena Vanita of the Metropolitan Police . . . Good evening, Commander."

Baxter's superior appeared on the screens in front of a generic backdrop of London:

"Good evening, Ms. Hall."

All too aware of the ambitious journalist's ability to make a bad situation worse, Vanita had clearly decided it safer to negotiate the minefield of an interview herself.

"Would you say you're a religious woman, Commander?" blurted Andrea right out of the starting gate.

"I . . ." The look on Vanita's face suggested the interview had already veered out of her comfort zone. "If we could just stick to the—"

"I'm presuming from the lack of update that you *still* have no solid leads regarding these horrific murders—to all appearances, the work of a single twisted individual and yet carried out by people with no *apparent* connection to one another?"

"Well . . . we're still looking into—"

"Azazel."

"I beg your—"

"You've heard Pastor Jerry Pilsner Jr.'s theory, I assume?"

"Of course," replied Vanita, managing to complete her two-word sentence. It had been almost impossible to avoid the fanatical man as he popped up on every television show that would have him.

"And?"

"And . . . ?"

"He has a rather *unconventional* explanation for what's occurring out there."

"He does."

"May I ask whether the police are giving any credence to his claims?"

Vanita smiled:

"Absolutely not. That would be a disgraceful misuse of vital resources."

Andrea laughed and Vanita visibly relaxed on-screen.

"Would it, though?" asked Andrea, lost in exaggerated thought. "I mean, here, as in the US, religious institutions of all faiths have been seeing record attendance this past week."

Vanita's expression changed as she foresaw the trap that the journalist was maneuvering her toward:

"And the Metropolitan Police respect these people's—"

"Are they foolish to believe in something, Commander?"

"Not at all, but—"

"So you're now saying that the 'fallen angel' theory *is* a valid branch of the investigation?"

Poor Andrea seemed awfully confused.

"No. I'm not saying that. I'm saying . . ." Vanita was floundering.

"I'm no detective," Andrea went on, "but isn't there some possibility, at least, that these murders are inspired by the Bible and perhaps even the notion of one of God's angels fallen from grace?"

Vanita froze while she calculated the path of least damage.

"Commander?"

"Yes . . . No. We—"

"Well, which is it?" Andrea threw her hands up in exasperation. "Surely the police would want to look into every—"

"Yes," interrupted Vanita resolutely. "We *are* looking into that possibility."

Suddenly, the camera pulled back, leaving the newsreader sat center stage, the wall of monitors stretching out several meters in either direction.

"Oh no," whispered Baxter, sensing a trademark Andrea Hall moment of sensationalist brilliance approaching.

The screens behind the news desk flickered and buzzed theatrically, obliterating Vanita's image and replacing it with an enormous set of tattered black wings, framed to look as though they had sprouted out from the award-winning reporter as she continued:

"There you have it," Andrea told her global audience, "the Metropolitan Police hunting fallen angels."

"What is she talking about?" asked Curtis.

"This is what she does," replied Baxter as she watched Andrea's animated mantle shed black feathers.

"But this is absurd!"

"Doesn't matter—not when *she's* saying it . . . Here it comes," said Baxter, bracing herself.

". . . So join me, Andrea Hall, tomorrow morning from six A.M. as we discuss every bizarre and terrifying turn in what the police are now calling . . . 'the Azazel murders.'"

"No!" Baxter groaned despondently. She switched off the television and shook her head.

"Are . . . are you all right?" Curtis asked softly.

"I'm fine," replied Baxter, remembering that she was wearing a towel and pulling it up to hide a little more skin. "I'm just going to go to bed."

There was an awkward pause as she waited for the woman to leave her in peace. Instead, Curtis took a seat at the desk in the corner of the room.

"I was actually hoping for a chance to speak to you alone," she said.

Baxter hovered in the bathroom doorway, trying to hide how uncomfortable she was feeling. She would have felt self-conscious standing half dressed in front of Thomas, let alone attempting to hold a conversation with a woman she had only recently met.

Curtis continued obliviously: "It's probably irrelevant anyway now that we know the counseling lead is solid, but I don't feel comfortable keeping it from you. The forensic pathologist found some irregularities in Glenn Arnolds's bloodwork."

Baxter tried to look surprised at the news, despite being able to see the corner of the document in question poking out from the folder on the desk.

"Basically, he wasn't taking his antipsychotic medication. In their place, he'd been taking others that made his mental state worse. For *reasons* . . . this didn't get shared with you, and I apologize for that."

"OK. Thanks for telling me." Baxter smiled. An emotional exchange while standing in her bra was too much for her. She just wanted it to be over. "Well, I think I might . . ." she said, gesturing to the shower.

"Of course." Curtis got up to leave.

Baxter was afraid that she might attempt to hug her on the way out and physically cringed when it inevitably happened.

"We're a team, right?" Curtis smiled.

"We certainly are," agreed Baxter, slamming the door in her face.

*

"Was getting thrown through a table not enough of a hint to take a hike?" whispered Lennox as she and Curtis headed into the field-office meeting room. She had just spotted Baxter trudging in ahead of them.

A young agent entered the room with the stack of printouts she had requested:

"Would you mind handing these out, Agent . . . ?"

"Rouche."

"Rooze?"

"For Christ's sake! Pick someone else," snapped Lennox.

Once everyone had taken their seats, she dived straight into the first item on the agenda, pointedly making no mention of Baxter's numerous injuries.

At the front of the room, Rouche's whiteboard of killers had grown an additional column:

US	UK	?
1. MARCUS TOWNSEND *(Brooklyn Bridge)* *MO: strangulation* *Victim: Ragdoll-related*	**3. DOMINIC BURRELL** *(Belmarsh Prison)* *MO: stabbing* *Victim: Ragdoll-related*	**6. ?** *(Westchester County)* *MO: gunshot* *Victim: psychiatrist and family*
2. EDUARDO MEDINA *(33rd Precinct)* *MO: high-speed impact* *Victim: police officer*	**4. PATRICK PETER FERGUS** *(The Mall)* *MO: blunt-force trauma* *Victim: police officer*	**7. ?** *(Brooklyn)* *MO: gunshot* *Victim: counselor*
5. GLENN ARNOLDS *(Grand Central)* *MO: Unpleasant* *Victim: -? station employee*		

"Footprints from Brooklyn are identical to those taken at the Bantham house," Lennox told the room. "Ballistics came back a match. Plus this is the first instance of an MO being repeated. I'm going to go out on a limb here and say that I don't think the deaths of these two men were part of the plan. Dead Puppets. No Bait. This is somebody acting out of desperation, somebody tying up loose ends. Anything to add to that?" she asked, looking to Rouche and Curtis.

"Only that this 'somebody' is no professional: Baxter gave him a good fight, and the three rounds he unloaded into East only did the job through blood loss, not because they hit any vital organs," said Rouche, "which certainly backs up the desperation theory."

"Can't be a coincidence that as soon as we start showing an interest in these people, they wind up dead," said Curtis.

"No. It can't," agreed Lennox. "Speaking of which, our repeat killer: we've got an approximate height and weight, along with a vague description of 'Caucasian male, brown eyes.'"

Baxter ignored the subtle jibe in the word "vague."

"Who did the apartment East was staying in belong to?" someone asked.

Lennox flicked through her pages of paperwork:

"A . . . Kieran Goldman. Apparently he and East were friends, and the property was sitting empty while he raised the funds to renovate it."

"So we've got nothing?" asked the same officer. "Unless Forensics come back with a name, we've got nothing?"

"Far from it," said Lennox. "Now we know the identity of the person masterminding this. Now we *finally* know who's holding the strings."

"We do?"

A room of blank faces waited for her to continue.

"I give you our Azazel . . ." Thanks to Andrea Hall, the name was being adopted by more and more journalists every minute, to the point where even the FBI were now referring to the case as if it were the work of a body-swapping fallen angel.

Curtis's heart sank when Lennox held up a photograph of

their missing British psychiatrist. Not only had she killed an innocent man, now she had come face-to-face with the FBI's most wanted, flirted with him like an idiot schoolgirl, and let him be on his way.

"Alexei Green," stated Lennox. "Green made five separate trips across the Atlantic to visit East and Bantham in the last year alone. As we already know, he was Dominic Burrell's prison counselor. What we didn't know before was that the cleaning company our cop-killing arsonist, Patrick Peter Fergus, worked for had been contracted to service Green's offices, giving Green plenty of opportunities to recruit, manipulate, or persuade him through unofficial channels."

"Green's motive being . . . *what* exactly?" asked Baxter.

Lennox shot her daggers but answered professionally: "We're still looking into that. But Green is the link between all of our Puppets. This is him, people. Apprehending Alexei Green has *got* to be our number-one priority."

"I'm not convinced," said Baxter. "Involved: definitely. Coordinating: why?"

"I agree," Rouche backed her up.

"Do you?" asked Lennox impatiently. "Perhaps this will change your mind: after we interviewed him, East made a single phone call during the taxi ride back to Prospect Park. Anybody want to hazard a guess as to who he called?"

Nobody did, suspecting that it was safer to remain quiet.

"You got it: Alexei Green. East had gone out of his way to keep himself and his family hidden. He had done a good job of it too, until he placed his trust in the wrong person. He phones Green for advice. Half an hour later, someone turns up on his doorstep to murder him."

Rouche was confused:

"If Green's still using his phone, why can't we find him?"

"He isn't. It was a burner, and the call was too brief to trace anyway."

Rouche was even more confused:

"So how do we know it even belonged to Green?"

"We were listening in on the call." Lennox shrugged. "Do you *really* think we would let our most promising lead just walk out of here because he flashed a fancy lawyer at us?"

Rouche was impressed by the special agent in charge's underhanded tactics. She had put on a convincing show at the time, but he now recalled Ritcher's displeasure that he and East had been separated from their belongings.

"The evidence is mounting: Alexei Green is holding all the strings, and we're going to throw everything we've got into finding . . ." Lennox trailed off on seeing the distracted faces of her audience. She followed their gaze out through the windows to the main office, where people were rushing about frantically.

She opened the meeting-room door and caught a young officer as he jogged by:

"What's happening?"

"We're not sure yet. Something about a body in a—"

Every phone in the office seemed to go off at once. Lennox hurried over to the nearest desk and answered, her eyes growing wide as she listened attentively:

"Curtis!" she shouted.

The special agent jumped to her feet, Baxter and Rouche following her out.

"Times Square Church, off Broadway!" Lennox barked without further explanation.

As they obediently hurried out, they could hear Lennox shouting orders across the room:

"Can I have everybody's attention? We have just been alerted to a *major* incident . . ."

CHAPTER 21

Tuesday, 15 December 2015

10:03 A.M.

No one had spoken a word as they sped across the city with Curtis behind the wheel. The NYPD radios had not paused for breath as flustered transmissions cut over one another, and the dispatchers sent more and more resources to the scene every time a unit came clear from another call. What little information the officers at the church had been forced to pass over the open channel had been chilling:

". . . bodies everywhere . . ."

". . . strung up from the walls . . ."

". . . Everyone's dead."

Curtis had to mount the pavement to get through the gridlocked traffic as they drew nearer to West 51st Street. Two blocks out, a young officer waved them through the hastily organized road closure on Broadway. He dragged a flimsy plastic barricade across the icy sludge, opening up the deserted street for them. Curtis accelerated toward the crowd of police cars abandoned across the junction ahead, their flashing blue lights fanning out in all directions.

They skidded to a stop outside Paramount Plaza, as close as they could get to their destination, and ran the rest of the way on foot. Baxter was convinced they were heading in the wrong direction as she scanned the uniform buildings for anything resembling a church, exhaust-stained facades lining both sides of the street. She was even more confused when she followed Curtis and Rouche through the doors of a grand old theater.

The ornate 1930s lobby was an uneasy fusion of decadence, messages assuring that *all* one really needs in life is God, and police officers wearing traumatized expressions, suggesting that perhaps God was having an off-day.

A set of doors stood open, allowing glimpses into the auditorium beyond. Baxter could see flashlights sweeping across a golden ceiling and the top of a bloodred curtain, drawn closed as if in anticipation of a show.

She followed her colleagues through the doorway.

Just three steps into the magnificent hall, they stopped.

"Oh my God!" whispered Curtis, while Rouche regarded his surroundings in utter disbelief.

Baxter pushed between them but immediately regretted doing so. The old picture-house-turned-theater, reborn a church, had gone through a final metamorphosis, a depraved mutation: a living manifestation of hell on earth. She felt light-headed as her eyes drank in the scene before her. She had forgotten the feeling, the same plunging reaction that she had experienced on first laying eyes on the Ragdoll suspended in front of those large windows in that filthy Kentish Town apartment.

Countless wires crisscrossed overhead, running from stage to balcony, from ceiling to carpeted floor, ornate wall to ornate wall—a steel spiderweb hanging above the tiered rows of plush red theater chairs. Bodies like trapped insects, twisted into unique and yet disturbingly familiar contortions, unnatural and deformed, naked and scarred.

In a daze, Baxter led her colleagues farther into the auditorium . . . further into hell.

The exploring flashlights threw ominous shadows across the walls, distorted likenesses of disfigured subjects, and a hushed murmur emanated from the dozens of police officers already inside as they weaved between the horrors. Nobody was giving orders or pulling rank, presumably because, much like Baxter, no one had any idea what to do.

A roving flashlight passed over a body above them, the beam reflecting brightly off the dark skin. Confused, Baxter drew closer, an eerie creaking sound becoming louder as her eyes ran the lengths of the bent limbs, contorted more violently than the others, fractured in on themselves.

"Do you mind?" she asked a passing officer, adopting an appropriate stage whisper.

Pleased to have somebody to tell him what to do, he shone his light skyward . . .

"There are others," he informed them as the wooden limbs swayed gently. "Not sure how many."

They were staring up at a full-sized but featureless replica of the people suspended in the air around them—the head an eyeless oval, sinister expressions formed in the grains of the polished wood . . . a marionette floating before a theater stage, a familiar word gouged through its hollow body, "Bait." Glancing around the darkened room, it was impossible to tell which of the twisted shapes surrounding them were real.

A moment passed and then Curtis stepped away from them. Holding her identification high above her head, she addressed the room: "Special Agent Elliot Curtis with the FBI! *I* will be taking the lead on this crime scene. Everyone is to report to me, and any press contact is to go through me . . . Thank you."

Baxter and Rouche shared a look, but neither said anything.

"Curtis, stay close!" Rouche hissed as she moved farther from them to stand among the seats in the very center of the room, the theater's real stage, an arbitary point around which all the hanging bodies seemed to be facing. "Curtis!"

She ignored him, assigning an officer the unenviable task of counting up the exact number of dead versus wooden mannequins.

Baxter took a few steps toward the closest suspended body, placing the victim in his sixties. His mouth gaped open like the recent wounds torn into his chest: "Bait." Even in the subdued lighting, she could make out the bruised-blue-colored skin of the dead. He had been strung up so that the tips of his toes were just brushing the old red carpet.

She was startled by a loud thump above them but then saw the beam of a flashlight emitting from the balcony as one brave officer checked the upper level. Curtis gave her an anxious smile from the center of the room, standing below the body of a man just a few rows over.

The hushed murmur became a gentle hum as more uniformed officers filled the hall, a tide of blue retreating from the streets of the city to amass in a single room like moths buzzing around a flame. More flashlights shone across the darkened hall.

The additional light fell over four other suspended corpses nearby, causing Baxter to notice something that she had not before. She fumbled around for her phone, aimed its weak light up at a body hanging in midair just below the balcony, and then at the lone figure contorted agonizingly up on the stage. She hurried over to a female victim, positioned with her back to her. Ducking beneath the wires anchoring the woman in place, she shone the light across her exposed chest.

"Baxter?" asked Rouche. He had noticed her erratic behavior and rushed over to join her. "What is it?"

"Something . . ."

She whipped her head around and illuminated the lean, pale body that Curtis was still standing in front of.

Curtis looked over at them quizzically.

"Baxter?" Rouche repeated.

"Bait," she replied distantly.

"What about it?"

"They're all Bait. Every one of them," she explained, looking around in concern. "So where are the Puppets?"

A drop of blood landed on her cheek. She raised her hand to it instinctively, smudging it across her face.

Rouche looked up at the body beside them, the familiar word carved across the slight frame, streaks of crimson still snaking down past her navel.

"The dead don't bleed," he mumbled, pulling Baxter away.

This time, she didn't fight back but turned to him with terrified eyes as her makeshift flashlight beam fell over Curtis's victim—a spectral white in the glow of Baxter's light.

Curtis beckoned them over, wanting to know what they were talking about, when the muscles beneath the sallow skin behind her twitched and one of the long white arms unwrapped itself from the wire, a glint of light reflecting off something in its closed hand . . .

Before Rouche could reach for his weapon, before either of them could even call her name in warning, the reanimated corpse had swept its hand across her throat in a single gentle motion.

Baxter stood openmouthed as Rouche fired three deafening rounds into the man's torso, causing him to jerk violently against the taut wires that held him in place.

In the moments that followed, the only sound in the silent hall was the metallic hum of the web vibrating.

Curtis's wide eyes met Rouche's own as she comprehended what was happening. She removed her hand from her neck to find it dripping with dark blood. Copious amounts poured down her white blouse like the stage curtain descending. Baxter was already running toward her as she swayed and dropped out of sight behind a row of chairs.

"Everybody out!" Rouche shouted. "Get out!"

Several of the figures around them had begun freeing themselves from their contortions. The shouts of panicking police officers were amplified to ear-splitting levels by the hall's natural acoustics as they scrambled toward the daylight.

The spider had come.

There were reckless gunshots.

Rouche heard a bullet pass within inches of his head.

A cry from above—a split second later, the officer from the balcony landed in a grotesque heap at his feet.

Rouche raised his weapon and ran deeper into the hall after Baxter.

There was a huge, rattling bang from the other side of the room, different from a gunshot, followed by cries of desperation from the evacuating officers. Rouche did not have to look back to know what the sound had been; it had been the sound of hope dying; it had been the sound of heavy wooden doors slamming shut and sealing them inside, inside a place that no longer belonged to God.

He found Baxter crouched over Curtis's body as the massacre continued all around them. She was feeling for a pulse and listening for breaths, a bloody hand pressed over the mortal wound:

"I think I can feel a weak pulse!" she gasped in relief. She looked up at Rouche.

"Get her gun," he ordered emotionlessly.

The words didn't even register with Baxter: "We've got to get her out of here."

"Get . . . her . . . gun," Rouche repeated.

Baxter stared up at him in disgust.

A blur of white suddenly sprinted full pelt at Rouche. Caught off guard, he was only able to fire a single shot, which struck his attacker in the lower leg, sending him crashing into the chairs across the aisle but granting a few seconds of respite. Rouche leaned over Curtis's body and pulled her firearm from its holster. He then hauled Baxter roughly to her feet as she struggled against him.

"Let go of me! She's still alive!" cried Baxter as he dragged her away from Curtis. "She's still alive!"

"There's nothing we can do for her!" he shouted, but Baxter couldn't hear him over the sound of her own protests, the echoing gunshots, and the sickening sounds of death as the officers trapped by the exit were cut down with crude weapons: makeshift blades, tools, and wire. The few people still clawing at the doors were surrounded. "There's nothing we can do for any of them."

He was forced to let go of Baxter when the man he had wounded sliced at them with a jagged piece of metal, tearing a saw-toothed line of flesh from Rouche's waist. Rouche stepped back and winced as he held his side in pain. He gripped the gun he had taken from Curtis by the barrel and struck the floored man forcefully with the heavy handle, knocking him unconscious. He then offered the weapon to Baxter, who just stared at it in her hands.

Several bodies were still hanging motionless around the hall. There was no way to tell whether they were dead, marionettes, or patiently lying in wait. Rouche had neither the inclination nor the time to get close enough to find out because two more pale figures emerged from the darkness at the back of the room, running down the aisle toward them.

"Baxter, we've got to go . . . We've got to go!" he said firmly.

She was still looking longingly to where they had abandoned their friend when the chair beside her burst into a spray of splinters and stuffing.

Someone was shooting at them.

As they sprinted for the stage, the gunman up on the balcony fired inexpertly around them, bringing one of the wooden marionettes crashing to the floor, before running out of bullets. Rouche led the way up the steps to the side of the stage. As they ascended, he watched the lone figure twisted in the spotlight for any sign of life.

Several sets of thirsty eyes turned in their direction as they hurried between the curtains and into the darkened backstage area.

Rickety ladders climbed the walls, towering over them, while thick, knotted ropes dangled overhead like nooses. Somewhere, they could hear their pursuers coming for them.

The thud of bare feet on wooden floorboards chased them as they negotiated the claustrophobic bowels of the old building, guided solely by the "Fire Exit" signs burning green arrows through the gloom. They kept their weapons raised as they passed open doorways, the endless junctions slowing their progress through the grubby corridors.

There was a noise directly behind them.

Rouche spun on the spot and watched the darkness.

He waited, but the only movement came from a rusty bucket swaying gently on one of the ropes that they had disturbed.

He turned back to Baxter to find that she was gone.

"Baxter?" he hissed, staring down three possible corridors she might have taken. The wild shouts and slapping of running feet seemed to surround him. "Baxter?"

He made a decision and started down one of the corridors, based solely on the fact that it was marginally better lit than his other two options. Halfway along, the muffled echoes of excited voices doubled in volume as three ghostly shapes came around the corner ahead of him.

"Oh shit," gasped Rouche, turning and sprinting back the other way.

He felt as though he was on the verge of falling face-first into the floor as his legs struggled to keep pace with his desperation to escape. He tore across the junction where he had lost Baxter and continued straight on as the shouting behind him grew more crazed, more frenzied, the hounding predators sensing the hunt's imminent end.

Rouche didn't dare look back but fired shots blindly behind him, which did nothing more than pepper the featureless wall. He shouted Baxter's name, hoping that the panic in his voice would prompt her to run if she was still able. The gunshots became clicks, the last of his ammunition gone. He leaped over an empty paint can, only to hear it clatter across the floor a few seconds later.

They were gaining on him.

He reached a sharp corner and hit the wall hard, feeling a grasping hand against his face as he propelled himself away. At the far end of the corridor, framed thinly by daylight, stood an emergency exit. He sprinted toward it, his pursuers' breath in his ears, and threw himself against the bar to burst out into the blinding light.

The stutter of automatic gunfire greeted him, followed by a barked order:

"ESU! Do not move! Drop the weapon!"

His eyes watering in the cold air, Rouche complied.

"Slowly get to your knees!"

"It's OK. It's OK," a familiar voice insisted. "He's with me."

The dark blur dominating Rouche's vision became an ESU officer wearing full tactical gear. Rouche recognized the buildings opposite and realized that the church's extended network of corridors and storerooms had spat him back out onto West 51st Street, two buildings along.

The armed officer lowered his weapon and strode past Rouche to where two naked bodies lay in the open doorway. Rouche took the dismissive action as an invitation to get up off the ground and sighed in relief when he saw Baxter, but she neither returned the gesture nor approached him.

"Are they inside yet?" Rouche asked the ESU officer urgently. "There's a woman, an FBI agent, who—"

The officer cut him off:

"They'll be breaching the doors to the auditorium any moment now."

"I need to be there," said Rouche.

"You need to stay right here," the man corrected him.

"They might not find her in time!"

Rouche turned to approach the main entrance when the armed officer raised his AR-15 assault rifle.

Baxter hurried over to intervene:

"We're OK," she called to the officer before stepping into Rouche's path. She shoved him. He held his chest in pain. "Are you trying to get yourself killed?" she asked. "You told me you didn't want to die, remember? You promised me."

"She's still in there!" said Rouche. "Maybe if I can ... If I could just ..."

"She's gone, Rouche!" Baxter shouted over him, before dropping her voice to a whisper: "She's gone."

A muffled rumble ... and then the front wall of the church was blown out over the street as an enormous fireball twisted and retreated to the hiss of shattering glass. Baxter and Rouche stumbled backward, holding their hands over their ringing ears as a cloud of smoke engulfed the entire road around them. It stung Baxter's eyes until she could no longer see. She could feel the grit rubbing under her eyelids and then felt Rouche take her hand. She had no idea where he was leading her until she heard a car door creak open.

"Get in!" he shouted, slamming it behind her as he ran around to get in the other side.

She was able to breathe again and rubbed her eyes until she could open them. They were inside one of the patrol cars abandoned in the middle of the intersection. She could only just make out Rouche's face as a river of dirty smoke rolled past the windows—a premature nightfall.

Neither of them spoke.

Baxter was trembling as she took stock of the previous twenty minutes.

And then there was a second explosion.

Baxter grasped Rouche's hand as she started to hyperventilate. The sound had not come from the church this time but from somewhere close by; however, they were blind to anything beyond the interior of the patrol car. Baxter closed her eyes as a third bomb blast went off. She felt Rouche's arms around her when a fourth and final explosion reverberated through them.

Gradually, the daylight started to return as the smoke around them thinned. Baxter pushed Rouche off her and climbed out of the car, holding her sleeve over her nose and mouth to form a makeshift face mask. She couldn't see the ESU officer anywhere out on the street, suspecting that he had sheltered inside after the first blast. Rouche climbed out on the other side of the car.

The first licks of fire began coloring the sky over the heart of the city as enormous plumes of black smoke coiled toward the heavens, an image all too familiar over the New York skyline.

"Where is that?" asked Baxter, unable to tear her eyes away.

"Times Square," whispered Rouche.

The silence was chased away as a thunderous wall of sirens, alarms, and humanity approached like an avalanche.

"Oh." Baxter nodded in a daze as they stood there, helpless, watching the city burn.

SESSION ONE

Tuesday, 6 May 2014

9:13 A.M.

Despite his hurry, Lucas Keaton knew that he wouldn't be able to leave the house knowing that the photo frame was hanging askew. Even if he tried, he'd only end up turning back five minutes down the road and making himself later still. The rapping on the front door continued as he walked over to the picture and very gently raised it up on one side. He made a valiant effort not to focus on the memory entombed behind the glass . . . but his will was as weak as ever—the countless hours he had lost to this wall, immersing himself in a past bathed a rose-tinted shade of perfect.

He could no longer even hear the sound of the urgent knocking as he gazed at the snapshot: surrounded by his wife and two sons, all cheesily sporting Universal Studios–branded attire.

Lucas focused on his past self. He'd adopted a thick beard back then, the beginnings of middle-aged spread already starting to show beneath the tacky gift-shop T-shirt, unattractive wiry hair covering far more of his balding head than it managed to now. He was wearing his well-practiced photo face, the same disingenuous impersonation of happiness normally reserved for his press and publicity obligations.

He might have been there with them in person, but his mind was elsewhere, on more important matters, and he despised himself for that.

The person at the door reverted to the shrill doorbell, excusing Lucas from his self-loathing. He hurried up the stairs, checking his tie as he passed the large mirror in the entrance hall.

"I'm so sorry to pester you, Mr. Keaton, but we're going to be late," apologized his driver the moment he opened the door.

"No need to apologize, Henry. I wouldn't make it anywhere on time *without* you pestering me. I'm sorry for keeping you waiting." He smiled.

Henry climbed straight into the front seat, having chauffeured his multimillionaire passenger enough times to know that he hated having doors opened for him.

"Somewhere different this morning," stated Henry conversationally as he started them on their journey.

Lucas failed to answer immediately. All he wanted was to sit in silence:

"I'll be all right making my own way back afterwards."

"You're sure?" asked Henry, leaning forward in his seat to glance skyward. "Looks as though it might rain."

"I'll be fine," Lucas assured him. "But I expect you to bill me for the return journey and go get yourself a nice lunch somewhere instead."

"That's very kind of you, sir."

"Henry, I hate to be unsociable but I've got a few emails to catch up on before I get to this . . . meeting."

"Say no more. Just let me know if there's anything you need."

Satisfied that he hadn't upset the man, Lucas took out his phone and stared down at a blank screen for the remainder of the journey.

In his time, Lucas had met more celebrities, captains of industry, and world leaders than he could count, yet sat in the minimalist waiting room of Alexei Green's practice, he had never felt so nervous. While filling out the form handed to him on arrival, his foot had shaken constantly. He had found it difficult to hold the pen in his clammy hand, and he'd managed to bite his thumbnail so short that it was now outlined with bright red blood.

He stopped breathing altogether when the receptionist's phone went off.

Seconds later, the door across from him opened and an unusually handsome man stepped out. Perhaps because he'd been analyzing a photograph of his own thinning hair, Lucas found himself unable to take his eyes off Green's, which he wore in the slicked-back style that all the movie stars were currently sporting— he looked like one of them.

"Lucas, I'm Alexei," Green greeted him, shaking his hand with the sincerity of an old friend. "Please, come in, come in. Is there anything I can get you? A tea? Coffee perhaps? A glass of water?"

Lucas shook his head.

"No? Well, come and take a seat." Green smiled, closing the door softly behind them.

Lucas hadn't said a word in over twenty minutes. He fiddled with the zip of his jacket while Green watched him patiently. When Lucas glanced up at him, the two men briefly made eye contact before he quickly reverted his gaze to the jacket in his lap. Moments later, he burst into tears, sobbing into his hands, and still Green did not say a word.

Almost five minutes passed.

Lucas wiped his red eyes and exhaled deeply:

"Sorry," he apologized, nearly setting himself off again.

"Don't be," Green said soothingly.

"It's just . . . you . . . No one can understand what I've been through. I am *never* going to be OK again. If you love someone, I mean *truly* love someone, and you lose them . . . you shouldn't be OK, should you?"

Green leaned forward to address the troubled man, passing him a handful of the "man-sized" tissues he kept on his desk.

"There's a big difference between being OK and accepting that something was completely out of your control," Green said kindly. "Look at me, Lucas."

He tentatively met the psychiatrist's eye once more.

"I genuinely believe that I can help you," Green said.

Smiling as he dabbed his eyes, Lucas nodded:

"Yes . . . Yes. I think you might be able to as well."

CHAPTER 22

Tuesday, 15 December 2015

2:04 P.M.

Baxter sent three identical text messages: one to Edmunds, one to Vanita, and then one to Thomas:

I'm OK. Coming home.

She had switched off her phone and taken one of the few trains still running out to Coney Island. She just needed to be away from Manhattan, from the traumatized people, from the four dark clouds hanging above the city, blotting the blue sky: a killer's calling card.

One by one, each of the other wary passengers had gotten off along the way. Alone, Baxter stepped out into the almost deserted subway station. She wrapped herself up against the wind, stronger and colder than it had been back in the city, and headed for the beach.

The fairground was closed up for winter, the skeletal frames of the frozen rides surrounded by boarded-up booths and stalls, oversized padlocks on show.

To Baxter, the scene revealed the true emptiness beneath the surface, nothing more than an illusion of bright lights and loud music to distract from its insubstantial offerings. It was the same

principle that would have attracted hordes of people to Times
Square that morning, the world-famous tourist trap, where people
from all over the planet chose to stand and gawk up at illuminated versions of the advertisements that normally had to fight
so hard for attention.

Although she knew her anger was both unreasonable and mis-
placed, she felt sickened by these companies' attempts to shove
their various products down everyone's throats. There was just
something about the hollowness of dying in the glow of a Coca-
Cola sign that made it feel that much more wasteful.

She didn't want to think about it any longer. She didn't want
to think about anything, especially about Curtis, about how they
had abandoned her in that terrible place to die.

As much as she had blustered and protested at Rouche's cowardice, she knew that she had let him lead her away, that had her
heart truly been set on staying, nothing could have separated her
from her colleague's side. *That* was why she was so furious with
him: he knew. It had been a joint decision.

They had left her behind.

She continued along the boardwalk, past the funfair, nothing
but sea and snow stretching out in front of her . . . and just kept
walking.

The next morning, Baxter got up early and skipped breakfast to
avoid running into Rouche. It was a beautiful, crisp winter's day,
without a single cloud in the sky, so she picked up a takeaway
coffee and walked to Federal Plaza. After passing through security,
she took the lift up to the subdued office.

She was the first one into the meeting room and automatically
took the seat in the far back corner. After a moment she realized
why. She and Wolf had always claimed the back row as their own
during staff meetings and training sessions. The two troublemakers
messing around out of sight.

She smiled, then felt angry with herself for getting nostalgic:
the time that Finlay had unwisely nodded off during a political-

correctness session. Over the course of twenty minutes, she and Wolf had gradually pulled his chair around until he had been facing the back of the room. The look on his face when the trainer realized and started bellowing at him had been priceless. He had called Finlay a "lazy jock bastard," which had brought the session to an abrupt close.

Baxter had far too much on her mind to start thinking about such things. She got up and moved to the seat in front.

The room filled up at five minutes to nine, with an atmosphere of restless anger. Baxter made sure to avoid eye contact when Rouche came in and started looking for her. With no other chairs free, he was forced to take a seat in the generally avoided front row.

All her efforts to avoid dealing with the loss of her colleague had been in vain. Twenty seconds after entering the room, Lennox switched on the enormous touch-screen display and brought up a photograph of Curtis, smiling genuinely in full FBI dress uniform, her skin still absolutely flawless, even at that size.

Baxter felt as though she had been punched in the gut and looked around the room to keep her eyes busy, knowing that they would fill with tears if she didn't.

A caption at the bottom read:

Special Agent Elliot Curtis
1990–2015

Lennox lowered her head and stood silently for a moment. She cleared her throat:

"I guess God just needed another angel."

It took all of Baxter's self-restraint not to storm out of the room, but then, to her surprise, Rouche got to his feet and walked out.

A strained pause later, Lennox commenced the meeting. She announced that they would "regrettably" be losing Baxter that afternoon and went on to thank her for her "invaluable" contribution to the case. She then stressed that the work was only just beginning for the rest of them, that they would be liaising closely with Homeland Security and the NYPD Counterterrorism Bureau "going forward," before introducing the agent who would be assuming Curtis's role.

"We, as law-enforcement agencies, as a nation, allowed ourselves to be manipulated yesterday morning," Lennox told the room. "We will *not* make that mistake again. With the luxury of hindsight, it is all so obvious now: piggybacking off the fame of the Ragdoll case to spark initial media interest, the grotesque spectacle at Grand Central to ensure the whole world was talking about it, killing our own to provoke a disproportionate response . . . Bait."

An uncomfortable silence followed Lennox's summation. They had been warned all along that they were being goaded into something and not one of them had seen it coming.

"We threw everything we had at them." Lennox paused as she glanced down at her notes. "Between the church and Times Square we lost twenty-two of our own yesterday, including NYPD officers, an entire ESU team, and, of course, Special Agent Curtis. The total death toll thus far has reached one hundred and sixty souls. We're expecting that to increase significantly, however, as the cleanup operation continues and we lose more hospitalized victims to their injuries."

She glanced up at the photograph of Curtis:

"We owe it to each and every one of these people to hunt down and punish those responsible . . ."

"Oh, I'm gonna punish them all right," someone muttered.

". . . while honoring our colleagues by maintaining the very highest standards of professionalism that they would expect of us," Lennox added. "I'm sure you're all sick of listening to me by now, so I'm going to hand you over to Special Agent Chase."

Curtis's replacement got to his feet. Baxter had already decided to hate him out of principle but was pleased to discover that it was also completely justified. Chase was wearing half his body armor around the office for no other conceivable reason than he thought it looked cool.

"OK," started Chase, who was clearly sweating beneath the unnecessary layers. "We've managed to identify two of the vehicles involved in yesterday's attacks."

The photographs slowly filtered out across the room. One had captured a white van in an alleyway, the other a second white van parked in the middle of the pedestrianized area.

"As you can see, we've got two identical vehicles: fake plates, positioned strategically for maximum damage," said Chase.

"In an alleyway?" asked a female agent near the front.

"Human and structural," clarified Chase, tensing to support the piece of paper in his hand. "The van in the alleyway was positioned to bring down the billboards and New Year's ball. We were already on high alert. On *any* other day, these vehicles would have been flagged and intercepted before they got within ten blocks of Midtown. We dropped our guard for less than an hour and we paid the price for it."

"And the other two explosions?" someone asked.

"The final detonation was underground, in the subway but not on a train. We're assuming in a rucksack or similar, but that one's gonna take a while to trace. The one in the church looks like it was triggered by the doors. Our best guess—the hollow wooden mannequins reported were packed with C-4. They detonated the moment our boys breached."

Chase held up a recent photograph of the long-haired British psychiatrist:

"Our primary suspect, Dr. Alexei Green, appears to have dropped off the face of the earth. He thinks he can hide from us. He's wrong. He believes he's smarter than us. Also wrong. None of us rest until we have this bastard in handcuffs. Now, let's get to work."

Baxter settled into her window seat on the plane. It had taken her almost an hour and a half to negotiate the enhanced security checks that had been implemented the previous afternoon. She had been summoned to Lennox's office following the meeting for an insincere farewell and had waited for an opportune moment to escape without having to see Rouche again. It had been rude to leave without saying goodbye, but she didn't trust him. She found him irritatingly eccentric at times, downright weird at others, and now his face served only as a reminder of the worst experience of her life, horrific and shameful in equal measure.

She was glad to be rid of him.

After spending the evening roaming the city streets aimlessly, she was exhausted. She had walked miles. When she had finally returned to the hotel, the thoughts she had been trying to outrun had caught up and prevented her from getting a moment's rest.

She removed the cheap plastic earphones from the pocket in front of her, found a radio station to fall asleep to, and closed her eyes.

The gentle hum of the engines faded in, accompanied by the soothing sound of warm air blowing into the cozily lit cabin. Baxter pulled the blanket up around her and shifted position to get comfortable again when she realized that she had not fallen asleep with a blanket.

Instantly wide-awake, she opened her eyes to find a familiar face inches from her own, openmouthed and snoring quietly:

"Rouche!" she exclaimed, waking at least seven people in the vicinity.

Rouche looked around in bewilderment for a moment: "What?"

"Shhhhh!" someone hissed behind them.

"What's wrong?" Rouche whispered in concern.

"What's wrong?" replied Baxter, still rather loudly. "What are you doing here?"

"Where?"

"On the . . . Here! On the plane!"

"Madam, I'm going to have to ask that you keep your voice down," said a waspish flight attendant from the aisle. "You're disturbing your fellow passengers."

Baxter just stared at her until she tottered off again.

"Working off the educated assumption that yesterday's events constituted the conclusion of the US attacks, we have to prepare ourselves for the possibility of a similarly sized attack in the UK," Rouche whispered almost inaudibly. "Alexei Green is our best lead, and he was last seen in London shortly after Cur—" He stopped himself from saying her name. "Shortly after we were at the prison."

"Curtis," spat Baxter. "You *should* say her name. It's gonna haunt us both for the rest of our lives either way. We had guns. We should've tried. We just left her there to die!"

"We couldn't have saved her."

"You don't know that!"

"Yes, I do!" Rouche snapped in a rare moment of anger. He waved apologetically at some miserable old woman across the aisle and lowered his voice: "I do."

They sat in silence for a moment.

"She wouldn't have wanted you to die for her," Rouche continued softly. "And she knows you didn't want to leave her."

"She was unconscious," Baxter bit back.

"I mean now. She knows. She'll be looking down on us and—"

"Oh, will you shut the *fuck* up!"

"You shut up," someone in front mumbled.

"Don't you *dare* start spouting your religious shit at me. I'm not some idiot child whose hamster just died, so keep your sky-fairy bullshit to yourself, OK?"

"OK. I apologize," said Rouche, holding his hands up in a gesture of surrender.

Baxter wasn't done, however.

"I'm not gonna sit here listening to you console yourself with some fantasy that Curtis is up in some wonderful place right now thanking us for letting her bleed out onto a dirty floor. She's dead! Gone! She felt pain and then nothingness. End of story."

"I'm sorry for bringing it up," said Rouche, shaken by the venom of Baxter's tirade.

"You're supposed to be intelligent, Rouche. Our entire careers are built on collecting evidence, on solid facts, yet you're happy to believe that there's some old bastard sat up on a cloud somewhere waiting for us all like some geriatric Care Bear. I . . . I just don't get it."

"Could you just stop? *Please*," said Rouche.

"She's gone, all right?" said Baxter, only now realizing that she was crying. "A cold slab of meat in a freezer drawer somewhere because of us. And if I've got to live with that for the rest of my life, you're damn well going to live with it too."

She put her earphones in and turned to face the window, still breathing heavily after her outburst. All she could see was her own reflection in the dark glass as her furious expression gradually relaxed into something resembling guilt.

Too stubborn to apologize, she closed her eyes until she eventually drifted back off to sleep.

Once back at Heathrow Airport, Rouche had been as amiable and pleasant as always, which only made Baxter feel worse. She had ignored all of his attempts to engage with her and had pushed past to disembark before him. Her suitcase had been one of the first to come off the plane. She snatched it off the baggage carousel and wheeled it outside to wait for Thomas.

Ten minutes later, she heard a case rolling up behind her, so focused intently on the pickup point until she heard it roll away again. Out of the corner of her eye, she watched Rouche heading toward the taxi rank. Looking down at her bags, she was surprised to find her garish hat and gloves now sat on top of it. She shook her head:

"I am a horrible, horrible person," she whispered.

CHAPTER 23

Thursday, 17 December 2015

9:34 A.M.

"Morning, boss!"

"Morning."

"Welcome back, Chief."

"Thank you."

"Bollocks. She's back."

Five minutes after arriving at New Scotland Yard, Baxter had to fight her way through an onslaught of mostly friendly greetings in order to reach the sanctuary of her office.

Thomas had driven her back to his house that morning, where she had treated herself to a quick shower and a change of clothes. They had enjoyed a breakfast together while Echo sulked in the corner, incredulous that Baxter would leave him in a strange place for almost an entire week. But for the first time ever, arriving at Thomas's house had felt like coming home . . . Thomas had felt like home.

Not entirely clear what time or even what day it was anymore, Baxter had headed into work.

Quickly closing the door to her office, she shut her eyes and exhaled deeply, leaning against the flimsy wood in case anybody else attempted to wish her a good morning.

"Good morning."

She slowly opened her eyes to find Rouche sitting behind her desk. He looked irritatingly wide-awake and full of life.

There was a knock at the door.

"Yes!" called Baxter. "Oh, hi, Jim."

An older, mustached man entered and took an inquiring look in Rouche's direction:

"Morning. I was just here for our *interview*," he said carefully.

"It's fine," she assured him, turning to Rouche:

"Jim's the man in charge of the 'search' for Detective Fawkes," she explained.

"So," said Jim, not even bothering to take a seat, "seen Wolf?"

"Nope."

"Great. See you next week, then," he told her, closing the door behind him.

Baxter braced herself for the next visitor, but none came.

"I'm in your seat," said Rouche, getting up to relocate onto one of the cheap plastic chairs. "I've scheduled a meeting with the T-Branch section chief at Thames House. Half ten. I hope that's all right? Then we're back here with SO15 at twelve."

"Fine."

"I thought we'd go together," he added carefully.

"Did you?" sighed Baxter. "Fine, but I'm driving."

"Keep breathing. Keep breathing. Keep breathing . . ."

The breathalyzer beeped twice before the youthful officer removed it from Baxter's mouth. His colleague was lying facedown on the pavement, fishing what was left of the road bike out from beneath the Audi. The Lycra-clad cyclist was being checked over by a paramedic, despite only suffering a few minor grazes. Rouche, meanwhile, was sat quietly on the curb looking visibly shaken.

"So are we done here?" Baxter called to everybody involved.

After a noncommittal response, she removed a business card from her pocket and handed it to the seething cyclist as she passed. Rouche got up unenthusiastically and they climbed back into the car. A few additional bits of carbon fiber clattered across the concrete as they reversed off the pavement and continued on their short journey to Millbank.

"Stick those in the glovebox, will you?" said Baxter, handing him a stack of the Metropolitan Police business cards that she had given to the cyclist.

Rouche took them off her but then paused:

"You realize these have Vanita's name on them, don't you?" he asked.

Baxter frowned at him as though he were being thick.

Rouche was still staring at her, waiting for an explanation.

"I seriously can't have any more insurance claims against me," she told him. "I was on my final warning from Transport about eleven accidents ago. I'll get some Finlay Shaw cards made up when I get a chance . . . 'Finlay' could be a girl's name, right?"

"Absolutely not," said Rouche.

"Well, *I* think it could. And it's fine!" Baxter assured him. "He's retired. He won't mind."

Rouche still looked uncertain.

After a few minutes of quiet, in which they moved approximately five feet through the gridlocked traffic, Rouche attempted to spark a conversation:

"Boyfriend must be glad to have you back," he said casually.

"I guess." Baxter yielded to social etiquette by reciprocating the comment, which she reeled off with the emotion of a robot: "It must be nice for your family to have you around a bit more."

Rouche sighed: "They'd already left for work and school by the time my taxi driver had finished showing me the sights of London."

"Shame. We'll try to finish at a decent time tonight so you can get back to see them."

"I'd like that." He smiled. "I was thinking about what you said about Curtis and—"

"I don't want to talk about it!" Baxter shouted over him, all the raw emotion from the previous day returning in an instant.

The silence swelled.

"Well, don't *not* talk either!" said Baxter angrily. "Can we just talk about something else?"

"Like what?"

"Like anything. I don't know. Tell me about your daughter or something."

"You like kids?" Rouche asked.

"No."

"Of course not. Well, she's got bright red hair like her mum. She likes singing, although God help you if you find yourself within earshot when she does."

Baxter smiled. Wolf had often said the same about her. After arresting a drug dealer who had pulled a knife on him, he had asked her to serenade their prisoner while he went to find them some lunch.

She pulled the car up to block a busy junction.

"She loves swimming and dancing and watching *The X Factor* on Saturday nights," Rouche continued. "And all she wants for her birthday is Barbie, Barbie . . . and more Barbie."

"At sixteen?"

"Sixteen?"

"Yeah. Your friend, that FBI agent, said she was the same age as his daughter: sixteen."

Rouche looked lost for a moment and then laughed:

"Wow. Nothing gets past you, does it? McFarlen is *not* my friend. I thought it would be easier to go along with it rather than tell him he'd got it all completely wrong. She's six . . . Close, though." He smiled.

Finally, Baxter rolled them off the junction and onto a pedestrian crossing.

"What's her name?"

Rouche hesitated for a moment before answering: "Ellie . . . Well, Elliot. Her name's Elliot."

Chief of Section Wyld leaned back in his chair and shared a look with his colleague. Baxter had been talking for ten minutes straight, while Rouche nodded along silently.

Wyld appeared surprisingly young to hold such a prominent position in the security services and radiated an indissoluble confidence.

"Chief Inspector," he interrupted when she showed no sign of slowing down. "We appreciate your concerns . . ."

"But . . ."

". . . and you coming to us with this, but we are already well aware of your investigation and have a team working through the intel sent over by the FBI in relation to this."

"But I—"

"What you have to understand," he said forcefully over her, "is that the US and New York City, in particular, were already at a 'Critical' threat level, meaning that an attack was imminent."

"I know what it means," said Baxter childishly.

"Good. Then you'll understand when I say that the UK has been maintaining a somewhat discomforting but reassuringly consistent status of 'Severe' for the past fifteen months."

"So put it up!"

"It's not quite as easy as just pushing a button, I'm afraid." Wyld laughed patronizingly. "Do you have *any* idea what it costs the country every time we ascend a terror alert? Billions: the visible armed presence on the streets, mobilizing the military, people not going to work, a halt in investment from overseas, stock prices plummeting. The list goes on and on . . .

"To declare ourselves 'Critical' is to admit to the rest of the world that we're about to take a big hit and there's not a damned thing we can do to stop it."

"So it's about money?" said Baxter.

"In part," Wyld admitted. "But it's more about us being absolutely one hundred percent positive that an attack is coming, and we're not. Since settling at 'Severe,' we have prevented seven serious terror attacks that the public know about and many, many more that they don't. My point, Chief Inspector, is that if there *was* going to be an incident related to the Azazel murders . . ."

"They're not called that."

". . . we would have heard something about it by now."

Baxter shook her head and laughed bitterly.

Rouche recognized the look and quickly stepped in before she could say something irreparable to the MI5 officers:

"You can't be suggesting that Times Square being leveled less than ten minutes after the massacre at the church was just a coincidence?"

"Of course I'm not," snapped Wyld. "But have *you* considered that the attack may have been opportunistic in nature? That this imminent terror attack was brought forward to take advantage of the NYPD's major incident?"

Both Baxter and Rouche remained quiet.

"The FBI have already ascertained that the crude materials used at the church bore no resemblance whatsoever to the devices detonated down the road. And this whole 'UK mirroring the US' theory: we've only had two murders here, both as widely reported across the Atlantic as they were domestically. Even *you* have to admit the very real possibility that the Times Square church massacre was their endgame all along."

Baxter got up to leave. Rouche followed accordingly.

"Have you had a message yet?" she asked on her way out of the door. "Has anybody claimed responsibility for all that devastation and death?"

Wyld looked to his colleague in exasperation: "No. No, they haven't."

"Know why?" she asked, now out in the corridor. "Because it's not over yet."

"Dickheads!" hissed Baxter the moment they stepped out onto Millbank, the grand arched entranceway to Thames House looming above as a cold wind blew across the river.

Rouche wasn't listening. He was busy reading through the emails on his phone.

"They've found one of the killers from the church still alive!"

"Really? How?"

"Buried beneath a load of debris in one of the backstage corridors apparently, away from the worst of the blast. He's comatose, but Lennox is insisting they wake him up against the doctor's orders."

"Good for her," said Baxter. She didn't like the special agent in charge but knew that Vanita would never make such a brave decision. It was the detectives' job to make these difficult choices and hers to sacrifice them when they did.

"They say he'll more than likely suffer lasting brain damage as a result of being brought round early."

"Even better."

"If he does, it won't end well for Lennox. They'll want their pound of flesh."

"Yeah." Baxter shrugged. "A common side effect of doing the right thing, unfortunately."

At 8:38 P.M., Edmunds stumbled through his front door and was confronted by the smells of talcum powder, fresh poo, and toast, and the sound of Leila screaming as loudly as her little lungs could manage.

"Alex? Is that you?" Tia called from the bedroom.

Edmunds glanced into the kitchen as he passed, which looked like it had been ransacked. He climbed the stairs to find Tia cradling their daughter. She looked absolutely exhausted.

"Where have you been?"

"Pub."

"The pub?"

He nodded innocently.

"Are you drunk?"

Edmunds shrugged sheepishly. He'd intended to have only the one drink, but Baxter had an awful lot of awful news to catch him up on. Now that he thought about it, keeping up with her always tended to leave him feeling dodgy the following day.

"I told you this morning," he said, picking things up off the floor as he walked across the room.

"No," Tia corrected him. "You just said Emily was coming back today. Or am I supposed to deduce that once *she's* back in the country, of course you'll run straight out to go drinking with her?"

"We've got a case!" blurted Edmunds.

"No . . . you . . . don't! *She* has a case! *You* work in Fraud!"

"She needs me."

"You know what? This weird, little relationship you two have . . . it's fine. If you want to run around after her like some pathetic lapdog, you just go right ahead."

"Where's all this coming from? You love Baxter! You're friends!"

"Oh, *please*!" scoffed Tia. "The woman is a train wreck. She's rude to the point of being farcical. She's more opinionated than anybody I've ever met, and she's as stubborn as a mule."

Edmunds went to argue, then realized he did not really have a retort for any of those perfectly valid points. He suspected that Tia had been practicing this Baxter-slamming tirade.

Leila started crying even louder at her mother's raised voice.

"And have you seen how many wines she can put away in a night? Jesus!"

Edmunds's stomach grumbled in agreement. Another valid point.

"If you like domineering women so much, how about this: go drink a pint of water, eat some toast, and sober up," yelled Tia. "You're taking care of Leila tonight. I'm sleeping on the sofa!"

"Fine!"

"Fine!"

She threw a teddy bear at him on his way out. He picked it up and took it downstairs with him, remembering how awkward Baxter had been when she'd handed it to him on Leila's first birthday. It made him sad to think of how difficult she found even the simplest interactions with people.

He loved Tia more than anything and could understand her point of view, but she could not imagine the things that his best friend had been through, the devastating horrors and loss she'd suffered in the past week alone. He was going to do anything and everything in his power to help her through this.

She needed him.

INITIATION

Tuesday, 24 November 2015

9:13 P.M.

She knew it was her turn.

She could feel their eyes on her, and still she didn't move.

A fleeting glance behind her confirmed what she had already known: that the only way out might as well have been on the other side of the world.

She couldn't make it.

"Sasha?" a voice said softly in her ear.

Alexei was standing beside her. She needed to remind herself to address him formally in front of the others. He didn't let just anybody call him by his first name, but he had told her that she was special.

"Why don't you come with me?" he said kindly, holding his hand out to her. "Come on."

They walked between the others. For those on Sasha's left, the ordeal was already over, but the anxious wait for those on her right had been drawn out a little longer by her cowardice.

Green led her to the front of the room, to where a red smear had been dragged across the polished floor, one of her "brothers" having lost consciousness halfway through. A man she didn't recognize regarded her emotionlessly, a bloody blade waiting in his hands. He wouldn't clean it, not before disfiguring her—that was the point. They were one now, equal, connected.

"Ready?" asked Green.

Sasha nodded, taking short, rapid breaths.

He moved behind her to unbutton her blouse and slide it off her shoulders.

But as the stranger brought the blade toward her, she flinched, stumbling backward into Green.

"I'm sorry . . . I'm sorry," she apologized. "I'm OK." She stepped back up to the dead-eyed man, closed her eyes, and nodded.

He raised the knife once more . . . She felt the cold metal push against her skin.

"I'm sorry. I'm sorry. I'm sorry," she said, beginning to cry as she moved away. "I can't."

While she sobbed in front of her audience, Green embraced her tightly: "Shhhh . . . Shhhh," he soothed her.

"I'll do whatever you want me to, I swear," Sasha told him. "This means *everything* to me. I just . . . can't."

"But, Sasha, you *do* understand why I'm asking you to do this for me?" asked Green.

A violent branding couldn't have been as painful as the look of betrayal he shot her.

"Yes."

"Tell me . . . In fact, even better, tell us all," said Green, releasing her.

She cleared her throat:

"It shows you that we would do anything for you, that we are yours, and that we will follow you anywhere, do what you say without question." She looked again at the curved blade and started to weep.

"Good. But you know you don't have to do anything you don't want to," Green assured her. "Are you positive you can't do this?"

She shook her head.

"Very well . . . Eduardo!" Green called. A man stepped out into the gauntlet of his peers. He pulled at his fresh bandages uncomfortably. "You and Sasha are friends?"

"Yes, Ale— Sorry. I mean Dr. Green."

"I think she could use you right now."

"Thank you," Sasha whispered as Eduardo approached them, putting his arm around her.

Green squeezed her hand affectionately, then let go.

They had made it halfway back down the room before he addressed them again:

"Eduardo," Green called, stopping them where the entire audience could see. "I'm afraid Sasha has decided that she isn't one of us . . . Kill her."

Stunned, Eduardo turned back to say something, but Green was already walking away, disinterested, his sentence passed. He turned to face Sasha, unsure what to do.

"Eddie?" she gasped, watching the look on her friend's face change. She couldn't even see the exit now through the wall of onlookers. "Ed!"

His eyes filled with tears, and then he struck her with a disorientating fist to the face.

Grasping out as she fell, his bandages tore away in her hands.

All she could focus on, as he kneeled down over her, was the word etched into his chest. And in her final moments, that brought her some solace, because it wasn't her friend driving her skull into the room's hard floor . . . He was already gone.

CHAPTER 24

Thursday, 17 December 2015

3:36 P.M.

The glass walls muffled the shouts from outside as Lennox and Chase marched across the entrance hall of Montefiore Medical Center. Someone, almost certainly the comatose man's reluctant doctor, had informed the media of the situation developing inside and they had turned out in force. Behind the cameras, picket boards bobbed in and out of sight: campaigners protesting against the FBI's decision to prematurely wake a man with a life-threatening brain injury.

"Christ! These people's memories are short," muttered Lennox as they followed signs toward the intensive-care unit.

Chase had not heard. He was keeping pace with his superior while deflecting phone calls on her behalf. He made an irritating creaking sound with every step as his various pieces of body armor rubbed against one another:

"Yes, I understand that, sir . . . Yes, sir . . . And as I said before, she's not currently available."

A middle-aged man in a long brown coat seemed overly interested in them as he approached from the other direction. Lennox was about to alert Chase when the man pulled a camera and audio recorder out from his pockets:

"Agent Lennox, do you believe the FBI is above the law?" he asked accusingly as Chase shoved him up against the wall. Lennox continued down the corridor without pausing. "Judge, jury, and executioner—is that how it works now?"

As Chase restrained the struggling man, he continued to shout after her:

"The family have *not* given their consent!"

Lennox maintained her confident demeanor as she passed between the two police officers on the door and entered the ICU. Inside, the atmosphere was even more tense. A defibrillator sat ominously on a cart in the corner. Three nurses fussed over wires and tubes while the doctor prepared a syringe. Not one of them acknowledged her as she regarded the man in the bed.

He was as scrawny as a schoolboy, despite being in his twenties. Severe burns covered most of his right-hand side. Even the four-letter lie cut into his chest had spilled over onto his flank: a Puppet masquerading as Bait, a killer masquerading as a victim. A sturdy neck brace held his head in place, while a thin, bloody tube protruded from the tiny hole that had been drilled through his skull.

"I just want to reiterate how strongly I advise against this," said the doctor, without taking his eyes off the syringe in his hands. "I am one hundred percent against performing this procedure."

"Noted," said Lennox as Chase entered the room. She was glad to have at least one person on her side.

"The risks involved in inducing consciousness with a brain injury like this are immense, exacerbated exponentially when considering his previous mental health history."

"Noted!" repeated Lennox more forcefully. "Shall we?"

The doctor shook his head and stood over his patient. He plugged the first of the syringes into a port, an access point into the closed system of intravenous tubes and medications flowing into the bedridden man. Very, very slowly, he depressed the plunger, clouding the clear fluid already inside.

"Crash cart ready," the doctor instructed the room. "We need to keep intracranial pressure as low as possible. Constant monitoring of pulse and blood pressure. Here we go."

Lennox watched the motionless body, refusing to show even a glimpse of her inner turmoil. Whatever happened, her career at the Bureau was more than likely over. She had created a nationwide PR incident, ignored direct orders from above, and lied to the doctors to procure their compliance. She just hoped that it would prove to be worth the sacrifice, that this sole surviving enemy might just give them something that they had been missing the entire time.

The man gasped. His eyes sprang open and he attempted to sit up, the tubes and wires keeping him alive pulling him back down.

"OK. OK. Andre? Andre, I need you to stay calm for me," the doctor said soothingly, resting a hand on his shoulder.

"Blood pressure's 152 over 93," one of the nurses called out.

"I'm Dr. Lawson, and you are in Montefiore Medical Center."

The man looked around the room. His eyes grew wide with fear as he regarded horrors that nobody else could see.

"Heart rate ninety-two and still climbing. BP's too high," said the nurse anxiously.

"Don't die. Don't die," Lennox whispered to herself as the man started thrashing around.

Dr. Lawson reached for a second syringe and twisted it into another port. Within seconds his patient stopped fighting and became drowsy to the point of sleep.

"BP's dropping."

"Andre, I've got someone here who needs to ask you a few questions. Would that be all right?" asked the doctor, sealing the deal with a kind smile.

The man nodded groggily. Dr. Lawson stepped aside to allow Lennox through.

"Hello, Andre." Lennox smiled, setting the tone for the friendliest interrogation in history.

"Try to keep it simple. Short, direct questions," warned the doctor as he moved back to monitor his patient's vital signs.

"Understood." She turned back to the man in the bed. "Andre, do you recognize this person?"

She held up a photograph of Alexei Green, looking every bit the wannabe rock star with his beautifully kept chin-length hair. Andre struggled to focus on the picture. Eventually, he nodded.

"Have you ever met him?"

On the edge of sleep, Andre nodded again: "We . . . all . . . must," he slurred.

"When? Where was this?" asked Lennox.

Andre shook his head as if he couldn't remember. In the background, the steady beeps were building momentum. Lennox looked back at Dr. Lawson, who made a gesture that she interpreted as "move on." Reluctantly, she obeyed. She stared down at the letters sliced into the man's chest, "Bait," cut halfway through his emaciated body:

"Who did this to your chest?" she asked.

"'Nother."

"Another? Another what? Another . . . Puppet?" She almost whispered the last word.

Andre nodded. He huffed and panted as he struggled to form his words:

"All of us . . . to-gether."

"What do you mean, 'together'?"

He did not respond.

"When you were at the church?" she asked.

Andre shook his head.

"You were all together somewhere before the church?"

He nodded.

"And *this* man was there?" She held up the photograph of Green once more.

"Yes."

Lennox turned to the doctor excitedly:

"How old would you say these scars are?" she asked.

He got up and examined the wounds, causing Andre to flinch when he prodded a tender section just below the armpit.

"Rough guess, based on scabbing, inflammation, and infection: two, maybe three weeks."

"That coincides with Green's last visit to the US," confirmed Chase from the back of the room.

Lennox turned back to the patient:

"Did you know the church was going to blow up?"

Andre nodded shamefully.

"Did you know about the other bombs?"

He stared up at her blankly.

"OK," said Lennox, taking her answer from his expression. "Andre, I need to know how that meeting was arranged. How did you know where to go?"

Lennox was holding her breath. If they could just work out how these people were communicating with one another, they could intercept the messages before anybody else had to die. She watched the exhausted man struggling to remember. He brought his hand up to his ear.

"Over the phone?" she asked skeptically. Her team had thoroughly scrutinized the previous killers' phone records, messages, apps, and data.

Andre shook his head in frustration. He raised a hand to the electronic display above his bed.

"A computer?"

He tapped his ear.

"Your phone screen?" asked Lennox. "Some sort of messages on your phone?"

Andre nodded.

Confused, Lennox turned to Chase. He acknowledged the unspoken order to share this important information immediately and left the room. Lennox could tell she wasn't going to get much more out of the man but would question him until the doctor stopped her:

"Did these *messages* say anything else? Were there any instructions for after the church?"

Andre started whimpering.

"Andre?"

"Heart rate increasing again," called the nurse.

"What did they say, Andre?"

"Blood pressure's rising!"

"That's it. I'm sedating him," snapped Dr. Lawson, stepping forward.

"Wait!" yelled Lennox. "What did they tell you to do?"

He was whispering something under his breath, searching the room again for his invisible tormentors. Lennox leaned in closer to hear what he was saying.

". . . one . . . every . . . ill . . . ryone . . . ill everyone . . . Kill everyone . . ."

Lennox felt her firearm slide out of its holster: "Gun!" she shouted.

She grabbed the weapon in the man's hands as a round fired into the wall. The monitoring equipment was flashing and beeping frantically as the struggle continued. Dr. Lawson and the nurses were all crawling across the floor. Another shot shattered the light overhead, showering the bed in broken glass. Chase rushed back into the room and threw himself on top of the bedbound gunman, a second pair of hands easily overpowering the weakened man.

"Knock him out!" Chase ordered the doctor, who scrambled to his feet and reached for one of the syringes.

As they kept the gun pointed safely at the exterior wall, consciousness drained from his patient bit by bit until the weapon dropped out of his limp hand.

Lennox holstered the gun and smiled at her colleague in relief: "Last twenty seconds aside, I think that went pretty well!"

Baxter turned off the obnoxious breakfast radio show and watched the entrance to Hammersmith Station, the hail exploding into icy patterns as it struck her windscreen.

After a few minutes, Rouche emerged from the station with his phone pressed to his ear as usual. He waved in the direction of Baxter's black Audi and then hovered in the doorway while he finished his call.

"Are you kidding me?" Baxter muttered to herself.

She honked her horn angrily and revved the engine until Rouche jogged through the downpour to climb into the passenger seat. Empty Tesco sandwich boxes and half-drunk bottles of Lucozade crunched under his feet.

"Morning. Thanks for this," he said as she pulled onto Fulham Palace Road.

Baxter didn't reply, switching the radio back on, only to find the show more annoying than ever. She soon turned it off again and resigned herself to making conversation:

"How's coma-bastard doing?"

The entire team had been made aware of the FBI's progress overnight.

"Still alive," said Rouche.

"That's good . . . I guess. Should mean we can hold on to Lennox for a bit longer."

Rouche looked at her in surprise.

"What? She's the first manager I've ever met who actually did something I would do," said Baxter defensively. She decided to change the subject: "So, they forgot to check the killers' text messages, then?"

The rain outside was intensifying.

"I believe it's a little more complicated than that," replied Rouche.

"Uh-huh."

"They're going to try decrypting the . . . fragmented . . . errrm . . . data store . . . the Internet," explained Rouche, explaining nothing. "Anyone searched Green's place again since?"

"Where do you think *we're* going?" said Baxter.

They continued along the high street. Rouche stared out at the illuminated shops longingly:

"Hungry?" he asked.

"No."

"I skipped breakfast."

"Sucks to be you." Baxter huffed and pulled over.

"You're the best. Want anything?" asked Rouche, already climbing out into the rain.

"No."

He slammed the door behind him and dodged the traffic to enter the bakery across the road, his mobile phone lying forgotten on the passenger seat. Baxter looked down at it for a moment and then focused her attention back on the bakery; however, her gaze slowly returned to the passenger seat. She rapped her fingers anxiously against the steering wheel.

"Screw it!"

She snatched the phone off the leather. The screen was locked—she swiped her finger across it—but not password-protected. She clicked on an icon and started scrolling through the call log.

"Who the *hell* are you calling all the time?"

A list of outgoing calls flashed up, the same number reappearing time and time again: a London area code, almost every hour throughout the previous afternoon and evening.

A moment's indecision.

She glanced back at the bakery, heart racing, pressed the "call" button, and held the phone up to her ear.

It started to ring.

"Come on. Come on. Come on."

Someone answered: "Hello, my lov—"

The car door opened.

Baxter hung up and tossed the phone back onto the passenger seat as Rouche sat down. He was soaked through, his graying hair darker, making him look younger. He shifted his weight and pulled the phone out from under him before dropping it into his lap.

"I got you a breakfast bap," he said, offering it to Baxter. "Just in case."

It did smell delicious. She snatched it off him and quickly pulled into a gap in the traffic.

As Rouche unwrapped his bacon-and-egg roll, he noticed that his phone was glowing against his trousers. His eyes flicked across to Baxter, who was focusing intently on the flooded road. He watched her carefully for a few moments and then swiped his finger across the screen to lock it once more.

CHAPTER 25

Friday, 18 December 2015

8:41 A.M.

"Would you just calm down for a moment!" hissed Edmunds as he rushed out of the Fraud office and loitered in the corridor with his phone pressed to his ear. He had managed to steal an impressive three hours of sleep, more than Tia tended to average, but the recent run of sleepless nights had his weary body demanding payback.

When his boss suddenly stepped out of the lift a little farther along the corridor, Edmunds backed into the disabled toilet and lowered his voice to a whisper:

"I'm sure there's a perfectly reasonable explanation."

"For lying to me time and time again ever since I joined this case?" whispered Baxter.

She was standing in the massive master bedroom of Alexei Green's rented penthouse apartment in Knightsbridge. The floor was littered with expensive clothes, while the wardrobe and drawers stood empty. The mattress had been eviscerated, spilling springs and stuffing across the rug beside the window, which looked out over the Harrods building to the southeast. The television had been removed from the wall, its rear panel separated from the screen.

The search team had done a thorough job.

Baxter could hear Rouche rooting through the mess in another room.

"Think about it—I *literally* watched them find something in front of me at the 33rd Precinct and he denied it. The toxicology report that Curtis . . ." She paused. "I found it screwed up in his jacket pocket, and now he's lying about where he was last night."

"How do you know?"

"Why would he be phoning home every hour through the night if he was already there?"

"Maybe you should have asked his wife when you spoke to her," suggested Edmunds unhelpfully.

"I didn't have time," hissed Baxter. "So considering this, the whole weird situation with his family, and the fact that he doesn't even seem to know how old his daughter is—one minute she's sixteen, the next she's six—I just think . . . something's not right."

"When you put it like that . . ." said Edmunds. He paused. "But being a crappy father isn't illegal. What does his personal life have to do with our case?"

"I don't know! Everything . . . Nothing."

She went quiet when Rouche emerged from the second bedroom and entered the hallway. He yawned widely and stretched his arms, revealing his pasty abdomen. He waved cheerfully and then moved into the kitchen.

"I've got to get in there," Baxter whispered.

"Where?" asked Edmunds. "You mean his house?"

"Tonight. I've already offered to drop him home. I'll ask to use the bathroom or something. If that fails, I'll just have to force my way in."

"You can't!"

"I don't see another way. I can't trust him, and I need to know what it is he's hiding from me."

"I don't want you doing this alone," said Edmunds.

"So you admit there's something suspicious about all this?"

"No. But . . . just . . . I'll meet you there, all right? Let me know what time."

"Fine."

Baxter hung up the phone.

"Pretty girl," said Rouche, standing in the doorway, making Baxter jump guiltily.

He was holding up a canvas print of Alexei Green and a beautiful woman. They looked happier than any couple she had ever seen, effortlessly upstaging the incredible scenery behind them, which was shamelessly pulling out all the stops, the sun setting over a tranquil fjord.

"We need to identify her," said Baxter as she barged past him. "I'm done in here anyway."

"This is a waste of time," said Rouche, placing the canvas back onto the pile of mess in the spare room as he followed her down the corridor. "The Met have already been through every inch of this place."

"'Cause I didn't know that."

"I'm just saying."

"Whatever," Baxter replied as she stepped into the beautifully appointed kitchen. The granite work surface sparkled under the spotlights, the gray city stretching out into the distance beyond the balcony that choked the building's upper levels. "Know what else isn't here? A single reason why Alexei Green would want to blow up half of New York. Why risk it all when he had so much to—" She stopped when she noticed him staring at her. "What?" She started to feel uncomfortable when he failed to look away. "What, Rouche?"

"Top floor, right?"

"Yeah."

He rushed toward her. Baxter instinctively clenched her fist, but then relaxed when he stepped around her and pulled open the balcony door. A cold wind snaked through the spacious apartment, animating the discarded paperwork and photographs. She followed him out into the rain.

"Bump me," said Rouche.

"I beg your pardon?" Baxter had a dangerous edge to her voice.

"Bump me up," said Rouche. "Onto the roof."

"Oh!" Baxter sighed in relief. "Yeah . . . No."

Undeterred, Rouche climbed up onto the wet railings.

"Jesus, Rouche!"

He reached up and grabbed the edge of the flat roof before unsuccessfully attempting to pull himself up. Avoiding his floundering legs, Baxter gave him an undignified shove in the right direction until he finally scrambled up and disappeared out of sight.

Her phone went off:

"Baxter," she answered. "Uh-huh . . . Yep . . . Fine." She ended the call. "Rouche!" she shouted up, the freezing rain stinging her face.

His head popped over the ledge.

"Anything up there?" she asked.

"Roof," he answered, a little embarrassed.

"Tech team's got something for us." She politely pretended not to notice when he split the crotch of his trousers clambering back down. "Shall we?"

"OK. So this is pretty exciting," said Techie Steve, bustling around the various wires that linked laptops to flashing boxes to other flashing boxes to mobile phones. "I've taken a second pass at our Mall killer's phone."

"Which wouldn't have been necessary if *someone* had done their job properly in the first place," said Baxter accusingly.

"Well, let's not start pointing fingers." Steve smiled awkwardly, as Baxter was literally pointing at him. "Anyway, I found something. That"—he gestured to the expensive new phone on the table—"is Patrick Peter Fergus's."

He typed something on his laptop.

There was a cheery ping.

"I think you've got a text," he prompted Baxter excitedly.

Rolling her eyes, she picked up the mobile phone and clicked on the familiar messaging icon:

"'Hi, boss. Winky face,'" she read aloud.

"Wait for it," Steve told her, barely able to contain himself as he counted down the seconds on his watch. "OK. Why don't you read it to me again?"

Baxter groaned. Losing patience, she glanced back down at the screen to find that the short message had vanished. Confused, she clicked back to the list of previous texts from Fergus's assorted contacts:

"It's gone!"

"Self-deleting one-read-only messages," Steve told her proudly. "Or 'suicide texts,' as I've just coined them. That phone has been installed with a clone messaging app. It looks like the standard one. It even *acts* like the standard one 99.9 percent of the time. That is, until it receives a text from a particular set of numbers, in which case *that* happens and the content becomes unrecoverable."

Baxter turned to Rouche, who looked to be struggling to keep up with the conversation:

"What do you think?" she asked him, while Steve fiddled with his equipment, a huge grin on his face.

"I think . . . this guy might *actually* wet himself if we ask him to send another one," he whispered, making Baxter snigger.

"Just so I'm up to speed," said Rouche, looking over the equipment, "we're *now* saying that Patrick Peter Fergus was a sixty-one-year-old tech genius Santa Claus?"

"Definitely not," Steve told him. "This is some proper clever stuff. *This* was done at manufacturing level."

"Where?"

"I'm working with the Americans on that right now as they have far more recovered devices to work with than I do."

"You said we had something to work with *now*," Baxter reminded him.

"We do." He smiled. "The server at S-S Mobile's headquarters in California, where all of these suicide texts originated from, each and every one sent out by a different number. We might not be able to recover the data from the devices but there *will* be a record of them at source. The FBI should be sharing the files with us within the hour."

Baxter looked almost happy, or at least a little less miserable than usual.

Steve typed another short message and hit the "return" key with satisfaction.

The phone pinged in Baxter's hand:

You're welcome ;-)

The printer in the main office continued to swallow page after page, churning out hour after hour of work for Baxter and her team to wade through.

The capital's underbelly had excelled itself during an abnormally busy night, limiting the resources available to sort through the mountain of messages the FBI had retrieved from the S-S Mobile server. Baxter had been able to assemble a team of only six, most drafted in on their day off.

She removed the lid from her highlighter:

They don't understand you, Aiden, not like we do.
Know that you are not alone.

"What *is* this shit?" she whispered, placing the page onto a separate pile.

After four hours, the general consensus was that these bizarre snippets of pontification, provocation, and instruction wouldn't have been enough to coerce even the most susceptible of minds alone. Rather, these insidious communications waking them in the night only to vanish without a trace had served to contaminate their thoughts between sessions—those hours of privacy devoted to molding the vulnerable into weapons.

"What *is* this shit?" Rouche didn't whisper from the next desk over. He looked up at the board, where details of three gatherings, on both sides of the Atlantic, had been extracted from the messages. Having all already taken place, the relevant CCTV footage had been requested.

"It's like he's probing their paranoia, their sense of worthlessness," said Baxter, highlighting another message, more than aware that she sounded just like Edmunds with his university psychobabble she always found so irritating. "He's promising them greatness and purpose, things they're never going to achieve alone."

Rouche waited for her to gather her thoughts.

"It *is* a cult," she told him. "Not in the traditional sense, but it's still a shared mass hysteria fulfilling the wishes of a single person."

"Our Azazel," said Rouche. "Dr. Alexei Green."

"Chief!" a detective shouted from across the room, a sheet of paper in her hand as she waved it excitedly above her head. "I think I've got something . . ."

Baxter rushed over to her, Rouche close behind. She snatched the sheet out of the woman's hand and read through the short message:

Sycamore Hotel, 20 December, 11 a.m.
Jules Teller welcomes you one final time.

"Well?" asked Rouche.

Baxter smiled, handing him the supposedly unrecoverable message.

"Jules Teller?" he asked, the name sounding familiar.

"That was the name their last gathering was booked under," Baxter clarified. "This is it. This is Green. And now we know *exactly* where he's going to be."

"What's that?" asked Rouche, looking back at the rear seats as Baxter drove him home through the rush-hour traffic.

"Homework."

"Can I help?" asked Rouche, reaching for the box.

"No! I got it."

"There must be hours of it to get through!"

"I said, I got it."

Rouche gave up and stared out at the half-arsed seasonal displays in the shop windows. A tatty motorized Santa Claus waved at him with what little remained of his right arm. Depressed, he turned back to Baxter:

"We've got two days."

"Huh?"

"According to the messages, we've got two days," he elaborated, "until Green's gathering. How do you want to play it? Check out the venue in the morning?"

"I'm not sure there's much point in planning tomorrow," said Baxter.

"What's that supposed to mean?"

Baxter shrugged, but after a few moments, she continued:

"No one's putting a foot inside that place before Sunday."

Rouche was still watching her carefully, the throwaway comment playing on his mind.

"For the first time, we're one step ahead," said Baxter. "Green has *no* idea we've found the messages. This is our *one* shot. We can't risk spooking him."

"Left here!" Rouche reminded her.

Baxter swung the wheel and hit the curb as the car skidded onto the leafy street. She recognized Edmunds's dilapidated Volvo as they passed it and pulled up outside Rouche's similarly dilapidated house.

"Ta for the lift. I can make my own way in in the morning if it's easier?"

"It is."

"OK, then." Rouche smiled.

He stepped out, waved awkwardly, and then ascended the perilous driveway.

In the rearview mirror, Baxter watched Edmunds get out of his car. She waited until Rouche had disappeared inside before climbing out into the chilly night.

She nodded to her friend, took a deep breath, and then made her way up toward the weathered front door.

CHAPTER 26

Friday, 18 December 2015

6:21 P.M.

Overgrown ivy framed the doorway, the leaves trembling in time to the first frozen raindrops of the night.

Baxter had almost knocked twice, but her hand had been stayed by the realization that by doing so, she was instigating the bitter end of her partnership with Rouche.

Between the warped wood and the frame, a solitary slit of orange light cut through the darkness to settle over the shoulder of her jacket. She glanced at Edmunds, who had taken up position on the opposite side of the road, and smiled uncertainly before turning back to the house.

"OK," she whispered, knocking sharply against the wood.

When there was no reply, she knocked again more loudly.

Eventually, she heard the sound of footsteps approaching across the floorboards. A lock clunked and then the door opened a few cautious inches. Baxter watched the metal chain pull taut as Rouche peered out from between the gap:

"Baxter?"

"Hey," she said through an embarrassed smile. "Sorry to do this, but I think the traffic's gonna be shit trying to get back into Wimbledon and I'm absolutely bursting for a wee."

Rouche did not respond immediately, his face disappearing

momentarily from view, revealing the tattered wallpaper behind and the dust particles crashing into one another in their haste to escape the dying house.

An eyeball returned to address her:

"It's not . . . it's not really a great time."

Baxter took a small step forward, still smiling, as if her colleague's cagey behavior were perfectly normal:

"I'll be in and out. I swear. Two minutes, tops."

"Ellie . . . She's caught something at school and really isn't feeling too good at all and—"

"You *do* remember the lift I just gave you across London, right?" interrupted Baxter, taking another small step toward the opening.

"Yes, of course I do," replied Rouche quickly, clearly aware of how incredibly rude he was being. "Do you know what? There's actually a Tesco just down the road. They've definitely got toilets in there."

"A Tesco?" asked Baxter, unamused, edging forward.

"Yeah."

Rouche clocked the drastic change in her, noticed the way that her eyes were searching what little space he could not block with his body.

They stared at each other for a long moment.

"Guess I'll just head there, then," she said, watching him.

"OK. I'm really sorry."

"No harm done," she told him. "I'll be off, then."

"Good nigh—"

Baxter lurched forward. The chain tore from the wood with the force of the impact as she shoved the door back violently into Rouche.

"Baxter!" he shouted, scrambling to push back against her. "Stop it!"

She wedged a foot between the door and the frame, and jolted when her eyes fell on the huge bloodstain dried deep into the sanded wooden floorboards.

"Let me in, Rouche!" she yelled as he crushed her boot in the narrowing gap.

He was stronger than her.

"Just leave me alone! Please!" called Rouche desperately as, with one final effort, he threw his full weight against the door, slamming it shut. "Just leave, Baxter. I'm begging you!" his muffled voice pleaded from inside.

"Shit!" she shouted when she heard the lock click again. "What happens next, Rouche, is on you!"

She kicked the blocked entrance with her injured foot before limping back down the driveway. Edmunds met her halfway up and offered her his hand, knowing full well that she would refuse it.

"Blood on the floor," she announced.

"You're sure you want to do this?" asked Edmunds, already making the call to the control room. It was answered immediately. "Baxter?" he hissed while cupping his hand over the speaker. "Are you sure? You can't be wrong about this."

She considered for a fleeting moment: "I'm not wrong. Get a team down here."

The door surrendered without a fight, separating from its hinges in a shower of splintered wood and scattering screws. The first members of the Armed Response Unit rushed inside, accompanied by a chorus of barked orders, to secure the man sitting quietly on the bare hallway floor.

Rouche remained still, his head lowered.

"Are you armed?" the team leader yelled, unnecessarily, down at him, watching the CIA agent's empty hands cautiously.

Rouche shook his head:

"Dismantled. Kitchen table," he mumbled.

Keeping his weapon trained on the subdued man, the team leader sent another officer to go and check the kitchen while his colleagues moved through the tumbledown property.

Baxter and Edmunds followed the last armed officer inside, pausing on the threshold to estimate the pints of blood required to soak such a large area of floor. The broken door rocked underfoot as they crossed it and took their first breath of the stale, dusty air. A single, yellowed lightbulb swung from the ceiling, illuminating sections of the peeling wallpaper, which looked at least forty years old.

Baxter immediately felt right at home because it was the sort of place where she had spent the majority of her working life: the rotten truth hidden behind closed doors, the darkness that the veil of normality had been concealing; it was a crime scene.

She turned to Edmunds:

"I wasn't wrong," she told him, attempting to sound smug but unable to hide the confusing mix of relief and sadness that she was feeling.

They passed an open door to their right, where damp patches climbed the walls of the empty room. Rainwater had stained sections of the floor. Baxter moved on, stepping over Rouche in the hallway and trying to ignore the look of betrayal that he shot her.

From the foot of the wide staircase, the house looked even more derelict than it had from the entrance. Deep cracks ran up the exposed plaster. Several of the stairs were rotten through, with crude spray-painted crosses warning where to avoid placing one's weight. On the ground floor, the scene in the kitchen looked like the aftermath of a bomb blast, resurrecting images of New York that Baxter prayed to one day forget.

"You head up. I'll stay down," she told Edmunds.

She stole another glance at Rouche, who was sat on the floor between them. It was clear that he had given up, sitting with his face in his hands, the back of his white shirt ruined by the filth of his own home.

As Edmunds risked his life playing stair roulette, Baxter entered the rubble-strewn kitchen. The dividing wall to the neighboring room lay in pieces across the floor. The few remaining cupboards showcased a depressing array of canned foods and packets of instant unpleasantness. Exposed live wires protruded from behind broken tiles, offering a merciful way out to anyone unfortunate enough to be faced with the prospect of a Rouche household dinnertime.

"Bloody animals," one of the armed officers muttered under his breath. "Who lives like this?"

Baxter ignored the man and walked over to the patio doors to look out over the dark garden. She could just about make out a colorful and cared-for Wendy house, something for the ruined family home to aspire to. Long grass obscured its walls, threatening to swallow it up entirely.

Upstairs, Edmunds could hear the team searching the rooms either side of him. Entire sections of the ceiling lay fragmented and trodden into the ancient carpet, and he could hear water dripping somewhere above him. Had it been earlier, he was confident that he would have been able to see daylight shining in through the roof.

A long white wire ran across the landing to the home's first sign of inhabitancy: an answering machine placed on the floor at the top of the stairs. An LED display flashed in warning:

Message box full

He moved on, away from his colleagues, and, with an uneasy feeling in the pit of his stomach, approached the closed door at the far end of the corridor. A sliver of light escaping beneath the whitewashed wood quickened his pulse as a familiar feeling returned to him. The door seemed to glow against the rest of the dark house, beckoning him, just as the solitary light shining down over the Ragdoll corpse had drawn him in.

He knew he didn't want to see whatever lay beyond, but his vault of nightmares still sat relatively empty in comparison to Baxter's. This would be one horror he'd invite to haunt him in order to spare his friend.

He braced himself, twisted the ornate doorknob, and slowly pushed the door open . . .

"Baxter!" he yelled at the top of his lungs.

He could hear her recklessly negotiating the deathtrap of a staircase as he stepped back out into the corridor and gestured to the officers that everything was all right.

She came stomping over to join him: "What?" she asked, looking worried.

"You were wrong."

"What are you talking about?"

Edmunds sighed heavily:

"You got it wrong," he said, nodding toward the open door.

She gave him an inquiring look and then stepped around him to enter the small but beautifully decorated bedroom. An intricate mural had been painstakingly hand-painted across the back wall behind a narrow bed that overflowed with stuffed animals. Fairy lights sparkled where they'd been draped over the shelves, lending a magical ambience to the rows of pop CDs.

Beside the Barbie Dream House in the corner of the cozy room, three photographs stood on the windowsill: a darker-haired Rouche smiling broadly as a gorgeous little girl laughed from his shoulders, stuffed toy in hand; an even younger Rouche and his beautiful wife holding their baby daughter; a picture of the girl in the snow, stood beside the familiar Wendy house in an unfamiliar garden. She looked to be trying to catch snowflakes on her tongue.

Finally, Baxter looked down at her feet. She was standing on a sleeping bag that had been laid out over the fluffy carpet beside the bed. Rouche's dark blue suit jacket was folded neatly beside the pillow, obviously placed carefully so as not to disturb anything in the perfect little room.

She wiped her eyes.

"But . . . he phones them all the time," she whispered, feeling physically sick. "She answered the phone to me and you said there was someone in when you were here . . ." She trailed off when she realized Edmunds was gone.

She picked a silly-looking penguin up off the bed, recognizing the soft toy from one of the photographs. It was wearing an orange woolly hat, much like her own.

A moment later, a woman's voice filled the empty house:

"Hello, my love! We're both missing you so, so much!"

Baxter placed the toy back onto the bed and listened in confusion as the vaguely familiar voice grew louder and louder until Edmunds reappeared in the doorway holding the flashing answering machine in his hands.

"OK, say good night to Daddy, Ellie . . ."

Finally, an abrupt beep signaled the end of the recorded message, leaving Baxter and Edmunds standing in silence.

"Bollocks," sighed Baxter, marching out of the room to stand at the top of the staircase. "Everybody out!" she ordered.

Curious faces appeared in doorways.

"You heard me: everybody out!"

She herded the disgruntled officers down the stairs, over Rouche in the hallway, and out into the rain. Edmunds was the last to leave. He loitered at the broken front door:

"Want me to wait for you?" he asked.

She smiled appreciatively: "No. Go home," she told him.

Once they were alone, she silently took a seat on the dirty floor beside Rouche. He appeared too lost in his thoughts even to notice. Without the luxury of a door, the pelting rain had started to flood the far end of the hallway.

They sat quietly for several minutes before Baxter built up the courage to speak:

"I'm a shit," she announced decisively. "A complete and utter shit."

Rouche turned to look at her.

"That slightly annoying, geeky, ginger guy who just left . . ." started Baxter. "He is *literally* the *only* person on this entire shitty planet that I trust. That's it. Just him. I don't trust my boyfriend. Eight months together . . . but I don't trust him. I get reports into his finances because I'm so scared he's trying to use me or hurt me or . . . I don't even know what. Pathetic, right?"

"Yep." Rouche nodded thoughtfully. "That *is* pathetic."

They both smiled. Baxter huddled up tighter to keep warm.

"It was just after we'd bought this wreck," started Rouche, looking around at the broken house. "We'd gone into the city. Ellie . . . She was getting ill again . . . Her little lungs . . ." He trailed off, watching the rain intensify at the end of the hall. "Thursday, 7 July 2005."

Baxter put her hand over her mouth, the date ingrained into every Londoner's memory.

"We were on our way to see a specialist at Great Ormond Street. We were sitting on the Tube as normal one moment; the next, we weren't. People were screaming. Smoke and dust everywhere, scraping at my eyes. But none of that mattered because my daughter was in my arms, unconscious but still breathing, her little leg all bent out of place . . ." Rouche had to pause for a moment to compose himself.

Baxter hadn't moved. She waited for him to continue, her hand still covering her mouth.

"Then I saw my wife lying under a pile of rubble a few feet away, where the roof of the train had come down on us. I knew I couldn't save her. I *knew* I couldn't. But I had to try. I could have got Ellie out then. People were already running down the tunnel towards Russell Square. But you've got to try, right?

"I start pulling at these sheets of metal that I have no hope of ever moving, when I should have been getting Ellie out instead. All that smoke and soot: she couldn't cope. And then another part of the roof falls in, just as it was always going to. Everybody left down there starts to panic. I panic. I grab Ellie to follow the others down the tunnel when someone shouts that the tracks might still be live. Suddenly, nobody's leaving. I *know*

I can get her out, but I just wait there because nobody else is leaving . . . *nobody.*

"The crowd had made its decision, and I mindlessly obeyed. I didn't get her out in time. I could have . . . but I didn't."

Baxter was speechless. She wiped her eyes and just stared at Rouche, amazed that he was strong enough to carry on after all he had been through.

"I know you blame me for leaving Curtis behind in that terrible place, but—"

"I don't," Baxter interrupted. "Not anymore. I don't."

She hesitantly put her hand on his. She wished that she wasn't so awkward, otherwise she would have hugged him. She wanted to.

"I just couldn't make the same mistake twice, you know?" Rouche told her, running his hands through his graying hair.

Baxter nodded as a timer switch clicked, illuminating the lamp in the corner.

"OK. Your turn again," said Rouche with a forced smile.

"I let Wolf . . . Sorry, Detective Fawkes," she clarified. "I let him go. I had him in handcuffs. I had backup moments away . . . and I let him go."

Rouche nodded as though he had suspected as much: "Why?"

"I don't know."

"Sure you do. Did you love him?"

"I don't know," she answered honestly.

Rouche considered his next question carefully before asking it: "And what would you do if you ever saw him again?"

"I ought to arrest him. I ought to hate him. I ought to kill him myself for making me the paranoid wreck that I am today."

"But I didn't ask what you *ought* to do." Rouche smiled. "I asked what you *would* do."

Baxter shook her head: "I honestly . . . I don't know," she replied, ending her turn. "Tell me about the blood in the doorway."

Rouche didn't answer her immediately. He calmly unbuttoned his cuffs and rolled up his shirtsleeves to reveal the deep pink scar torn into each of his forearms.

This time, she did hug him, for some reason recalling one of Maggie's pearls of wisdom to a distraught Finlay the night her cancer returned with a vengeance: "Sometimes the things that nearly kill us are the things that save us."

Baxter kept the thought to herself.

"A couple of days after I got out of hospital," Rouche explained, "birthday cards started arriving for my wife. I just sat there by the door reading through the pile and . . . I guess it wasn't my time."

"I drink too much," Baxter blurted, confident that she and Rouche no longer had any secrets from one another. "Like . . . *too* much."

Rouche laughed at her inappropriately cheery admission. Baxter looked offended but then couldn't help smiling.

They really were both as messed up as each other.

They sat in a comfortable silence for a few moments.

"I reckon that's enough sharing for one night. Come on," said Baxter, getting to her feet and offering him one of her frozen hands. She pulled him up, took out her keys, slid one off the metal ring, and held it out to him.

"What's this?" asked Rouche.

"Key to my apartment. There's no way I'm letting you stay here now."

He went to argue.

"You'll be doing me a favor," she told him. "Thomas will be over the moon when I tell him we're going to play house for a little while. The cat's already at his. It's perfect. There's really no point even trying to argue about it."

Rouche got the distinct impression that was probably true.

He took the key from her and nodded.

CHAPTER 27

Friday, 18 December 2015

10:10 P.M.

Rouche loaded the dishwasher while Baxter finished stripping the bed in the other room. He was afraid to touch anything in her surprisingly ordered apartment, which would serve as his temporary home until the resolution of the case or he was called back to the US. He could hear her across the hall, swearing as she struggled to stuff the provisions for an indefinite period into two small holdalls.

She emerged from the bedroom a few minutes later, dragging the bloated bags behind her.

"Arse," she sighed, spotting her workout clothes draped over the treadmill. She collected them up and found a zip pocket to shove them into. "Right. I'm off, then. Help yourself to . . . whatever. There are some emergency toiletries below the sink, if you need them."

"Wow! You are well prepared!"

"Yeah," she replied cagily. The moment had passed to explain why she still kept, and had even restocked, the supply of men's toiletries in her bathroom cabinet—one of the more pathetic parts of herself still hoping that they might come in useful one day. "Well, help yourself. Good night!"

It dawned on Rouche too late that perhaps he should have offered to help her with her bags when there was a crash out in the hallway, followed by a particularly offensive expletive. Deciding it safer to pretend he hadn't heard, he went through to the bedroom. A selection of threadbare soft toys had been hastily stuffed beneath the bed, making him smile.

He had been touched by the amount of effort Baxter had gone to in making him feel welcome in her home. He switched the bedside lamp on and the main light off, immediately making it feel a little more like Ellie's cozy room. He unpacked the three photographs from the windowsill and lost a few minutes in their happy memories. Finally, he unrolled his sleeping bag across the carpet and got changed for bed.

Baxter arrived at Thomas's house a little after 11 P.M. Abandoning her things in the hallway, she went through to the dark kitchen to pour herself a glass of wine. Still peckish, thanks to the stingy fish-and-chip shop owner on Wimbledon High Street, she raided the fridge for dessert. Irritatingly, Thomas was on one of his sporadic health kicks, meaning that her only options were chocolate-less fruit slices or a suspicious-looking bottle of green slime that the Ghostbusters would certainly have considered evidence of paranormal activity.

"Ahhhh! Don't try it, funny!" yelled Thomas from the doorway.

Baxter peered around the fridge, eyebrows raised. He was standing in his boxer shorts, anchored by a pair of tartan slipper boots, and was wielding a badminton racquet above his head menacingly. He almost toppled over in relief when he saw her:

"Oh, thank Christ! It's you! I nearly"—he looked down at the ridiculous weapon he'd selected—"well, swatted you, as it happens."

Baxter smirked and picked up her drink: "'Don't try it, funny'?" she asked.

"It was the adrenaline," replied Thomas defensively. "Something about not trying anything and not wanting any funny business got a little jumbled up on delivery."

"Uh-huh," said Baxter, smiling into her wineglass.

"That's right," said Thomas, placing a reassuring hand on her shoulder. "You drink up. You've had a hell of a fright."

Baxter spluttered up her wine laughing.

Thomas handed her the kitchen roll:

"I didn't know you were coming round," he said as she dabbed at the fresh pink spots on her blouse.

"Neither did I."

He brushed her hair away from her face, revealing some of the more stubborn scabs that were yet to fully heal.

"You look like you've had a rough day," he said.

Baxter's eyes narrowed.

"In an effortlessly beautiful and refreshed sort of way, of course," he added quickly, making her soften. "So what's going on?"

"I'm moving in."

"Right . . . I mean, right! That's great! When?"

"Tonight."

"OK!" He nodded. "I mean, I'm delighted, but why the sudden rush?"

"There's a man living at my place."

Thomas took a moment to process that one. He frowned and opened his mouth.

"Could we talk about this tomorrow?" asked Baxter. "I'm exhausted."

"Sure. Let's get you to bed, then."

Baxter left her unfinished glass in the sink and followed Thomas out.

"Forgot to mention we're in the spare room for the time being," he informed her as they climbed the stairs. "Echo's fleas have laid claim to ours. There's been a bit of a siege, but I let off a second Nuisance Nuke this evening, which will hopefully kill the last of the little bastards."

This might have been infuriating news any other time, but Thomas looked incredibly proud of the genocidal finale to his microscopic war and the words "Nuisance Nuke" had sounded so absurd in his toffy tones that she could only laugh as he led her up to bed.

*

The next morning, Baxter entered Homicide and Serious Crime Command with a slight swagger to her step thanks to the pair of boxer shorts she'd had to borrow from Thomas, having forgotten to pack any underwear. It being so early on a Saturday, she didn't expect to see anyone important, but she entered her office to find Vanita in her chair and a well-dressed man in his fifties sat opposite.

Baxter looked puzzled: "Shit. Sorry . . . Wait, am I . . . ?"

"You are," Vanita assured her. "This is *my* office . . . until you resume normal duties."

Baxter looked blank.

"None of this ringing any bells?" asked Vanita patronizingly.

The man with his back to Baxter cleared his throat and got to his feet, pausing to do up the top button of his tailored suit.

"Sorry, Christian. I forgot you two hadn't actually met," said Vanita. "Christian Bellamy, Detective Chief Inspector Baxter. Baxter, this is our new commissioner . . . as of yesterday."

The handsome man was sunbed-brown. His full head of silver hair and chunky Breitling watch added to the impression that he was far too wealthy to concern himself with paid employment beyond the occasional business lunch or poolside conference call. He had a winning "vote me" smile, which had evidently done its job.

He and Baxter shook hands.

"Congrats," she said, letting go. "Although, I actually already thought you were anyway."

Vanita forced a laugh:

"Christian moved over from Specialist, Organised and Econom—"

"Really don't need his whole life story," Baxter interrupted, turning back to the man. "No offense."

"None taken." He smiled. "Long story short: I was only acting commissioner."

"Well," said Baxter, checking her watch, "I was only *acting* interested. So if you'll excuse me . . ."

The commissioner burst into laughter:

"You certainly don't disappoint!" he told her, unbuttoning his jacket to sit back down. "You are everything Finlay promised and more."

Baxter stopped on her way to the doorway.

"*You* know Finlay?" she asked dubiously.

"Only for about the last thirty-five years. We worked robbery together for a time, in here for a while after that, before our careers took different paths."

Baxter considered that a rather smug way of feigning tact. The underlying sentiment: Finlay had been left stagnating in the same dead-end position while his leathery friend ran out of rungs at the top of the ladder.

"I dropped in to see him and Maggie yesterday evening," he told her. "The extension's looking good."

Baxter caught Vanita rolling her eyes:

"I haven't seen it," she said. "Been a little busy."

"Of course." The man smiled apologetically. "I hear we've had a promising development."

"Yes. *We* have."

The commissioner ignored the tone:

"Well, that is good news," he said. "When it's all over, though, you must drop by. I know he'd love to see you. He's been worried sick."

Baxter was a little uncomfortable with how personal the conversation had suddenly become.

"Well, my partner's here," she lied, leaving the room.

"Do pass on my regards when you go visiting, won't you?" the commissioner called after her as she escaped to the kitchenette to make herself a coffee.

By mid-morning, Saturday, the temperature had soared to a sweltering 6 degrees Celsius thanks to the blanket of dark cloud that never seemed to stray too far from the capital. Miraculously, Baxter managed to find a space on the main road. They were

parked a hundred meters from the Sycamore Hotel, Marble Arch, which according to several of the recovered suicide texts would be the venue for Green's final gathering.

"Oooo! They've got a screening room," announced Rouche as he flicked through their website on his phone. He looked out at the hotel. "D'ya think anyone's watching it?"

"Probably," replied Baxter. "We're here for external exits, access, and vantage points only."

Rouche puffed out his cheeks. "Only one way to find out."

Baxter grabbed his arm when he opened the car door to climb out:

"What are you doing?"

"Exits, access, and vantage points . . . Can't see much from here."

"Someone might recognize us."

"You maybe. Not me. Which is why I brought you a makeshift disguise from the flat."

"Apartment," she corrected him.

"Apartment. I hope you don't mind."

He handed her the baseball cap he had found on the coat stand.

"It's a three-part disguise," he explained when she looked decidedly unimpressed.

"Happen to bring me anything else from home?" she asked, eyebrows raised.

He looked blank.

"Anything at all . . ." she pushed him.

"Oh, your pants! Yeah." He smiled, producing a carrier bag of underwear.

She snatched it off him and tossed it into the backseat before getting out onto the pavement.

"Part two of the disguise: we're in love," said Rouche, taking her hand in his.

"And part three?" huffed Baxter.

"Smile!" Rouche told her before mumbling: "No one's gonna recognize you then."

*

Special Agent Chase struggled to restrain his colleague.

"For Christ's sake, Saunders," shouted Baxter. "Do you have *any* idea how much paperwork you create every time you get yourself punched in the face?"

The Homicide and Serious Crime meeting room was populated with the team of territorial Met detectives, SO15 officers, and jet-lagged FBI agents who would be involved in Sunday's operation. Baxter had been briefing the various teams on her external assessment of the venue.

Overall, the meeting was going much as expected.

MI5 had sent along a token agent, who had quite clearly been instructed not to disclose a thing but to report back with in-depth details of what was being discussed, in what must have been one of the most blatant acts of espionage ever employed. Rouche, as the sole representative of the CIA, was attempting to discreetly hand Baxter the loose pair of underwear that had fallen into the bottom of his bag.

Fortunately, no one noticed apart from Blake, who looked absolutely crushed.

"That conference hall should be covered in cameras by now," Chase told the room, to the nods and mumbled agreement of his men.

"And how do we know it's not being watched?" asked Baxter impatiently. "How do we know they're not going to search the hall for cameras or bugs or meathead FBI agents hiding behind the curtains?"

Chase ignored the laughter from the other side of the room:

"They're crazies, not spies!"

The MI5 agent looked up from his laptop as if someone had called his name, affirming the general consensus that he was probably the worst secret agent in the business.

"Crazies they may be, but crazies who have managed to coordinate attacks on two different continents without anybody being able to stop them," Baxter pointed out. "If we spook even *one* of them . . . we could lose *all* of them. We stick to the plan: passive surveillance on the five entrances, the hotel's CCTV routed through to facial recognition here. We plant a fake porter or receptionist armed with a high-powered microphone in case we can't get anybody in there. The moment we get confirmation that Alexei Green's inside, we go in."

"And if Green's a no-show?" asked Chase challengingly.

"He'll show."

"But if he doesn't?"

Then they were screwed. Baxter looked to Rouche for support:

"If we're unable to verify that Green's in attendance, we hold until the last possible moment," said Rouche, "and then we raid the hall as planned. If we can't get him there, we'll get to him by questioning his roomful of accomplices."

"Quick question," blurted Blake, cup of tea in hand. "The bit about getting someone 'in there.' What's up with that?"

"We need visual confirmation," said Rouche, simply. "He's the FBI's most wanted. Anyone who's seen a paper knows his face by now. It's likely he'll obsure or change his appearance."

"Granted, but you can't *actually* expect one of us to just waltz inside, with absolutely no idea what's going to happen when those doors close, to sit in the middle of an audience made up purely of murderous psychopaths?"

The room fell deathly silent.

Rouche looked back at Baxter, stuck, consenting that perhaps it didn't sound the most inspiring plan when put like that.

She just shrugged: "Anyone got any better ideas?"

SESSION SIX

Wednesday, 11 June 2014
11:32 A.M.

The tailored white shirt landed in a crumpled ball on the bathroom floor, the warm coffee seeping into the Egyptian cotton. Selecting a replacement from the master bedroom wardrobe, Lucas started to pull it on in front of the mirror.

He sighed at the sight of his paunchy body, an angry red mark across his chest from where the scalding drink had branded him. He did up the buttons as quickly as possible, tucking himself in as he rushed back down to the living room, where a rake-thin man in his mid-sixties was sat tapping away on his BlackBerry.

"I'm so sorry about that," said Lucas, lifting his chair out of the wet patch on the floor and taking a seat. "I keep doing things like that at the moment."

The man watched him carefully: "Is everything all right, Lucas?" he asked.

Although there in a professional context, the two men had known each other for years.

"Fine," he replied unconvincingly.

"I just mean . . . that you seem a little out of sorts, if you don't mind me saying. Nothing's *prompted* our meeting today, has it?"

"Not at all," Lucas assured him. "This is just something I've been putting off for a while. I feel I've been remiss in not taking care of it sooner, after . . . well, after . . . after . . ."

The older gentleman smiled kindly and nodded:

"Of course . . . So, this is all refreshingly simple. I'll just run through the gist of it: 'I revoke all former wills and testamentary dispositions made by me . . . I appoint Samuels-Wright and Sons, Solicitors, to act as the executors of this will . . . Subject to the payment of debts, funeral, and testamentary expenses, I leave my residuary estate in its entirety to the Great Ormond Street Hospital Charity.' Blah. Blah. Blah. 'Lucas Theodor Keaton.' All sound about right?"

Lucas hesitated for a moment and then, failing to steady his shaking hand, removed a USB memory stick from his pocket. He held it out to his acquaintance:

"There's also this."

The solicitor took it from him and looked at it inquisitively.

"It's just a message . . . to whom it may concern . . . should the time come," Lucas explained self-consciously. "To explain why."

Nodding, the solicitor placed the memory stick into a pocket of his briefcase:

"That's a very thoughtful touch," he told Lucas. "I have no doubt that they'd want to hear from the person who's leaving them this . . . frankly staggering sum of money." The man was about to get up, but then he paused. "You're a good man, Lucas. Few who have reached your dizzying heights of wealth and influence remain impervious to all of the ego and bullshit . . . I just wanted to tell you that."

When Lucas arrived for his appointment with Alexei Green, the psychiatrist was occupied with a stunningly attractive woman. Although engaging with her politely, he appeared utterly uninterested in the very clear signals that she was putting out:

"I mean it. *Literally* the day after I attended your lecture on everyday applications of behavioral neuroscience, I submitted a request to alter the focus of my thesis."

"Ah, well, you've got behavioral neuroscience to thank for that . . . I couldn't possibly take the credit," Green joked.

"I know it's cheeky to ask this, but even just an hour talking with you would be . . ." The woman made an excited squeal, placed a hand on his arm, and laughed.

From the doorway, Lucas watched in awe as she swooned over the psychiatrist, intoxicated by his charm.

"I'll tell you what . . ." started Green.

The receptionist rolled her eyes.

". . . why don't you have a word with Cassie over there and she'll find us a time to do lunch next week?"

"You're serious?"

"You're at that event in New York next week," Cassie's bored voice called from behind the desk.

"The week after, then," Green promised, finally noticing his patient loitering in the doorway. "Lucas!" he called. He had to give the woman a gentle shove in the right direction to get her moving as he welcomed him into his office.

"You know, it's OK to be angry with the person . . . with the people who did this to you and your family," said Green delicately.

The sun disappeared behind a cloud, throwing the office into gloom. All of a sudden, the ornate lampshade, oversized chairs, and solid wood desk, which usually gave the room a homely ambience, appeared stale and dead, the psychiatrist, too, merely an ashen copy of himself.

"Oh, I am angry," Lucas told him, gritting his teeth. "But not with them."

"I don't understand," said Green, a little sharply. He quickly amended his tone: "Imagine that I was the man who had traveled into Central London that day carrying an explosive device with the sole aim of murdering as many people as possible. What would you want to say to me?"

Lucas stared into space while he considered Green's question. He got up and started to pace the room. He could always think more clearly when he was moving:

"Nothing. There isn't a single thing I'd want to say to him. There would be as little point in me taking my anger out on him as there would an inanimate object . . . a gun . . . a knife. These people are no more than tools, brainwashed and manipulated. They are but puppets for a cause far bigger than themselves."

"Puppets?" asked Green, a mixture of interest and skepticism in his voice.

"They behave like wild animals when they're set loose," Lucas continued, "drawn towards the greatest concentration of their prey, and we . . . we cluster together in these enormous numbers, unconsciously baiting them, playing the odds that our luck will hold out, that it'll be somebody else's turn to die. And all the while, the people *actually* holding the strings, just like those responsible for our protection, play us all like chess pieces."

The words looked to have struck a chord with Green, whose gaze was fixed firmly on the window across the room.

"Apologies for the monologue. It's just that . . . I find it really helpful talking to you," admitted Lucas.

"Sorry?" asked Green, a million miles away.

"I was saying, I was wondering whether we might be able to increase the frequency of our sessions, perhaps meet twice a week from now on?" Lucas asked, attempting to hide the desperation in his voice. "I appreciate that you're away next week, though . . . New York, wasn't it?"

"Yes. That's right." Green smiled, still mulling Lucas's words over in his head.

"You go often?"

"Five, six times a year. Don't worry—I won't have to reschedule our appointments often," Green assured him. "But yes, of course. If you are finding our sessions beneficial, we can certainly step them up. But as you're making *such* impressive progress, I wonder whether I might try something a little bit different with you . . . a fresh approach, if you will. Do you think you might be ready for that, Lucas?"

"I do."

CHAPTER 28

Saturday, 19 December 2015

2:34 P.M.

In true tradesman style, Special Agent Chase abandoned the van across two disabled parking spaces. He handed his colleague a stepladder before dragging a toolbox out of the back. Dressed in matching overalls, the two men entered the lobby of the Sycamore Hotel and made their way toward the reception desk, where offshoots of tinsel hung limply over the floor like dying ivy.

As they proceeded across the lobby, Chase noted that the first, unassuming signage had already been put out in preparation for the following day's illicit gathering:

20 December—11 A.M.
Managing director of Equity UK, Jules Teller,
on the effect of the economic downturn on equity prices,
the resulting precipice on which the financial markets now stand,
and what this means to you.

Chase had to hand it to their enemy: who needed an army of ferocious security guards policing their privacy when you could use equity prices and the financial markets as an equally effective deterrent?

Clocking that both of the receptionists were otherwise engaged, they followed signs down a corridor to the modest conference hall.

The room was, thankfully, empty. Row upon row of threadbare chairs faced the barely elevated stage. The hall smelled musty, the beige walls making it feel hazy and tired.

If Jules Teller's mind-numbing equity talk had been a real event, thought Chase, this would have been the place to hold it.

They closed the door behind them and set to work.

Following the disastrous meeting earlier in the day, Lennox had made her position quite clear to her exported lead agent: the investigation may have led them to London, but this was still an FBI case and Alexei Green was at the top of their most-wanted list. His instructions were to disregard Baxter's paranoid order to stay away from the hotel and set up cameras and microphones inside the hall. The moment they had eyes on Green, Chase and his men were to move in on their target, leaving Baxter and her people to scoop up his fleeing audience.

As an experienced undercover agent, Chase at least acknowledged Baxter's concerns that the hotel may be under surveillance. He had learned the hard way that it was always better to be overly cautious regarding such matters. As such, he and his colleague carried out a genuine repair to the set of double doors, replacing two of the greasy hinges as they placed their first camera. The entire time, they remained in character, speaking only about the job at hand in passable English accents, just in case anybody was listening in.

Within fifteen minutes they were done. Three cameras and a microphone in situ, four squeaky hinges replaced.

"That wasn't too 'ard, was it, guv?" Chase's colleague smiled, the American under the common misconception that all English people speak like they're about to clean a chimney for Mary Poppins.

"Tea?" suggested Chase, supressing a burp as he patted his belly, method actor through and through.

They packed up their equipment, whistling as they worked, and headed back out to the van.

*

The Met's investigation was going nowhere fast.

They had managed to take DNA samples from the keys Baxter had used to attack Phillip East's killer, but, predictably, these had not matched anyone in the system. A team was still wading through the CCTV footage in relation to the three previous gatherings.

The search for Alexei Green's patients had so far only turned up perfectly pleasant, scar-free examples of his past and present clients, all of whom maintained that Green was a kind and genuine man who had helped them through difficult times. Several patients remained unaccounted for. Baxter had assigned a team the task of obtaining emergency contact details for each of them, attending addresses in the hope they might stumble upon one of Green's Puppets.

The FBI had made no secret that they were searching everywhere for Green and his assorted minions. So he had dispersed his army, who would reconvene only once more before unleashing whatever horror they had in store for the people of London.

Sunday's gathering would be their one opportunity to end it.

By late afternoon on Saturday, Baxter had had enough.

They were going through the motions but all knew that they were biding their time until the following day. She spoke once more to Mitchell, the undercover officer whom she had chosen to enter the conference room. Then, satisfied everything was in hand, she left Rouche with an ex-colleague of Green's, made her excuses, and headed out to Muswell Hill underneath another dark gray sky.

She parked up beside a familiar tree, but it took her a moment to recognize the once-familiar house behind it, which had sprouted an extra room over the garage and a shiny new Mercedes on the driveway. She could hear drilling as she stepped out of the car and walked up to ring the bell.

A well-presented woman in her early fifties opened the door. She had sparkling blue eyes, which contrasted with her jet-black hair, tied up into a 1950s-style bun. Her dark denim jeans and slouchy jumper were covered in paint, but it looked more like a fashion statement.

"Hello, trouble!" she exclaimed in her upper-class diction before embracing Baxter and planting a rose-red lipstick stain on her cheek.

Baxter eventually managed to squirm out from the woman's grasp:

"Hi, Maggie." She laughed. "Is he in?"

"He's *always* in now," she sighed. "I don't think he knows what to do with himself. I told him this would happen if he retired, but . . . you know Fin. Anyway, come in, come in!"

Baxter followed her inside.

Finlay was one of her favorite people in the world, but every time she saw Maggie, she marveled at how her ugly old friend had ever managed to woo and keep hold of such an attractive, unfailingly lovely, well-bred woman. "Punching above my weight" was always his answer when quizzed on it.

"How are you?" asked Baxter, the question carrying significantly more weight than usual when directed at someone who had been so ill for so long.

"Having a good patch. Can't complain." Maggie smiled as she led her into the kitchen. She started fussing over teapots and cups while Baxter waited patiently.

She could tell that Maggie wanted to ask her something: "What?"

The older woman turned around with an innocent look, but dropped it almost immediately. They had known one another far too long for pretense:

"I was just wondering whether you had heard from Will."

Baxter had been expecting the question: "No. Nothing. I swear."

Maggie looked disappointed. She and Wolf had grown incredibly close over the years, to the point where he had spent a couple of Christmases with them before the arrival of the grandchildren:

"You know you can tell me in confidence, don't you?"

"I *do* know that. But it doesn't change the fact that he hasn't contacted me."

"He'll come back," Maggie told her.

Baxter did not appreciate the reassuring way in which she said it.

"If he does, he'll be arrested."

Maggie smiled at that:

"This *is* Will we're talking about here. And it's OK to miss him. We all do. None more than you, I'm sure."

She had been witness to enough interactions between Baxter and Wolf over the years to know that their relationship went far deeper than mere friends or colleagues.

"You still haven't met Thomas," said Baxter, changing the subject and yet not really changing the subject at all. "I'll bring him with me next time."

Maggie smiled encouragingly, which only annoyed her more.

The drilling upstairs ceased.

"You head up. I'll bring the drinks."

Baxter climbed the stairs, following the smell of fresh paint, and found Finlay on his hands and knees securing a floorboard in place. He didn't notice she was there until she cleared her throat, at which point he dropped what he was doing, groaning as his back and knees clicked, and got up to embrace her.

"Emily! You didn't tell me you were popping round."

"Didn't know."

"Well, it's a treat to see you. I've been worried with all that's been going on. Sit down," he insisted, before realizing that it wasn't much of an offer. An entire corner of the sawdust-covered floor was still propped up against the wall waiting to be laid, leaving a dangerous gap to fall through. Sealant and paint cans littered what remained of the space between the ancient tools. "We can go downstairs," he offered on second thought.

"No, it's fine . . . Place is looking good."

"Aye, well, it was either this or move," he told her, gesturing to the room. "We want to help out with the kids a bit more now that I'm—"

"Bored?"

"Retired," Finlay corrected her with a wry smile. "At least, we will if Maggie ever decides on a color."

"Big extension. Fancy new car on the drive," said Baxter, sounding more questioning than impressed.

"What can I say? Pensions were actually worth something back when I started. You're going to get bugger all, mind." He paused to check whether Maggie had heard him use a curse word. "So . . . should I be worried about you?"

"No."

"No?"

"It'll be over by lunchtime tomorrow." Baxter smiled. "You'll hear all about it when Vanita totters out to tell the world how she saved the day by sitting behind her desk doing arse all."

"What's happening tomorrow?" Finlay asked, looking concerned.

"Nothing you need to worry yourself about, *old man*. We're basically just watching the FBI do their thing," she lied, knowing full well that he'd insist on tagging along if he thought, even for a moment, that she might need him. She had already had to lie to Edmunds for precisely the same reason.

He gave her a searching look.

"So I met our new commissioner this morning," she told him. "Asked me to pass on his regards."

"Did he now?" asked Finlay, deciding to take a seat on the floor after all.

"Seems very keen on you. Who is he, anyway?"

Finlay rubbed his dirty face wearily as he considered his reply.

"He's Fin's oldest friend," Maggie answered on his behalf from the stairs as she made her way up with a tea tray and the swear jar. "Almost inseparable they were when we all first met. More like brothers."

"You've never mentioned him," said Baxter, surprised.

"Oh, I have, lass. The time our murder victim came back to life on us?" Finlay reminded her. "The time we made the largest drugs bust in Glasgow's history? The time he took a bullet in the arse?"

"They were *all* about him?" She had heard the stories so many times that she knew them off by heart.

"Aye. Not that any of that makes him commissioner material in the slightest."

"He's just jealous," Maggie told Baxter as she rubbed Finlay's balding head affectionately.

"I'm not!" he said gruffly.

"I think you'll find that you are!" Maggie laughed. "They had a bit of a falling-out a long time ago," she explained to Baxter, who raised her eyebrows, knowing the definition of a "falling-out" in Finlay's dictionary. "Punches were thrown, as were tables and chairs. Insults were exchanged, as were broken bones."

"He didn't break any of my bones," Finlay mumbled.

"Nose," Maggie reminded him.

"Doesn't count."

"But they put all that behind them," she assured Baxter, before turning back to her husband. "And it was you who got me in the end, wasn't it?"

Finlay squeezed her affectionately: "Aye. Aye."

Maggie gave him a kiss on the forehead and got up.

"I'll let you two talk," she said, heading back downstairs.

"Just because *we're* old friends," Finlay told Baxter, "it doesn't mean *you* can trust him any more than any other pencil-pushing manager. Usual rules apply: stay well clear unless absolutely unavoidable. But if he does give you any hassle, you just send him to me."

Rouche was wide-awake. He had been staring into the darkness for hours, playing with the silver cross around his neck, thinking about the imminent operation. The din rising up off Wimbledon High Street had intensified as the weekend revelers filled the restaurants and bars, boozing away their self-restraint before making the journey from one overcrowded establishment to the next.

He sighed and reached up to switch the bedside lamp on, illuminating the patch of Baxter's bedroom floor that he had made his own. Giving up on his aspirations of a good night's rest, he

climbed out of the sleeping bag, dressed quickly, and headed out
to find himself a drink.

Thomas rolled over and patted the flat duvet beside him. He didn't
open his eyes right away, while his muddled thoughts struggled
to remember whether Baxter had even come up in the first place.
Eventually deciding that she probably had, he slid out of bed and
headed downstairs to find her fast asleep in front of the television. A dated episode of *QI* was amusing itself, while the dregs
of a Cabernet Sauvignon edged ever closer to the rim of the tilted
wineglass in her hand.

Thomas smiled down at her. She looked so peaceful. Her face
had relaxed, removing the persistent scowl from her expression,
and she had curled up into a ball, taking up just one cushion of
the three-seater sofa. He leaned over to scoop her up in his arms.

A strained squeal later, she hadn't moved an inch.

He adjusted position and tried again.

Perhaps it was the angle she was sitting at, perhaps the stodgy
pasta bake he'd whipped up for dinner, or perhaps the fact that
his biweekly games of badminton had failed to bulk him up as
much as one might have hoped. In the end, he elected to leave her
where she was. He draped her favorite blanket over her, turned
up the heating a little, and kissed her on the forehead before
going back upstairs.

CHAPTER 29

Sunday, 20 December 2015

10:15 A.M.

"This is bullshit!" Baxter snapped before hanging up the phone on Vanita.

The rain had been hammering down all morning, playing havoc with the comms as she'd attempted to organize the four Armed Response Unit teams at her disposal. She was standing on the top level of a multistory car park that provided the FBI with an elevated view of the nearby hotel. She stormed over to Chase, who looked even bigger than usual, actually having reason to adorn himself in body armor for once.

"You stood my officer down?" she yelled over the rain.

Chase turned to her with a bored expression:

"I did. We no longer require him," he said dismissively as he headed back toward the surveillance unit. "It's all in hand."

"Hey, I'm talking to you!" shouted Baxter, following him.

"Look, I appreciate the Met lending us use of their men and resources, but this is an FBI operation, and unless I misunderstood your superior, there really is no reason for you to still be here."

Baxter opened her mouth to argue when Chase continued:

"Rest assured, if we get anything of relevance out of Green, we will, of course, send it over to you."

"Send it over?" asked Baxter.

They had reached the van. The rain was falling harder, creating a mist above the roof of the vehicle as the drops exploded against the metal. Chase pulled on the handle and slid the side door open to climb in, revealing a rack of monitors that showed three separate feeds from inside the conference hall.

Baxter suddenly understood why her undercover officer was no longer required: Chase and his team had disregarded her order to stay away.

"Oh, you arseholes!"

"As I said, it's all in hand," said Chase unapologetically as Baxter stormed off.

"Baxter!" he called after her. "If I see you or Agent Rouche trying to interfere with *my* operation, I *will* order my men to intercept and detain you!"

Baxter emerged from the car park and jogged to her Audi out on the street. She climbed in and let out an angry scream of frustration.

Rouche, bone-dry and halfway through a bag of Cadbury Crunchie Rocks, waited politely for her to finish.

"Vanita has let Chase take charge of the operation. The whole place is rigged with cameras. They've stood Mitchell down. In fact, we've all been stood down," was her abridged version of events.

"She knows I don't work for her, right?" asked Rouche, offering Baxter a chocolate to cheer her up.

"Makes no odds. Chase's threatened to 'intercept' and 'detain' us if we interfere, and I reckon he's enough of a dick to make good on that promise too."

"And there was me thinking we were all on the same side."

"Where did you get that idea?" asked Baxter, exasperated. "Something Chase said didn't sit quite right with me. I'm starting to get the distinct impression that the FBI are just going to grab Green and piss off straight back to the States, leaving us to clean up the rest of this mess."

Rouche nodded. He'd suspected much the same thing.

They both stared out at the gloomy scene before them.

"Twenty-eight minutes to go," sighed Rouche.

There was a knock against the driver's window.

Startled, Baxter turned to find Edmunds smiling back at her. "What the . . . ?"

He jogged around the front of the car and opened the passenger door to find Rouche staring back at him.

"Edmunds," said Edmunds, holding out his wet hand.

"Rouche," said Rouche, shaking it. "I'll just . . ." he suggested, pointing into the back.

Rouche swapped seats, allowing Edmunds to climb in out of the rain. He moved a pair of ancient trainers, some oily Chinese takeaway packaging, and a novelty meter-long Jaffa Cake box onto the seat next to him.

"What are you doing here?" Baxter asked her friend.

"Helping." Edmunds smiled. "Figured you could use it."

"Do you remember the part where I told you I didn't need any help?"

"Do you remember the part where you used both the words 'please' and 'thank you'?"

"Ah." Rouche nodded.

She turned her angry gaze on him: "Ahhhhhhhh, what?" she demanded.

"Well, you only use pleasantries when you're lying," he replied, looking to Edmunds for support.

"Exactly," agreed Edmunds. "Also, have you noticed the way that when she gives you a really good insult, she kind of nods to herself afterwards, as if to say, 'Yeah, good one, me'?"

Rouche laughed out loud: "She *does* do that."

They both fell silent as they interpreted the new expression that had formed on her face.

"How did you find us?" she asked through gritted teeth.

"I've still got a *few* friends in Homicide," said Edmunds.

"Have *you* ever noticed the way that when *you* tell a lie, really stupid, unbelievable shit comes out of your mouth?" Baxter asked him, nodding subtly to herself. "You haven't got *any* friends in Homicide. Everyone hates you."

"Harsh," said Edmunds. "Fine—I might not have any friends there, but Finlay still does. He knew there was something up as well."

"Please *God* tell me you haven't dragged Finlay into all this?"

Edmunds looked a little guilty: "He's parking the car."

"For Christ's sake!"

"So," he said cheerfully, "why are we just sitting around?"

There was a rustling sound from the backseat.

"The FBI have shut us out," Rouche told him through a mouthful of Jaffa Cake. "We need to know what's going on in there, but they've stood down Baxter's man and will arrest us if we interfere."

"Oh," said Edmunds, absorbing half an hour's worth of drama in just a few seconds. "OK. Keep your phone on, then," he told them, before climbing back out into the rain.

"Edmunds! Where are you going? Wait!"

The car door slammed and they watched him walk away toward the entrance of the hotel.

Rouche was impressed. He hadn't believed anyone capable of handling Baxter so well.

"You know, I quite like your ex-boss," he told her, oblivious to his faux pas.

"My . . . what?" she asked, turning on him.

He cleared his throat. "Twenty-three minutes to go."

Edmunds was relieved to get out of the rain, until he remembered that by doing so, he had entered a building populated with murderous, self-mutilating cult members. With checkout time fast approaching, a seemingly endless stream of people was passing in and out of the hotel. He walked through the lobby, dirty footprints stalking him across the floor as he followed the modest signage. At the end of the corridor, a set of double doors stood open, leading to an apparently empty hall.

Edmunds took out his phone and dialed Baxter, pretending to be searching his pockets for his key card should anyone be watching.

"Is there another conference room?" he whispered in greeting.

"No. Why?" asked Baxter.

"It looks completely empty from where I'm standing."

"And where are you standing?"

"Down the corridor. Ten meters away."

"There's still twenty minutes before it's due to start."

"And not *one* person has showed?"

"You don't know that for sure. How much of the room can you see?"

Edmunds took a few steps forward, glancing behind him to ensure he was alone.

"Not much . . . I'm going to take a closer look."

"No! Don't do that!" panicked Baxter. "If you're wrong . . . if anybody's in there, you could blow the whole thing."

Edmunds ignored her and continued toward the silent room. More of the vacant seating came into view.

"Still no one," he reported under his breath.

"Edmunds!"

"I'm going in."

"Don't!"

He passed through the double doors and stepped into the completely empty conference hall. He looked around in confusion.

"There's no one here," he told Baxter, equal parts relieved and concerned.

He spotted a piece of white paper taped up to the inside of the door and walked over to read it, only then noticing the mobile phone placed subtly against the frame—one beady eye, a camera, facing toward him, no doubt streaming his image elsewhere. Yet another set of eyes watching the empty room.

"Oh shit," he said.

"What?" asked Baxter down the phone. "What's wrong?"

"They've moved it."

"What?"

"They've moved the meeting . . . to the City Oasis, across the road," said Edmunds, already running back out. "We're in the wrong building!"

CHAPTER 30

Sunday, 20 December 2015

10:41 A.M.

Edmunds burst from the Sycamore's lobby, afraid that he might have just blown the entire operation. At least whoever was watching would have seen only a lone civilian entering the hall, which had to be preferable to an armed tactical team.

Before being drowned out by the weather, he had heard Baxter relaying his discovery to the FBI. He held his phone in his hand, the call still connected, as he rushed across the busy road and entered through the revolving glass doors of the City Oasis Hotel.

Marble pillars lined the grand reception area, a coachless coachload of people scattered across the space as they sheltered from the rain.

Edmunds searched the various signs for directions:

← CONFERENCE SUITES

He accidently kicked over someone's suitcase and jogged toward the appropriate hallway. As he reached it, he spotted two large men, clearly security, standing outside a set of doors at the end of the corridor, a large crowd filling the room behind them. He took a casual glance in their direction and then continued walking, bringing his phone back up to his ear.

"Baxter? Are you there?"

He could hear her yelling at someone in the background: "Yeah. I'm here."

"Conference suite 2," he informed her.

The van accelerated down the service road at the back of the hotel, coming to a halt outside one of the rear entrances. The sliding door opened and the team clambered out, a series of clicks and beeps accompanying them as they prepped their equipment and tested their comms.

"Sure they've got the right building this time, boss?" asked one of the men.

The team leader, professionally, ignored the comment.

"I want you to run to the end of the building and see how many more exits we've got to cover," he told his mouthy colleague. He checked that his Airwave radio was set to the appropriate channel and pushed the "talk" button to speak into his headset. "Team 4 in position. Sitrep to follow."

The FBI surveillance unit pulled up alongside Baxter's Audi on the main road. The car behind honked its horn angrily but grew noticeably more patient when the armed FBI agent climbed out.

Baxter approached Chase as he passed orders to the teams.

"Team 3, be aware there is a second access point just around the corner from your position. All units, all units, Trojan is about to enter the building. Repeat: Trojan is about to enter the building."

Baxter rolled her eyes.

With Mitchell halfway back to New Scotland Yard, Chase's own "undercover" agent stepped out of the van. The man could have been Vin Diesel's younger, buffer brother. Even Chase was dwarfed by his imposing colleague, who looked absurd dressed in a baggy jumper and jeans.

"Go!" Chase ordered, sending his agent off down the road.

Baxter shook her head and resumed her phone call with Edmunds:

"You've got the FBI agent heading in now," she told him.

"OK. What does he look like?" Edmunds whispered back.

Baxter was still watching the man waddling uncomfortably away from them.

She shrugged. "Like an FBI agent trying not to look like one."

"I've got eyes on Chase's agent," said Edmunds, peering over the crowds in the lobby before rushing back to the vantage point he had found.

Several corridors led to the conference suites. He had discovered that the next one along spat him out at the door to suite 3, fifteen meters along from the guarded entrance. He glanced around the corner and caught a side-on glimpse of the imposing men behind the open door. The hum of voices spilling out into the corridor suggested scores of people inside, perhaps more, and he had seen two others arrive just while he'd been watching.

"OK," he whispered into the phone. "I've got a partial visual on the door."

"He's still making his way through the lobby," Baxter informed him.

Edmunds watched as a greasy-haired woman approached the doorway. In the split second that she was in view, she had done something strange.

"Hold on," he whispered, risking stepping out from his corner to get a better angle.

The door was still blocking his view.

"What's wrong?" Baxter asked urgently.

"I'm not sure. Tell him to wait."

There was a pause.

"He's already in the corridor," was Baxter's tense reply.

"Shit," hissed Edmunds, weighing up his options. "Shit. Shit. Shit."

"Should we abort? . . . Edmunds? Should we abort?"

Edmunds had already made his decision and was halfway to the set of open doors with his phone pressed to his ear. One of the thick-necked men peered around the wood when he heard him approaching, clearly not expecting anyone to come from that direction. As he reached the doorway, Edmunds smiled pleasantly at the man, noting the greasy-haired woman behind him, who was bearing her open blouse to his colleague, no doubt producing her mutilated invitation to gain entry.

Edmunds broke into inane chatter:

"I know! If it ever stopped raining we might." He laughed, turning down the main corridor, where the FBI agent was approaching from the other direction.

Both men were far too experienced to give in to the urge to make eye contact, to pass a subtle nod or shake of the head as to whether to proceed or not, knowing that the man in the doorway would be watching their every move.

Edmunds passed the brawny man without breaking stride, unable to tell him that he was less than six seconds away from being discovered.

He didn't dare increase his pace.

"Yeah, not in England, right?" He laughed loudly into his phone before whispering: "Abort! Abort! Abort!"

Behind him, the FBI agent was just three steps from the doorway when he veered off to the right and ambled casually along the corridor that Edmunds had just come down.

"There's got to be another entrance!" Chase yelled into his radio, desperately trying to salvage his floundering operation. He stormed back over to his surveillance vehicle.

"Chase! Chase!" called Baxter, to get his attention.

He paused for a moment to look at her.

She stuck her middle finger up at him: "You're welcome . . . you *prick*."

She knew it wasn't a particularly constructive thing to say, but she'd never claimed to be perfect. Chase looked genuinely hurt for a moment, not that she cared, and then he continued speaking to his agent:

"A window? Is there any way that you could take another pass, or maybe we can take out the guards?" he tried.

Baxter walked away and leaned against her car. She noticed a fresh scratch on the passenger door and rubbed at it absent-mindedly as she resumed her phone conversation with Edmunds.

"You just saved the whole operation from these idiots," she told him, "but they're still talking about sending someone in."

"If they do and Green's not in there, we've lost him," said Edmunds.

Her phone started buzzing against her ear. She looked at the screen.

"Hold on. I've got another call . . . Rouche?"

"I've got an idea. Meet me in the café across the road." He hung up.

"Edmunds?" she said. "Sit tight. Rouche has got something. I'll get back to you."

She ended the call and scanned the shopfronts on the other side of the street.

ANGIE'S CAFÉ

Soaked through and freezing cold, she weaved between the passing traffic and entered the café, triggering a shrill bell above the door. A visible layer of grime seemed to cover every conceivable surface, including Angie herself.

Rouche was sat at one of the big beige tables, serviettes wedged beneath one of the legs, a disposable plastic cup of coffee between his hands. The moment he saw her, he got to his feet and walked into the toilets. Baxter checked the time. They had just over ten minutes until the meeting was due to start, perhaps even less before Chase and his movie-star doppelgängers charged in and ruined everything.

Feeling tense, she strode across the room, ignoring the looks from the arse-crack-exhibiting clientele, and entered the toilets, using her shoulder to push the door open rather than risk touching the handle. Confronted with the two options, made even clearer by the addition of graffitied private parts, she pushed on the door to the men's and stepped inside the revolting room.

A cold draft poured in from a high frosted window. Two yellowed urinals were overspilling with blue hygiene disks, not that it appeared anybody considered their presence any more than a polite suggestion anyway, opting instead for the piss-covered floor.

Rouche had draped his suit jacket over the side of the cubicle and was washing his hands in the only sink.

"We couldn't talk out there?" she asked, glancing at her watch again.

He seemed distracted, like he hadn't even heard her.

"Rouche?"

He switched off the hot tap and Baxter realized that he hadn't been washing his hands but something *in* his hands. Without a word, he handed her the sharp steak knife he'd taken from the kitchen.

She looked down at it in confusion.

He started to unbutton his shirt.

"No! No way, Rouche! Are you crazy?" she said, finally catching up.

"We need to get in there," he said simply. He slid off his shirt.

"We do," said Baxter evenly. "But we can work out another way."

They both knew that wasn't true.

"We don't have time for this," said Rouche. "Either you can help me or I can do it myself and make even more of a mess."

He went to take the knife off her.

"OK! OK," she said, looking ill.

She tentatively stepped up against him and placed her left hand against his bare shoulder. She could feel his warm breath on her forehead.

She brought the knife up to his skin and hesitated.

The door behind them swung open and a bulky man froze in the entrance. They both turned around and glared at him. His eyes flicked from Baxter to Rouche to the discarded shirt to the weapon she had pressed to his chest.

"I'll come back," he mumbled, turning on his heel and leaving.

Baxter faced Rouche once more, secretly appreciative of the extra few moments to steel herself. She deliberated about where to start and then pushed the tip of the blade in gently until she drew blood, slicing a thin line downward until Rouche took hold of her hand.

"You're going to get me killed," he told her shortly, trying to provoke her. "You've seen these people's scars. If you can't do it properly—"

"This is for life, Rouche. You know that?"

He nodded: "Just do it."

He removed his emergency tie from his trouser pocket, folded it over on itself, and bit down hard.

"Do it!" he ordered again, muffled by his makeshift gag.

Baxter winced and sank the blade into him, forcing herself to ignore his involuntary gasps of pain, the way that his muscles were quivering beneath the skin, the rapid breaths against her hair, as she tore the letters across his chest.

At one point, he staggered back against the sink, almost losing consciousness as his own warm blood soaked into the waistband of his trousers.

While he took a moment, Baxter stared in revulsion at what she had done to him and retched. Her hands were covered in his blood.

PUPPL

Rouche looked at her incomplete handiwork in the mirror.

"You didn't think to mention before that you've got shitty hand-writing?" he joked, but Baxter was too traumatized even to smile.

He shoved the gag back into his mouth, stood up straight, and nodded.

Baxter dug the blade back in to finish the final letters:

PUPPET

The second she was done, she dropped the knife into the sink with trembling hands and ran into the cubicle to vomit. When she emerged, less than a minute later, she was horrified to find that Rouche had devised one final torture for himself.

He had the knife in one hand, a lighter in the other, heating the stained blade from beneath.

She didn't think she could take any more.

"Cauterizing the wounds," he explained. "I need to stop the bleeding."

He didn't ask her to help.

He pushed the flat side of the metal into the deepest wound, to the sickening hiss of burning flesh, and worked his way around from there.

Bent over the sink, he turned to her, eyes watering, struggling to catch his breath.

"Time?" he asked, barely able to speak.

"Ten fifty-seven."

He nodded, wiping the blood away with coarse paper towels: "Shirt."

Baxter stared at him blankly.

"Shirt, please," he said, gesturing to the floor.

Baxter handed it to him, unable to take her eyes off his disfigured chest until he covered it.

She took out her mobile:

"Edmunds? I need you to get into a good position . . . Rouche is coming in."

CHAPTER 31

Sunday, 20 December 2015

10:59 A.M.

Edmunds felt sick.

Just moments earlier, Baxter had informed him of the sacrifice that the CIA agent had made in order to keep their operation alive.

Edmunds watched as Rouche entered the hotel through the revolving doors. He looked ashen and sweaty, unsteady on his feet as he fiddled with his suit jacket in an attempt to hide his bloody shirt.

"Eyes on Rouche," he told Baxter, fighting the urge to rush over and help him. "This isn't going to work," he said worriedly. "I don't think he's even going to make it to the door."

"He'll make it."

Rouche staggered across the reception area holding his chest, attracting several inquiring looks before having to steady himself, just out of sight of the two men guarding the doors. His legs suddenly gave out beneath him. He slumped against the wall, smearing a red mark onto the cream paint.

Edmunds had unconsciously taken a few steps toward him, but paused when Rouche gave him a subtle shake of the head.

The numbers on Edmunds's watch rearranged themselves with a buzzy electrical beep: 11 A.M. He could see the two men down the corridor checking their own wrists.

"Come on," he whispered under his breath, his eyes darting from Rouche to the men in the doorway and back again.

Rouche pushed himself off the wall. He could feel his shirt sticking to his skin and tried to tell himself that it was sweat rather than blood that had saturated the material. It felt as though he had a gaping hole in him. He could feel the breeze that snuck in with each revolution of the door, inside him, as if it were blowing straight through him. Unable to pinpoint any specific source of the pain, his brain told every last nerve in his body that it was burning.

He forced himself to stand up straight and stepped around the corner into the corridor, walking purposefully toward the open doorway. The two men watched him carefully as he approached. Behind them, the audience looked to have taken their seats, and the hum of conversation was dying down.

The two men appeared to be brothers, both sharing the same sharp features and imposing way of being fat. Rouche approached the bigger of the two, in a psychological display that he had nothing to hide. He nodded curtly.

Eyeing him warily, the man directed him just inside the doorway, tactically positioning Rouche so that he could no longer see the other man behind him.

He gestured to Rouche's chest.

Gritting his teeth, Rouche unbuttoned his suit jacket, feeling the wounds ripping back open as he slid his arm out of the sleeve. He didn't need to look down to assess the damage; the expression on the man's face was enough.

His white shirt was now no more than a red-and-brown rag clinging to him, a bandage in need of changing. Suddenly, there was a large, rough hand over his mouth, the stink of nicotine-tainted skin, and a tree trunk of an arm locked around his throat.

"We've got a problem!" Edmunds told Baxter. "They know something's wrong."

"Are you sure?" she asked him, unable to hide the panic in her voice. "If we're blown, we need to move in now."

"I can't say for sure . . . I can't see them."

Baxter's voice went distant for a moment:

"Prepare to breach," she told someone in the background. Her voice then returned at full volume. "It's your call, Edmunds."

"Hey! Hey! Hey!" said a softly spoken man as he rushed over to the scene in the doorway.

Several members of the audience had noticed the disturbance and were watching avidly. Rouche was struggling in vain against the arm around his neck. His shirt had been torn open to reveal the word, rendered almost illegible from where it had bled over the lines, like a poorly colored-in picture.

"What's going on?" the newcomer asked the two doormen.

He was in his late forties, and had an ironically kind face beneath his neat beard considering where they were.

"You told us to act on anything suspicious, Doc," said the taller brother. "His scars are fresh," he explained unnecessarily.

The doctor gently pulled Rouche's shirt open and winced at the mess beneath. He met Rouche's eye and gestured for the other brother to let him speak.

Rouche gasped as the hand moved away from his mouth and the arm around his throat slackened a little.

"My, my, what a mess you have made of yourself," the doctor said, calm but suspicious. He waited for an explanation.

"I cut them into myself every morning," said Rouche. It was the best answer he'd been able to come up with.

The doctor looked undecided. "Who invited you here today?" he asked Rouche.

"Dr. Green."

The answer, although possibly true, was of no use. The FBI had made Alexei Green one of the most famous people on the planet almost overnight. The man stroked his chin as he regarded Rouche:

"Kill him," he said with a pained shrug.

Rouche's eyes grew wide as the arm tightened around his throat. He kicked out and pulled desperately at the asphyxiating appendage when something caught the doctor's attention:

"Stop!" he ordered. He took hold of Rouche's wrists and raised them out in front of him. "May I?" he asked politely, as if Rouche had any choice.

He unbuttoned Rouche's cuffs and rolled the shirtsleeves back to reveal the jagged line of scar tissue torn into his forearms. The doctor delicately ran his fingers along the wrinkled and raised pink skin.

"Not so fresh." He smiled at Rouche. "What's your name?"

"Damien," Rouche croaked.

"You need to learn to follow instructions, Damien," he said, before addressing the two doormen: "I think we can safely say that Damien is one of ours."

Rouche was released from the chokehold and gasped for air, staggering two strides forward so that Edmunds would be able to see him in the open doorway.

"Excellent work," the man told the two brothers. "But I think you owe Damien here an apology, don't you?"

"Sorry," said the taller man, staring at his toes like a chastised child.

The man who had restrained Rouche, however, turned to face the wall. He began punching it as hard as he possibly could.

"Whoa! Whoa!" said the doctor, taking hold of his damaged hands. "Nobody's angry with you, Malcolm. I was only asking you to apologize to Damien. It's polite."

The man couldn't meet his eye: "Sorry."

Rouche waved off the apology graciously, despite still being bent over struggling for breath, and seized the opportunity to remove the earpiece from his pocket.

"You take a moment," said the doctor, resting a hand on Rouche's back. "When you're ready, find yourself a seat."

Still bent double, Rouche glimpsed Edmunds in the lobby, phone to his ear, as the heavy doors between them were pulled together and locked, sealing him inside.

The doctor walked away.

Forcing himself upright, Rouche re-dressed himself, quickly poking the two-way earpiece into place while taking his first proper look around the hall. In comparison to the depressing venue across the street, the room felt modern and light. He quickly counted the number of chairs in the back row and the number of rows standing between him and the stage to estimate the size of the audience. The stage itself stood perhaps five feet above the floor, with a large projector screen hanging down as a backdrop. The doctor who had permitted him entrance climbed the steps in the center to join two other people whom Rouche did not recognize.

"I'm in," he mumbled. "Between thirty-five and fifty suspects."

He spotted a vacant seat toward the end of a row and side-stepped his way through, facing the rear of the room. Just as he reached the chair, everybody around him got to their feet and he found himself staring into a sea of faces.

His first instinct was to run, even though he knew he had nowhere to go, but then they broke into rapturous applause.

Alexei Green had taken to the stage.

Rouche turned around to see the long-haired man waving to his adoring audience. To make his entrance a little more memorable, he had dressed in a sharp suit with a metallic-blue sheen and, perhaps more importantly, had projected behind him an enormous photograph of the Banker's suspended body set against the New York skyline.

Rouche joined the applause, conscious that he was somewhere within that photograph, one of the indistinguishable crowd of emergency-service personnel staring up at the corpse from the safety of the bridge.

"Obs on Green," he almost had to shout over the cheers and intensifying applause as the image changed: a crumpled black truck replaced the Banker, its back end protruding from the entrance of the 33rd Precinct like the handle of a knife.

Rouche recalled seeing what was left of Officer Kennedy's body in the morgue, a good man by all accounts. He remembered the dirty rope still wrapped around his right wrist from where he had been bound to the hood before being driven through the wall of a building populated with his friends and colleagues.

Rouche clapped harder.

"All teams: move into position," Chase ordered into his radio.

"Thirty-five to fifty people in the audience," Baxter told him.

"Between three-five and five-zero perps," Chase helpfully translated into American.

Baxter moved away from the mobile surveillance unit to resume her other conversation:

"Edmunds, evacuate the lobby. They're coming in."

Edmunds looked around the crowded space in concern: "Yeah . . . No problem."

"Do you need any help?" she asked.

"No, I'll be all right. I've got Fi—"

Finlay shook his head, having joined Edmunds a few moments earlier.

"I've got things covered," he corrected himself before hanging up.

"She'd only fret if she knew I was in here," Finlay explained. "Let's just get these people out and she need never know."

Edmunds nodded. They split up and began shepherding people outside as quietly as they could through one set of doors as the armed officers rushed inside through another.

Rouche risked a glance around the room, expecting Chase and his men to be joining them imminently. There were three exits, one on either side of the stage and the large double doors through which he had entered. He had already warned Baxter that there were two makeshift security personnel on each exit, none of whom appeared to have heard the arrival of the tactical teams, who were undoubtedly mere inches away from them behind the wooden doors.

He returned his attention to Green as the psychiatrist jogged down the steps at the front of the stage to join his followers, his floppy hair held in place by the headset microphone. Rouche had to hand it to him—he was a charismatic and charming public speaker, exactly the sort of magnetic personality suited to inspire the impressionable.

"Our brothers and sisters have made us so, *so* proud," he told the room passionately, his voice cracking.

He appeared to be set on meeting every eye in the audience as he roamed up and down the aisle. A woman at the end of a row wrapped her arms around him as he passed, falling out of her seat as she wept in delight. Rouche noticed one of the doormen moving in, but Green held up a hand to signal that he was fine. He stroked the woman's hair and then lifted her chin to speak directly to her.

"And we, in turn, are going to make them equally as proud."

The room applauded the idea enthusiastically as he continued: "And one very fortunate person, sitting in *this* room *right* now, just a little sooner than the rest of us." Green smiled, finally able to detach himself from the woman.

Rouche used the comment as an excuse to take another look around the hall as the audience searched the faces of their neighbors for their unidentified champion. By the time Rouche turned back, Green was at the end of his row. Just two people sat between them. He was three meters away at most.

The police would breach at any second.

Rouche wondered whether he could reach him.

Green must have noticed him staring because he was looking right at him. His eyes flicked down to Rouche's soiled shirt, but he did not falter:

"Two days, my friends. Just two more days to wait!" he shouted, firing up his audience as he continued up the aisle, out of reach, to the sound of thunderous applause.

On seeing the looks of adoration on the faces around him, Rouche understood the necessity for this risky final meeting: these people worshipped Green. There was nothing they wouldn't do to earn his approval, even dying for him, and in return all they asked was that he love them back. They had *needed* to see him this one last time.

And now, they were entirely his to command.

"Do not breach. Do not breach," Rouche mumbled, hoping that Baxter was still listening. Green voluntarily offering up his plans would be a far more reliable way of extracting them than the defiant silence or self-preserving half-truths of an interrogation. "Repeat: do . . . not . . . breach," he said again, raising his voice.

The tapping of rain against the skylights transformed into a sudden shower of hailstones to complement the applause.

"Each of you already knows what is expected of you," Green told the room, his tone now serious. "But know this: when the eyes of the world fix on Piccadilly Circus and witness our glorious victory for themselves, when they carry their dead up out of the ground to be counted, *that* is when they will finally take notice. *That* is when they will finally understand . . . that we are not 'damaged.' We are not 'afflicted.' We are not 'weak.'"

Green shook his head dramatically before raising both of his arms up into the air:

"Together we . . . are . . . strong!"

The room was on its feet once more, the roar from the crowd deafening.

Chase and his handful of FBI agents were in position at the two sets of doors adjacent to the stage and therefore adjacent to Green. He was in the middle of a whispered argument with Baxter.

"For Christ's sake, Chase. Just give him a minute longer," she said.

"Negative," replied Chase, able to raise his voice a little as the applause continued inside the room. "He's eyeballed Green. We're going in."

"He said not to breach!"

"Goddamn it, Baxter! Keep this channel clear!" he snapped. "We're going in. All teams. All teams. Breach! Breach! Breach!"

*

The ovation faltered as the three sets of double doors shook fiercely against their metal locks. It was Green who reacted first, backing away toward the stage, where his alarmed colleagues were getting to their feet. The fear on the faces of their leaders spread through the crowd like a contagion. Rouche started shoving his way out into the aisle as, behind him, the main doors yielded.

The crowd surged.

He was suddenly pinned against the wall as the people at the end of the rows were thrown into him, the audience moving as a single entity. Green had reached the stage by the time the exits either side of him finally burst open.

"FBI! Get down! Get down!"

Rouche was fighting desperately to break free of the crush as the crowd moved as one again, swelling toward this fresh opening. The wave of bodies crashed over the FBI agents, the audience not dispersing in all directions as expected but concentrating on a single point.

The crowd swallowed up two of the armed officers as the first shots were fired. But still they pushed on. Rouche could see Green, surrounded by his entourage, making a beeline for the open doors. Shoving someone over, Rouche managed to break free of the herd. He clambered over rows of seats, positive that the overwhelmed officers had not spotted Green heading toward them and were in no position to intervene even if they had.

There was the crack of a gunshot.

The man in front of Rouche dropped to the floor, leaving only open space between him and a panicking officer. The order to use deadly force had evidently been given once the police started losing control. He could see that the officer had not recognized him, that amid the chaos, and in his self-mutilated state, he appeared no more than another of Green's fanatical followers.

The officer took aim, the heavy gun clicking in anticipation.

Rouche froze. He opened his mouth to say something but knew he would never get the words out in time . . .

The assault rifle fired just as a swarm of people engulfed the officer, wasting the gunshot into empty air. The man was shoved onto the floor. Rouche was trying to reach him when a second wave of people, flowing into the path of least resistance, swept him up, trampling the floored man.

He was carried through the doors and into the corridor outside. The majority of the audience stampeded toward the lobby, but then Rouche spotted Green climbing through an emergency exit at the far end of the hallway.

The glass had been smashed. He climbed out through the jagged pane and into the service area at the back of the hotel. Beyond the Armed Response vehicle, Green was running toward the main road.

"Baxter!" Rouche shouted, pushing the earpiece hard against his skull. "Green's outside. On foot towards Marble Arch."

He was unable to decipher her distorted response.

He sprinted around the side of the building and onto the street, where people were huddling together beneath storefronts and doorways. The frozen raindrops felt excruciating as they struck his burning chest.

Rouche thought he'd lost him, but then Green tore across the road in front of the three grand archways, his coiffed long hair now dark strips stuck to his face.

"Oxford Street!" Rouche yelled as he rounded the corner, unsure whether Baxter was even still receiving his comms in the deteriorating weather.

Green was putting more and more distance between them as Rouche's body started to fail him, no longer able to ignore the damage to which he had subjected it. The hail felt more like ball bearings striking him, his painful breathing returning.

Green was confident enough to pause and watch as Rouche slowed to walking pace, every last drop of adrenaline spent. He scooped his hair out of his eyes, laughed, and started walking away.

Rouche was on the verge of collapsing when Baxter's Audi sped past.

The car mounted the pavement meters ahead of Green and made contact with the wall of a building, cutting him off. Caught off guard, Green deliberated between the busy road on one side and the lingerie shop on the other when Rouche tackled him from behind, the metallic suit tearing as he dragged him to the ground.

Baxter rushed out of the car and contributed a knee to the back of Green's neck, pinning him to the pavement as she secured the handcuffs.

Utterly exhausted, Rouche rolled onto his back, the sleet easing into the first graceful snowflakes as he stared up into the blank sky. He was gasping for breath, holding his chest, and yet, for the first time in as long as he could remember, he actually felt peaceful.

"Rouche?" shouted Baxter. "Rouche?"

He could hear her speaking to someone.

"Ambulance . . . 521 Oxford Street . . . Yeah, it's an Ann Summers shop . . . Police officer injured. Multiple deep lacerations, severe blood loss . . . Please hurry." Her voice became louder. "They're on their way, Rouche! We got him. We got him! It's over."

He slowly turned his head to watch as she pulled Green up onto his knees, somehow managing a smile . . . but then his eyes grew wide.

"Rouche? Are you all right? What's wrong?" she asked as he started crawling back over to them. "I don't think you should move. Rouche?"

He cried out in pain as he dragged himself across the freezing concrete. He reached up and ripped the rest of Green's saturated shirt open to reveal the familiar word scarred into his chest:

PUPPET

"Shit," gasped Baxter as Rouche rolled onto his back again. "Why would he . . . ? Oh shit!"

Green smiled up at her triumphantly.

"He was never the one holding the strings," Rouche wheezed, his words turning to mist above him. "We haven't stopped anything."

CHAPTER 32

Sunday, 20 December 2015

12:39 P.M.

Chase was furious.

His botched operation and subsequent failure to apprehend Green himself had, at least temporarily, countermanded the FBI's claim to the prisoner. Baxter was all too aware that this situation would be short-lived with her spineless commander throwing the fight in her corner. As such, she had arranged to interview Green the moment he arrived at Homicide and Serious Crime Command.

The rest of his followers had been distributed across a number of local stations based on a complex algorithm calculating current workload against predicted operational demand, written by a man in IT. A man who, as chance would have it, had been briefly mistaken for the Ragdoll Killer and unjustly robbed of his lunch almost eighteen months earlier. The officers on duty were conducting interviews based on a set of questions that had been written and circulated by Chase.

Baxter had expected Green to delay proceedings by demanding a lawyer; however, to her surprise, he had made no such request, an ill-advised decision on which she intended to capitalize. With Rouche in the hospital, she had reluctantly asked Saunders to join her. As much as she disliked the loudmouthed detective constable, he was so vile that he had proven to be the unit's most effective investigative interviewer time and time again.

They made their way to the interview rooms, where the officer on guard opened the door to room 1. (Only new staff to the department ever used the pristine room 2.) Green sat patiently at the table in the center of the room. He smiled at them pleasantly.

"You can wipe that shit-eating grin off your face for a start," Saunders barked at him.

Baxter wasn't used to being the good cop.

For the first time ever, Saunders looked quite professional. He was still dressed in uniform from the operation and was holding a file full of paperwork in his hands, which he slammed down threateningly on the table as he took a seat. It was, of course, just a copy of *Men's Health* he'd tucked inside a plastic folder, but she thought it was a nice touch.

"If you think you've beaten us, you are sorely mistaken," Green told them, tucking his hair behind his ears.

"Is that so?" asked Saunders. "That's strange, because I thought we'd arrested all your batshit-crazy friends, all of whom are spilling their guts to our colleagues at this very mome—"

"How many?" Green interrupted.

"All of them."

"How many precisely?"

Saunders faltered over the question.

Green smiled smugly and leaned back in his chair.

"So, including however many escaped your poorly executed raid this morning, plus all of those I instructed not to attend, I'd say that makes you . . . *fucked*."

To buy himself a moment to think, Saunders picked up the file and flicked it open to appear as though he was checking something. It was, in fact, yet another article on how to achieve a six-pack in just six weeks, which in theory would have put the magazine out of business after a month and a half if any of them actually worked.

Feeling instantly fatter, he closed the file and turned to Baxter with a shrug.

"I suppose he's right," said Saunders, before slapping himself on the forehead theatrically. "Do you know what? I've done something really bloody stupid! I've already arranged to meet that woman on Tuesday. What was her name again?"

"Maria," Baxter reminded him.

Green tensed.

"And you'll never guess where I've asked her to meet me."

"Don't say Piccadilly Circus Underground Station!" Baxter shook her head in pantomime dismay.

"See," said Saunders, turning back to Green, "I figured, as your sister, she might recognize any ex-colleagues, friends, possibly even patients of yours. Legitimate request, I'm sure you'll agree. She'll be there all day."

Green's change of mood was verification that the Tube station was indeed the intended target.

"She means nothing to me." Green shrugged quite convincingly.

"Really?" asked Saunders. "You know, I was the one who interviewed her the day we realized it was you."

"One of *you* interviewed me," said Green, speaking over him, meeting Baxter's eye. "At the prison. That's right. An agent . . . Curtis, wasn't it? How's she doing these days?"

Baxter's back straightened. She clenched her fists.

Saunders swiftly continued: "*I* was the one who had to tell her what an evil piece of shit her brother really was. She didn't believe it at first. She defended you passionately. It was . . . *pathetic* watching her belief in you crumble like that."

The comment landed.

Green glanced at him before returning his gaze to Baxter: "You must have left her," he said, watching her closely. "If you're sitting here, to save yourself, you must have abandoned her in there."

Baxter's eyes narrowed. Her breathing quickened.

Saunders was also watching her. Should she lash out at Green, the interview would be over, and he'd be protected by the Met's self-imposed red tape and army of crusading bureaucrats.

It had become a race to see who broke first.

"I know you're not like the rest of them," said Saunders. "You don't believe in any of this. You're doing this for a payday, aren't you?"

Their handsome suspect gave them nothing:

"From what little I know of knife wounds," Green spoke over him, "they very seldom kill instantly."

Baxter's hands were trembling with anger, her jaw set.

"So what was it?" Saunders shouted. "Money or their silence? Hang on. You're not some sort of pedo or something, are you?"

"I don't think she could have been dead when you left her. She wasn't, was she?" smirked Green, taunting Baxter.

She got to her feet.

Realizing that his current angle wasn't working, Saunders changed tack:

"Who's Abby?" he asked. "Sorry. I should have said, who *was* Abby?"

For no more than a split second, Green's eyes filled with emotion. He turned to address Baxter once more, but it was too late—Saunders had found his "in" and was going for the jugular:

"Yeah, your sister mentioned her. She died, right? What would she think about all this? I wonder. Think Annie would be proud of you? Think Annie would—"

"Abby!" Green yelled at him. "Her name is Abby!"

Saunders laughed:

"Honestly, mate, I couldn't give a toss. Oh, wait . . . Unless you killed her?" He leaned forward in interest. "In which case, I'm all ears."

"How fucking *dare* you," spat Green, now a red-faced version of his former self, deep frown lines betraying his age. "Fuck you . . . both of you. I am doing *all* of this *for* her."

Baxter and Saunders shared the briefest of glances, knowing how significant that aggravated admission could be, but Saunders wasn't done yet:

"That's all well and good—doing this as some form of fucked-up tribute to Amy . . ."

"Abby!" Green screamed again, spraying the table in spittle as he fought against his restraints.

". . . but do you *really* think anyone's gonna give a second thought to you or your dead bitch of a girlfriend after the bombs start going off?" Saunders laughed bitterly in Green's face. "You're nothing, no more than a distraction, a warm-up act for the main event."

Both Baxter and Saunders held their breath, aware that he had just played his hand.

Slowly, Green leaned as close to Saunders as his handcuffs would permit. When he finally spoke, it was in a whisper tainted with rage and hate:

"Come see me on Tuesday, you smug piece of shit, 'cause I promise you—you *are* going to remember her name: A-B-B-Y." He counted the four letters out on his fingers before sitting back in his chair.

Baxter and Saunders turned to one another. Without a word, they got up and hurried out of the room.

They had what they needed.

"I'd like to see MI5 try to tell us there's no threat of another attack now," scoffed Baxter as they marched across the office collecting up the team en route to the meeting room. "And find out where we are on the deceased girlfriend."

"We've got a serious problem," announced a detective the moment Baxter stepped through the door.

"Oh, but things were just going so well!" She could never remember the manly young woman's name: Nichols? Nixon? *Knuckles?* She decided to play it safe: "Go ahead, Detective."

"We've finished eliminating suspects in custody versus the self-deleting phone messages . . ."

"Suicide texts!" Techie Steve's voice called from under a desk somewhere.

"Thirteen of Green's Puppets remain unaccounted for."

"*Thirteen?*" Baxter winced.

"And . . ." the woman continued guiltily, "of the Puppets processed so far, at least five of them have no prior history of mental illness and no record of ever visiting any psychiatrist, let alone one of *our* psychiatrists. It confirms that, as in New York, this thing is much bigger than just Green and his patients. We've only been focusing on a very small piece of the puzzle . . . Just thought you should know."

Baxter made a sound: the combination of exhaustion, disappointment, and concern manifesting itself as a concise, but pathetic, squeak.

The woman smiled apologetically and took a seat.

"Hey," whispered Saunders. "What did Knuckles want?"

It bloody *was* Knuckles!

"Just to piss on our fireworks," sighed Baxter as she walked to the front of the room and brought the team up to speed.

Blake raised his hand.

"For Christ's sake, Blake," she shouted. "You're a grown-up. Speak!"

"Would Green really have confirmed how many bombs they're planning?"

"Makes sense—same as New York. Plus, Saunders got it out of him."

"Oh." Blake nodded, requiring no further explanation.

Chase looked blankly between them.

"He was provoked," Blake explained.

"How's facial recognition going?" Baxter asked the room.

"The City Oasis has sent their footage to us," said one of the FBI tech team. "We're comparing video between both hotels to ensure we haven't missed anyone."

"And the three people onstage with Green?" she asked.

"One was shot and killed while trying to escape."

Baxter huffed.

"She pulled a knife on me!" one of Chase's agents said defensively.

"Dr. Amber Ives," the man continued. "Another psychiatrist and bereavement counselor. Numerous occasions for her to run into Green—seminars, mutual colleagues." He checked his notes. "A second, who was with Ives, did manage to escape."

Everyone looked accusingly at the FBI agent:

"There were a *lot* of people!"

"And the third?" asked Baxter, losing patience.

"Is being transferred here right now. Says he wants to make a deal."

"Well, that's progress," said Baxter. "But continue working on the assumption he's gonna give us shit all in the meantime." She turned to Saunders. "Really great work in there," she complimented him, before addressing Chase: "We're done with Green. You can fight with MI5 over him now."

Baxter hesitated on the threshold of Rouche's private room in St. Mary's Hospital as the snow fell heavily outside the window. For a split second, she was back inside the dark church watching the thin line appear across Curtis's throat, her memories lured back there by Green's taunts . . .

Rouche looked dead as he slept, his head hanging forward over his chest, where the weeping wounds bled through the bandages. His arms were positioned unnaturally, each linked to a drip bag on a pole, the trailing tubes snaking up and off the bed like wires holding him in place.

His eyes flickered open and he smiled wearily at her.

She shook the image and walked toward the bed, tossing him the family bag of Crunchie Rocks she'd picked up from the newsagent's in the foyer, a touching gesture, ruined only by the restricted movement in Rouche's medicine-fed arms and his resultant shriek as the projectile landed dead center of his bloody bandages.

"Bollocks!" she gasped, rushing over to place them on the wheelie bedside-cupboard thing instead.

She picked up the remote control to turn down the Christmas movie, which she secretly recognized as *Harry Potter and the*

Half-Blood Prince, the similarities between their situations dawning on her as Albus Dumbledore imparted a grave warning to his students that their enemy's greatest weapon was them themselves.

She hit the "mute" button and sat beside Rouche.

"So when are they letting you out?" she asked.

"Tomorrow morning," he told her. "They've got to pump me full of antibiotics until then so that I—and I quote—'don't die.' At least I can breathe again now."

Baxter looked at him quizzically.

"I had a rib poking into my lung," he explained. "Since the prison."

"Ah." Baxter stared guiltily at the bandages wrapped around him.

"I'm gonna get some funny looks down at the pool now," joked Rouche.

"Maybe they can do something," said Baxter. "Skin grafts or something?"

"Yeah," he said. "Yeah, I'm pretty sure they can."

He wasn't very convincing.

"There are those people who transform tattoos into other things," she suggested hopefully. "Get rid of exes' names and stuff."

"Yeah." Rouche nodded. "They could make it say . . . Buppet?" He pulled a face.

"Puppies!" Baxter suggested, straight-faced, before they both burst out laughing at the absurd suggestion.

Rouche held his painful chest: "So what did you get out of Green?"

Baxter filled him in on their interview with the pseudo-leader and what they had gleaned from the captured doctor, Yannis Hoffman, who had provided them with complete details of his patients, three of whom were among the thirteen Puppets still at large. A medical doctor specializing in cancer and palliative care, he had been recruited by Alexei Green directly, whom he had believed to be the sole architect of the murders. Vitally, however, and earning himself the reduced prison sentence he'd been seeking, the doctor had confirmed an exact time for the attack: 5 P.M. Rush hour.

"And get this," she added. "Green's girlfriend was killed in the Norway terror attacks."

If that revelation upset Rouche, he didn't show it: "Motive?"

"Vulnerability," Baxter corrected him.

"None of this was ever about the Ragdoll case?"

"Only to ensure that the entire world was watching," said Baxter. "Just a very clever distraction, using some very vulnerable people, to set off some very big bombs. They used the worst parts of us against us, made possible by our own craving for bloodlust. And people haven't been this excited since the Ragdoll murders."

She'd clearly been thinking a lot since her interview with Green.

"It's genius," she continued. "I mean, who's watching their back for someone sneaking up on them when they're consumed with fighting one another? They made us kill ourselves."

CHAPTER 33

Sunday, 20 December 2015
6:03 P.M.

The snowflakes glittered as they fell through the headlight beams of Baxter's Audi. The car had picked up a fresh grating noise and been pulling to the right ever since taking a chunk out of the Oxford Street Superdrug earlier that afternoon. The first niggling doubts had set in regarding the likelihood of it passing its upcoming MOT.

Baxter switched off the engine. A sharp hiss of air escaped from under the hood, suggesting yet another fault to fix/cover up. Either that or the car was literally sighing in relief at completing this latest journey unscathed.

On spotting the group of sportswear-clad youths loitering at the entrance to the park (the morbidly obese one apparently wearing it ironically), she unplugged her satnav and tucked it under the seat. Gloves on. Hat on. She grabbed a bag from the passenger seat and crunched along the path to Edmunds's maisonette.

She rang the doorbell. As she waited, she noticed a set of dead Christmas lights trailing down the brickwork that looked to have been severed in half. Down the street, a bottle smashed and laughter rang out over the quiet houses. She heard the sound of Leila crying before the hallway light came on and Tia struggled to unlock the front door one-handed.

"Merry Christmas!" Baxter smiled, making a real effort. She held up the bag of presents that she had collected from her flat on the way over. "Merry Christmas, Leila," she cooed, reaching out to stroke the baby, much as she would Echo, while using the same silly voice she adopted to call him for his dinner.

Tia tutted and then disappeared back down the hallway, leaving Baxter stood on the doorstep like an idiot.

"Alex!" she heard Tia call, the sound coming from around the side of the property. Leila was still crying. "Alex!"

"Yeah?"

"Your girlfriend's at the door. I'll be upstairs," she told him as Leila's cries faded away.

A few moments later, Edmunds came rushing down the hallway, brushing snowflakes out of his hair.

Baxter was almost positive that the socially acceptable way to handle situations such as this was to pretend that she had heard nothing and then to drop in passive-aggressive comments about Tia whenever the conversation permitted.

"Baxter!" Edmunds smiled. "Why are you still out there? Come in."

"What the *hell*'s her problem?" she blurted, unable to help herself.

He waved it off. "Oh, she thinks you're a bad influence on me . . . and I missed a one-year-old's birthday party or something this morning . . . *and* there was something else too," he said cryptically as he closed the front door behind her and walked through to the kitchen, where the open back door invited the night inside.

She handed him the bag of gifts, only to receive an even larger one in return.

"Drink?" he offered.

"No . . . I shouldn't stay," she said, looking pointedly up at the ceiling, deciding to go down the passive-aggressive route anyway. "I just came round to . . . I just had to . . . I . . ."

Edmunds recognized the telltale awkwardness that preceded Baxter bestowing a compliment or praise.

". . . I just wanted to say . . . thank you."

"You're welcome."

"You were looking out for me . . . like usual . . ."

There was more? Edmunds was astounded.

". . . and you were brilliant today . . . like usual."

"*Actually*," said Edmunds, "I think it's *me* who needs to thank *you*. Today . . . this last fortnight really has made me realize just how much I miss this. *God,* I miss it: the danger, the excitement, the . . . *importance* of it all. Tia's pissed off with me, well, with us, because I *kinda* handed in my notice this afternoon."

Baxter's face lit up: "You're coming back!"

"I can't."

She deflated.

"I need to have a life. I need to think about my family. But at the same time, I can't waste away behind a desk in Fraud any longer either."

"So . . . ?"

"I want to show you something."

Confused, Baxter followed him outside and across the wedge of snow illuminated by the kitchen light to the rickety shed.

"Da-naaaa!" sang Edmunds proudly, gesturing to the in-no-way "da-naaaa"-worthy eyesore.

His enthusiasm dissipated with Baxter's underwhelming reaction.

"Bollocks," he said, realizing why the unveiling had not earned the anticipated response. He stooped down to pick up the home-made sign. "Stupid bloody thing won't stay up," he explained, hooking it back on to the wood. "Da-naaaa!"

ALEX EDMUNDS—PRIVATE INVESTIGATOR

He opened the flimsy door, which almost dropped off its hinges, to reveal the office he'd set up within. Lit by the cozy glow of a desk lamp, his laptop sat atop the work surface beside a printer and a cordless phone. An oil heater in the corner warmed the tiny space. There was a coffee machine, a kettle, a hose hooked over a bucket to form a makeshift sink, and even a "client seating area" (second stool).

"So what do you think?"

Baxter didn't answer right away, taking another long look around the shed.

"It's just temporary, of course," Edmunds insisted when she failed to respond. "Just while I get myself set up and . . . Are you crying?"

"No!" replied Baxter, her voice cracking. "I just think . . . I think it's perfect."

"Oh my God! You *are* crying!" said Edmunds, embracing her.

"I'm just so happy for you . . . and it's been such a hard couple of weeks." She laughed, before bursting into tears.

Edmunds continued to hold her as she sobbed against his shoulder.

"Christ!" she said, her mascara smudged across her cheeks, laughing as she composed herself. "I've snotted on you. I'm so sorry! I'm gross."

"You're not gross," Edmunds assured her.

It *was* a bit gross.

"Leila already dribbled food all over this top anyway," he told her, pointing to it. In actual fact, he suspected that stain had also come from Baxter.

"'Means something more to him,'" she said, wiping her eyes, reading one of the half-formed ideas scrawled onto the sheets of paper that littered the wooden wall behind him.

"Yeah," said Edmunds, ripping the sheet down to decipher his own handwriting. "Puppet . . . Bait. Why carve *those* particular words into themselves and their victims?"

"A sign of loyalty?" suggested Baxter, still sniffing. "A test?"

"I'm sure his disciples see it that way—a brand of unity, of being a part of something, but I can't help feeling that it means something else entirely to our . . . *Azazel*." He used the name reluctantly. "Something personal."

He hesitated before continuing:

"Baxter, I don't think you are going to be able to stop what-ever's coming."

"Cheers for the confidence boost."

"It's just . . ." He looked concerned. "Look at the amount of work that must have gone into persuading Glenn Arnolds to stitch another man onto his back, building him gradually to that level of delusion, systematically substituting his meds like that—all tai-lored solely to that one person. This is beyond obsession . . . This is someone's sole purpose on this earth . . . and that terrifies me."

Ten minutes and a cup of shed tea later, Baxter was on the doorstep, bag of presents in hand.

"Oh, I almost forgot," said Edmunds. He rushed back down the hallway to fetch something. He returned with a white envelope, which he tucked into the top of the present bag. "Last one, I'm afraid. Listen, Baxter—"

"Do myself a favor and don't open it?" she interrupted, know-ing Edmunds was once again about to voice his opinion on them spying on Thomas.

He nodded.

"Merry Christmas," she said, giving him a peck on the cheek before walking back out into the night.

Baxter returned to the house to find it empty. She had completely forgotten that Thomas was out at one of the numerous work dos scheduled over the festive season. She placed the bag of presents beneath the Christmas tree and two things slowly dawned on her: One, Thomas had purchased a tree. Two, thanks to everything going on, she hadn't actually bought him a single present yet.

With Echo asleep in the kitchen, Rouche spending the night in the hospital, and Thomas no doubt getting pawed at by Linda "the Cougar," she wished she had dropped in on Finlay after all. She hadn't wanted to intrude on his and Maggie's evening with the grandchildren so had thanked him for his help over the phone and arranged to pop around to see him after Christmas.

Suddenly feeling very alone, and resolute not to start thinking about the other people, the ones she had lost from her life over the past year and a half, she kicked off her boots and went upstairs to run herself a bath.

Baxter picked Rouche up from the entrance to St. Mary's Hospital at 8:34 A.M. Still buzzing from the pain meds, he was irksomely cheerful company for a Monday-morning rush hour. As they escaped the queue for one junction just to join another for the next, she didn't have high hopes of them making their 9:30 A.M. meeting with MI5 T-Branch, who were, all of a sudden, taking the threat against national security very seriously indeed.

Rouche turned up the radio.

". . . morning, the UK's terror threat level has been elevated to 'Critical,' meaning that the security agencies believe an attack on the country to be imminent."

"About *bloody* time," said Baxter. She looked over at Rouche and caught him smiling to himself. "How has *any* of this given you reason to smile?" she asked him.

"Because there isn't going to be an attack. We're going to stop them."

Baxter jumped a set of traffic lights:

"I like your optimism—PMA and all that—but—"

"It's not about optimism. It's about purpose," he replied as the news bulletin moved on to the story that both Betfred and Ladbrokes had ceased taking bets on a white Christmas. "I've spent years drifting aimlessly, wondering why I survived that day and my family didn't . . . Now I know . . .

"Just think about the innumerable decisions and chance events required to lead me out of that Underground station a victim of a terror attack a decade ago, only to find myself in the position to prevent one tomorrow. It's like history repeating itself, giving me a do-over. It's like I *finally* understand why I'm still here and, at last, I have a purpose."

"Look, I'm glad you're feeling more upbeat and everything, but our priority is that Underground station and whatever these shits have planned for it. *We* need to handle it. We can't let them manipulate us like in New York. We can't pull resources from elsewhere in the city, no matter what happens down there, no matter what happens to us. The *diversion* is our responsibility. The bombs are the security services'. We're not going to be involved with that side of things . . . Sorry," she added, feeling guilty for raining on his parade.

"Don't be." Rouche smiled. "You're right, but I just *know* that by playing our part tomorrow, we'll stop this from happening."

Baxter forced a smile to humor him.

"We're getting ahead of ourselves," she pointed out. "We might still have one more murder to deal with before then. And if our stitched-together Gemini man is anything to go by, it's going to be absolutely horrific."

"Unless we've already arrested that particular Puppet."

"Because we're just *that* lucky," scoffed Baxter bitterly.

The traffic started moving more freely. Rouche kept quiet while Baxter changed lanes and overtook a procession of buses. The sporadic sweeps of the windscreen wipers had already compacted the beginnings of a snowman around the edges of the glass.

"We could . . ." Rouche hesitated, trying to form a more compelling argument. "We could wait until five to five and then evacuate the station."

"I wish we could," said Baxter. "But we can't."

"But if we—"

"We can't. If we do that, we're risking them dispersing across the city again and then they could attack anywhere. At least this way, we know where they'll be and we'll be prepared."

"We're using innocent people as *bait* . . . Why does that sound so familiar?" he asked. He didn't sound accusatory, only regretful.

"Yes, we are, but I don't see another option."

"I wonder if someone said something similar about me and my family back in 2005."

"Maybe they did," Baxter said sadly.

She felt a little disgusted with herself for her callous assessment of the situation. She suspected that Rouche was going to struggle with their day of strategic meetings, regarding people's lives as no more than figures on a graph. Sacrifice one digit here, save two there.

She suspected that she was going to struggle with it too.

By 6:04 P.M. Baxter was exhausted. As expected, the day had consisted of back-to-back meetings. Security had been doubled on the London Underground and at all major attractions. The five largest A&E departments in the city were on standby to implement their Major Incident Protocols, while the London Ambulance Service had arranged additional cover through private providers.

The Puppet interviews had continued throughout the day without any major revelations. It had been futile to threaten or bargain with Green's fanatical followers when they had no interest whatsoever in self-preservation. Green himself had been in the hands of MI5 overnight, being subjected to whatever enhanced interrogation techniques they could throw at him; however, the lack of communication suggested that they were yet to break the psychiatrist.

The department had spent the entire day on tenterhooks but reports of a final grotesque murder somewhere within the city never came. As such, the uninterrupted hours had left Baxter feeling as well prepared as possible for the Puppets' final act.

It was a strange feeling, knowing what might happen, a betrayal to every soul she'd passed on the street not to warn them. She wanted to call everyone in her phonebook, shout from the rooftops that people should stay out of the city, but to do so would only be to delay the inevitable and to sacrifice their one advantage.

She spotted Rouche waiting to say good night as she filed some paperwork. By then she felt as though there was nothing more they could do to prepare. She packed up her bag and walked over to him.

"Come on," she yawned. "I'll give you a lift back. I need to pick up a couple of bits anyway."

*

Baxter and Rouche had made it as far as Vincent Square before both their phones went off in unison. They shared an exhausted look, anticipating what was coming. Rouche put the call on speakerphone.

"Agent Rouche," he answered. "I'm with DCI Baxter."

Baxter's phone immediately stopped buzzing in her bag.

"Apologies, Agent Rouche. I'm aware you've both left for the day," started the woman on the phone.

"It's fine. Go ahead."

"One of Dr. Hoffman's patients, an Isaac Johns, just used his credit card to pay for a taxi."

"OK," he said, presuming there was more to the story.

"I called the taxi firm and got put through to the driver. He said the man was very intense, told him that he was dead anyway, that he'd go out while he still had his dignity, in a way that people would remember. According to Hoffman's statement, Johns was recently diagnosed with an inoperable brain tumor. The driver had already called it in. A unit from Southwark has been dispatched."

"Location?" asked Baxter as she switched on her sirens and maneuvered out of the traffic.

"The Sky Garden," replied the woman.

"In the Walkie-Talkie?" asked Baxter, using the building's nick-name.

"That's the one. Apparently he was heading for the bar, which is on the thirty-fifth floor."

The wheels spun against the slushy road as Baxter sped down Rochester Row, heading north.

"Stand them down," she shouted over the noise, "and back us up with an armed unit. We're seven minutes out."

"All understood."

"Have you got a description?" asked Rouche.

"Caucasian, 'built like a brick shithouse,' short hair, dark suit."

Rouche hung up as the colors of the city flashed by. He took out his firearm and checked it:

"Here we go again."

Baxter stifled a yawn: "No rest for the wicked."

CHAPTER 34

Monday, 21 December 2015

6:29 P.M.

"Come on. Come on," Baxter uttered under her breath as the LED numbers ascended toward their destination.

Rouche had already unholstered his service weapon, but doubted that this latest Puppet could have smuggled anything illicit through the airport-style security check on the ground floor.

31 . . . 32 . . . 33 . . . 34 . . .

The lift slowed to a gentle stop.

"Ready?" asked Rouche.

The doors parted; music and the soft hum of sophisticated conversation greeted them. They shared a pleasantly surprised shrug before Rouche quickly concealed his gun and they stepped into the cavernous space to join the smartly dressed queue waiting to be seated.

As moodily lit as the city sparkling in the background, the immense cage of steelwork was glowing pink, an enormous arch of glass and metal reaching fifteen meters overhead, greedily laying claim to a little more of the sky.

While they were waiting, they scanned the busy hall for anyone matching the description they'd been given, only to find that at least a third of the clientele were wearing dark suits and that a person's brick shithouse–ness was a difficult thing to judge while seated.

A smartly attired man gestured for them to step forward. A not-so-subtle look down over Baxter's practical winter outfit and then back up via Rouche's crumpled suit ended in a condescending smile.

"Good evening. You have a reservation?" he asked skeptically.

Rouche flashed the man his identification.

Baxter leaned in close to speak quietly:

"Detective Chief Inspector Baxter. Don't react!" she told him when he suddenly recognized her and looked around for a supervisor. "I need you to check your list. Do you have a reservation for an Isaac Johns?"

A brief pause; then the man ran his finger down his clipboard of names: "Johns . . . Johns . . . Johns . . ."

"Really think he'd use his real name?" Rouche asked her.

"He used his own credit card," replied Baxter. "He's got nothing to lose now. I don't think he cares."

"Johns! Found him!" the man exclaimed. Several people looked in their direction.

"Again," said Baxter patiently, "don't react."

"Sorry."

"Which table? Don't turn round! Don't point!"

"Sorry. Beside the window. Right-hand side. Closest to the doors, as he requested."

Baxter held the man's gaze as Rouche glanced across the room:

"Table's empty."

"Did you see what he looked like?" she asked the man.

"He was . . . tall . . . and big, as in muscular. He was wearing a black suit and tie . . . like he was going to a funeral."

Baxter and Rouche shared a look.

"OK," she told him. "I want you to carry on as normal. If you see him, I want you to walk over to us very, very slowly and whisper it in my ear. All right?"

He nodded.

"Start on the terrace?" she suggested to Rouche.

Unexpectedly, she linked arms with him. They walked through the bar under their camouflage of happy couple and out onto the terrace, the tip of the Shard sparkling white in the distance like a snow-capped mountain. As they strolled over to the metal railing, snowflakes blew around them from all directions before scattering over the twinkling metropolis below.

The only people braving the cold were a shivering couple toasting champagne glasses and some accommodating parents being led outside by their excited little girls. From the relative privacy of the dark terrace, the indoor space was lit in neon pink, allowing them to search the room of faces without attracting attention.

"Perhaps he went home," said Rouche optimistically, but then he spotted their well-dressed assistant pacing around the room searching for them. "Or perhaps not."

They hurried inside and then followed the man's directions back past the lifts to the toilets. There, they were confronted with a row of identical cubicles, the shiny black doors promising a more pleasant setting than the last set they had occupied together.

Rouche took out his weapon: "I'll go in. You keep watch."

Baxter looked like she might hit him.

"We don't know for sure he's in there," explained Rouche, glad he was armed. "Plus, there might be more than one of them. I need you watching my back."

"Fine," Baxter huffed, slumping against the wall to stay out of the path of the harassed waiters struggling to cope with the demands of simultaneous Christmas parties.

Rouche made his way down the narrow corridor of partitioned bathrooms to find the first two standing empty.

"Someone's in here!" a woman's voice called from the third when he tried the door.

"Sorry!" he shouted over the sound of a hand-dryer as the next door along unlocked.

Fingers wrapped around the handle of the weapon inside his jacket, he relaxed when an elderly gentleman wobbled out, giving him a rosy-cheeked smile.

Rouche passed one more vacant cubicle before reaching the final black door, propped closed despite clearly being unlocked. With his gun raised, he kicked the flimsy piece of wood open. The door swung back loudly into the side of the empty room.

Against the back wall stood the lid from the cistern; beside it, a rubber bag had been discarded, dripping water onto the floor. On the back of the door hung a large black suit jacket and tie. Rouche turned to leave, kicking something metallic across the floor. He walked over and picked up a brass nine-millimeter bullet.

"Shit," he said to himself, rushing back out into the main room.

"He's not in th—" Rouche started, colliding with an overladen waiter, who dropped his tray of precariously balanced glasses across the floor. "Sorry," Rouche apologized, looking around for Baxter.

"Entirely my fault," the young man responded politely, even though it entirely wasn't.

"Did you see a woman waiting out here?"

Then came the sound of chair legs scraping across the floor as people abandoned their tables.

Rouche hurried toward the uproar and shoved his way through the crowd moving away from the glass windows.

He paused.

He could see Baxter out in the dark. She was standing by the railing as her hair blew wildly in the wind. A few meters from her, huddled in the corner beside the glass, the young family was cowering, the father crouching defensively in front of his two daughters.

Weapon first, Rouche slowly stepped outside.

Free from the glare of the lights reflecting in the glass, he finally understood the situation; there was one other person out on the terrace with them, behind Baxter.

A muscular arm was holding her still, a small pistol pushed up under her chin.

In the other hand, a second weapon was pointed at the family in the corner.

"Rouche, I presume," said an unfittingly high-pitched voice from behind Baxter, only a sliver of a face visible behind his human shield.

He pronounced it correctly, meaning that Baxter had either given up his name or, more likely, she had called out to him.

"Mind putting that down?" asked the man pleasantly, pulling the hammer back on the gun beneath Baxter's chin.

She gave a subtle shake of her head, but Rouche hesitantly lowered the weapon.

"Isaac Johns, *I* presume," said Rouche, hoping that his calm tone was catching. "You all right, Baxter?"

"She's fine," Johns answered on her behalf.

"I leave you alone for one minute . . ." Rouche laughed, casually taking a step toward them.

"Hey! Hey! Hey!" yelled Johns, dragging Baxter backward, losing Rouche the ground he'd just made up.

He was as imposing as his description had promised. Although Baxter's slender frame was insubstantial cover for the man's bulk, his vital organs, and therefore any hope of an instant kill, were safely out of sight.

"So what's the plan, Isaac?" asked Rouche, keen to get Johns talking. He had already registered the difference between this man and the other killers: he appeared calm and in control. He was *enjoying* his moment in the limelight.

"Well, it *was* to get our audience to decide which of them"— he gestured toward the huddled family—"lives or dies. But then I spotted Detective Baxter here and simply couldn't help myself. So that responsibility has, regrettably, fallen to you."

The man was momentarily distracted by his indoor audience. Rouche slowly raised his gun a couple of inches, just in case an opportunity presented itself.

"No!" yelled Johns, careful to keep Baxter between them. "Tell those people if *anyone* leaves, I'll start shooting. *These* people have the right idea: get your phones out. It's OK. I *want* you to film this. I *want* the world to hear Rouche make his decision."

Satisfied that enough cameras were about to capture his moment of triumph, Johns turned his attention back to Rouche.

"So which is it, Rouche? Who would you like me to kill, your colleague or a completely innocent family?"

Rouche looked anxiously at Baxter.

She gave him nothing.

With the barrel of the gun pressing into her chin, she couldn't move at all, let alone create an opportunity for him to take a clean shot. He then looked over at the family, recognizing all too well the look of utter desperation on the father's face.

There were shouts from inside as the first armed team arrived.

"Stop!" Rouche called back to them. "Don't come any closer!"

When one of the officers failed to obey the order, Johns fired a warning shot, which ricocheted off the wall close to the younger girl's head before cracking the glass barrier that separated them from the sky. The officers inside raised their hands and remained with the watching crowd.

In the quiet that followed, Rouche could hear the little girl's teeth chattering. She was only five or six, freezing to death while Johns protracted the ordeal under a pretense of hope.

There was no choice to be made. This was no game. He intended to kill them all, and Baxter knew it too.

After all the theater, all the media-seducing horrors increasing in spectacle and ambition, there was still one simple, despicable act left in their arsenal, something worse than all the mutilated bodies put together—the public execution of an innocent child. They had already proven capable of it, having murdered the entire Bantham family behind closed doors. Rouche was confident that Johns wouldn't hesitate to pull the trigger.

The falling snow was hindering his vision. He was careful to keep his trigger finger moving before it could stiffen and slow in the cold.

"It's decision time!" Johns shouted to his audience. "Speak up so that the world can hear you," he instructed Rouche. "Who do you want to die? Answer or I'll kill them all."

Rouche remained silent.

Johns groaned in frustration: "OK . . . Have it your way. Five seconds!"

Rouche met Baxter's eye. She had no way out.

"Four!"

He glanced at the family. The father was holding his hands over his younger daughter's eyes.

"Three!"

Rouche sensed the room of camera phones at his back.

He needed more time.

"Two!"

"Rouche . . ." said Baxter.

He looked at her desperately.

"One!"

". . . I trust you," she told him, closing her eyes.

She heard Rouche move, the crack of a gunshot, the air whistling past her ear, the shattering glass, and the muffled impact all at once. She felt the pressure release beneath her chin, the restricting arm fall away . . . the presence behind her vanish.

When she opened her eyes again, Rouche looked shaken, still standing with the weapon pointed directly at her. She watched a bloodstained snowflake dance in the air between them before it plunged over the edge of the building to join the rest of the crime scene five hundred feet below.

Her temple began to throb from where the bullet had grazed her as their backup ran out to join them. The traumatized parents were sobbing inconsolably in relief and shock, in desperate need of some words of reassurance, just somebody to tell them out loud that they were safe.

Rouche slowly lowered his weapon.

Without uttering a word to any of them, Baxter headed back inside, swiping a bottle of wine from one of the vacated tables as she passed, before sitting at the deserted bar to pour herself a generous glass.

CHAPTER 35

Monday, 21 December 2015

11:20 P.M.

Rouche parked the Audi outside number 56, a powder-blue town house set on an affluent side street, the designer wreaths adorning the doors more fashion statement than decoration. Outdoor Christmas lights pulsed in white and gold, content in the knowledge that there wasn't a single plastic Santa Claus in sight. Old-fashioned lampposts lined the street, stark black towers against the snow, like urban lighthouses warning of the hidden dangers concealed just below the surface. Their warm orange glow was charming but served as a reminder as to why the rest of the city had upgraded to uglier varieties that actually gave off some light.

Rouche trod in a puddle of slush as he stepped out of the car and slipped around to the passenger door. He pulled it open and Baxter dropped out. Half catching her, he dragged her across the pavement to the bottom of the steps that led up to the front door. Rouche could feel the wounds beneath his bandages stinging as he picked her up, ringing the doorbell with a carefully aimed swing of Baxter's feet.

An energy-sapping forty seconds later, he heard someone rushing down the stairs. The locks clicked and then a man, who had apparently been playing badminton in his pajamas, peered around the door before throwing it wide open:

"Oh my *Christ,* she's dead!" gasped Thomas as he looked down at Baxter's limp body in his arms.

"Huh? No! God, no! She's just drunk," explained Rouche, turning Baxter's top end toward Thomas as proof. Her head lolled forward, and her mouth hung open. Reasonably confident that she was still with them, he gave her a shake. She groaned. "*Very* drunk," he added.

"Oh . . . right," said Thomas, relieved and surprised in equal measure. "God, I'm sorry. Do come in. I'm being extremely rude. Ummm . . . Shall we get her up to the bedroom, then?"

"Bathroom," suggested Rouche, struggling to support her, suspecting that Thomas's use of the word "we" meant that he wouldn't be taking her off his hands after all.

"Bathroom. Of course." Thomas nodded, closing the front door behind them. "It's upstairs."

"Fantastic," puffed Rouche, staggering across the hallway.

He was a little surprised by Thomas. He was certainly handsome in a wholesome catalog-cardigan-model sort of way, but he'd been expecting someone . . . Now that he thought about it, Rouche had absolutely no idea what he'd been expecting.

He followed Thomas through the bedroom and into the en-suite bathroom, where he was finally able to deposit Baxter next to the toilet. Almost instantly, she reanimated and pulled herself up to the bowl. Rouche held her hair back for her as she was sick. Thomas, meanwhile, crouched on the other side of her with a glass of water.

"Thomas, by the way," he introduced himself, habit making him offer out a hand that Rouche was clearly unable to take. "Right. Sorry," he said, taking his unshaken appendage back.

"Rouche."

"Ah, you're Rouche." He smiled, looking down in concern as Baxter slumped back onto the floor between them. "I've never seen her like this before," he admitted, flushing the toilet.

Rouche managed to hide his surprise both that Baxter had chosen to share her ongoing struggle with him but not with her boyfriend of eight months and that Thomas could possibly be that utterly unobservant.

It was Thomas's turn to grab a handful of Baxter's hair as she climbed back up the toilet.

"What happened?" he asked.

Rouche didn't feel it was his place to say. What Baxter chose to tell him was her business. He shrugged apologetically: "Open case and all that."

Thomas nodded, suggesting that Baxter had already used that line on him before. He changed the subject:

"You and Emily must be very close."

"Who?"

Baxter raised a floppy hand.

"Oh, Baxter! I suppose we . . . Yeah," said Rouche, realizing just how much they had been through together during their short time on the case, a lifetime's worth of horrors. "Yes," he said decisively. "She's very, very special."

Baxter vomited loudly.

Rouche was back on hair-holding duty.

Once she was done, he got to his feet.

"It looks like you've got everything under control here," Rouche told Thomas. "I can show myself out." Then he remembered something. "I've got a . . . silly present for her out in the car."

"You're more than welcome to put it under the tree with the others," said Thomas. "And, please, take the car tonight. I can drop her at work in the morning."

Rouche nodded appreciatively and went to leave.

"Rouche."

He turned back.

"She doesn't really tell me everything that's going on," started Thomas, submitting his entry for Understatement of the Year. "Just . . . you know, if you could . . . just . . . look after her."

Rouche hesitated. He wouldn't make Thomas a promise he couldn't keep.

"One more day," he said evasively before leaving the room.

*

Baxter woke up in Thomas's arms. The cold bathroom tiles pressed into her bare legs and she was instantly conscious of her scar even without looking at it. Her trousers were crumpled up in the corner, but she was still wearing her sweat-dampened shirt. They were both wrapped in a bath towel, and Thomas was wedged uncomfortably between the toilet and the wall.

"Shit," she whispered, angry with herself.

She wriggled out of his hold and slowly stood up, swaying as she adjusted to the new altitude. Carefully, she headed downstairs.

The Christmas-tree lights were blinking, a lone source of light and warmth in the dark house. She crossed the room and slumped down in front of it, crossing her legs as she watched the colorful bulbs take turns to shine. After a few hypnotic minutes, she noticed the pretty angel peering down at her from the top of the tree. Lennox's "reassuring" words about their fallen colleague returned to her like an unwelcome voice inside her head: "I guess God just needed another angel."

Baxter got to her feet, reached up, and tossed the fragile ornament onto the sofa. Feeling better, she began sorting through the pile of presents to which she had not contributed.

She had adored Christmas when she was younger. But in recent years the degree of celebration had only extended as far as the usual five festive movies in December and perhaps crashing somebody else's Christmas dinner, on their insistence, should she get out of work in time.

She reached for the remote control and switched on the television, turning the volume down until it was barely more than a buzzing in the speakers. She was irrationally excited to find a Christmas-themed rerun of *Frasier,* and then, unable to keep the smile off her face, she started separating the presents into three piles. Most were for her, of course. Echo hadn't had a bad haul, but Thomas's was pathetic.

She picked up an unfamiliar and oddly shaped gift to read the tag:

Merry Xmas, Baxter. His name's Frankie.
Rouche x

Intrigued, fueled by the excitement of her private mini-Christmas, and in need of an approximate price so as not to look tight/ overly keen when reciprocating the gesture, she tore the wrapping paper open and looked down at the orange-hatted penguin in her hands, the same stuffed toy that she had admired back at Rouche's house . . . that had belonged to his daughter.

She stared at the silly-looking bird. Her disbelief that Rouche would want her to have something of such importance was outweighed by a feeling of unease, a suspicion that he no longer felt he needed it, that whatever final test they were about to be confronted with, he did not expect to be coming back.

She placed Frankie on her crossed legs and pulled the large gift bag from Edmunds and Tia closer. She reached inside and found the blank white envelope sitting on top.

She had forgotten all about it.

She took it out and held it in her hands, just above Frankie, reminding her of her unfounded suspicions about Rouche, her initial irritation with Edmunds, her best friend, who pleaded with her every time not to take his illegal reports on Thomas. She pictured Thomas, be-toweled and more than likely stuck in the bathroom upstairs, where he had spent the night taking care of her.

She realized that she was smiling just at the thought of her bumbling boyfriend. She tore the envelope into several pieces, showered the rubbish over the tattered wrapping paper, and continued dividing out their presents.

CHAPTER 36

Tuesday, 22 December 2015

9:34 A.M.

Baxter followed the signs for the Bakerloo line, descending deeper beneath the city into Piccadilly Circus Underground Station. She had tied her hair up into a ponytail and plastered herself in the few items of colorful makeup that had been gifted to her over the years—most a not-so-subtle hint from her mother to "stop looking like a vampire." The disguise was effective enough, however, and she had barely recognized herself in the mirror after she'd finished.

She followed the crowds onto the platform. Halfway along, she spotted her destination and stopped outside a gray door adorned with the London Underground logo and a sign that read:

NO ENTRY—STAFF ONLY

She knocked, hoping she was in the right place and not trying to gain entry to a cleaning cupboard.

"Who is it?" a female voice called from inside.

Several people were within earshot, and she was not about to yell her name in front of them after going to the trouble of painting herself up like a clown.

She knocked again.

The door opened a cautious inch, but then Baxter shoved her way through into the darkened room. The woman quickly locked the door behind her, while the two other technical officers continued setting up the racks of monitors, radio base units, frequency boosters, computers, and encrypted relay stations, converting the sparse office into a fully functional tactical command station.

Rouche was already there, sticking an assortment of maps up next to a list of radio call signs.

"Morning," he greeted her.

He reached into his pocket and handed over her car keys, making no mention of the events precipitating the need to borrow them in the first place or of her alarmingly colorful new face.

"Thanks," Baxter replied curtly, shoving them into her coat pocket. "How long till we're all up and running?"

"Ten . . . fifteen minutes?" one of the people crawling around under the tables replied.

"We'll come back then, then," she told the room ineloquently.

Rouche took the hint and followed her out onto the platform to speak in private.

By the time he'd returned to the flat the previous night, footage of the shooting had already spread to every major news channel in the world, immortalizing him in grainy video as he saved Baxter's life. As a result, he had neglected to shave that morning, the dark shadow a notable change to the clean-cut agent's appearance. He had also combed back his quiff, exposing the grayer layers beneath, a look that actually suited him far better.

"You're a bit of a silver fox today, aren't you?" Baxter smiled as they strolled to the far end of the platform, passing a huge poster for Andrea's book.

"Thanks. And you . . . well, you . . ."

He was struggling.

"I look like a bingo nan," said Baxter, unamused, amusing Rouche. "The FBI have elected to grace us with their presence," she said quietly. "They wish to 'assist in any way possible to bring to a close these atrocious acts of barbarism.' Translation: they can't piss off back home without Green, but MI5 aren't done waterboarding him yet, so they might as well stick around and shoot somebody."

"Yeah, I'd worked that much out myself," said Rouche, a subtle nod toward the enormous ponytailed man standing a little farther along the platform. "Steven Seagal over there's been choosing a chocolate bar for nearly an hour now."

"For Christ's sake," huffed Baxter. "Report from the night shift: two more Puppets were picked up overnight."

"So . . . ten to go?"

"Ten to go." She nodded.

"And our Azazel, whoever he may be," added Rouche.

They stood silently for a moment as a train clattered to a stop.

Baxter used the interruption to compose what she wanted to say, although she didn't feel as though she could admit to opening his gift early and would probably have avoided the inevitably emotional conversation anyway.

"We're both gonna get through this," she told him, watching the train departing to avoid his eye. "We're *so* nearly there. I know you believe that today is some sort of test or something, but we can only do what we can do. Don't take any stupid risks or—"

"Do you know what I was thinking about last night?" Rouche interrupted. "I never answered your question."

She looked puzzled.

"How someone who's supposed to be intelligent and spends their life looking for evidence could ever believe in something as groundless and illogical as . . . 'sky fairies,' wasn't it?" he asked with a smile.

"I really don't want to get into this right now," said Baxter, cringing at the memory of her vicious outburst on the plane.

"This is the *perfect* time to get into it."

Another train decelerated into the station before a mass game of musical chairs played out over ten seconds of chaos, the losers' forfeit: hold a diseased pole or fall over the moment it sets off again.

"I was like you," started Rouche. "You know, before. I thought faith was just something for the weak—a delusion to help get them through their overwhelming lives . . ."

The way that Rouche had described it reminded her of how she had felt about counseling before it had saved her.

"... but then, when what happened ... happened, I just couldn't even process the idea that I'd lost them forever, that I'd never get to be with them again, to hold them, that my two girls and everything they were was just gone. They were too important, too special, to just not exist anymore, you know?"

Baxter was struggling to hold it together, but Rouche seemed perfectly composed, just trying to articulate his thoughts:

"The second I thought about that, everything just sort of made sense: they weren't really gone. I could *feel* it, and now I've been led back down here today and ... Am I making any sense at all?"

"I prayed this morning!" Baxter blurted, before putting her hand over her mouth as if she'd given up an embarrassing secret.

Rouche looked at her suspiciously.

"What? I don't even know if I did it right, but I thought, What if I'm wrong? What if there *is* someone or something out there and I don't? There's just too much at stake today not to, right?" Baxter's cheeks went bright red, but fortunately, the garish assortment of colors somewhat diminished the effect. "Oh, shut up," she snapped when she caught him smiling at her. She quickly moved on to her real point. "While I'm making a complete fool of myself, I might as well tell you what I prayed for."

"That we stop these sick bastards from—"

"Well, obviously! But I also prayed for you."

"Me?"

"Yeah, you. I used my one and only prayer I'm ever going to make on *you*. I prayed that you'd make it through today with me."

The unexpected revelation looked to have had the desired effect.

Whether Rouche's God wanted him to live or die that afternoon was out of their hands, but Baxter hoped he might now, at least, pause for a moment before actively inviting it.

*

"What time is it?" groaned Baxter, her head in her hands and lit by the bluish light of the monitors in the makeshift command unit.

"Ten past," replied Rouche, keeping his eyes on the live camera feeds from all over the station.

"Ten past what?"

"Three."

She sighed heavily:

"Where the hell are these shits?" she asked the room.

The heightened terror threat level had resulted in an interesting day in the capital. A man had been arrested attempting to smuggle a knife into the Tower of London; however, all signs were pointing toward stupidity rather than mass murder as the driving force behind his actions. There had been a bomb scare at an event in Kensington Olympia. That, too, had ended anticlimactically with an irate, but admittedly forgetful, exhibitor learning that his missing laptop had been subjected to a controlled explosion.

Baxter and her team of twelve had detained five people throughout the day due to suspicious behavior. Although none had been involved with Green and his minions, it had highlighted the alarming number of weird people roaming the city at any given moment.

"Where are the MI5 guys?" Baxter asked. She didn't raise her head off the desk.

"Still in with the FBI on the Piccadilly line platform," someone answered.

She made a nonspecific noise in acknowledgment.

"Weirdo alert!" Rouche called out.

Baxter looked up excitedly. A man in a Santa hat, clearly concealing some sort of live animal inside his jacket, strolled past one of the cameras. She was just glad for something to do.

"Let's check it out."

Back at New Scotland Yard, Constable Bethan Roth had been assigned the task of reviewing camera footage relating to the case but of too poor quality to be utilized by facial-recognition systems. Over the week, she had compiled an entire album of fuzzy screenshots, which, after being processed through image-enhancement programs, had led to the arrest of two more Puppets.

She had spent the day studying footage from the Sky Garden security cameras, watching the narrowly evaded disaster play out from every angle. The current black-and-white video was as mind-numbing to watch as the two hours of people passing in and out of shot as they visited the bathrooms.

She was reviewing a recording from the indoor bar area. Unable to see any of the action out on the terrace, she could tell when Rouche had taken his shot only by the reaction of the crowd. Several people turned away, others continued filming, phones extended, and one elderly lady fainted, taking her zombie-looking husband down with her.

She leaned forward to select the next video file when one of the monochrome figures in the background caught her attention. She rewound the footage and watched again as the crowd reacted accordingly to seeing a man killed in front of them.

Bethan kept her eyes fixed on the dark figure at the back.

Just as the fainting woman dropped out of frame, he turned away and walked calmly toward the exit. Everything about his demeanor, even the way that he walked, suggested a complete emotional detachment to what he had just witnessed.

Bethan zoomed in but couldn't find anything better than a pixelated circle where the man's face should have been.

She had an idea.

She loaded up the footage from outside the toilets again and continued from where she had stopped watching. After a few moments, the unidentified man rounded the corner and passed beneath the camera, making sure to keep his head lowered at all times.

"Bastard," whispered Bethan, now positive that she was onto something.

She replayed the snippet of video in slow motion, wondering what the shiny circle on the ground could be. She zoomed in further: a tray surrounded by broken glass. She zoomed in further still until the reflective surface dominated the entire screen and started flicking through frame by frame, her eyes wide in anticipation.

A shadow spilled over the upturned tray; a few clicks later, the top of the man's shoe entered the frame. She continued clicking.

"Come on . . . Come on . . ." Bethan smiled. "Got you!"

Framed in a circle of silver, a workable image of a middle-aged man's face.

"Boss! I need you over here!"

CHAPTER 37

Tuesday, 22 December 2015

3:43 P.M.

Blake pulled up outside the property at the same moment as the Armed Response Unit. En route, he had been passed the information the team had cobbled together at short notice on their new prime suspect.

Lucas Theodor Keaton was the multimillionaire owner of a telecoms company that had been bought out in the 1990s, providing him with a healthy payoff and a place on its board. From that time on, he had concentrated predominantly on his charity work and on helping start-up businesses.

Encouragingly, S-S Mobile, whose servers had contained the hidden messages, was a subsidiary of Keaton's original Smoke Signal Technologies. In addition, the depot that supplied all the compromised mobile phones had links to this little-known parent company.

Keaton had a wife and two children, all deceased.

He and the two boys had been caught up in the 7/7 bombings. Although Keaton had escaped relatively unscathed, one of his sons had been killed outright. The other had succumbed to his injuries over a year and a half later, following which Keaton's wife had taken her own life by fatal overdose.

"Cheers for that," Blake had said to his colleague on the other end of the line, now feeling suitably depressed.

"But it gets worse."

"Worse than him losing his entire family?"

"His brother"—the constable back at New Scotland Yard clicked about on his computer—"had taken his place attending a charity event back in 2001 over in the States . . ."

"Don't say it!"

". . . September 11."

"Jesus Christ!" Blake almost started to pity their prime suspect. "How unlucky can one man be?"

"The brother had no business whatsoever at the World Trade Center. He was just walking past at the wrong time."

"Reckon this Keaton bloke's cursed or something?"

"All that money and he's had the most miserable life imaginable. Goes to show, doesn't it?" was the constable's rhetorical farewell before hanging up.

With Saunders engaged with the operation at Piccadilly Circus, Vanita had sent Blake alone to accompany the team to Keaton's enormous Chelsea residence.

As the armed officers hurried up the steps to break through the front door, Blake sheltered out of the wind behind a postbox to light up a cigarette. Despite the prestigious postcode, the leafy street wasn't a particularly pleasant place to be: almost a third of the houses appeared to be undergoing major building works— lorries, vans, and even a mini-crane were scattered among the sports cars in the resident parking bays. The noise was obtrusive.

"Mate!" Blake called to one of the passing construction workers, producing his identification. "What's going on? Street falling in or something?" he asked, wondering whether it might be in some way relevant.

"This?" asked the rotund man, gesturing to the mess. "Nah. With property prices at such a premium, every square inch you can stake a claim to counts. So some enterprising billionaire, becoming stir-crazy confined to his measly ten bedrooms, realized that directly beneath his basement, everything down to the Earth's core was wasted space that he could be utilizing . . . and now they're all at it."

Blake was a little surprised by the articulate response.

"Course, if I started digging through the floor of my place, I'd just end up in the kebab shop downstairs," the man added with a sigh.

"Detective!" a member of the Armed Response Unit called from the doorway. "All clear!"

Blake thanked the well-informed, kebab-scented man and hurried into the house. The entrance hall alone was larger than his entire Twickenham flat. A sweeping wooden staircase ascended from the mosaic floor, the other seven officers already lost within Keaton's sprawling home. Fresh flowers burst from expensive vases, and a large portrait of the family hung on the back wall.

"If you're in a hurry, I'd start on the third floor," the team leader advised Blake with a knowing nod.

Blake started in the direction of the staircase.

"Sorry. I meant down," the officer clarified, pointing toward the corner. "The third floor down."

Descending the stairs, Blake's phone made a quiet beep as he lost signal. There, just one level beneath the property's wholesome facade, the first signs of a tainted mind began to bleed through.

The room appeared to have been an office at some point in the past, but now the walls were suffocating beneath pictures of the happy family: another professionally commissioned portrait beside casual holiday snaps, hand-drawn sketches neighboring their photographic counterparts, each and every one of them framed and hung with precision.

"Computer in the corner," Blake told the officer, expecting it to be in the van by the time he resurfaced. "Phone there . . . and this picture," he said, choosing what looked like the most recent, based on the ages of the two boys—gap-toothed smiles and matching haircuts.

They moved on, the temperature dropping as the stairs creaked underfoot, the stale air thickening in their lungs. To Blake, it felt as though they were sinking deeper into Keaton's subconscious . . .

This was where he slept.

A small camp bed stood unmade against the far wall, surrounded by what could only be described as a shrine. Items of jewelry, clothing, childish drawings, and toys sat in ordered piles around the bed. Candles had melted into the wooden floor around the perimeter.

"Christ!" Blake jumped, only just noticing the depiction of the crucified Jesus hanging on the wall behind them: feet and wrists nailed to the wooden cross, hands dangling uselessly, a tangled crown of thorns tearing into his head: a violent inspiration for the atrocities of the previous few weeks.

Blake frowned and reluctantly took a step backward into the room to read what had been scrawled in finger-paint either side of the Son of God:

WhEre tHe FuCK weRE yOu?

He almost tripped over the cushion on the floor as he took a photograph of the wall to include in his report.

"Moving on?" he suggested eagerly to the officer.

As the temperature dropped another couple of degrees, they negotiated the narrowing staircase to the property's lowest level.

They'd made it two steps into the room before Blake's heart sank.

Books, journals, folders, diagrams littered every conceivable surface—stacked several feet high or else adding to the paper floor underfoot—years of work, the harvest of an obsessive mind.

They had less than an hour.

Two other officers were already sorting through the mess, a recovered laptop bagged up and ready for transport.

"This pile contains just about every newspaper story on the Ragdoll murders," one of them called across. "On the desk is everything we've found so far relating to Alexei Green. This Keaton guy's completely obsessed with him from the looks of it—been collecting stuff on him for years."

Blake moved over to the stack of articles and CDs, handwritten notes labeling Green's various interviews and talks at conferences. He picked up a journal and flicked it open, the first page simply titled "Session One," followed by what looked like a word-for-word transcript of Keaton's first meeting with the psychiatrist.

The lead officer was reading over his shoulder:

"Looks as though this Keaton was just another recruit, then."

"But he can't be," whispered Blake, looking again at the mind spilled out in ink around them.

There was a crash as one of the officers knocked a precarious stack of books across the floor. Very calmly, he leaned down to take a closer look at what he'd uncovered:

"Boss?"

"What?"

"Do ya wanna get the bomb squad boys down here?"

The team leader looked concerned: "I don't know. Do I?"

"Doesn't look live . . . homemade, but still . . . yeah, I think so."

"Shit . . . Everybody out!" he ordered.

"I'm staying," Blake told him.

"Live or not, first sign of an explosive, I am to get everybody to safety."

"If Keaton's our man—" Blake started.

"He's not!"

"But *if* he is, we *need* what's down here. Get your men out. Get these computers to the tech guys, and get the bomb squad here . . . *please.*"

The officer looked torn, but then collected up the recovered laptop and followed his men up the stairs, leaving Blake alone to wade through Keaton's thoughts.

He quickly picked the journal back up, opened it to Session One, and skim-read the page. Aware of their time constraints, he skipped forward to Keaton's ninth session with the psychiatrist, rapidly losing hope that they had found their Azazel after all.

SESSION NINE

Thursday, 3 July 2014
2:22 P.M.

". . . and the world just carried on as if nothing had happened," said Lucas, lost in his own thoughts. "I have *nothing* left. I go home to an empty house, a mausoleum of everything they were, every night. I can't throw any of it away. It's all I have left of them, but I feel like I'm drowning in memories every time I step inside . . . I can still smell my wife's perfume . . . Are you all right?"

Green quickly got up from his seat to pour himself a glass of water.

"Yes. Fine . . . fine," he said, but then his face scrunched up as he began to cry. "I am *so* sorry. This is so unprofessional. I just need a moment."

"Was it something I said?" asked Lucas in concern, watching Green compose himself.

Outside, it started to rain harder. It must have rained all day.

"Maybe this isn't such a good idea," said Lucas, getting to his feet. "All I seem to do is upset everyone."

"It's not you, Lucas," Green said quickly. "It's me and my own issues."

"Why?" Lucas asked innocently. "Did . . . did you lose somebody too?"

"Let's just focus on you, shall we?"

"You can tell me."

"No, I can't," said Green firmly.

Lucas got up and started heading for the door.

"Lucas!"

"Everything you say is bullshit! I pour my heart out to you twice a week, but there's no trust here," he told the psychiatrist, hurt.

"Lucas, wait! OK. OK. Yes!" said Green. "You're right. I apologize. We *do* have a trust, and yes, I *did* lose somebody very, very special to me."

Keaton closed his eyes, exhaled in victorious relief, and let his flicker of a smile fade before slowly returning to the sofa. He lingered, pausing to stand over Green as the cool and collected psychiatrist finally broke down.

He leaned down to address the troubled man, passing him a handful of the "man-sized" tissues he kept on his desk:

"Please . . . tell me about *her*."

Blake urgently flicked through the pages to find the final entry—Alexei Green and Lucas Keaton's eleventh session together.

SESSION ELEVEN

Thursday, 10 July 2014

6:10 P.M.

"Why the *fuck* are we the ones who got punished?" asked Keaton, pacing around the room as Green listened. "*Still* being punished! We are good people—my family, your beautiful Abby, were good people!"

He sighed heavily as he stared out the window, the early evening sunshine warming his face:

"These Ragdoll murders," Keaton started casually, "you're following them, I presume?"

"Isn't everybody?" replied Green, utterly drained by the conversation. He hadn't managed a decent night's sleep in over a week.

"Can you name the victims? Actually, let's make it a challenge. Can you name them in order?"

"Why, Lucas?"

"Just . . . humor me."

Green let out an exasperated groan:

"Fine. Well, there was Mayor Turnble, of course, and then Khalid's brother. Something Rana? . . . Vijay Rana. Jarred Garland, and the other day it was Andrew Ford . . . Again, why?"

"Immortalized—a backpedaling politician, the brother of a child-murdering serial killer, a greedy and opportunistic journalist, and, finally, a disgusting, alcoholic specimen of human refuse. Their unworthy names etched into history simply because they died in an 'entertaining' fashion."

"I'm tired, Lucas. What's your point?"

"I have an admission to make," announced Keaton without

turning around. "I did some research into the Oslo and Utøya attacks."

"Why would you do that?" asked Green. "I don't understand why you'd—"

"The news stories mainly," Keaton continued, speaking over him as he dominated the conversation. "'Seventy-seven dead,' 'multiple casualties,' 'several victims.' Want to know how many acknowledged Abby by name?"

Green didn't reply.

"None. Not *one* that I found even bothered to report that your fiancée had been taken from you."

Green started to weep as Keaton walked back over to sit beside him:

"All those people out there got to carry on with their lives, while ours crumbled . . . and they couldn't even be bothered to learn their names!" shouted Keaton passionately, tears pouring down his cheeks. "*None* of them has suffered as we have . . . None of them."

Keaton paused a moment to read Green's expression.

"I'm not much to look at, Alexei. I know that. I'm successful, but people don't listen when I speak . . . not really. And all the preparation and manipulation in the world isn't going to get them to do what I need them to do. I need them to surrender themselves to me . . . to *our* cause, entirely."

"Puppets?" asked Green, glancing up, recalling their previous conversation on the futility of holding an inanimate object accountable for its actions.

"Puppets." Keaton nodded encouragingly. "I need someone who can inspire them, someone for them to look up to, someone to *lead* them . . . I need you."

"What are you saying?" asked Green.

Keaton placed a hand on his shoulder:

"I'm saying, what if there was a way to make things right? A way to make these self-obsessed masses understand what happened to us. A way to ensure that every *fucking* person on this planet knows the names of my family, knows the face of your beautiful Abby and exactly what she meant to you."

There was a long pause as Green absorbed what Keaton was saying to him.

Slowly, he placed his hand on top of his and turned to face him: "I'd say tell me more."

CHAPTER 38

Tuesday, 22 December 2015

4:14 P.M.

Baxter received an urgent radio call requesting that she return to the command unit/Bob's break room. She was handed the phone on her arrival.

"Baxter," she answered.

"It's Vanita. Just a courtesy call to bring you up to speed. About an hour ago, the Central Forensic Imaging Team pulled an image from the Sky Garden footage, which they have since matched to surveillance from New York."

"Why am I only just hearing about this now?" asked Baxter.

"Because nothing beyond the boundaries of that station concerns you right now. Both MI5 and SO15 have all the details. As I said, just a courtesy call. So I sent Blake—"

"What did you send Blake for?" Baxter interrupted as Rouche entered the room. "Hang on. I'm putting you on speaker."

"I sent Blake to the address," Vanita continued, "and he's confirmed it: Lucas Theodor Keaton, forty-eight. I'm sending details over to you now. Prepare to be underwhelmed . . . Ladies and gentlemen, meet our Azazel."

They crowded around the computer as one of the technical officers brought up the email. Keaton's forgettable face stared out from the screen, his sensibly styled hair receding from his temples at the rate one would expect of a man of his age.

"That's him?" asked Baxter.

"That's him. His company facilitated the hidden messages *and* supplied the mobile phones. Numerous flights to and from JFK this past year, building in frequency. He last flew back Tuesday night," Vanita added, significantly.

The other phone went off. Rouche hastily answered it and commenced a whispered conversation.

"On Blake's recommendation, the security services are prioritizing targets with religious connotations. Seems this Keaton might have some sort of spiritual agenda, which would certainly explain the New York church," Vanita told her.

"OK," Baxter replied distractedly.

"I'll let you get back to work," said Vanita, hanging up.

Rouche tore a map from the wall and urgently traced his finger across the paper.

"What is it?" asked Baxter.

"Three of our missing Puppets have just flagged up within a quarter mile of each other."

"So they've dispatched armed units, right?"

"They have," answered Rouche, tapping his finger on a location almost dead center of the three sightings. "They're heading to Baker Street Station. I'm going."

"No," said Baxter. "They can handle it. I need you here with me."

"I can get ahead of them."

"We need to stick together!"

"Baxter," he sighed, a rumbling underfoot as another train slowed along the northbound platform. "Just trust me on this. That's where I need to be. It's three stops away. I'll be back in time." He picked up his coat.

Baxter grabbed hold of a sleeve.

"You're not going!" she told him.

"I don't work for you," he reminded her, letting go of the coat.

"Rouche!" she yelled after him, following him up the stairs toward the other platform.

He jumped into a carriage just as the doors slid shut, Baxter only moments behind.

"Rouche!" she shouted again as the train started moving off. On the other side of the glass, he waved apologetically. She threw his coat to the floor in frustration. "Rouche! Shit!"

Baxter had instructed the technical officers to disseminate Keaton's details and photograph to the teams, while she read up on his tragic history and the accompanying documents from Blake. An uncropped version of the family photo had been included, the smiling faces blissfully unaware of the misery to come.

"He's Rouche," she mumbled to herself, shaking her head, or rather, he was what Rouche could have become.

The two men's stories were disarmingly similar, even down to the religious proclivity, and yet where Keaton had allowed his hate and sorrow to consume him, Rouche had poured all of that negative energy into helping people.

She smiled; maybe something more than coincidence had led him back there after all.

Rouche stepped out onto the platform at Baker Street. Photographs of the three suspects had been sent to him en route. He had his phone at the ready to refer to as he followed the black-and-yellow "Way Out" signs above ground.

"Baxter, are you still reading me?"

"I am."

She didn't sound happy with him.

"I've just arrived at Baker Street, heading up to intercept the targets at the main entrance. I'll deal with CFIT directly but will keep you updated."

"Great."

He jogged up the left side of the escalator, swiped through a ticket barrier, and allowed the current of commuters to wash him out onto the pavement.

The mouth of the station was a chaotic free-for-all, with a *Big Issue* seller, Wham!-singing busker, and sorry-looking homeless man with an even sorrier-looking dog all vying for space in the busy entranceway.

Rouche made it across to the wall bordering the congested road and changed the channel on his radio, his earpiece picking up the tail end of a transmission to the FBI unit.

"Rouche here. I'm in position at the entrance. Did I miss anything?"

"Suspect Brookes has been apprehended," a female voice informed him.

"Nine to go," he whispered to himself.

He scrolled through the photos on his phone to see which of the faces he could now forget. He looked up at the endless parade of people approaching from either direction, their features obscured beneath hats, hoods, and umbrellas, as the woman continued:

"Armed units still one minute out. Remaining suspects arriving at your location imminently."

Rouche scanned the faces as they passed through sporadic patches of light. And then he recognized one of them.

"Obs on the fatter one," he announced.

"Richard Oldham," his earpiece corrected him.

Rouche wrapped his fingers around the handle of his weapon:

"Moving in to intercept."

He paused for a split second, waiting for a gap in the human traffic, when he spotted a second familiar face coming from the opposite direction.

"Shit! Obs on the other one now as well," said Rouche. He glanced between the two men on an apparent collision course. "How far out's my backup?"

"Forty-five seconds."

"If I move on one of them, I lose the other," he said, now barely having to turn his head to keep sight of them both.

"Forty seconds."

It was clear that the two men had never met. They came within a couple of meters of each other without so much as a second look before shuffling through the station's entrance.

"I'm following them in," he informed CFIT as he pushed through the herd walking dirty slush over the yellowed floor, struggling to keep the two men in sight as they veered left.

"Heading down to the Bakerloo line towards Piccadilly," Rouche updated them. He quickened his pace as he descended the escalator. "Train's coming!"

The people around him had heard it too. The sound of hurried footsteps surrounded him as the doors of the train slid open, releasing scores of people against the current. He shoved his way through them just as the doors were closing but was relieved to find both men still stood on the platform.

"Targets not on train," he mumbled as people began filling every conceivable space along the platform. "Be advised: one suspect is carrying a large rucksack."

He was curious as to why both men had deliberately delayed their journey. Just then he noticed a disheveled woman sitting on one of the benches, who had also made no effort to board the train.

"Tell my backup to hold out of sight," said Rouche, attracting a strange look from the Japanese tourist standing next to him. "Have you got a visual on a female, forties, blue jacket, black jeans, sat far end of the platform?"

"Wait one," replied the CFIT officer in his ear.

As he waited, the woman picked up her plastic carrier bag and got up to stand at the edge of the platform. He glanced behind him to see that both suspects were displaying similar intentions of boarding the next train.

"They're about to get on a train. Tell the team to move in."

No sooner had Rouche said it than a swarm of armed officers had surrounded the two men and pinned them to the ground. When he looked back at the blue-jacketed woman, she was walking away toward the very end of the platform.

The train came clattering in as one member of the team gently unzipped the heavy rucksack that their suspect had been carrying.

Rouche was straining to see over the crowds.

He checked his watch: 4:54 P.M.

He needed to get back to Baxter.

Unable to reach the rear of the train in time, he stepped up into the wall of people congregated in the nearest set of double doors, which juddered and reopened twice before eventually closing behind him. Ignoring their very British tuts and eye rolls, he pushed through the crowd to the less populated belly of the carriage.

"What was in the bag?" he asked the CFIT officer in his ear.

After a brief pause, she replied: "Explosives of some sort . . . It's been made safe . . . Disposal unit's two minutes out."

He momentarily switched channel on his radio:

"Baxter, I'm on my way back to you."

"Whatever."

"Seven to go . . . *and* we've just obtained one of four," he told her carefully, unable to say any more in the packed carriage.

"Might be two of four in a minute," she replied. "Apparently the MI5 guys came tearing out of here a few moments ago. Just get back here."

He switched his radio once more to catch the end of a transmission: ". . . a suspect." There was a pause. "Agent Rouche, did you copy last?"

"Negative. Repeat, please."

"Confirmed: the woman in the blue jacket *is* another suspect."

"Received," replied Rouche, weaving through the wall of commuters.

He reached the end of the carriage and peered through to the next, hoping to spot the woman, but was unable to see a thing beyond the people pressed up against the other door.

"The next station is . . . Regent's Park. Exit here for . . ." an automated voice announced.

Everyone leaned in unison as the train decelerated. Dense crowds rolled past the windows as they came to an abrupt stop.

Rouche stumbled out onto the platform and fought through the throngs of people to climb aboard the rearmost carriage.

"Excuse me. 'Scuse me . . . Sorry," he muttered as he squeezed between them.

He glanced up at the Tube map as he moved through the train; just one station stood between them and Piccadilly Circus.

He checked his watch again: 4:57 P.M.

"Sorry . . . Excuse me." He was halfway through the carriage when he spotted the familiar blue jacket. The scruffy woman was sat with her hands placed protectively over the carrier bag in her lap. "Obs on target."

"Where are you, Rouche?" Baxter whispered under her breath as she watched a constant stream of people pour onto the already flooded platform.

The orange numbers on the display above counted up the seconds toward 5 P.M.

"Team 3: radio check," she barked confidently into the radio, despite her heart galloping in her chest.

"Reading you loud and clear. Over."

There was a bang from somewhere within the crowd.

"Team 3 on me!" Baxter ordered as she hurried toward the disturbance.

A flustered businessman was holding a split bag as he attempted to collect up his Christmas shopping before any more fragile items could get stamped into the ground.

She sighed in relief, her nerves already shot to pieces:

"False alarm. Stand down."

On her way back to her post, she received an update from one of her constables: an explosive device, matching those used in Times Square, had been recovered from a homeless shelter in Clapham, the bag's owner having been one of those arrested overnight.

Two of four.

*

Rouche was just five paces from the seated woman when his ear filled with distortion and the CFIT officer's voice returned.

"Agent Rouche, be advised: one additional suspect believed to have boarded your train at the last station. Backup en route."

"Send details," Rouche replied, before shoving his way through to the woman in the blue jacket.

He dragged her out of her seat and pushed her face-first onto the floor, restraining her arms behind her back. Some of the appalled passengers attempted to intervene.

"It's OK! It's OK! I'm CIA," Rouche told them, producing his identification. "And you're under arrest," he shouted down at the squirming woman.

The Good Samaritans retreated back to their seats, sharing their fellow passengers' thinking that it was probably best to move as far away as was possible in the packed space.

Rouche had managed to handcuff one of the struggling woman's hands by the time the train pulled into Oxford Circus. Keeping one eye on his prisoner, he scanned the crowds scrolling past for any sign of his backup. Dozens of people alighted, but they were instantly replaced with more, filling the carriage in front and behind him.

He snapped the second handcuff closed and patted the woman down before dragging the plastic carrier bag out from beneath her. Keeping one hand pressed against her back, he reached in and removed the tarnished meat cleaver from inside. He was about to place it on the floor beside him when he realized how many children were among the frightened faces watching him.

"It's OK. I'm with the CIA," he repeated for the sake of the newcomers. He deliberated for a moment and then gestured to the muscular man who had just taken a seat behind him. "Can I borrow you?"

"Me?" the man asked uncertainly. He scratched at his beard as if he were still getting accustomed to it and then got to his feet.

Rouche placed his service weapon on the floor while he rewrapped the meat cleaver in the bag and held it out to him: "I need you to hold this for me," Rouche told him.

His helper looked uneasy.

"Just hold on to it and make sure you don't touch what's inside."

The bearded man tentatively took it from him and sat down, holding the green plastic bag in his lap just as the woman had done.

As the doors slid closed once more, Rouche spotted two armed officers running out onto the platform too late.

The train started to pull away.

"Agent Rouche! Agent Rouche!" the voice called in his earpiece, louder than before . . . panicking.

"I've just secured the woman. I'm about to start looking for—"

"Agent Rouche! Three more suspects just boarded your train! Repeat: *three* additional suspects."

"Copy that," said Rouche slowly, looking up at the carriage full of faces. "I need you to get a message to DCI Baxter immediately: the train is the target, not the station."

He felt his phone buzzing frantically in his jacket pocket as they sent through the details.

"The train is the target," he repeated, reaching for his weapon.

Unbeknown to Rouche, a clean-shaven image of the muscular man had just downloaded onto his phone.

Unbeknown to Rouche, the man had gotten to his feet to stand over him.

Unbeknown to Rouche, it was the tarnished meat cleaver that cut the first powerful blow through him.

CHAPTER 39

Tuesday, 22 December 2015

5 P.M.

"Get these people out!" Baxter yelled over the prerecorded emergency announcement.

She had reacted immediately to Rouche's relayed message; however, the sheer numbers bottlenecking up the stairway had brought the evacuation to a complete standstill as the orange display continued counting above their heads: 17:00:34.

"DCI Baxter," a voice buzzed urgently in her ear. "I still can't get hold of Agent Rouche."

"Just keep trying," she replied as she grabbed the arm of a passing staff member. "We need to close the station! You *have* to stop people coming in."

The man nodded and hurried away as Baxter's radio went off again.

"What?" she shouted in frustration.

"Apologies. I'm patching you through to a DI Lewis with the Imaging Team."

"Now?!" asked Baxter as the automated male voice announced the imminent arrival of the train.

"We've just spotted Lucas Keaton on a CCTV feed from five minutes ago. Trying to get you updated information now."

"That's good news . . . Where?"

"He's there . . . at the station . . . He's down there with you!"

Baxter looked in concern at the heaving crowd, trying to picture the photograph she'd shared with her team.

"Description?" she requested.

"Wearing a dark jacket, dark jumper."

Everyone was wearing a dark jacket with a dark jumper.

She went to push the transmit button to relay this latest development when a piercing squeal of feedback tore through her ear. Instinctively ripping the earpiece out, she noticed her colleagues react in similar ways, sharing anxious looks as the transmission broadcast snippets of distant screaming, warped and distorted, a mutilated choir of voices.

"Rouche?" she murmured, but only static clicks answered her. "Rouche, can you hear me?"

There was a rumble on the tracks.

Baxter turned her back on the crowd and stared into the dark mouth of the tunnel, the horrific noises still emitting from the earpiece in her hand a chilling prelude to an unknown horror.

Slowly, she moved to the edge of the platform. A delicate spiderweb above her began to quiver in anticipation.

A clattering emanated from the darkness, a galloping sound, vibrations underfoot of a monster advancing. The warm breeze preceding it was stale and laced with metal like blood-tainted breath, and then two bright eyes pierced the gloom as the train rushed toward them.

Baxter's long hair was blown across her face as the first smeared window flashed by, a dirty crimson veil concealing what lay within.

There were screams as people started to panic, climbing over one another in a desperate bid for escape, blocking the stairway down toward the Piccadilly line platforms as well. Nightmarish images flashed by, scenes from inside the brightly lit carriages lingering longer as the train slowed: people running for the doors, bodies pressed up against the glass, a face crying for help, blood-covered hands reaching skyward for a god that was never coming for them.

Baxter realized that the tiny speaker she was holding had gone quiet and tentatively placed it back in her ear as a set of double doors came to a stop in front of her. Beyond the smudged windows, the carriage lights flickered intermittently behind cracked casings. She could no longer hear the noise of the stampeding crowd behind her, only the set of cheerful beeps assuring that this was just a stop like any other.

The metal doors slid apart . . .

As hundreds of panicking passengers burst free of the train only to find themselves still trapped, a body slumped out onto the platform at Baxter's feet; the glazed look in the man's eyes confirmed that he was beyond saving. An electrical popping accompanied the failing lights as she stepped up into the carriage, struggling to comprehend the devastation.

There were gunshots somewhere farther along the platform and then the hollow thud of bare feet running toward her.

Spinning around, Baxter held her arms out defensively, by pure luck catching the woman's hand as she slashed at her. They dropped to the carriage floor, the tip of the stained knife slicing through her lip on impact.

The feral woman was on top of her, her shirt hanging open to reveal the scarring beneath as she pushed her entire weight down onto the knife. Baxter cried out as she struggled to hold the woman at bay, her arms trembling with the effort.

The knife inched closer, scraping across Baxter's front teeth when she turned her head away from it. Recalling Rouche's advice at the prison, she reached up blindly and tore at one of her attacker's eyes.

The woman shrieked and recoiled as Baxter kicked out at her and scrambled backward. Her attacker thrashed around like an injured animal for a moment before rushing at Baxter once more.

Two much closer gunshots sounded as a pair of gaping wounds disfigured the scar-tissue tattoo that adorned the woman's chest. She released the knife in her hand, dropped gently to her knees, and then slumped forward onto the floor.

"You OK, boss?"

Baxter nodded and got to her feet, holding a hand over her throbbing lip.

"Rouche!" she called, checking faces as she stepped between the injured.

"DCI Baxter," said a voice in her ear.

"Rouche!"

"DCI Baxter!" the voice demanded.

She held a finger to her ear:

"Go ahead," she answered as she continued the search.

Two more gunshots were fired nearby.

She winced, having missed the transmission: "Go again."

"DCI Baxter, we've lost sight of Lucas Keaton."

Rouche gasped for air.

Pinned to the floor of the rearmost carriage, he could feel his own warm blood trickling down his neck from the deep wound in his shoulder. He was trapped beneath the deadweight of his muscular attacker, whom he had shot five times in order to cease the indiscriminate massacre. He had been immobilized by the excruciating pain in his chest where the panic-stricken people he'd managed to save had trampled him in their desperation to escape. Something was grating inside him every time he took a breath.

He could feel heavy footsteps resonating through the floor.

"Clear!" someone shouted.

The footsteps moved closer.

Rouche tried to call out, an inaudible gasp all he could muster . . . He tried again.

He heard the boots step right over him and start moving away.

"Please!" Every time he exhaled, he had to fight even harder to force the air back into his lungs.

"Hey . . . Hello. It's OK. Take my hand," he heard one of the voices say. "You close your eyes for me, all right?"

"We've got someone trapped under here!" another shouted. "I need some help!"

Rouche filled with hope and couldn't understand what was happening when the voice then announced: "OK. I've got her. I've got her. Let's go."

He listened to the footsteps change pitch as they reached the solid platform floor, leaving him alone with the dead once more.

"Baxter!" he tried to call out, barely able to hear his own whispered cry for help.

His breathing was becoming shallower, his muscles fatiguing beneath the weight pressing down on him as he surrendered to the realization that he was going to bleed out onto the dirty vinyl floor long before anybody found him.

He had failed.

Baxter ran back out onto the platform and stared into the sea of people fighting their way above ground. Fear had spread through the crowd like fire catching, every individual blinded by self-preservation, each and every one consumed by panic, all oblivious to the detrimental effect that their actions were having . . . all but one.

As a group of people stumbled forward, Baxter spotted a face on the far side, eyes not pointed upward toward safety like the others but watching the train, watching them, as they searched for survivors.

Their eyes met across the crush.

It was Keaton.

She hadn't recognized him from the photograph but from the key-shaped wound torn across his right cheek from where she had, unknowingly, confronted him at Phillip East's Brooklyn hideout.

She opened her mouth to broadcast his location.

And then he was gone, swallowed up by the surging crowd.

"Team 3: continue the search," Baxter's voice ordered through Rouche's earpiece, dragging him back to consciousness. "Teams 1 and 2: your target is Lucas Keaton. Man the exits. We can't let him leave the station."

The name was like a shot of adrenaline to Rouche's failing body, muting the pain enough for him to slowly pull his pinned arm out from underneath the heavy man and wrap his fingers around the brown pole protruding from the carriage floor. Feeling his chest ripping and cracking under the strain, he gritted his teeth and dragged himself free, kicking the bearded man's limp body off him as he took an agonizing but euphoric breath.

The handcuffed woman on the floor had not survived the evacuation stampede.

Rouche reached for his service weapon and staggered to his feet, panting from the exertion required to achieve so little.

He allowed himself a nod skyward.

He hadn't failed.

He was precisely where he needed to be.

CHAPTER 40

Tuesday, 22 December 2015

5:04 P.M.

"Police! Move!" yelled Baxter, as the heaving throng inched gradually toward the blocked stairway. She scanned the crowd for Keaton. After a moment, she spotted him. He was already at the foot of the stairs, glancing back anxiously, looking for her.

As he began his scramble above ground, she could see that he was holding something.

"Eyes on Keaton!" she shouted into her radio. "Bakerloo stairway, heading up. Be advised: suspect has something in his hand. Treat as a trigger until we confirm otherwise."

A gap opened up in front of her. She pushed through, gaining several meters in just a couple of seconds.

"Disarm by any means necessary."

"Baxter, can you hear me?" wheezed Rouche as he ascended the emergency stairwell at the far end of the platform, his damaged microphone screeching back at him uselessly.

He was still able to hear the rest of the team's transmissions as he joined the hordes rushing toward fresh air. Holding his wounded shoulder, he struggled against the current, searching for where the endless river of people was emerging from.

There was a loud crackle of distortion in his ear.

A moment later, he spotted a dark shape on the ground up ahead. Flickering between hurrying legs, he could make out the shape of a body-armored officer lying facedown at the top of the escalators.

"Shit!" He looked back at the sea of people disappearing through exits all around him.

With slightly more space to maneuver, the evacuees were now moving at walking pace toward the waiting night.

They were running out of time.

He ran blindly into the crowd, barging a route through the crush as he searched in desperation for Keaton.

"Officer down! Officer down! Top of the Bakerloo escalator," Baxter announced into the radio, only realizing that it was Special Agent Chase as she checked for a pulse.

She didn't find one.

At each of the exits, a lone FBI agent faced the impossible task of locating a single face among the army of people advancing toward them. Meanwhile, London Underground staff struggled to hold a swarm of inconvenienced commuters at bay outside the station's entrance.

Out of the hundreds of people hurrying away from her, just one glanced back.

"Keaton's ten meters from Exit 3!" she updated the team. "Do . . . not . . . let him out!"

She started pushing forward, relief washing over her when she spotted Rouche beyond the open ticket barriers, making a beeline for Keaton.

"Rouche!" she called after him.

He was too far away to hear her.

Rouche had noticed the man with the scar looking back every few seconds.

The man, however, had failed to notice Rouche.

Following directions to Regent Street, St. James's, and Eros, he was only a few congested meters behind as they started to pass the threshold into the building storm.

"Keaton!" Rouche tried to yell, pointing toward him, his hoarse whisper almost inaudible. "It's Keaton!"

The agent hadn't heard him, but Keaton had, looking back to discover just how close his pursuers were.

Rouche caught sight of the black device in his hand as Keaton lowered his head and passed within inches of the FBI agent, breaking into a run the moment he emerged into the freezing night.

Rouche clambered up the stairs to join the mayhem on the street, the metal wings of Anteros silhouetted against the iconic neon signage. The evacuation of the station had spilled out onto the road, bringing the heart of the city to a complete standstill, car headlights stretching as far as the eye could see in every direction.

Beneath the starless sky, the blue snow fell unabated, lit by the flashing lights of emergency-service vehicles. The sudden drop in temperature burned his lungs. A stabbing, short, sharp coughing fit deposited watery blood into his hand as he spotted Keaton running southeast along Regent Street.

Rouche took off after him along the busy pavement, weaving between the oversized jackets and armfuls of shopping bags, the warm blood trickling down his sleeve painting a meandering trail for Baxter to follow.

Baxter waited for a break in the frantic transmissions.

It sounded as though every siren in the city was wailing, her earpiece crackling with harried updates from SO15 as they closed in on another of the bombers:

"Requesting air support," she panted into the radio. "DCI Baxter in pursuit of . . . Lucas Keaton . . . along Regent Street . . . towards the park."

Nearly twenty meters behind, she reached the crossroads with Pall Mall, almost colliding with a scooter that was darting in and out of the stationary traffic. She continued along Waterloo Place, the bronze figures that reside there emerging ominously out of the blizzard.

Baxter sprinted between them, her radio buzzing in her ear, fighting to make itself heard over the howling wind as she reached the steps that descended toward the dark void that was St. James's Park.

"Lost sight of suspect," one of the assorted voices announced in her ear as she eavesdropped in on their operation. "Does anyone have eyes? Does anybody have eyes on suspect?"

"Confirmed: northeast corner of the square . . . No clear shot."

Rouche couldn't breathe and he was losing ground, Keaton's spectral silhouette flickering on the far borders of his vision.

Suddenly, the roar of helicopter rotor blades sliced through the night air, a searchlight blinding him before sweeping toward the entrance of the park, illuminating the monument standing guard—a dark angel, rendered in blackened bronze. Azazel.

And then it was gone, the circle of light chasing blindly after Keaton as Rouche stamped dark footprints across the pristine frozen scene. Ahead of him, the snow-laden weeping willows were bent double over the icy water, as if the lake had lured them in, only to freeze while they drunk greedily from it.

The city had disappeared, nothing but the storm existed beyond the borders of the park. As they reached an open space, Rouche released the magazine from his gun and reloaded.

He ceased his pursuit and took aim, the frozen lake reflecting the spotlight back up at the heavens.

Keaton was no more than a shadow, growing smaller with every passing second.

Trying to suppress the pain in his chest, Rouche extended his arm, lining the sight dead center on the figure's back. He embraced the wind against his face, judging its speed and direction, adjusting accordingly, waiting until the beam bathed his target in light.

He exhaled to steady his limbs and then very, very gently squeezed the trigger.

"Take the shot!"

"Civilian down! Target wounded . . . No visual. Repeat: I no longer have a visual."

Baxter had been distracted both by SO15's transmissions as they hunted their prey and by the trail of bright red blood staining the ground when the crack of the gunshot cut through the snowstorm. She could see that Rouche had stopped up ahead, but Keaton had been engulfed by the whiteout.

Her throat burning, she caught her breath and continued after them.

Keaton had dropped to the ground instantly, framed in the unsteady circle of light.

Rouche walked over to the injured man, who was reaching desperately for the device a few feet away; long, gasping breaths rose up from his prone form like clouds of smoke.

"Rouche!" Baxter shouted in the distance, her voice barely audible.

He looked up to see her running toward them.

As Keaton dragged himself over to the small black box, Rouche stooped down to pick it up, discovering that it was a mobile phone.

A little disconcerted, he flipped it over to look at the screen. A moment later, he tossed it away from him and turned to Keaton with a murderous expression.

Six feet away, the uploaded video, destined to be viewed by tens of millions of people across the world, entertained itself as flake by flake it was claimed by the snow.

During the forty-six-second film, a tearful but unremorseful Keaton claimed responsibility for everything, all the while holding up photographs of his family crudely annotated with their names and the dates on which they died . . . Not once did he make any mention of Alexei Green or his beloved lost fiancée.

"Rouche! We need him! We need him!" yelled Baxter as she watched her partner press his gun into their prisoner's temple.

A spotlit performance on a dark stage.

"Where is it?" she heard him shout over the noise of the helicopter somewhere overhead, suggesting that the recovered device had not been what they had hoped.

She had almost reached them.

"Shots fired! Shots fired!" her earpiece buzzed. "Suspect down."

Rouche struck Keaton viciously with the heavy weapon, but the man simply smiled up at him through bloodied teeth as the snow turned crimson beneath him.

"Rouche!" Baxter shouted, sliding up to them.

She dropped to her knees, sinking into the powder, then pulled at Keaton's clothing as she searched desperately for the source of the blood loss. Her fingers found the gaping exit wound beneath his shoulder before her eyes did. Sliding the sleeve of her jacket up over her hand, she pushed it deep into the wound.

"What's the target?!" Rouche demanded.

Baxter could see the utter desperation on her colleague's face, the realization that his one chance to redeem himself was slipping away from him:

"He can't tell us if he's dead, Rouche! Help me."

Sat on the wet floor of the filthy Underground toilets, Green's last remaining Puppet began to weep to the relentless hum of the helicopter circling overhead.

He had never felt so alone.

He could hear them above him, scurrying around the entrance as they repositioned themselves, their overladen footfalls like the padding feet of a hound whose quarry had gone to ground.

He cried out in frustration and pulled at the chunky vest that he had been entrusted with, the wires and components pressing uncomfortably into his back.

Despite all that Dr. Green had told him, had taught him, he had allowed himself to be herded into a deserted street and, like a timid animal, had taken the only refuge available to him . . . had taken their bait.

"Aiden Fallon!" an amplified voice boomed, all distortion and malice. "You are completely surrounded."

Aiden put his hands over his ears, but he couldn't block out the voice:

"Remove the vest and come out slowly or we *will* have no choice but to force detonation. You have thirty seconds."

Aiden looked around the rancid room that would serve as his tomb, an appropriate memorial for someone who had failed as utterly as he. He only wished that he could see Dr. Green one last time, to tell him that he was the greatest friend he'd ever had and that he was so sorry for letting him down.

"Fifteen seconds!"

Aiden slowly got to his feet, wiping his hands on the fabric of his trousers.

"Ten seconds!"

He caught sight of himself in the dirty mirror. He really was the most pathetic excuse for a man. Maintaining eye contact with his reflected twin, a smile formed on his face as he tugged on the short cord dangling from his chest . . . and felt the fire engulf him.

"Rouche, help me here!" winced Baxter, shoving more of her jacket sleeve into the life-threatening wound.

There was an explosion somewhere in the distance.

Rouche staggered away from Baxter and their dying prisoner to stare out over the trees, the spotlight abandoning them as the helicopter was rerouted toward an orange glow in the sky. He wore an expression of confusion and disbelief, unable to comprehend that they had failed, that he'd never had any greater purpose . . . that there really was no plan.

All any of them could do was watch the sky fall and catch snowflakes.

"Rouche!" Baxter called as she struggled to stem the bleed beneath her hands. Her earpiece distorted with overlapping transmissions. "Rouche! We don't know what's happened yet."

"What more could we have possibly done?" he asked, his back still to her.

She couldn't be sure whether he was talking to her or to *somebody* else.

Anxiously, she watched him raise and lower the gun in his hand.

"Rouche," said Baxter as calmly as she could over the confusion crackling in her ear, her sleeve sodden and cold with Keaton's blood. "I need you to leave . . . for me . . . *please*."

He turned back to her with tearful eyes.

"Just go, Rouche . . . Walk away," she pleaded.

She glanced nervously at the weapon in his hand.

She couldn't lose him, couldn't lose another friend to the undeniable allure of a glorious and violent retribution.

"Are you going to kill me, *Rouche*?" Keaton wheezed weakly, having heard Baxter use his name.

"Keep quiet!" Baxter hissed. She needed to call in for an ambulance but couldn't move her hands any more than she could interrupt the urgent radio traffic.

"Do you *honestly* think I care?" Keaton continued, slurring a little from the blood loss. "I've achieved what I needed to in this world. There is nothing left for me here."

"I said, shut up!" Baxter snapped, but Rouche was already making his way back over to them.

"My family are with God, and wherever I'm heading, it can only be better than here," Keaton told them. He looked up at Rouche expectantly as he kneeled down beside him.

Sensing the situation rapidly deteriorating, Baxter risked removing a hand from Keaton's chest to push the transmit button on her radio:

"DCI Baxter requesting an emergency ambulance to St. James's Park. Over."

She looked across at Rouche with imploring eyes as she returned her hand to the wounded man's chest.

"I wonder if He's here . . ." Keaton spluttered on noticing the silver cross dangling around Rouche's neck, ". . . right now . . . listening to us," he said, watching the night sky for any sign. "I wonder if He's *finally* paying some *fucking* attention!"

Rouche couldn't help but recall the literal translation of Azazel's name: *Strength over God.*

He forced it from his thoughts.

"A year and a half . . ." coughed Keaton, half laughing, half crying. He adjusted position in the snow to make himself more comfortable. "A year and a half I visited that hospital room to sit at my son's side, much as you are now. A year and a half I quietly prayed for help . . . but it never came. You see, He doesn't hear you when you whisper, but He can hear me now."

Rouche watched the man beneath him dispassionately.

They were alone, the park silent bar the tinny buzzing of Baxter's earpiece, Keaton's labored breathing, and the wind.

"Rouche?" Baxter whispered, unable to decipher the look in his eyes.

Slowly, he reached around and unclipped the metal crucifix from around his neck, the silver cross spinning on its chain as he held it out.

"Rouche?" she repeated. "Rouche!"

He looked at her.

"We still don't know what's happened, but whatever it was, *none* of this is your fault. You *do* know that, don't you?" she asked.

To her surprise, he smiled as if a crippling weight had been lifted from his shoulders:

"I know."

He let the necklace slip through his fingers and fall into the discolored snow.

"Are we OK here?" she asked him, her eyes flicking back down to Keaton.

Rouche nodded.

"Call it in," she told him with a relieved sigh, her friend proving, yet again, just how strong he really was.

Looking down at the man one final time, he removed his phone from his pocket and struggled to his feet.

As he began to walk away, snippets of MI5's transmissions filled Baxter's ears.

"Rouche, I think it's OK!" she called after him excitedly, the bleed between her fingers slowing. "They're saying they got him! They're saying it was contained! . . . One fatality . . . the bomber!"

Unable to help herself, Baxter smiled down at Keaton triumphantly:

"Did you hear that, you *fucker*?" she whispered. "They got him. He's dead."

Keaton rested his head back and closed his eyes in defeat, habit prompting him to recite the words bestowed to him on too many occasions during his cursed time on this earth: "I guess God just needed another angel."

Rouche froze midstride.

Baxter hadn't even realized that she'd removed her bloody hands from his chest, her eyes blurring with tears—Curtis's beautiful face all she could think of.

She never heard the crunch of snow underfoot.

She didn't feel the warm blood spray across her face in time to the muffled gunshot, didn't understand why the body should shake so violently . . . as three more bullets tore through it.

Rouche was standing over Keaton, tears streaming down his face.

She looked up at him blankly as he pulled the trigger again . . . and again . . . and again . . . until he'd reduced the corpse to no more than a fleshy mess in the dirty snow, into nonexistence, until the weapon clicked with empty rounds.

"There is no God," he whispered.

Baxter just sat there, staring openmouthed at her friend, who took a few unsteady steps and then collapsed to the ground.

A sigh of relief escaped Rouche's broken lungs.

He could hear Baxter calling his name as she scrambled over to him.

But he just smiled sadly, raised his head to the falling heavens . . .

. . . and stuck out his tongue.

EPILOGUE

Wednesday, 6 January 2016

9:56 A.M.

"...is...no...God."

Agent Sinclair stormed past the mirrored window on his way out of the interview room.

"Nice job. Thank you for your *cooperation*, Detective Chief Inspector. Now, we're done," Atkins sighed, dabbing at his sweaty forehead while he collected up his things.

Baxter waved him off sarcastically as he hurried out after the enraged FBI agent, an hour of shameless arse-kissing no doubt ahead of him.

"Boss as diplomatic as ever," scoffed Saunders, grinning back at Vanita and the man in the corner as an important-looking American saw himself out of the cramped viewing room.

Vanita groaned:

"Why can't she just be civil? Just for twenty *bloody* minutes? Am I really asking *that* much?"

"Apparently so." Saunders shrugged.

The man in the corner nodded in agreement.

"Don't *you* start. You shouldn't even be in here," she told him, massaging the building headache in her forehead.

Baxter brusquely dismissed the consultant psychiatrist, assuring her that she was absolutely fine and had no interest in "talking anything through."

Apparently forgetting that there might be, and indeed were, people still watching, she placed her head in her hands and slumped down onto the table.

"And where do you think you're going?" Saunders asked the man in the corner, who was no longer in the corner but making his way out of the room.

"I want to see her," he replied simply.

"I'm not sure you're *totally* grasping this whole 'under arrest' thing," said Saunders.

The man looked to Vanita, who appeared almost as tired and resigned as Baxter did.

"We had an agreement," he reminded her.

"Fine," she said with a dismissive wave of her hand. "It's not like this mess could get any worse."

The man smiled cheerfully, turned, and stepped out into the corridor.

"We're all gettin' fired for this," said Saunders, watching him leave.

Vanita nodded: "Yes. Yes, we are."

Baxter heard footsteps approaching, neither the regimented march of the American nor the lazy shuffle of Atkins.

She groaned into her hands.

A metal chair scraped across the floor, and then she felt the flimsy table rock as this latest annoyance took a seat opposite her. She let out an exasperated sigh and lifted her head, her breath escaping her as violently as if she had been kicked in the gut.

The imposing man smiled awkwardly at her, deliberately leaning back in his chair a little, just in case she decided to take a swing at him, his dark, wavy hair longer than she had ever seen it, but the bright blue eyes unchanged—able to look right through her, just as they had when he'd walked out of her life.

Baxter could only stare blankly at him, incapable of even processing another devastating assault on her emotions.

"So . . . hey!" he tried casually, as though they'd seen each other only the previous day. He placed his handcuffed hands on the table between them as he attempted to come up with something profound to say, something to render the year and a half of silence trivial, something to restore her faith in him.

In the end, Wolf settled on:

"Surprise!"

ACKNOWLEDGMENTS

I'm still not entirely sure what I'm doing but I am lucky enough to have a long list of very nice and supportive people looking after me. They are . . .

My family—Ma, Ossie, Melo, B, Bob, KP, Sarah, and Belles.

From C+W—My wonderful agent Susan Armstrong, Emma, Jake, Alexander, Dorcas, Tracy, and the much missed Alexandra.

From Orion—My editor Sam Eades for putting up with me, the cloud of vapey smoke that is Ben Willis, the best copy editor in the business Laura Collins, Claire Keep, Katie Espiner, Sarah Benton, Laura Swainbank, Lauren Woosey, and the rest of the Hachette team in the UK and around the world.

Last but not least, a sincere thank-you to all the readers for keeping me in a job and for your endless enthusiasm for these characters and their messed-up lives that I take so much pleasure in destroying. I don't really do social media and certainly don't do reviews but apparently you're out there, so thank you!

AUTHOR Q&A

1. Baxter takes center stage in this novel. How has she changed since the events in *Ragdoll*?

Hangman picks up the story almost eighteen months after the Ragdoll murders. In that time, Baxter has made valiant efforts to get on with both her personal life and her career; although, it becomes apparent that these attempts to forget about Wolf are in fact driven by him and the void that he has left in her life. She's as irritable and blunt as ever, and yet her friendship with Edmunds has somehow blossomed into something special.

2. Tell us about Rouche. Was it hard introducing a new lead character? How did his character develop?

Writing *Hangman*, I realized that these are actually Baxter's books. She's the real lead. *Ragdoll* was Wolf's story and *Hangman* may be driven by Rouche and his secrets, but Baxter is the constant. She's the one getting swept up in these characters' imploding lives.

Rouche himself is a very different protagonist to Wolf. He is affable and relaxed, spiritual and selfless . . . and perhaps just a little bit odd.

3. Much of the action is set in New York, with those dramatic set pieces. How much research did you do? Did you visit?

I have been to New York in the past but it was important to me to make it feel as though Baxter was a tourist in an unfamiliar place. Truth be told, when I first started thinking about writing a sequel to *Ragdoll*, I decided from the outset to make life as hard for myself as possible: I wanted to know whether I could drop my main character, do a cringe-worthy relocation to New York City, and still write a book that was better than the first.

4. How hard was it to write a story that connected to *Ragdoll* but also entertained new readers too?

Very hard. I am writing these (first?) three Ragdoll books as a trilogy. They are all interconnected and overlap and reference each other. There's no way to get round the fact that people will get far more out of the book if they've read *Ragdoll* but it does work as a self-contained story as well. It's a difficult balance to bring new readers up to speed, remind casual readers of *Ragdoll* of certain things, while not alienating the fans who already know these characters inside out. That is, of course, the dilemma faced by every sequel, of any medium, ever made.

5. Humor plays a large part in *Ragdoll*. How do you weave this humor into *Hangman*?

In exactly the same way. I'd say there's even more humor in *Hangman,* but I suppose there would have to be to balance out the darkness and despair. I really put these characters through the wringer in this book but that just makes those sparks of genuine warmth and camaraderie and affection all the brighter.

6. You write cinematically. Are you inspired by film and TV?

I am and I don't think that these books would work otherwise. I don't like to get too bogged down by the constraints of reality and I feel that although gruesome, those are moments of "movie gore." The entire point of these books is to entertain, not to upset or disturb anybody.

7. How has life changed for you since *Ragdoll*? What are the highlights of being a successful author? Any drawbacks?

Life's been great, thank you. Cliché answer—but I've met so many really great people ever since this all started, and I mean that—like genuinely only one person who I thought was a bit of a nob . . . Well, maybe two. Definitely no more than three. But that's pretty good going for a year and a half of being a writer. I get to travel, which is fantastic. The downside being that after getting flown out, put up in a hotel, fed, and watered, people tend to expect me to do some form of public speaking at the end of it, which never ceases to strike me as unreasonable.

8. Have you started book three? Do you know how the series will end?

I have started book three. As mentioned earlier, I've planned these books as a trilogy so do actually have a pretty good idea of how I want it to end. Beyond the trilogy, who knows?